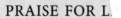

Laura Jane Willliams (she/her) is the author of four novels, a novella, and three works of non-fiction. The rights to her international bestseller *Our Stop* have been sold for television and her books have been translated into languages all over the world. She loves romance, being a parent, and Mr Kipling's French Fancies – the chocolate ones are best, but strawberry will do. Laura is currently writing her next book.

Fiction by the same author

Our Stop
The Love Square
The Lucky Escape
The Wrong Suitcase (novella)

One Night With You

LAURA JANE WILLIAMS

avon.

Published by AVON
A division of HarperCollins*Publishers*
1 London Bridge Street
London SE1 9GF

www.harpercollins.co.uk

HarperCollins*Publishers*
1st Floor, Watermarque Building, Ringsend Road
Dublin 4, Ireland

A Paperback Original 2022

First published in Great Britain by HarperCollins*Publishers* 2022

A catalogue copy of this book is available from the British Library.

ISBN: 978-0-00-836547-9 (PB)
ISBN: 978-0-00-851856-1 (TPB)

Typeset in Minion by Palimpsest Book Production Limited,
Falkirk, Stirlingshire
Printed and Bound in the UK using 100% Renewable Electricity
at CPI Group (UK) Ltd

MIX
Paper from
responsible sources
FSC™ C007454

This book is produced from independently certified FSC™ paper
to ensure responsible forest management.

For more information visit: www.harpercollins.co.uk/green

For the love of my life,
the one who calls me mummy

PART ONE

1

Nic

'Bro,' Ollie says to me down the phone, his words thick with the drowsiness of sleep despite it being just after 3 p.m. 'I'm so sorry. Don't have a cob on or nothin' – I overslept. I've only just woken up and seen your messages. Last night got a bit wet and wild, and—'

'Nah, come off it,' I tell him, rolling my eyes so hard that it actually kind of hurts. Wet and wild? I don't even want to *ask*. I raise my hand as I gesticulate a 'stop' sign, like he's the one in front of me and not half of Ealing Broadway heading home to make a start on their weekend tea. 'I knew you'd be MIA,' I mutter frustratedly. 'Honestly – I ask you for one simple thing, and you get distracted from helping me, your brother of thirty-one years, by a *one-night* stand—'

'*Two*-night stand,' he corrects me.

'You get distracted from helping me by a *two-night* stand,' I clarify, my eyes rolling even harder. 'With a very nice woman whose name, as you well know, you should have got right

3

the first time. *How* you got a second chance I'll never understand. Truly. And now I don't even know where Maple Avenue is. This is why I needed you, Ollie. I don't know what I'm doing! Google Maps has me going around in circles.' Ollie makes grumbles of protestation at my rant, but it doesn't slow me down. I'm on one. 'You're such a letdown! I never ask you for help. And this is why!'

A woman in a rain mac and rubber boots looks over her shoulder at me in fright. I'm shouting. I'm two days into the alleged adventure of a lifetime and I'm dripping wet, lost, and running fifteen minutes behind. I hate being late. Not to mention now I've got no clue on how I'm supposed to get the sofa I'm about to pick up home. I'm going to have to hold out hope for one hell of an obliging Uber driver. Although, I suppose this *is* London. The drivers have probably seen worse. Last night, after I left Ollie at the pub, I saw a rat the size of a guinea fowl stood on its hind legs, drinking a can of full-fat Coke. Earlier I saw six fully dressed clowns climb out of a Prius being driven by a man in a leotard. Every time I thought the final clown had disembarked, another one came out. It was remarkable, really.

'The yelling,' Ollie whimpers, dramatically. 'Too much yelling. Not enough congratulations for night *número dos* with the sexy Spanish señorita.'

I shake my head and smile in spite of myself. Ollie is ridiculous, and knows exactly how to play me – he thinks I've got absolutely zero game with women myself and assumes that by illuminating his own prowess, I'll soften in the face of his '*accomplishments*' . . . which I'd *never* admit to, but I kind of do. I've got no idea how to play the field – not really. Something tells me not to use Ollie as my reference point, despite his obvious successes, but he's the only other bachelor I know. Everyone back home in Liverpool is seeing someone and has been for ages. It's that kind of place.

'You're a blert,' I say, shaking my head. 'You know that, don't you?'

'Yes,' he says, plainly. 'I do. But I'm also a blert who got very, very lucky last night.'

It's impossible to stay mad at him. He's a typical younger sibling: his grades weren't as good as mine were, he never got told off as much I did when we were kids, and somehow his refusal to take responsibility for *anything* comes off as roguish and charming. He could snog your wife and crash your car, and you'd still end up buying him a pint. It defies the laws of physics *and* logic, how much he gets away with.

'I can come and meet you now?' he offers. 'She just left. I'll need a shower though. I'll tell you what, every inch of these bedsheets is covered in—'

'I'M HANGING UP NOW!' I declare, utterly convinced I don't need to know a single further detail. 'I'LL-FIGURE-SOMETHING-OUT-PLEASE-STOP-TALKING-BYE!'

I shake off thoughts of his dirty bedsheets, returning to the task in hand. It's hard, stepping into a new life. But I'm doing it. I've never had to search for courage more than I did in deciding to start from scratch, and even though I've already wanted to kick something in frustration ten times today I'm still dead proud that I'm actually doing it. I tell you something – actually building this new life isn't half as scary as the decision to leave my old one. It took me months. Years, even. I try to remember that every time I wonder what I'm doing. Safe doesn't mean better. Safe can just mean safe. Alive but not living. Miserably comfortable. Well – not anymore for me, thanks.

I look around.

Maple Avenue, the street sign says to my surprise.

Excellent. I might have found where I'm supposed to be going by accident, but I've found it all the same. Thank God.

2

Ruby

'I don't know if you've misunderstood the definition of helpful,' I say to Jackson, who is slouched up against the radiator on the floor, playing with the tape dispenser Candice stole from work to help with the packing. 'But shredding the tape I need for these boxes? Decidedly counter-productive.'

'Not if my dastardly plan is to keep you from leaving.' He pouts, scratching the short afro stubble of his shaved hair. 'Honestly. If you wanted us to express our unending admiration and love, these are quite the dramatics to establish feeling appreciated.'

The pink of his bottom lip juts out, and I wonder who he is to make accusations of theatrics. He'd give Liza Minnelli a run for her money.

I know it comes from love. He's been like this all week. I don't think either of them genuinely thought I'd go. When I first told them I was thinking of getting my master's, they didn't take me seriously, but then I secured my second interview. I could have applied to Brighton or even somewhere in London, but Manchester is the best course in the country so when I got in – and with a partial scholarship, I mean come on! – there was no way I could turn it down, even if they not-so-secretly hope that any second now I'm going to declare that I've changed my mind and stay.

'Heads up, bevvies coming through,' Candice announces, jutting open the bedroom door with her hip, her hands cradling three Aperol Spritz. Her brunette crop is standing up in spikes on her head, a result of her having spent most of the day on the sofa watching Disney movies as a way to ignore the unfolding scenes in my room.

'Candice, I can't drink yet – look at everything I've still got to do!' I exclaim, gesturing to the piles of stuff strewn across the room as Jackson greedily paws at the glasses, taking one for himself and one for me. He holds mine out, but I immediately discard it on the mantelpiece. We live in a big old Victorian semi, and, because we'd rather split the rent four ways than three, we make do with the tiny box of a dining room beside the kitchen as a living room and use the front room – working fireplace and all – as a bedroom, in addition to the two doubles upstairs, and a single room at the back. For the past two years we've rented the small one out mostly as short-term lets to students studying English, who happily pay over the odds to be near the Central Line, which in turn means that me, Jackson and Candice get rent below the odds. It's naughty, but this is London: it's eat or be eaten when it comes to finding a place to live that you can actually afford – and the landlady doesn't care as long as the money lands in her account on time.

'Bottoms up, gang,' Jackson cheers, waving his glass in the air. The pair of them look at me with such expectation that

I join them in spite of myself for what we call 'first blood' – the first few sips of the first drink of the night (or afternoon, it seems) when it whets your appetite for more. I do feel bad, leaving them. We've been the three musketeers for so long. But if I don't act the tough guy, I'll sob and sob and that won't help anyone.

'To the traitor,' Candice says, a coy smirk offsetting her harsh words.

'To the traitor,' Jackson echoes, and shaking my head I take a sip too. I haven't said as much to them, but I'm actually excited to leave London behind. This city has exhausted me. It's too dirty, too expensive – just too *hard.* I've never been able to escape the feeling that this isn't the place for me. I don't know if Manchester is, but at least it's closer to my parents and sister over in the Peaks. Candice and Jackson would rather die than return to the area where they were born.

My attention is caught by the screen of my phone lighting up. Ah. Of course. Behind every woman trying to move on is an ex who can sense she's almost over him. It's a message from Abe.

Surely you're not leaving without saying goodbye?

I swipe left on it, so it deletes without even opening.

'What time is it?' I ask, determinedly pushing him from my mind and piling more books into a box for Jackson to tape up. 'The sofa guy is late. He should have been here by now.'

'Bet he's stopped for some essentials after my text,' Candice sing-songs, joining Jackson on the floor. There's nowhere else to park themselves: as far as furniture goes there's only my bedframe and mattress left, which is strewn with a mixture of half-packed boxes and charity bags, and the love seat, which, though empty, has already been cleaned for collection – if the guy ever shows up.

'Deodorant, breath mints, condoms . . .' continues Candice, still teasing me about the man buying my couch.

I scowl. Jackson catches it and laughs.

'Is the sweepstake up to twenty quid that she'll shag him, or twenty-five?' he goads.

I give him a dirty look. 'Why is it so hard to believe that I can last all year without a man between my thighs?' I sigh. 'As my best friends, aren't you supposed to be more supportive than this? It's like you *want* me to fail.' I'm trying to guilt them into shutting up so add for emphasis, 'After everything I've been through as well . . .'

Jackson fishes the orange slice from his drink to squeeze out the juice into his glass. 'Au contraire,' he says, licking his fingers and not one bit bothered by remorse. 'We want you to succeed, my darling.'

'New city,' Candice says. 'New outlook, new life. All of that is a wonderful plan . . .'

'But . . .' Jackson adds. 'It's like we continue to remind you: you cannot leave London with Abraham Lawson as the last man to have been inside you. We'd be worse friends if we *didn't* get you a better parting memory than that.'

'I asked Jackson if he'd take one for the team, but he refused.' Candice giggles.

'I couldn't think of anything worse.' Jackson shrugs.

'Charming!' I say. 'I love you too.'

'Be like snogging my sister,' he explains. 'Improper. My services can only lie in teasing you into compliance. It's for your own good. You won't be making very good art if you don't satiate Little Ruby.' He says *art* like it's in air quotes, but I'm more put out by him calling my lady parts *Little Ruby*.

10

'Well,' I say, waving him over with a wag of a finger to signal which boxes can be taped shut now. 'You didn't really send that text, and there's only us three celebrating tonight, so if you aren't going to cleanse my palate yourself, we're rather in a tough spot, aren't we?'

Jackson laughs. The whole 'joke' started last week when Candice had seen me arranging the pick-up with him as I typed on Facebook Marketplace at the breakfast bar, said he was hot in his photo, and before I knew it pulled up his every social media profile on her phone, just from a name and the fact that he used the same photo for all of them. By the time Jackson had added his own Inspector Clouseau skills to the mix, they'd established that he was new to London, originally from Liverpool, and was crisp off a break-up. He'd won an award for outstanding achievement from his university – University of Liverpool, joint degree in Economics and Politics – and was headhunted for some sort of graduate scheme at a financial consultancy. He played a bit of football, and did this thing called LARPing, which we'd had to google. It's Live Action Role-Playing, where people dress up as characters and act out pretend settings in the real world.

There was a particularly disorientating photo of him dressed in chain mail with a sword belt slung low on his hips, geotagged in Scotland. It was easy to tell by how everything fell that he was ripped, and he was even fitter without his glasses on. By the time our deep dive into who the stranger buying my sofa was had finished, we'd polished off two bottles of champagne Candice had 'been gifted' (aka stolen, or 'reclaimed as payment in kind', as she sometimes frames it) from work, and were each as randy for him as the other. I liked his abs, Candice liked his shoulders, and Jackson said he couldn't help but notice the size of his hands.

'I really did let him know that it's his public duty to help you out,' Candice teases.

'You wouldn't bloody dare,' I growl, eyes playfully narrowed.

And yet when the doorbell goes, my tummy does a double dip. With Candice, you really can never be totally sure.

'I'll get it!' she cries, leaping up enthusiastically. She's revelling in the success of winding me up.

'Poor bloke.' Jackson laughs, as I finish labelling a box of books. 'I wouldn't leave her alone with him for too long.'

I pause, digesting what he's saying, and then put what I'm doing down. From here I can just about hear Candice say hello and the deep, manly tones of a quiet reply.

'You know what she's like,' Jackson presses.

I raise my eyebrows, muttering, 'Her middle name honestly may as well be "menace".'

Jackson sniggers.

'Not that you're any better,' I point out, and he simply gestures to the air like there's no other way it could possibly be.

3

Nic

'Rubes!' the statuesque brunette who answered the door warbles down the hallway. 'Your sofa guy is here!'

'Coming!' a voice chirrups from somewhere in the bowels of the house. The brunette looks me up and down and then smiles. It makes me nervous.

'How's it going?' she asks.

'Sound, yeah,' I reply, not really knowing how else to respond. I add, when she doesn't say anything else: 'Wet.'

'Hmmmm,' she ponders, as if she's mentally scoring my rain-soaked outfit, or my face – or maybe even my character – out of ten. I've got no idea if the amusement tugging at the corner of her mouth signifies doing well on her imaginary scorecard, or terribly. If it's my chat she's judging, I'd imagine I'm at a zero. Chit-chat about the weather? Ollie wouldn't approve of that. To be fair though, I'm not here for conversation. I'm here for furniture, and then a nice takeaway for tea in my new flat, on my new sofa. Admittedly I'll be alone for it, but still. I need to tick this errand off my list and then crack on.

'I'm here, I'm here,' the voice in the house sing-songs again, as a shadow steps out from the obscurity of the hall. She looks at the sky before she looks at me, taking in the unseasonably rainy August day. Some bank holiday weekend. It hasn't stopped raining across the whole country all summer, on and off, and it's worse today than it has been in ages. If we don't get some sun before winter arrives the whole country will go crackers – it's been awful. 'Urgh,' she notes to herself, as the sky spits again.

I look at her. She's holding the last dregs of what looks like a spritz, and wearing tiny shorts with an oversized T-shirt that falls off the shoulder, and not a scrap of make-up, her blonde hair piled high on top of her head. There's a dance of dusty freckles across her nose and high up on her cheeks, and her eyelashes are thick and dark, brushing upwards, framing her lovely face. I can't help but notice that she's not got a bra on, made apparent by her nipples' curiosity to the cold air. The things are like thick bullets, aiming right for me.

'Hi,' she says, dragging her gaze from the clouds to look at me. 'I'm Ruby.'

And it's so bizarre – so uncanny. But as we look at each other, I have this . . . *reaction.*

She's an angel. An actual, heaven-on-earth angel. Her face, her long, elegant neck, the creaminess of her skin and the way her collarbone arcs like poetry, telling the story of her body. The rise and fall as she breathes. Her smell – like coconut and exotic flowers. Surely she must feel it too. Lightning replaces the blood in my veins. I'm on fire.

'Nic,' I try to say, but tongue-tied by the rush of thoughts collapsing into each other it comes out as a cough. Shit. If you only get one chance at a first impression, I'm royally cocking this up. I look away and take a moment to catch my breath. *Be cool,* I tell myself. *Just be yourself.*

But even as I think it, I wince at my own advice. I don't know why *just be yourself* is said so often. 'Myself' is a massive geek who has only ever had a single girlfriend in his life. I've only even kissed four people, and one of those was mouth-closed because I was eleven. *Just be yourself* is fine if you're Justin Bieber or any of the Hollywood Chrises. To be Nic Sheridan is to be introverted, shy and chronically laughable. Google 'definition of uncool' and they show a photo of my face. Ask an impartial panel to rank the world's men from most suave to most tragic and I can save you the trouble of finding my name by having you flick to the bottom of the list. It was ever thus. I'm clever and organised and know how to calculate competitive interest rates on my stocks and shares ISA, but I can't talk to women for crap. Until recently I've been in the same relationship since school. I've never learned how because I never needed to.

And yet . . . *This* woman. It's like cherubs are singing and spirits are calling me and I ache, everywhere, at the impossible sight of perfection. My soul knows who she is. We've spent lifetimes together before. She's got the most cracking body, but that's still the least interesting thing about her.

I can't get this wrong.

I think I might be staring.

I can't help it.

I rang the doorbell, and Love answered.

(Well. Love's friend. But then Love showed up in hotpants.)

I'm going to have to be anyone *but* myself.

4

Ruby

This guy is looking at me like he's planning to murder me cold and fry off my limbs in duck fat to hide the evidence.

'Urm,' he says, after opening and closing his mouth like a trout. I remember seeing an old episode of *ER* where a woman just shut down as she stood talking to Dr Carter, like her plug had been pulled and she was powering down. This is scarily reminiscent. I hope he isn't in need of an ambulance, or medical assistance. I don't have time! I promised Candice and Jackson I'd be done by six so we could have our last 'family meal'. It's important to me that our last night is good, quality time. If this man is dying on our doorstep it'd be a huge inconvenience for all involved, no offence to him.

'Nic,' he manages, coming back to life after a small coughing fit, extending a hand that he has the sense to wipe on his jacket first. He doesn't break eye contact. It's really intense. 'Here for the sofa.'

Really, *really* intense.

16

I don't recall the woman on TV staring like this when she had her stroke. I think this might just be his face. It's a handsome face, though, brooding as it is. He's actually even more attractive than he looked in his profile picture.

That was just us being drunk and silly though. No way am I going to try and sleep with the guy I am selling my couch to. It's The Year of Me in less than nine hours. I don't even want to *look* at a man in The Year of Me. No distractions. No diversions. No disruptions, despite the campaign the other two have been waging for my one last hurrah.

Those eyes, though. Can men have come-to-bed eyes? On second thoughts, it's actually not an axe-murderer stare. He's looking at me like he's waded through the desert for weeks, and I'm a tall glass of iced water. His pupils have dilated and he's smiling like a goon. And his dimples . . . you could lose an afternoon in his smile. Wow. I can't help but inanely grin back, now the shock of his presence has settled. He's *gorgeous*.

Curse Candice and Jackson for putting silly sexual thoughts in my head! I have bigger fish to be frying. I can't be mentally undressing dashing men in damp jackets right up until the last hour of my celibacy. Anyway, he's gone the colour of a Christmas bauble now, all red and shiny. I think he's disconcerted by my dawdling, which is fair enough really. I *am* staring.

'Invite the poor man in,' Jackson stage-whispers from the doorway of my bedroom, breaking the spell. 'He's getting rained on!'

I snap out of my daydream and rearrange my features into something I hope conveys friendly, but detached. Back to business.

'Right then,' I say, reminding myself to smile. 'Come in.' He crosses the threshold and I notice him about to slip off

17

his trainers. It feels pervy to notice he's got massive feet, but jeez. The man could've water-skied here. You know what they say about men with big feet, et cetera . . .

'Don't worry about your shoes,' I add. 'We're a shoes-on house. It's okay.'

The sofa guy – Nic – issues a funny guffaw sound before responding: 'If it's all the same to you, I will slip 'em off. Mum'd go mental if she thought I'd trampled through somebody's house. I've got a sore back-of-the-head even thinking about it!'

Over his shoulder I see Candice looking pointedly at his arse with her glimmering big brown eyes as if to say: *sweet, huh?* I gently shake my head at her to warn her to pack it in before she makes me laugh, but he sees, casting his eyes back at her in confusion.

'Just through here,' I say, distracting him. 'Excuse the mess. I'm halfway through packing up my life.'

'No worries,' he declares, as he follows where I'm pointing and crosses into my room in front of me. Behind him it's impossible not to notice that Candice has a point about his arse. 'I'm halfway through *un*packing my life, so I get it.'

Nic sees Jackson then, who has been lingering in my room listening.

'How do,' he says with a little wave. 'I'm Nic, here for the sofa.'

'Isn't she *beautiful*?' Jackson gushes.

I can *feel* Nic redden once again as he replies, stiffening: 'You what?'

'The love seat?' Jackson says, but he knows full well what he is doing. It immediately feels unkind. *We're not laughing at you,* I want to say, *the guys are laughing at me.* I have an urge to reach out a hand to Nic's so he feels protected,

18

somehow, so he knows I'm on his side and we're not total monsters who can't control themselves. Plus it would be a great excuse just to have that human touch, that connection, I think, noticing his thick biceps that taper off into manly, dense wrists. I think of him holding that sword we saw in the photo. I think of how small my waist would feel in those substantial hands.

Bloody hell. *Focus*. What am I even doing, eyeing him up?

'Jackson,' I say, stepping in, waving my empty glass at him. 'You wouldn't mind pouring out another round with Candice, would you? In the kitchen?'

Basically, can you sod off? is the request behind my words. *You're making this awkward.*

Jackson smirks. 'I'll leave you two alone,' he states, and he deliberately brushes his shoulder against mine as he sashays by, nudging me in the direction of my buyer.

'Thank you.' I smile. Turning my attention back to Nic forces him to whip his head down, avoiding eye contact. It was the right thing, getting rid of everyone else. We *are* a bit of an intimidating bunch. We've been told that before. It's sweet, though, how easily he blushes. Whatever the opposite of a poker face is, he has it. Every emotion passes across his features like channels on a TV when you sit on the remote. It's disarming. Charming.

'It's all been cleaned down,' I explain, trying to get back on track. 'Vacuumed and brushed. All of that.' I gesture towards the two-seater love seat he's here to collect. 'Feel free to inspect it. The condition should be exactly as I described in the ad – there's just that mark at the side there, like you can see. I'm sad to be parting with her, to be honest. She just doesn't fit in the hire car, and if it doesn't fit in the car it has to be left behind. So . . . give her a good home.'

Nic crouches down and runs a wide, flat palm over the velvet upholstery, considering the lumps and bumps, examining the scuff but otherwise nodding his head. His eyes narrow in concentration, and I all but expect his tongue to dart out of his mouth like a little kid doing a class project. I'll bet he was adorable as an eight-year-old.

'We said sixty?' he asks, finally. His voice has settled into something lower now we're alone. Ruminating, you could say. I wouldn't mind a voice like that reading me a bedtime story, year of celibacy or otherwise.

'We did.'

'Great.' He nods. 'Yeah. I'm made up with that. I'll transfer you the cash right now, then I can get out of your way.' He stands and gets out his phone from his jacket pocket, and I realise that I'm weirdly aware of this stranger's smell: musky and manly. If we were in a bar, I'd let him buy me a drink. Am I mad if I say there's some sort of chemistry cracking off here? There's a vibe. First I was looking at his arse, now I'm rubbing my neck in a subtle gesture of flirtation. When did that happen? When did my body start flirting before my mind knew what was happening? I haven't meant to, but crap – I'm giving him *signs*. How unexpected! I think it was how he very first grinned at me. How can a woman resist a massive, boyish grin like that?

'No, gosh, don't worry. You're saving me from all this.' I half-heartedly gesture at the boxes with a flourish and give some deep eye contact. 'I'm grateful of a break. Take your time.' More eye contact. I linger, then look away. I can't help myself. I really am giving this man some game. Could it be that Candice and Jackson were right? Am I honestly going to crack on and lay it on thick, have a bit of fun before I go? Maybe I *should* get him to stay for a spritz . . .

'What's your sort code?' he asks. 'The transfer should be immediate.'

I give him my details, and, as he narrates the steps of paying me, I sneak another peek at him. His features are softer in real life than in the photos we saw on social media. Short dark hair, revealing a dense neck that narrows into the top of his jacket. His lips are full and his dusting of shadowy stubble adds a little rough to his look. We saw on Instagram that when he's clean-shaven he looks really, really young. I almost want to tell him I like the five o'clock shadow, but stop myself when I realise I'm not supposed to know how he looks without it. I wonder what his ex is like. I wonder who broke up with who. Before I can stop myself, I wonder what he likes in bed, if he's gentle or rough, how much time he spends on foreplay. *Ruby, calm down,* I coach myself.

An alert lets us know that the money has landed. I pick up my phone and wave it at him.

'Done!' I declare.

'Simple as that,' he says, smiling at the floor.

'Yeah . . .' I agree.

Neither of us knows what to say then. He taps his fingertips against his jeans as if waiting to be released. I look at them, the neat square tops of his nails, tapping out a staccato rhythm on his knees. I gather my courage, because I'm going to do it: I'm going to see if he wants to stay. Fuck it – why not? Then I feel his gaze on me so look up, and before my eyes meet his he looks away, above my head, to the empty space where my mirror used to hang.

'I should probably get going,' he offers.

Oh. I'm getting this all wrong. The vibe is all one-way. *Ooooops.* I should just let him get on with his day. He doesn't want to be here. Never mind.

'Shall I get Jackson to help you out with it?' I offer, releasing him from the jail of my attention. 'I'm sure he won't mind.'

He practically leaps up and runs for the door, which doesn't exactly make me feel great. I take the hint. At least with the sofa gone it's another job off the list, and we're another step closer to family dinner.

'Jackson,' I call, as I reach around to let Nic out. I needn't have bothered. Jackson is stood just outside the bedroom door with Candice, neither of them even trying to hide the fact that they've been statue-still and totally silent, listening in to the whole sofa-buying interaction.

'Do you mind helping?' I say, shooting daggers.

'Oh, absolutely,' he replies, unperturbed. 'It would be *my pleasure* to help.'

And there's something about the twinkle in his eye that makes my tummy flip once again. I try to shake my head to surreptitiously communicate Nic's not interested, but Jackson doesn't catch it.

'Right, mate – one end each? Don't forget to bend from the knees,' I hear him say, and I'm embarrassed at how disappointed I am that this good-looking man doesn't even want a bit of a flirt back.

5

Nic

I order an extra-large cab via the app on my phone. Fortunately, it's stopped raining.

'Is she your girlfriend, then?' I say to Jackson, because I have to know. I can't believe I'm never going to see her again. I didn't know what to do. I was so stupid back there, not knowing what to say and coughing and blushing and acting like I had the IQ of a two-year-old. Stupid, stupid, stupid. She couldn't get rid of me quick enough.

'Who, Ruby?' Jackson says. 'Nah, mate. Don't shit where you eat – that's my advice. We just live together, that's all. Well . . . Did. She's moving tomorrow. Hence the sofa sale.'

'Oh,' I reply. Not that it makes a difference what her relationship status is. I just proved, once again, how incompetent I am. This woman is moving anyway. I'll bet I didn't even register on her radar. Not a woman like that, and a bloke like me.

'Fit though, isn't she?' Jackson says. 'Ruby.'

I shrug.

'Come off it, don't tell me you didn't notice!'

I grin, just a bit, because I can't help it. Jackson has the same easy-going attitude that Ollie does. He makes me comfortable to relax around him.

'Ahh!' he says, hooting with a laugh. 'Look at your face! 'Course you noticed it, you big old perv. Well, you'll be pleased to know she's single.'

I look at the taxi app. Five more minutes. I'm praying the cabbie will even help me at the other end, if I tip well enough.

'You might have noticed I'm not very good with women,' I say to the end of the street, watching cars whizz by. 'So her being single doesn't help me very much.'

'Yeah,' Jackson says. 'I can't lie. I did spot that you were a bit . . .'

'Yeah,' I agree, not needing him to specify the word.

We stand.

'If you're accepting unsolicited advice,' Jackson says, eventually, 'the trick is to be where you are with them. That's what I find.'

I'm not sure I want romantic coaching at the side of a road with soggy clothes and a sofa to lift in less than four minutes, but . . . Well, somebody needs to help me, don't they? I didn't come all this way to be as meek and mild and useless as I've just been for the rest of my life. I might cringe when Ollie tries to help me, but that's not because I don't need it. It's the way he offers it. Jackson is talking like a person, not a caricature. He's making it easy to listen to what he has to say. I hate when other men put on some pissing contest I don't want to be a part of. Jackson seems sound, to be fair.

'What do you mean?' I ask cautiously. 'Go on.'

'Okay,' replies Jackson, turning to face me. 'Imagine there's this gorgeous bird, right?'

'Right.'

'And she's fit as fuck, right? She's got the eyes, the lips, the body, whatever. You look at her, and it's like, whoa!'

'Uh-huh . . .'

'Number one, she probably already knows it. Fit girls either know they're fit, and are sick of men like us ogling them like they're a piece of meat. Or they don't know how fit they are and so they get self-conscious. They assume we're making fun, or we've noticed something they're insecure about. You can be thinking, *God that's a good arse,* and she'll assume you're thinking, *Whoa, what a fat, disgusting pig of a woman with a bum like that!*'

'Girls don't talk to themselves like that,' I say, shaking my head. 'That's awful.' I never heard Millie say horrible things about herself. But then, Millie was quite self-assured; she was very practical about things like that. As soon as Ruby had opened the door there was an energy about her, a rawness. Millie was more . . . missionary. She liked to have a shower before we had sex and was always the first to get up to clean off afterwards. Millie was cerebral, in a way that made her body simply incidental, like she could honestly do without it. Ruby is body *and* mind. I can just tell, even after five minutes with her. I know I sound ridiculous but honestly – I've never felt this *struck* by another person before.

'Yes, they do,' Jackson insists. 'I've lived with those two for four years. I've heard it all. I don't know – diet culture, they say it's called. The way they think about their bodies isn't the same as the way we think about their bodies, basically.'

'Really?' I say. 'Because if I was a woman . . .'

'You'd be stood naked in front of a mirror all day, every day?'

'Yeah.'

'Same, mate.'

We both take a moment to digest what it might be like to be offered such mysterious powers.

'Anyway,' Jackson presses. 'We see a woman we like, and right away we've jumped ten steps ahead: how can I talk to her? How can I be alone with her? How can I kiss her, shag her, keep shagging her?'

'It's not always about sex,' I try to argue, but Jackson waves a hand.

'It is *always* about sex. It's always about sex until it isn't. It's always about sex until just after we've had sex, and then it's about . . .' He pauses, considering his conclusion. 'Something else. I think that's when we know, isn't it? After sex, there's this moment of *do I want you stay all night, or do I want you to go?* Do you know what I mean? It's like, once sex is out of the way then you see this person beside you for the first time. And you either want them around, or you don't.'

'You only know that *after* you've been with them?'

'Yeah, don't you?' Jackson replies, but before I can figure out how to make out like I know exactly what he's talking about he continues: 'Look. For women, right, they mostly don't sleep with you until they've already *decided* how they feel and what they want. That's where the trouble comes. It's not like that with men. Sleeping with men is way more straightforward.'

'Got a lot of experience with men, have you?' I jest, and it's supposed to be banter but comes out sounding pathetically homophobic. I regret it instantly.

'A bit, yeah,' says Jackson.

26

That's got me.

'I'm pan,' he continues. 'Pansexual. I fancy people, not genders. Men, women, non-binary . . .'

'Oh,' I reply, painfully aware that I shouldn't have even tried to make a joke about men liking men, or anybody else for that matter. This isn't 1952 for God's sake. 'That's really cool. Good for you.' I suddenly envy him, just a bit. Imagine liking yourself so much that you can just tell people who you are and not wait for the other shoe to drop?

He moves on, and the kindness of it makes me feel even worse for misspeaking. 'What I'm saying is this: if talking to women makes you nervous, try not to get too ahead of yourself. When I say be where you are, what I mean is don't think about her naked, or getting her naked. Focus on the now. Talk about what's right in front of you.'

'Like, literally? The sofa?'

'Try it on me,' Jackson says. I look at him and blink. 'Try it on me!' he repeats, and with it he flops down onto the chair, crosses his legs, and bats his eyelashes at me. 'Hello,' he says, in a high-pitched and silly voice. 'I'm . . . Bathsheba. I have a sofa for sale. Are you here to buy the sofa?'

I shake my head. 'This is . . . I'm not . . .'

He doesn't break character. 'Gosh, I wish I'd remembered to wear a bra today. I hope you can't see my boobies.' He pushes out his chest, realises I'm not biting, and then fixes his mouth into a straight line.

'How long until the taxi?' he asks, dropping his self-assigned role in exasperation.

I look at my phone. 'Oh,' I say. 'It's gone from three minutes back up to five. That's annoying.'

'Five minutes,' he says. 'You can play my little game for the next five minutes, can't you?'

I look back at the house, just in case anyone is watching us. I realise I actually really trust this guy. He doesn't have to be sympathetic towards me, but he is. London Nic needs to trust the process. London Nic needs to go with the flow and stay open to anything that could happen. That's what I've promised myself. Even if it means pretending to buy a sofa off a fella I've just met cosplaying as my schoolboy crush at the sharp edge of a West London cul-de-sac.

'Okay fine,' I say, sitting down beside him.

'Hello!' I begin, my voice brightening. 'Nice to meet you . . . Bathsheba. I'm Nic. Yes, I'm here to buy your sofa . . .'

6

Ruby

'What are they *doing* out there?' Candice says, holding the blind open with an elegant tanned finger and peering through. Jackson is waiting with the sofa guy to help him load the love seat into his taxi, and I peer over Candice's shoulder to see them, just beyond the front hedge, sat in rapt conversation as if the pavement is their living room and the rest of the street is where they live.

'Maybe Jackson is having a crack at the whip,' I observe. 'Nic might not fancy me, but one of you should get his number – you were right about his arse.'

'And did you see the size of his feet?' Candice exclaims, and I smile. We keep watching.

'But nah,' she decides. 'Jackson is hot for the new intern at work still, isn't he? Like, he's actually serious about her. Besides, he always does this. Befriends the waifs and strays. I smell a dodgeball tournament in young Nic's future . . .'

She's referring to Jackson's bi-weekly sports-fest, but I've already lost interest and turned my focus back to the job at hand. There's still loads to do.

'Hmm,' I mumble.

With the love seat gone, the room looks massive. I never really had leeway for the slim two-seater sofa, but with the dining-cum-living-room being so small, and there being somebody in the kitchen literally *all* the time, if I ever did want some time to myself it was a choice between either sacrificing the space, or relaxing on my bed – and that felt a bit teenager-y. I'd seen the sofa in the window of our local charity shop and all three of us had carried it home, Jackson swearing blind the whole time it wouldn't get through the door. But it did, and at the right angle in the corner, by the bay window, with a rug I got in Thailand and a little side table one of the neighbours had left out with a sign that said 'TAKE ME!', it's my favourite place in the whole house. Well, was.

'What shall we do about dinner?' I ask, pushing a pile of boxes and a twinge of sadness away as I look around the now very echoey space. Jackson and Candice have been in such denial about me going that they haven't bothered to look for my replacement, so the room will be empty until they find someone. They said they're not worried, though. There's enough cash in the housekeeping account to make up the shortfall and the box room normally gets let within twenty-four hours after the ad going live, so they reckon it will only take a few days to recruit their next housemate. I'm pretty sure they want to make sure this is still my home until the very last possible second.

We hear the front door go and Jackson's head appears around it. Candice and I look up at the exact same time.

'Hey,' he says. 'I'm going to help this guy take the sofa back to his place. Shall I pick up pizza on the way home? Sloppy Giuseppe's on the Green?'

'Not to sound rude or anything, but why are you helping him take the sofa home?' Candice asks.

'He needs help.' Jackson waves. 'And I'm a helpful person.'

'Uh-huh.' I laugh, reaching for my purse to give him my bank card. 'Sure you are.'

'I am!' he says, flapping my card away from him, refusing to accept it. 'Pizza, yes? The usual? My treat. As a parting gift.'

I blow him a kiss. 'Thank you,' I say. 'I suppose you'll be what? Half an hour? An hour?'

'Yeah,' Jackson says. 'He's only around the corner, and I'll walk from there. Do you mind calling ahead? Put in the order? It'll be quicker that way. I'm famished.'

'Done, and done,' says Candice, moving back to peer out of the window. Jackson sees her eyeing up the man outside.

'He doesn't have any friends here yet,' Jackson notes. 'I'm being neighbourly.'

It's Candice's turn to garble unconvinced noises.

'Wow,' defends Jackson. 'Way to make a man feel protective about caring. I think it says more about you than me that it's an issue . . .'

'I'm going to ban you from reading that psychology magazine if you keep saying stuff like that,' she says with a laugh, knowing he's right. 'Just go. You're distracting us anyway!'

'Back soon!' he sings, the front door clicking open and closed once more. I hear a burst of laughter as he joins Nic back out on the street, and move to join Candice in scrutinising them again, trying to establish what's so funny. I mean, fair play if Jackson is going to make a new friend. I feel a tug of something at my heart at the thought. They're allowed new friends, of course – it just stings I won't be here. I have vague worries of being replaced, but don't feel entitled to those worries since it's by my own volition that I'm going.

'He totally fancied you, you know,' Candice says, her eyes pointed in continued observation of the two men and the sofa.

'So you *were* listening from the other side of the door,' I reply. 'Unbelievable!'

She shrugs as if to say, *well duh.*

'Ruby,' she says, looking at me now. 'I cannot emphasise enough just how much you need a sexual exorcism from *that shit who shall not be named*. You had it right within reach just then; all you had to do was ask him to stay for a spritz, and you lost it. He really would have been happy to oblige. I could tell.'

'Your radar is off,' I dismiss. 'He couldn't leave fast enough.'

'My radar is never off,' she pushes.

'Well, whatever. I'm a boy-free zone now. I'm over it.'

'I could go and ask him to join us for that pizza . . .'

'Candice,' I caution. 'Please.'

'I'm just saying!' she tries again, though it's clear from her expression that she already knows it's fruitless.

I don't want my mood to sour. I'm not spending my last night talking about chuffing *men*. Everything that happened was awful, but at least some good has come from it. Jackson and Candice might not understand, but it's an undeniable truth: it's time to take control of my life, make a change, and own it. I want a fresh start and a Year of Me: twelve months, starting tomorrow, of total celibacy and absolute focus on my own self-discovery and creativity – if that doesn't sound too grand. I just feel like if I can wholeheartedly commit to myself this next twelve months, somehow it might alter the whole course of my life. I'm not where I'm meant to be yet, even if where I currently am is where the people I love are. That's what makes today so bittersweet. I just want to get a little tipsy, have a dance party, and lie on the living room floor until we can't keep our eyes open, swapping memories and promising to always be best friends. 'Just don't. I don't have the bandwidth for it. This is a brave face I'm putting on, in case you can't tell.'

She exhales and lets go of the blind. 'Me too,' she says, sadly. She gives me a hug, but we both pull away before the threat of crying looms. We can do that later, as well. 'I was only trying to help.'

'I get it,' I tell her, and the way she looks at me melts my stoic heart. She's wordlessly communicating with me, in the way only she can. I understand what she's saying and she's not even uttered a syllable.

'Seriously?' I say, knowing what she's getting at just from the way she blinks. She's not given up. 'We're seriously going to ask this man to hang out with us?'

She grins, impishly, letting me talk myself into whatever is going to happen next. It's her superpower, shutting up and letting other people babble away until she gets what she wants. Even as it's happening, I know I'm playing into her malevolent plan, but I am a mere mortal. I cannot refuse her.

'Fine,' I say, blinking back the threat of tears as it hits me, again, how much I'm going to miss her. 'Text Jackson. If Sofa Guy wants to come back for pizza – which he won't do, I'm sure – he's welcome. Maybe another person here will steer us away from morose and keep things celebratory and fun.'

Candice pumps her fist in the air in a dramatic gesture designed to make me laugh. 'Yes,' she squeals, as if she's won.

'You're an idiot,' I say, grinning in spite of myself.

'And you need to go make sure your bikini line is sorted,' she retorts. 'I'm telling you: my radar is perfect. You're about to get lucky.'

7

Nic

Well, it's official. I am back in their house and, every time Ruby speaks to me, I blush. She says a single word and something sticks in my throat and bleeds upwards, spreading like spilled wine towards my cheeks, the backs of my ears, my eyes. Then the blushing makes me even more nervous because I feel such a twat, and because I feel such a twat, I blush harder. It's humiliating.

'What did I say, man?' Jackson stage-whispers to me when Ruby disappears to find napkins with Candice. 'Just breathe. Be where you are, remember?'

I nod. 'Be where you are,' I repeat. I can hear the dull background noise of chatter behind the kitchen door.

'They're talking about you,' says Jackson.

He's clocked me trying to listen in, then.

'Are they pissed that I'm here?' I probe, and Jackson shakes his head. He had insisted I come back to the house with him after we'd delivered my sofa. In the taxi he'd told me about his job as an assistant talent manager and the crazy stories of what some of the roster get up to, and then, once we'd done the heavy lifting, a bit about what it was like when he first moved here whilst I made him a brew. It was really touching when he asked me to come and hang out, and to be honest I really appreciated being offered plans. Takeaway and Saturday night TV was fine by me for tonight, but you hear stories, don't you, about people relocating and then sitting in their flats all alone forever, with nobody to text to go for a pint. My brother is here, but he's not reliable – he invited me out at 9 p.m. last night, when I was about to go to bed. And of course pizza with Jackson is also a chance for pizza with Ruby, even if she is leaving. And Jackson knew it.

'The text says to invite you! Plus, you can practise what I taught you,' he'd offered, getting me hook, line and sinker. He'd even asked if I'd like to come and play dodgeball some-time as well. If I was seduced by him dangling Ruby's company, I was locked in by the suggestion that he and I could be friends.

I feel so awkward being here though. I wish I was better at knowing what to say, and what to do. I can be okay when I've warmed up, but shit, it takes me time to get going.

Ruby returns, Candice on her heels, handing over a fabric napkin to each of us, and I force myself to look her in the eye, just fleetingly. 'These are . . . pretty,' I say, and I'm quiv-ering so much that I have to snatch my hand away before she might see. I can't believe I'm using bloody napkins as a talking point, but Jackson promised me it would work. *Be where you are.*

'Thanks,' she says, brightly, settling in on the floor and tucking her bare legs under the coffee table. She wears life so lightly. She's clearly a happy person. Comfortable with herself. 'I actually got them as a gift for Candice last Christmas. We reached a low point, using toilet roll to wipe our hands when we ate, after we ran out of kitchen towel. I thought we were ready to graduate to proper linens.'

'Clever,' I admire, only that one word on the tip of my tongue. I scramble for something else to add. *Be where you are!* 'You need those napkin rings with each of your names on, so you know whose is whose.'

'I didn't think of that.' She nods appreciatively, considering it. 'We all have a special knot we do, so we know which is ours. But personalised napkin rings would be so much more sophisticated.'

'Personalised knots?' I ask. 'Like a sort of Girl Guides thing?'

She laughs. I've just made her laugh! She's got two tidy rows of pearly white teeth. She cocks her head back to issue a high-pitched giggle before she fiddles with the hair on top of her head, as if catching herself. I can't help but wonder what it would be like to press my lips up against that neck.

'I never made it that far actually,' she admits, but I'm finding it hard to focus: all I want to do is hear that giggle again.

Be.

Where.

You.

Are.

'I left after Brownies and discovered boys and nail polish and things you can't – and shouldn't – get badges in,' she continues. 'Do you want four cheese or the spicy *diavolo*?'

I realise she's motioning to the boxes.

'One of each, please,' I say. She plays mother and Jackson looks at me, nodding approvingly. I find myself pathetically wanting to keep her chatting just to hear her voice, but there's also a tiny part of me that wants Jackson's approval that I can. That his confidence in me isn't misplaced. He seems so sure I can do this. 'I can't choose, you see, because I'm a Libra. Balance is everything.'

To my surprise she exclaims: 'I'm Libra too! And Libra rising!' I take my food from her gratefully. When she smiles a dimple dips on one side of her mouth. It's adorably hot. 'Scorpio moon, though. So don't cross me. I've got a sting in my tail . . .' She issues a little laugh with it, and the others titter along too. It sounds like they all know full well what the sting in her tail is capable of, but I don't know what rising and moon mean. I rack my brains: she's responding to everything I say, like Jackson promised, and, when she talks, I want to say something else again. Handing off our thoughts to each other that way is wicked, man. I'm loving it.

Wait. Handing our thoughts off to each other? I'm describing conversation, aren't I? What I'm excited about is basic conversation.

'Triple Leo here,' Jackson pronounces, holding up a hand in admission. 'Star of the show, any which way, and never sorry about it. I'm a king in my castle.'

'You should be on TV,' I tell him. 'I know I've only just met you, but I feel like you shouldn't be managing talent. You could *be* the talent?'

Ruby and Candice guffaw, and Candice makes a vomiting sound at my suggestion. Jackson winks at me.

'These two are just jealous of my easy charisma,' he says. 'And anyway, fame doesn't interest me. It ruins people. I *could* be a relationship coach though,' he adds pointedly. 'Like that Grant Garby guy.'

Before I can scowl at him to shut up – I don't want the

girls to know what he's told me about how to keep my cool! Or that he's helped in any way! – Candice says: 'Jesus. It'd be a desperado to accept relationship coaching off you. You've never even had a proper relationship. Not in all the time I've known you!'

A shadow passes across his face, and I decide not to be mad at him. I wonder how he's never had a proper relationship, when everything he's told me to do is actually working. It's so funny – people can strike you as being one thing, and hide so many other truths about themselves. Not everyone is as they seem. In fact, hardly anyone at all.

'So what's brought you to London, then?' Ruby asks, clearly looking for a way to change the subject, as she lifts a slice of pizza to her perfect mouth. 'Jackson said you've just moved here?'

Everyone is being wonderfully accepting, like Jackson said they would be, and slowly I feel my nerves thaw like I'm stood in front of a cosy home fire.

'Yeah,' I say from my spot over on the far sofa, inwardly marvelling that *she* has asked *me* a question. It's almost as if she wants a conversation too!

'New job?' butts in Candice.

'Er . . .' I stall. I obviously don't want to get talking about finance. That'd kill the mood.

'Broken heart?' she presses.

I furrow my brow. Is it that obvious? Because I don't want to talk about that either.

'Candice . . .' says Ruby, as if she's warning her. It saves me from answering. 'Don't mind this nosy-pants.' She turns to me. 'She thinks she's being big and clever, but really it's a deflection tactic so nobody tries to penetrate her hard shell to see if there's a squishy, mushy heart under there.'

'Which there is,' Jackson interjects.

'Oh, but of course,' sing-songs Ruby, and then stage-whispering to me adds: 'You want to see her with the guy who delivers our post. She's putty in his hands.'

'I can hear you, you know,' Candice groans.

'I know you can.' Ruby grins. 'Giving you a taste of your own medicine is what keeps me going in this life. Honestly, Nic – she can barely form a sentence with him. He's her total opposite. Tall and gangly in the way only a man who walks 50,000 steps a day can be. All tanned from being out in the weather. Always smiling, permanently up for a chat. And if he rings the doorbell with a package Candice *has* to be the one to answer, but all she does is say hi and bye! We saw him at the pub once and they managed a whole five-minute conversation about laundry detergent and their favourite scents . . . It was a car crash. He looks at her all googly-eyed and she shuts him down because . . . actually Candice, why? I'm going to miss seeing you act a fool over him.'

'I *will* ask him out.' Candice pouts. 'Eventually. I'm just biding my time, waiting for my moment.'

'Timing *is* everything,' I acknowledge.

Ruby nods in agreement, and as Candice rolls up the last part of her pizza to make a tidy package to pop in her mouth, she says to me: 'Anyway. Ruby thinks she isn't going to miss us when she's gone, but she's wrong.'

'I am going to miss you!' Ruby cries. 'Of course I am. But that doesn't mean leaving is the wrong thing. I can miss you, and know it's right to take this scholarship.'

Jackson nudges into her shoulder. He's got the best spot in the room, down there on the floor beside her. Her cheeks are rosy from the food and the drink, and I can't lie: when she licks grease from her fingers I can't help but think rude thoughts. I'm trying not to, but I do. I think of holding her hair, a hand either side of her head, those fingers unbuttoning my jeans.

'Stop being earnest,' Jackson instructs. 'You're creeping me out.'

Ruby rolls her eyes.

'So you've all lived together for a while, I take it?' I ask. They seem like siblings, ribbing each other in the same way Ollie and I do. It's really lovely to see – and a bit over-whelming. Their in-jokes move at the speed of light.

'We have,' says Ruby. 'I moved here after uni and replied to the advert Jackson had put up.'

'And I met Ruby . . . what, Rubes, a year after that?' adds Candice. 'We ended up in the smoking area at an event I was a waiter at, and Ruby, as a guest, was hiding from . . .' She stops herself and turns her focus to the woman in question. 'Sorry,' Candice says to her.

Ruby shrugs. 'Some guy.'

'Some *arsehole* guy,' Candice clarifies, but then it's as if she's said too much and is pivoting quickly. 'And we shared a menthol and got chatting and followed each other on social—'

'And when the other room came up she saw Ruby's post about it . . .' says Jackson.

'And the rest is history!' finishes Ruby.

They pass the cues of the story off to each other effortlessly.

'And now, the story ends!' cries Candice, with mock hysterics. She flings the back of her hand to her forehead and wails. 'Jackson! How will we go on without her?'

I wait for more laughter, but we're interrupted by a small Asian man stood in the doorframe. You can practically hear us all turn to the disturbance in unison.

'Bao!' says Ruby vibrantly. 'We didn't hear you come in!'

Bao bows slightly in greeting, dipping his head and clutching his chest. 'Hello,' he says in stilted English. 'How are you today?'

Ruby returns the head bow. 'I'm good, thank you. How are you today?'

'Very well,' Bao replies, followed by a smile. 'Thank you. Please enjoy your meal.'

'There's plenty,' offers Jackson. 'Would you like some?'

Bao shakes his head. 'Now, I go,' he says. 'Thank you. Enjoy your evening, everybody.' He points a finger upwards, and everyone says goodbye.

'Let us know if you change your mind,' Ruby calls after him, kindly.

'I thought it was just the three of you,' I say, curious as to how Bao fits in with them all.

'We rent out the small room at the back to foreign students,' explains Jackson. 'Keeps things interesting. And cheap.'

I nod. They've got a great place here. Full lives and so much love. A feeling close to longing, or maybe jealousy, bubbles in my stomach. I want this in my life, too. I know I've been missing something, and seeing them together is making me realise what it is. It's fun. Plain and simple. I want more *fun* in my life.

'More beer anyone?' says Jackson, picking his up and taking the last swig.

'Please,' says Candice, handing over her empty.

'Sure,' I say. 'And am I okay to have that last slice of the *diavolo*? It's some proper good scran, is that.'

'Isn't it?' agrees Ruby. 'Giuseppe's will be a new staple for you now you're around here. I'm going to miss it almost as much as I'll miss . . .'

42

She pauses for dramatic effect.

'Well . . . You, Nic.'

The others don't even dignify her words with a rebuttal, but I've flashed up hotter than a summer heatwave. The others know she means *them*. She's going to miss them. *Why oh why* do I have to arrive right as she's leaving? I'm really enjoying being around her. Still, maybe if there's one like her down here, there will be more? Maybe? It seems unlikely, but like buying her sofa has taught me already: anything is possible if you let it be.

I really do fancy her, though. I admit it. I do. She's got her legs stretched out in front of her, occasionally flexing her feet to point her toes like a dancer warming up before going on stage. Her tiny toenails are painted lilac, I notice, like lavender.

'Rubes, come and help me?' Jackson requests. As they leave for the kitchen, I stuff more pizza into my mouth, fervently hoping that Candice doesn't ask me anything, so that it's quiet and I can listen in to what Jackson's saying.

'It's cool you'd come hang out with us,' Candice says, not giving me any such luck. 'Jackson's a good guy like that. He always wants to get everyone involved. He's kind of the glue that holds us together, really. I call them my London family – I don't really get on with my real family.'

I bob my head from side to side and exaggerate my chewing, the universal sign for 'Hold on – my mouth is full.'

'I don't know if he said,' I start, once I've swallowed. I can't just ignore her because I'm eavesdropping. 'But I only know my brother here. Jackson and I got chatting in the taxi and he's invited me to join his dodgeball team too. So I see what you mean about getting everyone involved.'

'I was on that team for a bit,' notes Candice. 'It's a good

43

group of people. Only reason I didn't stay is because of work – I'm a catering waiter, so do unusual hours. I had to book tonight off ages ago because of the bank holiday. Ruby did it for a month or so too, but it wasn't really her vibe. The dodgeball, I mean. Not the waiting on. She's much cleverer than that.'

Jackson and Ruby are laughing about something in the kitchen – one of them issues a high-pitched roar, the kind of laughter that's contagious. I can't help but smile too, and Candice clearly spots it.

'Do I sense a spark between you and our friend Ruby . . . ?' she presses, mischievously.

I instantly flush in awkwardness. 'What?' I say, shaking my head. 'No. I don't know. That's not . . .'

'Dude, chill,' she interrupts. 'We're not that serious around here. I didn't mean to embarrass you. It's cool.'

I feign a nonchalant wave, despite my glowing cheeks demonstrating that I am, indeed, embarrassed.

She holds her hands up like she's got nothing to hide. 'These are simply my words of encouragement, whilst we've got the chance.' She smirks, and then before I can ask her to clarify what she means – words of encouragement? – Ruby and Jackson are back from behind closed doors, three beers between Jackson's fingers as Ruby trails behind him. He gives me a not-very-subtle big thumbs up with his free hand. I don't know what that's supposed to mean, either. Something is going on, but I can't work out what.

'Did you miss us?' he says, giving me a wink. 'What are you talking about?'

'Secrets and lies,' Candice retorts, and she looks at Ruby, silently communicating something in *'girl'*. Ruby looks at me and blinks confusedly, before Candice reaches out and slaps her bum as she passes. Now I really don't understand what's happening. I look to Ruby, and she looks as bemused as I feel.

'Let's have a two-minute dance party,' Candice hollers then, and before I know it, they've turned all the lights off and we're swaying to a Jessie J song in the dark, screaming the lyrics at the top of our lungs and letting the gentle buzz of the booze gradually take hold. I don't even remember what I was so confused about. I simply dance.

8

Ruby

I'll bet Nic thinks we're bloody children in this house. Jackson has all but pimped one of us out, and I can't tell who. He didn't need my help getting the beers at all – he only wanted to let me know that he'd slipped a couple of condoms under my pillow.

'Just in case that's useful to know, darling,' he warbled into the fridge as he pulled out more Peroni. 'I'm not saying anything other than that.'

Which, of course, says it all. It makes me feel like he's brought Nic back here for the sole purpose of sleeping with me – I just can't tell if Nic knows that and is in on it, or if he's genuinely here to chill. He doesn't seem like that kind of guy – he asks great questions and is a good listener and, all in all, is solid company. Whatever his intentions, I have to admit that it's nice that he's here because, as I'd suspected, he's helping us keep our spirits up. There's nothing more our little group loves than an audience. I do keep snatching glances of him though. He's sent a tizzy through me more than once as he's maintained eye contact when he strikes up a conversation. And his laugh – oh my God, his laugh! He doesn't give it away freely but when he does it feels like an achievement. He's easy to be around. He's a bit awkward, sure, and he's certainly not my typical 'macho' type, but I find it surprisingly endearing: there's no bravado to him, only an earnestness that most blokes our age don't tend to have. Everyone wants to act so casual, so nonchalant; I forget what it's like to be around a man who is excited by stuff. He's sweet. Nice. I didn't think sweet and nice could also be hot but here we are.

Jackson doesn't give me time to get clarification on anyone's motivations, just tells me my tits look great and to remember I'm a queen, which makes me cackle with gleeful indignation even though what I really want to do is hook my finger into the back of his belt loops and tug him back so I can demand more information about Nic and the condoms and Jackson's suggestions we hook up.

As we re-enter the lounge, I catch sight of him and my stomach flips. Never mind Jackson: do *I* want to sleep with Nic? I suppose My Year of Me doesn't technically begin until tomorrow . . . so does that mean it comes into effect at midnight?

After The Abe Thing, Candice made me watch a movie where the main woman is celibate for a year as a way to focus on herself, and that's where I got the idea to take a year out to focus on myself. Rebuild myself. Because Abe did break me, if I'm honest. Somebody's friend-at-work's-sister's-auntie can be involved with a fella who has a girlfriend and you always think to yourself, *what an idiot – nobody ever leaves the girlfriend! Once a sidepiece always a sidepiece!* But I know first-hand now that it's too easy to judge. For years Abe had me under his spell, drawing me into his orbit, and I always thought we'd be together in the end. He promised me we would, that it was *circumstance* keeping us apart. He'd end up on a 'break' with his girlfriend, we'd spend two or three or four glorious weeks together, and then he'd disappear, saying they were trying again.

It happened over and over and over, and I let it. I was a willing participant. But that's why I held on for so long, tearing off pieces of myself for him even when he wasn't asking me to: I was desperate to prove what I thought was my love, eager to be chosen. I got so far in that I needed it to have all mean something, and I thought that if I could just prove how much I was willing to love him, in the end he'd love me back like I needed him to. But now I know better.

We dance wildly for the duration of a single song and all of this flies through my mind as I jump up and down and sing and shriek and think, *I'm going to miss this. I'm going to miss this so much it hurts.* I love Jackson and Candice with my everything. I wouldn't have survived the tumult of The Abe Thing without them. They've been my rock. We know everything about each other, inside and out. They are the real loves of my life. If I leave London with anything, it's the knowledge that they've been my little urban unit, and that's so special.

When the last note plays and the song stops, Jackson puts the light on again and I catch Nic looking sweaty and elated and happy and he says, sweetly, 'That was the best two minutes of my life!' I know what he means. Our two-minute dance parties are one of my favourite things. I like that he thinks they're awesome too.

I'm still looking at him when he proceeds to pull off his

jumper, revealing a tiny bit of toned stomach, chiselled like stone. Candice clocks it, but I look away before she can give me a *caught you!* wink. I didn't think he was interested, but he came back and now I get the feeling he might be. He's been looking at me when he thinks I don't notice. And now there are those condoms under my pillow . . .

Damn them both. Between Jackson in the kitchen, Candice asking him probing questions, and seeing that trail of hair from Nic's belly button down to . . . well, wherever it goes, I'm more than half wondering how seriously to take Jackson's prompt. We three really do know everything about each other, so it's possible they both know I really should have one last fling before I go. And now I'm thinking about it, to be honest, to mark my leaving, and to leave these crappy few years behind, to forget everything that has led up to this point and all that has transpired I really wouldn't mind one last night of passion before I set the timer on my Year of Me. Sort of like eating a tub of ice cream before starting a diet. A little treat to encourage good behaviour later. And, yeah – making the last person I went to bed with somebody other than bloody Abe.

Or maybe all this is the beer talking. I'm tipsy, not to mention generally hormonal and emotional at the prospect of saying goodbye.

'Here,' I say to Nic, holding out a hand to take his hoodie. 'Let me hang that up for you.'

Our hands brush as I take it and I note the way Nic's pupils dilate as he smiles in thanks.

'Cheers,' he says, smiling with only one side of his mouth, and there's something there, a suggestion that makes me think that the direction of the evening really can change, if, like Jackson and Candice have suggested, I want it to. He *is* handsome. And *little Ruby,* as Jackson calls it, *is* hungry for that 'ice cream'.

I beam at him again, and keep looking even when he glances away timidly. By the time he looks back, I think I've made my decision. If he wants the same, that is. Because with sudden clarity, I agree with everything Jackson and Candice have been telling me. Sod Abe, sod teary goodbyes – I deserve to leave London on a high note. And that high note could be Nic.

9

Nic

We drink our beers and stash the empty pizza boxes away and the three of them – Jackson, Candice and Ruby – start telling stories about everything they've got up to in the time they've lived together and been friends. I get the sense it's actually quite nice for them to have a relative stranger to regale, because they can pretend the stories are for my benefit when in fact they keep nudging one another or grabbing quick hugs or stroking one another's hair in flashes of affection, a poignant reminder that one of them is leaving.

I listen intently, laughing at the right parts and nodding sagely when needed, and after a while I realise Ruby is staring at me. I'd thought she was before, after the dancing, but quickly dismissed myself as being pitifully hopeful; it was more likely she was only checking the time behind me. I expect her to look away as I glance in her direction now, but she doesn't. She holds my gaze, and it almost gives me a hard-on. I just think she's so damned sexy, but also stunning – in a very old-school classic way – and fun. She's the full package. I smile back. We stay like that for a beat beyond friendly, until Jackson suggests tequila and corrals Candice into helping him in the other room.

The last time I had tequila was the month after the break-up, when I thought single blokes went out and drank and that's how a person met other people: doing shots after work with the team and bumping into a group from another place of work, out drinking with their team, hoping for the same. I got so bladdered that I actually threw up in my hand, at the bar. Chucked down the shot, felt it sting the back of my throat, and immediately spat it out, bringing up the dregs of the chicken salad I'd had for lunch with it.

I've not done shots since.

Ruby is looking at me again. It's just me, and her, and my circling thoughts of vomit. Proper seductive, me. *Not*.

'I've got a secret,' she says, coyly.

I knit the tops of my eyebrows together in question, narrowing my eyes. Every cell in my body is screaming: YOU'RE ALONE TOGETHER!!!!!!!!!!! I *cannot* fuck this up. The way she's looking at me . . . I refuse to do anything that might make that stop.

'Go on . . .' I say, noticing she's flushed. Her cheeks are pink, maybe from the drinks we've had, or maybe from the emotion bobbing under the surface for them all. It's a loaded night, all dancing and clowning around aside.

'I'm not proud of this, but . . .' she starts, and I've got no idea where this is going. 'We internet-stalked you. Well, they did. Jackson and Candice. And I looked too.'

'Oh,' I say, and I think I'm flattered. I suppose we did technically meet on Facebook, as 2009 as that sounds. That's where her sofa was for sale: Facebook Marketplace.

'I feel really naughty. I needed to come clean. To get it off my conscience.'

'Uh-huh,' I reply. I don't know how to respond. I've got Jackson's voice in my head telling me to say something, to keep her talking, but I'm so pleased by the way she's looking at me when she says the word 'naughty' that it's sending me right back to the tongue-twisted idiot who knocked on the door this afternoon. 'Well. That's . . . interesting,' I settle on. *Ask a question*, I coach myself. *Keep her talking with a question!* 'And what did you find . . . ?'

Good. That was a good thing to say. Her eyes noticeably widen.

'Lads' night out,' she replies, her voice getting softer and indicating the beginning of a list by raising a finger to count. 'Tagged pictures of a girlfriend that stopped suddenly, which Jackson said meant a break-up . . . graduate throwback Thursday photo . . . the role-play in Scotland . . .'

'Role-play?' I reply, genuinely amused. My voice is dropping to mirror hers, so that we're both leaning forwards to make sure we don't miss anything. 'The LARPing?'

'Is that what it's called?' she asks, smirking. 'There was chain mail involved anyway.'

She's flirting. I'm ninety per cent sure she's flirting. She's teasing me, she's maintaining eye contact, she's smiling a lot. That's flirting, isn't it? The way my heart has sped up, my mouth has dried, this feeling on my skin – that's definitely because of flirting.

I take a punt. 'Did you see the size of my sword though?'

She bursts out laughing. 'Subtle, Nic. Really subtle.'

When Jackson and Candice barrel back into the room, I manage to dodge the issue of shots by taking another punt at honesty: I told everyone the tequila story and *bam* – they were hysterical, and gave me another beer instead. They joked about not wanting to get the rug cleaned. We've all dropped quieter now, the evening having pushed into a crescendo of laughter and stories and given way into a comfortable lull. Ruby keeps stretching, reaching up and moving her arms and cricking her neck like a cat, enticing me without words. I don't think I'm imagining it. I hand-on-heart didn't come back in here for sex – I just wanted to be around her. To know what she's like. And if all that transpired from this night on Maple Avenue was the acquisition of a new dodge-ball team that would have been more than fine with me.

But I know now that there's more at play.

Jackson has sprawled back from his spot on the floor so that from the sofa Candice can tickle his back and play with his hair. Ruby keeps looking at me even when she's talking to somebody else, going undetected because they've both got their eyes closed and can't see us.

I tear the label off my empty bottle and when the small clock by the TV chimes midnight, Candice finally says, 'My loves, if it's all the same to you I'm going to hit the hay. I've got a fourteen-hour shift tomorrow.'

She stands up, forcing Jackson to sit upright and open his eyes as she pads across to Ruby to kiss the top of her head.

'I'll see you in the morning, babe,' she says sleepily, and Ruby nods.

'I'm leaving at nine,' Ruby replies. 'Sharp.'

Jackson lazily looks over at me and then across to Ruby, who is stretching yet again, the loose side of her T-shirt slipping down even further, and I know, without a shadow of a doubt, that it's for my benefit.

'That's me, too,' Jackson decides. He tells Ruby he'll make

breakfast at eight in the morning, and then asks me for my number so he can text the dodgeball team details.

'Nic . . . ?'

'Sheridan,' I say, and as I reply I look at Ruby again because he's looking at his phone. Neither of us grins this time. We're serious. She parts her lips a tiny amount and licks her bottom lip, her tongue gliding out and then slowly scooting back in. Jackson asks a question, but I don't hear him even when he repeats it.

'Yeah,' I say, not sure what I'm agreeing to. 'Sounds good.'

10

Ruby

He's over on one sofa, the one by the shelves of old DVDs we've always said we'd give to the charity shop and have never got around to. I'm on the sofa nearest the kitchen door. The candles are burning down to their nubs and the lamp is casting moody shapes over us, and as Jackson says goodnight and pulls the dining room door to, there's a timid pause. I look at Nic, Nic looks at me, and it crosses my mind that he might say his goodbyes as well. I don't want him to.

'Do you—' he starts, right as I say, 'Gosh, it's almost—'

We nervously laugh.

'After you,' he says. 'Sorry.'

'No, don't worry,' I insist. 'I've totally forgotten what I was even going to say.'

'Oh.'

His eyes scan the room. The music quietly plays.

I've got nothing to lose. If he rejects me, so what? Will it kill me? No. I'll live. Even with a dented ego, I'll survive.

Won't I? I'm leaving town, for crying out loud. I'm never going to see the man again.

I try to take a deep breath.

'Listen,' he says, and my heart sinks. He's going to go.

'Yes?' I ask.

'Forgive me for being so blunt but I was thinking . . . wondering, really. I suppose I was hoping, foolishly, even though we've just met and you're leaving in the morning . . .'

Oh my God.

I smirk. 'If you're asking if you can kiss me . . .' I instigate, and he looks at me with heartfelt eyes. In that second, I know with perfect clarity that we both want the exact same thing, and I let myself pause, adding some drama. Because, sod it, if you can't be utterly romantic and shameless and daring at a time like this, when can you? I feel like an actress in a film.

His eyebrows waver, just slightly, imploring me to finish the sentence. He might even be holding his breath. *I* might even be holding *my* breath!

'Then the answer is . . .' I continue, trying my best to look coquettish from under my eyelashes, the corner of my mouth twitching in a way I hope is cute and inviting. 'Yes, you may.'

There's a mischievous twinkle in his eyes, as he replies, cool as an autumn breeze and more self-assured than I've seen him all night: 'I'm not asking if I can kiss you, Ruby.'

I swallow, hard. I can't look away.

'I'm asking if I can take you to bed.'

He peels off my clothes slowly, like he's got all the time in the world to enjoy what he's about to do. When I'm naked, but still standing, he moves to kiss every part of my skin he can reach until he sits down on the edge of the bed, pulling me towards him by the hand, so he can kiss my chest, my stomach, lower and lower, until he can't bend that way anymore. He runs both hands down the outsides of my thighs, and then drags them back up the insides, tantalisingly close, before cupping my bum, jiggling it a bit.

'This,' he says, cheekily, quietly, 'is an excellent arse.'

'My arse likes you too,' I say, hands resting lightly on his shoulders, prompting a gentle spank with the flat of one hand. 'Easy boy,' I tell him, smirking, because I didn't *not* like that.

He opens his mouth and takes a nipple, then, sucking the tiniest bit and then letting his tongue perform circles, slowly, around and around. I moan, running my hands through his hair and closing my eyes to let the sensation wash over me.

'That's nice,' I sigh, and he moves to the other boob.

'This?' he asks, doing it again.

'Harder,' I instruct, and when the pressure is exactly right I tell him: 'Yes. Like that.'

He's firm and gentle, all at once, and I'm struck by how easy it is to tell him what I like. I'm never going to see him again – who cares if I'm bossy? He is, apparently, very good at taking direction. It's a turn-on.

'Take your clothes off,' I tell him, whispering but resolved. 'I want to see you.'

He pulls away from my chest and then holds my eye as he pulls off his T-shirt, then inelegantly pulls down his jeans. 'Socks too,' I say, and for a moment he's all legs and knees, bending over to do as I say and then standing – in more ways than one – to full attention.

'Very nice,' I admire, purposely letting myself stare, stating without words that I'm not going to rush either. Then, I reach out a hand and drop to my knees.

'Jesus,' he moans, but I'm only just getting started.

11

Nic

The faint chime of the living room clock tells us it's 2 a.m. She's still lying on top of me. I don't know what came over me, but the fact that I found the balls to seize the moment is something I will hold on to for the rest of my life. I've won the lottery.

'That was . . .' I say, and she hums agreement. But it's not exactly enthusiastic, and immediately I worry it wasn't as good for her as it was for me. Did she fake having a good time? Oh shit, I really, really hope not. Not even for my sake – for hers. If only she'd told me how to be better, what to do, given some instruction, I could have done it. I'm a quick study. I'm happy to learn. I am! And then I realise the shape of her under my arm has changed, and my chest feels wet.

'Hey, hey – are you . . . ?' I ask, craning my neck to get a better look at her. She is. She's crying.

'Ruby,' I say, panicking. 'Ruby? It's okay. What happened?

Did I do something? Are you hurt? Just talk to me please. Come on. I only want to make sure you're okay . . .'

'I'm fine,' she insists, turning her face away from me. 'I am, honestly. I'm fine. Sorry. Urgh. This is so embarrassing.'

My hand is at the small of her back, cradling just above her bum. I softly rub circles over it with my thumb, waiting for more information.

'Ruby . . . ?'

She lifts her face and uses the back of a hand to wipe her cheeks.

'I really am sorry,' she repeats, snottily self-conscious. 'I didn't know I'd feel this way. I'm fine, really. That was good – really good. Too good? I feel . . .'

It's killing me, waiting for her to decide how to explain. I know I sort of lost myself with her as we were doing it – it felt so, so good, like, teenage-fantasy, take mental pictures for the wank-bank good – but I didn't mean to miss any signs that she felt . . . well, I don't know how she feels. She's still not said it.

'I know this isn't about me,' I say carefully, trying to sound open to whatever she has to say but not selfish or self-centred. 'But I'm sort of freaking out that it's my fault you're crying?'

She sits up, then, putting both palms on my chest so that she's straddling me, looking down, all tits and face. I'm no longer inside her, but I like her there, the weight of her on me, letting what had just happened become a reality the longer her body continues to be wrapped around mine. If she wasn't right there in front of me I might almost believe I wet-dreamed it.

'This is mortifying,' she begins. 'But I can just be honest?'

She inhales and then lets out her breath slowly. 'I haven't been with anyone other than my ex in, like, years. And how you just made love to me – he didn't touch me with the tenderness you did in all the time we were together. A one-night stand has just been kinder to me than the man I thought I was in love with. Isn't that the most pathetic thing you've ever heard?'

She crumples back down and shifts her leg to roll off me, so that we lie side by side, and she issues an ashamed groan.

'I don't even know why I'm telling you this,' she continues. 'Actually, yes I do. I need to tell somebody, I suppose, and you're the one who's naked in my bed. I have a lot of feelings right now. Sorry. Oh God, I know this isn't what you signed up for, sorry. And now I'm waffling. Urgh.'

I flip onto my side so I can see her. What man would have her in his bed and not relish every atom of her, drink down every last drop? Who could willingly make a woman feel this way? She's the whole prize.

'Don't look at me,' she jokes. 'I'm literally still crying. This is so embarrassing.'

I reach out a hand and put it to her face, wiping away the tears that really are still there. She's good-humoured, laughing at herself for being emotional, but I feel for her. I honestly do. Because I was with Millie for all that time – we even talked about getting married, having kids – and it was never like it's just been with Ruby.

'I mean, same,' I say, eventually. Softly. 'If that helps. That was . . .'

'It was, wasn't it?'

'Uh-huh,' I say. 'If you didn't wake everyone up, I think I certainly did. That thing you did with your back arched that way? And the speed? I thought my head was going to explode.'

She giggles. 'Shut up,' she says. 'You're teasing me.'

'I'm not,' I insist. 'I'm deadly serious.'

She deposits a kiss onto my knuckles but doesn't say anything else. A car starts up outside the house, the noise reverberating through the walls, the headlamps lighting us up. We're still for so long I think she might have fallen asleep. But then, eventually, she says my name.

12

Ruby

'Nic?' I whisper again, staring at the ceiling. I can't tell if he's awake or not.

'Mmmmm?' he replies.

I can't help myself. A man doesn't treat a woman like he has just treated me without being one hundred per cent trustworthy. I could *smell* colours. He held me like he was worried he might break me, but was so precise and unhurried with his hands . . . with his mouth . . . I don't think I ever genuinely understood the big deal about sex until forty-five minutes ago. It was only supposed to be a hook-up, but is it crazy to say it felt more right with Nic than it ever has with anyone else? Ever?

And now the minutes are slipping away from me, the hours loaded against me. I'm leaving. The credits are about to roll on this life in London, and I've got to move and start anew. I'm petrified. I'm ready to admit that. I've been strong for Jackson, and for Candice, because I needed them to be strong for me. But I don't need to be strong for Nic, especially not now I've cried on him. It's a sweet relief. And of course, he knows better than anyone what I'm about to embark on: I think about what we saw when we stalked him online, the stories he's told tonight – I don't understand how a person is supposed to build something new like he has. Is. He can tell me how moving on – literally and emotionally, yes, but physically, somewhere else – is supposed to go.

'Your break-up,' I prompt. 'Was that her, or you?'

It's been two years with Abe of highs that were so heady I could barely breathe – and lows so crushing I could hardly function. It's been drama and chaos and only now, suddenly crystal clear in the arms of this stranger do I feel protected, like I can breathe. Nic is a safe port in the shitstorm I've weathered, and I'm not just saying that because he made me orgasm until I thought my legs were going to give out. Twice. Every piece of evidence I've got points to him being A Good Guy – and, crucially, he doesn't even know he is one. He takes it for granted that all the other men out there operate with the same courtesy and kindness he does. I can tell even from a few hours with him. He's a rare breed made rarer by the fact that he's got no idea, and it's knocked me sideways. What an unexpected turn of events.

'Me,' he replies, plainly, opening his eyes. 'But that doesn't make it any easier. It was proper devastating, breaking somebody else's heart. Nobody tells you that. All the songs, they're all about being dumped. Walking away is dead hard. Because you're not supposed to feel sad when you're the one who walked away, are you, because it was your choice. Except I didn't feel like I had a choice. If I had stayed with her it wouldn't have been fair. It would have been a lie. So I told her so.'

64

'And that's why you left Liverpool?'

'Yes and no,' he tells me.

He seems reluctant to talk about it.

'I'm being too personal,' I say, my heart sinking. I'm a magpie picking over the carcass of his experience for my own benefit, taking advantage of his gentleness because I need to feel better. 'Sorry. You can go to sleep if you want. It's all right.'

He scrunches up his nose.

'I don't want to be a boring bastard, that's all,' he says.

'It's the opposite of boring,' I insist. 'I'd like to hear it. It's . . . helpful. Would you tell it to me? All of it?'

So he does. He'd been with Millie since he was a teenager. He'd done great at school and even better at university. He'd saved for a house deposit and bought his first home, a tiny little terrace, when he was only twenty-three. Work was great, family was great, from the outside it was perfect.

'The whole path was laid out for me,' he explains, and he's not looking at me. He's looking at the ceiling too. It's easier to say things to a ceiling than a person, sometimes – I understand that. 'And I started to wake up feeling sick. I knew Millie was waiting for a proposal, and she'd always said she wanted to be a young mum. I knew her family, she knew mine, we had this whole routine: Monday night fajitas, Tuesday I'd play footy and come home late, Wednesday she'd be out with the girls, Thursday we'd watch a boxset and get a takeaway and Friday was date night in town. I'd go LARPing at the weekends and there'd be Sunday roast at either her parents' or mine, and then that was it. We'd do it all again the week after, and the week after that, and it was fine, but it was also awful. I had this feeling niggling away at the back of my mind that I ignored for months, maybe even a year.

Thinking about it, I might have always felt like that but I didn't know it could feel any different. Like I was drowning. Like my lungs were filling with water, drip, drip, drip, a tiny bit at a time and suddenly I wasn't so much sinking as sunk. Dying on the inside.'

He pauses, then, like he's sorry he's telling me so much.

'Well. Not dying maybe,' he corrects. 'But it was what can be referred to as a Shite Time.'

'I understand,' I say, gently, wanting him to carry on. Hearing somebody talk about what scared them into something new doesn't help, exactly, but it does make me feel less alone.

'I don't want you to think I'm a bad person,' he utters. 'I was damned if I stayed, damned if I didn't. I was stuck. I started to get the shakes and sweats and I was chucking up at weird times. Millie was so worried – she thought I might have some underlying cancer or something and *she* even cried to *me*, saying she didn't want me to die, that I had to get myself sorted out, seen to. I went to the GP and . . .' He lets out an uncomfortable sigh. 'I'm not proud of it, but he asked all these questions and I ended up crying, and he referred me to a therapist, but I didn't go. As soon as I'd cried to my doctor I knew the truth: I didn't love Millie.'

He looks so sad, like the memory haunts him. I know swapping tales of trauma can be a fake way to build intimacy – show me yours and I'll show you mine – but his truth makes me want to share as well. I want him to know that none of us know what we're doing.

'My ex,' I offer. 'We weren't ever really together. He had a girlfriend. I know that's horrible, but he used to tell me he wasn't happy with her, that he was searching for ways to leave her. He said that he wanted to be with me – but he never looked as sorry about it as you do. I know now that's because he wasn't ever telling the truth, in the end. He just wanted to have his cake and eat it. Men like Abe are the reckless cowards. What you did was brave.'

'He sounds like an idiot,' Nic says.

'We're all fools in love,' I sigh. 'Even hearing you call him an idiot makes me want to defend him, but that's a habit I'm trying to break.'

'That's fair,' he says. 'I wouldn't let anyone trash-talk Millie. Not that she did anything wrong.'

'What happened to your house? Did you sell it?'

He nods his head. 'Yeah. I'm just renting here though, until I know what's what.'

'Do you still talk to her?' I ask.

'No. It's too hard. I know from others that she's doing okay. I don't want to say I left because of her – I don't like to think I'm running away from anything. More like running *towards* something better. My brother has lived down here for a couple of years, and I've always liked visiting. So . . . Here I am. Seeking out adventure, I suppose. Seeing what's outside the town I grew up in.'

I smile. 'That's exactly how I try to think of moving, too,' I say. 'Not running away. Running towards something new.'

What I don't let myself say is that, lying here right now, I have this unnerving feeling that in running towards something new up in Manchester, I might be missing something wonderful that's just arrived in London. But that's so absurd. We barely know each other, really. And anyway, if I wasn't leaving I'd never have crossed paths with Nic in the first place, so it must have always been meant to happen like this. I had to be selling my stuff for him to buy it; he had to be arriving for me to be able to say goodbye. This moment, this night, it feels like the stars aligned precisely so I could have somebody else give me permission to embrace what happens next.

Maybe one night, twelve hours, is enough to make you see things differently, and that's a gift to make the most out of.

The clock in the living room chimes 5 a.m. It'll start to get light soon.

'What are you thinking?' I whisper, the postcoital cliché slipping out of my mouth before I can help it. I just want him to keep talking. I want to know everything about him before we go our separate ways.

He smiles at me, the dawn soft through the flimsy curtains, casting gentle light over one cheek and forcing the rest into shadows.

'I can't believe I only met you a few hours ago,' he admits, and the way he says it makes my heart soar.

Quietly happy he's said exactly what I've been feeling but still cautiously holding him at arm's length in case I seem too eager, I reply, 'You're very charming when you're trying not to be sincere, you know.'

'I can't believe my *first* night here is your *last* night here, that's all.'

'Life is nothing if not mocking of us,' I say, rubbing a hand over his chest.

'Deep,' he quips.

'I don't know what else to say,' I sigh. Lightly I add: 'I'm glad this was how I spent my last night though. Thank you.'

What I can't say is: *I'm scared.*

'Same,' he says. 'Maybe I'll see you in Manchester, or back here when you come and visit.'

I let his offer permeate the air between us. He's lovely, and kind, and he's exactly who I needed two years ago instead of the head-fuck that was Abe. But the thing is, I'm not the woman *I* was two years ago.

I've changed. This connection with Nic makes me wonder if there could be something more between us, but if I say I'll see him again, it'll be like I never truly learned anything. And isn't life supposed to make us keep repeating the same mistakes until we catch a bloody clue? I can't see him again, because I'm supposed to be savouring how to be on my own. I'm supposed to be going to find myself, letting the parts of me unfurl unimpeded, discovering how to be a phenomenal film-maker and deciding who I really am. I can't let myself be distracted by anyone. Especially not a man I met over Facebook Marketplace who paid sixty quid for my sofa. I have to be honest with myself – and with him.

'This can't be anything more than a one-night stand,' I find myself saying. 'I've committed to this course, as a sort of Year-of-Me thing. Do my degree, get creative, no distractions. Especially, you know – men.'

He takes a beat, but replies: 'Understood.'

'Sorry.'

'No, don't be,' he says. 'It's okay. I know what this . . .' He trails off. 'You're leaving. I just got here. We get one night.'

'We get one night,' I echo, relieved he's not pushing the issue. We're on the same page.

I decide, as a distraction of the best kind, because Cinderella always turns back into an everyday woman and reality always finds a way back in, to remind us both of what we're here for. I want to enjoy this man one more time, lose myself in him as we become one. Hours earlier, I decided I wanted to enjoy a man's body and have him enjoy mine, and it was so good that we should do it again before the horses are mice and the carriage is a pumpkin, and so my hand begins to meander down from his chest to tickle the very top of his leg, and he swells gratifyingly quickly.

'There is one thing we *could* do, if you wouldn't mind . . .' I mutter close to his ear. I want to feel the weight of him again. I want to feel and not think. I want it once more before the sun comes up and the spell is broken and this next part of my life begins.

I move an inch to the left and work my hand lightly.

'And what could that be . . . ?' he says, staccato from the pleasure.

He takes the hint and moves my hand from him then, disappearing under the covers until I feel his breath between my legs. It does the trick: soon neither of us is thinking very much at all.

PART TWO

PART TWO

13

Ruby

'Well. I've thrown myself into Manchester like my life depends on it,' I tell Janet, my degree supervisor, over vending machine tea in her office. 'Which, in a way, it kind of does. I've taken this massive leap by being here, and I'm determined for it to pay off. I've told myself I have to experience *everything*. And I'm not doing badly at it, to be fair. I'm proud of myself, if that doesn't sound too boast-y. I feel . . . oh God, I can't believe I'm saying it this way but – alive?'

Janet titters encouragingly, the bracelets on her wrist clanging together musically. 'No, no. We like *alive*. Alive is good! I'm pleased to hear it,' she replies. She has soft eyes and delicate gold earrings and chunky, trendy trainers. We have twenty minutes scheduled as a check-in to make sure I'm happy and have everything I need, and I know it's for everyone – I'm not special – but I appreciate getting the one-on-one time with her. Her lectures are so cool. In the past six weeks she's become a bit of a campus idol to me – how she thinks and how she articulates her ideas. Sitting in an armchair opposite her is the academic equivalent of grabbing a martini with Beyoncé. I mentally award myself a point for making her laugh.

'We don't like the term mental health here so much as mental *fitness*,' she offers. 'We like to make sure everyone has everything they need to be their best selves so they can do their best work. That's been my experience of creation, certainly. There needs to be space for it, and actually, making art means not just isolating creativity so that you save it all up and pour it into the course. For me, at least, creativity is compounded by letting it bleed into all areas of my life.'

'What do you mean?' I press. I'm desperately trying to concoct something clever to say back.

'I mean that creativity isn't simply choosing angles and subjects and narrative arcs, or saying the right thing in class. Creativity is a state of being whilst making movies and outside of all that. We like our students to be on campus because it's full immersion. Creativity is how we dress. The route we choose to walk through campus. Making a good risotto or setting the table nicely, you know? Creativity is a mindset, and the more you can indulge it, the better,' she says. 'That's what I mean. A state of overall flow, is what I'm saying. And it sounds like that's why you're so happy. Because you're in the flow.'

'The Element,' I offer. 'That's what Ken Robinson calls it.'

'I don't know his work,' she replies, and my belly gurgles at being able to teach her something.

'He says our element is the meeting point between our natural aptitude and personal passion,' I explain. 'That we need to have the right attitude and actively seek the opportunities.'

'You get what I mean exactly then.' She nods, smiling. 'It's like finding a way to be permanently "in the zone". What we create comes from that special place, but it's like an internal vibration that affects how we see the world, how we interact with it, and how the world then treats us.'

'Yes!' I say. 'And you're right. I'm finding that easier to do here than I ever have done before. It's addictive.'

'I knew I liked you.' She grins. 'You're always so astute in lectures.'

I let the sense of victory wash over me. Two points to me.

This past six weeks truly has been dizzyingly euphoric. At orientation the course leaders explained that the master's is twenty per cent lectures, eighty per cent independent study – and one hundred per cent coursework-assessed. I spent my birthday at a back-to-back screening of three Richard Linklater movies and, honestly, I think it was the best birthday I've ever had. I love that I'm the only person who can determine how well I do, and that they aren't forcing me into a box to do it.

'Don't get me wrong,' I continue. 'My reading list is sky-high and my "to watch" list even higher, but there's something about how you all frame it that makes me hungry for the full immersion, as you call it. Do you know what I mean? It's like a free fall into this thing that I've always known I loved, but now I don't have to make excuses for it being the thing I eat, sleep, and dream about.'

'That's why mental fitness is key,' Janet says. 'You're not here long. We want you to push yourselves as hard as you are reasonably able whilst you can. But you mustn't exhaust yourself doing so. It's a fine balance.'

'It was so hard to decide how to narrow down what to sit in on,' I tell her. 'But there's only so much time in a day. I could study here for three years and still not get around to taking every module I'd like to. It's so exciting. I feel like an

75

empty jug that's tried to fill itself from a drippy tap for years, and now it's full speed ahead with a bona fide hosepipe.'

She laughs. 'Now tell me,' she asks, changing tack. 'Have you made many new friends?'

I tell her that I've got a handful of people on the course who I know better than the others, but I talk to pretty much everyone about anything – we've all got so much to say. For the number of credits I need to graduate, they say it's about two hundred hours' worth of study, which I work out is twenty hours a week, give or take, to throw myself into the *theory* of film-making. The rest of the time I'm watching movies, talking about movies, critiquing movies, and then working on two interdisciplinary modules that are a requirement of the course. It's the thing I'm most excited about though: an independent project, where I can make my own documentary. I've picked classes in 'perspectives' to learn about ideas from other artists: the body in film, digital art activism and storytelling.

Campus itself is amazing too. As I leave our meeting, thanking Janet once again for her time, I marvel at all the big glass buildings and atriums, passing by airy rooms filled with state-of-the-art equipment. But the modernity is nicely offset by the natural setting; behind the buildings sit trees that must be older than the campus, judging by how big they are, already hues of gold and amber, the sun low in the sky and casting dramatic shadows everywhere. It makes me feel like the protagonist in an indie music video, especially now it's colder and I've permanently got a massive scarf looped around my neck and up to my chin, dancing behind me as I stride.

I can't help but feel part of something bigger, and knowing I'm here with the best of the best means I'm existing on about six hours' sleep a night because I'm just *too* happy. The only thing not working out is a sudden bad bout of thrush that my normal cream doesn't seem to be helping. But itchy fanny aside, I love the library, I love the beginning of autumn and the chill in the air contrasted with the warmth from the buzz inside.

I spot the coffee cart on the corner of where all the main paths intersect and notice that my new pal Mick is working, so decide to treat myself.

'How do,' he says, as the customer in front moves along and he sees it's me.

'How do,' I say back. 'The usual, please.'

I love Mick. He's proper Mancunian, saying words like 'sound' if something is good or 'buzzing' when something is great. He remembered my name after only going there twice, and even if I don't want coffee I stop by for something, just to experience neighbourly kindliness. He's as much a part of my routine as brushing my teeth or topping up my printer credits in the student hall.

'Won your Oscar yet?' he says over the din of steaming milk.

'Snubbed by the Academy again,' I retort, using my phone to pay on his card machine.

'There's always tomorrow,' he quips back. 'Or the day after.'

'Here's hoping,' I say, raising my cup at him as a gesture of goodbye.

I notice my phone flash with a text from Mum asking me to Sunday lunch this weekend so find a wall to set my coffee down on. I tell her I've got coursework to do this weekend, but I'll do my best to come down the week after. I feel a twinge of guilt – they're only forty minutes away – but even giving up a day here feels frivolous and wasteful.

I'm actually going to try and get to an exhibit on the origins of *la vie bohème* in 1880s Paris at the big museum in town. I'm not sure she'd like being turned down for an exhibit, though. I'm on campus so much that I have to book in days to head into town though, which I'm desperate to do because it's amazing.

Manchester is all old-meets-new, with wide streets and massive red-brick buildings beside glass-fronted offices. I took myself out for a cocktail at 20 Stories in Spinningfields, the posh bit of town, when I first got here. Just a way to mark to myself that I've arrived. All the museums are free, so I've been around the Manchester Art Gallery, People's History Museum, Science and Industry Museum, the Whitworth Gallery, and I've discovered the brilliant independent cinema, where the tickets are cheap enough to justify going a couple of times a week, even on my budget. I'm enjoying being *in it.* Everything feels charged and important and like it's a clue for what I should be doing – both here, and 'next'. I'm following the hunches and inklings as I watch this film or take this class or hear this snippet of conversation, adding everything to a sort of mental compost heap so it can sludge down and percolate and marinate into ideas. I'm not sure what I want to make in my independent project yet, or how I want it to look or sound or feel, but I am certain, even so soon, that this was absolutely the right thing. The Year of Me has begun.

'Hello,' a voice says, as I sit reading the newspaper in the atrium closest to where most of the graduate film-making classes are held. I've just been to a talk from a *very* famous BAFTA-winning writer, Veronica Latimer, who has just blown my mind with her explanations in building narrative arc to emotional stories, and now I'm doing exactly as she suggested and scouring local press for human interest stories that could be the special spark we're all looking for. I look up.

'Hello,' I say back, uncertainly, because I know his face, but I can't remember his name. He's tall and burly and bearded and has a tattoo across his knuckles that says MAMA. I glance down. His other knuckles spell out NANA. He always sits at the front of the classes we're in together – I think he's in my storytelling lecture. Barry? Barney? He's one of the few people I haven't been to the pub with. Come to think of it, I don't think I've ever seen him *off* campus. Only in class.

'Harry,' he says, smiling. 'I was just in the guest lecture? I sat behind you. Thought I'd introduce myself properly. Finally.'

He's carrying a tray with a cheese baguette and can of Coke. I gesture from it to the table and say, 'Do you want to join me? I'm Ruby.'

'Nice to meet you, Ruby.' He grins, kicking out a chair with his foot and sitting down. I move to close my paper so I'm not being rude, but he interrupts and insists: 'Please, by all means, keep reading. I'd never thought of the local paper as a place to start my research until Veronica Latimer said it just then. I suppose I always thought it was too . . . small-fry?'

'Same,' I reply, immediately enjoying that he has big ideas that he can articulate well. I study his expression: he's got a wide, open face and a crooked Roman nose, and he's all beard and strong shoulders so that he looks positively Viking. 'And what she said about the minutiae of one life speaking a wider universal truth to all of our lives? I felt that.'

'Me too. Like, isn't that why we share? So others can learn, and vice versa?' he enthuses.

'You know when Adele released "Someone Like You"?' I say, because he's looking at me like he's waiting for me to share my next thought. He nods, encouragingly. 'I remember lying on the floor of my bedroom and listening to it on repeat, and it wasn't because I cared about Adele's heartache, per se, it was that . . .' I pause, trying to find the words.

'Her articulation of *her* feelings gave *you* a language for your own?' Harry supplies, before biting off a huge chunk of his sandwich.

'Yeah!' I cry, astonished that he really must feel the same. 'Which I suppose proves the point: Adele's specific truth felt like my truth, but it felt like your truth, too, and millions of other people's. That's what made it such a hit. The totally personal becoming the absolute universal.'

Harry nods at the newspaper between us. 'So you got any leads?'

I like that we're not making small talk. I'd be happy to, I suppose, but getting right into the nitty-gritty of telling stories with somebody who gets it is a particular kind of joy, and it's exactly the kind of chat I hoped to get here. Plus, Harry seems about my age. A lot of the grads are closer to under-graduate age, some having even come fresh off their first degree and into their second so they're twenty-one or twenty-two, and I'm not being snobby when I say it makes me feel old, it's just fact. I've got almost a decade on them, and a lot has bloody happened in that decade. My early friendships have been nice so far, but it's not been as immediately easy as it is now, with Harry. He must be about thirty; I'd guess thirty-three if I was a betting woman. I'm committed to talking to anyone, but having somebody my age on the course is a comfort I didn't know I'd been searching for until this exact moment.

'I'm not sure,' I say. 'I'm trying not to discount anything, and so far there's . . .' I leaf back through the pages I've already thumbed, reminding myself of what's there. 'Lost dogs, a lottery win – but we're talking thousands, not millions – an arrest for misuse of company funds . . .'

'What's the old dude's story?' Harry gestures to a small colour photograph of a nonagenarian, waving the last stub of his baguette. He's eaten it in less than four bites.

'Oh,' I say. 'I didn't spot that one. Let's see.' I scan the story. 'JP, ninety-six years old . . . fell in love when he was fighting in the Second World War, came home and had four children with his wife of seventy years and . . . oh, that's sad.'

'What?'

'Well, his wife died, but it seems so has one of his sons. A rare blood cancer. He's raising money for a charity.'

'At ninety-six?'

'Yeah,' I say.

Harry chews the last of his food and says, 'Sounds like he's lived quite a life.'

I nod. 'It does. Can you imagine fighting in a war? Coming home and just getting on with life?'

'Truly, I cannot,' says Harry. 'My little brother doesn't even know the dates of the war. I remember spending ages on it at school, since it was so recent. But I suppose as more time passes and there are fewer survivors . . .'

'There are fewer people to encourage us to remember?'

'Something like that.'

'So it could be cool to talk to him about what? The war? Life after the war? Everything he's seen in almost a century?'

Harry shrugs. 'It's like Veronica said – who can be sure where the most interesting bit will be found unless you start digging.'

I'm so obsessed with this man! Five minutes ago, I was sat with a soggy egg and cress and my thoughts, and now here is a coursemate who thinks like I do and is saying all the right things and is giving me that excited anything-is-possible feeling that I love so much. He's beaming at me, and my skin tingles. He's cute. Not that I notice things like that in The Year of Me. Obviously. It's a transitory thought that leaves as quickly as it arrives.

'Okay,' I say. 'So he seems interesting. How do we even go about connecting with him? Do we just ask for a chat and hope he tells us something juicy? That seems like just using people. If he's actually very dull, do we just move on?'

'Well, three things,' intones Harry, cheerily. 'One, I'm loving the "we" here.'

I bow my head, as if to say *well, but of course – it was your idea.*

'Two, maybe we could do a tit for tat? See what he has to say, and at the very least make our class aware of the fundraiser and get a donation together. And three, can we contact him through the charity website?'

'So yeah?' I ask. 'You wanna investigate together?'

'I'm game if you are,' says Harry. 'Two heads are better than one, surely. It's not marriage, just a chat with a potential lead. We can decide what to do about it later.'

A man with a plan – that's attractive. I always end up being the organiser of stuff, but here is a chap who knows what he wants and how to go about getting it. I'm impressed.

'Okay, well . . . hold on,' I command, pulling out my phone. I see that Candice has tried to FaceTime and followed up with a message that says, simply, 'When's good?', but I swipe it from the screen with a mental note to reply later, so I can pull up my web browser. I google the charity and find the site, and it takes three more clicks to get a contact box up, where I type in a short message about being two young film-makers who want to set up a call with JP if he'd be willing to speak more about his story and life. I include my email address and phone number.

'Done,' I say. 'I've reached out.'

'And now we wait.' Harry nods.

Neither of us speaks. It occurs to me that all of this could be an excuse just to get chatting to me. Obviously I'm not Kendall Jenner or anything, but he did just come up to me out of the blue.

'Are you wondering if I'm hitting on you via the pretext of coursework?' he says, reading my mind.

'No!' I insist, too quickly, and it makes him chuckle.

'I'm not,' he says. 'Just to shoot straight, I'm gay. I am one hundred per cent engaging with you because you're the only other person on this grad scheme even close to my age, and I knew from the stuff you've said in class that you're clever.'

'An ulterior motive of a different kind, then . . .' I tease.

'It worked, didn't it?'

'It did.' I smile. I look at my watch – it's time for me to go. 'I don't suppose you want to wander down to the under-graduate open night to see what they've been making, do you?' I offer. I'm happy going to things on my own, but I like Harry, even after ten minutes of banter. Plus, if we end up working together it would be nice to know him more. 'I don't think it'll be very good, but . . .'

'But Veronica said that even in consuming art that feels underdeveloped, our critique of it will inform our education,' supplies Harry, citing the guest lecturer again.

'Are we a couple of geeks?' I say, pulling a face. 'I feel like between us we could transcribe her whole lecture.'

Harry waves a hand. 'I'm not here to waste a second,' he says. 'This course is my idea of heaven. I worked as a teller in a bank for three years to save up the money to be here. I'm not saying I *need* this course to change my life but, if it does . . .'

'You won't be mad about it,' I interject.

'I wear the geek crown with pride.' He grins.

'My kinda man,' I declare, as we walk to the recycling and get rid of our rubbish. 'I feel exactly the same.'

'Well then you're my kind of woman,' Harry says. 'Let's go and cause some trouble, baby.'

We weave through campus, a different place now it's dark. The shadows cast by the glass buildings onto the smooth, wide pathways dance across our faces, and we chat about how we ended up on the Manchester course and what our hopes are for it.

'I want to do exactly what the guest speaker said. Tell stories that speak to a wider truth. Documentaries, really – fiction's great, but there's so much about life you couldn't make up, don't you think?' Harry says.

'Absolutely,' I agree, waving at Mick by his coffee cart as he closes up for the day.

'How do,' he says.

'Evening,' I say in reply.

Turning my attention back to Harry I add: 'And I think there are so many new mediums afforded to us by technology that there's a sort of renewed hunger for it. Financially I don't know how it could work, but even one-minute videos on social media go viral if they're good enough, don't they? People love mini-insights into new worlds, other lives. Why else do we love stuff like *Big Brother* and reality TV?'

'That's so true.' Harry nods. 'I wonder if there's a way to utilise social to take people on the journey of a documentary getting made? So that by the time it's out there's a ready-built audience for it?'

'That's interesting,' I say. 'Yeah. There must be a way to build a community around it. It's kind of meta – you could get people interested in the story you want to tell. It becomes a sort of collective project, then, with everyone watching it come together in real time and still wanting to see the final doc. If that makes sense?'

'It really does,' says Harry. 'Yeah. I like the way you think. You've got my brain cogs turning now.'

'Same,' I say.

Before we reach the university gallery, we're interrupted by my phone pinging, alerting me to an email.

'Oh,' I say, taking a look at my screen. 'That was fast. They've replied. About the old man – although, sorry, I really should not refer to him that way.' I try again. 'They've replied about JP, the man from the paper.'

'And?'

I open my mail app and see emails from two fashion brands, the man in question – and a new one from Abe. I hit the checkbox to mark off the spam, including Abe's, deleting all of them unread. Then I open the one we want, skimming down the reply to pick out the top-line info. 'Okay. Well . . . It's his grandson writing back, and he says his grandfather would love to meet, and actually there's something they need our help with.' I look up at Harry, whose eyebrows have risen, impressed by this timely and positive development. 'So it's already mutually beneficial,' I say. 'Even without us saying about fundraising on campus.'

'I'm liking the sound of this . . .' He beams. 'It's a great start.'

'Shall I ask if they can do tomorrow? Strike whilst the iron is hot?'

'Go for it,' he says. 'I keep a car here, so I can drive us. Get his address?'

'Perfect,' I say, so excited I'm almost trembling. 'I'll write back now.'

We confirm the details of the meeting and, both equally buzzed by the promise of something interesting afoot, don't stop talking and swapping ideas for the rest of the night. I get another text from my mum, a missed call from Candice, and a DM from Jackson, but none of it is enough to pull my thoughts away from the here and the now, the total joy of everything I had hoped for feeling like it is working out exactly.

'Okay, so how do you feel about art as activism?' Harry asks me, and he has my full attention once more.

'Well . . .' I begin, and we talk for three more hours.

14

Nic

'Dude, come on! You can't need to take a leak again! We're three points up! We've got this in the bag! You've got a bladder smaller than my grandma's!'

I give a wave of surrender to a furious Jackson across the pitch. He's so mild-mannered and relaxed in real life, but put a sweatband on him and a switch is flipped. It's been six weeks since he helped me move my sofa – since I stumbled onto the doorstep of the house on Maple Avenue, and since I had what nobody else knows was my first ever one-night stand – and I've officially seen both sides of him. He calls himself Jumpy Jack when we play, coming up with 'strategy' and saying things like: *Get 'em where it hurts. That little blond will be out of puff within five minutes – run rings around him! Or: Look at that brickhouse of a bloke. He won't be fast, but he'll last the whole game. Keep the attack closer than flies on shit. That's a man whose arm will never tire and that's a danger to our leader board.*

Then we finish, and as long as we've won – which we do more often than not, to be fair, thanks to Jumpy Jack – the switch is flipped again and he shakes everyone's hand and becomes regular Jackson, inviting everyone to the pub. More's the luck, too, because I'm meeting loads of people this way. And by people, I mean . . . women. I've not gone on any proper dates yet, but I seem to be getting better at the whole 'good chat' thing. It's nice. Exciting. I want to embrace a different side of myself; someone more gregarious and out there. I don't want to sound wet but it's like I'm learning about myself, a bit. I always thought I was shy and introverted, but I'm not. Not really. I've got loads to say, it's just picking my moment to say it. I can see how most of the guys on my team don't even listen to anyone else most of the time; they just wait for the other person to take a breath so they can start talking. But Jackson's trick really helps me be present and relax – I ask questions, and women are just so *honest*. They tell you about being in therapy or what book they read before they asked for a raise at work and they're self-aware. Self-possessed. It's made me realise that all the guys I think of as being super confident actually aren't, really – they just act that way. Except Jackson. He's pretty legit. He's fast becoming my best mate here, as it goes.

Anyway, for saying I've been here less than two months I'm feeling great about my decision to move. Everything feels fresh and new and inspiring, and I know that I could have played dodgeball in Liverpool. I mean, of course I *could* have, but it's like when you go on holiday and get to try on a different part of your personality because the sun is shining. London Nic plays dodgeball after work and goes to the pub and chats with all sorts of people he never would have thought would want to chat with him. And no, I don't know why London Nic is talking about himself in the third person. Maybe he just can't believe it can all be this easy.

I didn't know so many people – let alone women – were into dodgeball, of all things. It's like somebody sent a memo out to everyone in the city saying it's the sporty in-real-life equivalent of a dating app. You don't swipe left or right at dodgeball, you simply pour all your sexual frustration into lobbing balls at each other twice a week and have a couple of pints and a bit of easy repartee afterwards. Ollie says I need to start asking for phone numbers, and Jackson says if I practise first dates with enough people, I'll get the first date that really matters right, so I have to 'get in the game'. Not that I'm looking for *The One*, obviously. I'm here for a laugh, to go with the flow.

London Nic says yes more than he says no, to all things from after-dodgeball drinks to new cuisine. (Memo to self though: don't let Jackson convince me to try Iranian-Mexican fusion again.) And besides, I can't quite shake thoughts of Ruby. I'm meeting wicked people, but man, with Ruby it was like . . . *bam.* I haven't had *the bam* with anyone else yet. Not that I've told Ollie or Jackson I feel that way. I knew what it was with Ruby and went into it eyes open. I don't want word to get back to her that I still mope over that night, like we had sex and I fell in love or whatever. Adults can fuck and then move on. I know that. I just haven't met anyone I want to move on with yet, that's all. Not to mention . . . well, embarrassingly, I'm having a bit of trouble in the old *sail ship* department, if you know what I mean.

I touch Zola's shoulder to signal to her to take my place on the court as I make my exit, returning the provocative wink she gives me with a roguish grin – we flirt, sometimes, at the pub. She's nice. A laugh. But as soon as I'm sure nobody is looking, I grab my water bottle to take with me and the façade quickly drops. I do it quickly, reflexively, because if anybody thinks to ask me why I need it to pee with, I will die. Actually, legitimately, one hundred and ten per cent die.

I can already feel the burning. It's been happening this way. I'm fine one minute and then . . . pain. Unimaginable, terrible pain.

I fill the bottle up at the fountain in the changing room, the pain in my kecks growing with every passing second. The water bottle reaches capacity and I'm *this close* to having an accident as I push through into the cubicle and sit down on the loo. As I pee, I pour water between my legs to ease the fire. It helps. I don't know why, but it does. I never knew having a wee could hurt so much. When I'm done, I sit, panting. It's got to be some sort of infection. It's been two days of torture now.

'You okay, Nic?' Jackson bellows through the emptiness of the changing room. I freeze. 'We won,' he continues. 'No thanks to you. They're up for the pub through, and I was going to get a kebab too? I'm starving.' His voice gets closer. 'Oh,' I hear him say, stood just in front of the line of urinals opposite my locked door. 'Time to drop the twins off at the pool, was it? Sorry.'

I don't say anything. The water bottle is empty now and it normally takes a minute or two for me to catch my breath and for the pain to properly subside. I need to go see a doctor. I'll do it tomorrow.

'Nic?'

'Yeah, great,' I manage to say through gritted teeth.

But I know Jackson, and he's not going to leave. We're in a silent stand-off as he waits for me to reappear. He knows there's something afoot that he's missing. He can sniff secrets out like a hound. I resign myself to the inevitable investigative looks, but don't make eye contact as I slip the lock across and go to wash my hands, the empty water bottle under my arm.

'You look white as a sheet,' Jackson observes, and he sounds legitimately concerned. I look up, and in the mirror am confronted with a deathly pallor. I'm sure I'll be okay. I'm fine until I'm not, and then I'm not until I am.

I catch Jackson's eye in our mutual reflections, and he slowly – deliberately – looks down to the water bottle and back again. I do the same. Ah, he's got questions.

'Tell Uncle Jackson,' he prompts, and I can hear some of the others trickling through the door to get changed. We don't tend to shower after, because it slows down getting 'first blood', as Jackson calls it, and if we all stink then no one's the odd one out. Thankfully, that means nobody comes to the back of the changing rooms to the showers and loos, where we are.

I shake my head.

'Is there burning?' he prompts, but I don't detect a single iota of judgement in the question. He's just asking, his tone as neutral as if he'd just said, 'Are there flowers in the vase?' or: 'Fishcakes for tea okay?'

I run the tap again and scoop up some cold water to my face. It feels good. When I stand back upright, I answer him. 'Yes,' I admit.

He nods. 'Testicles swollen?'

'Like dodgeballs.'

'Discharge?'

'I don't think so.'

'The clam,' he decides. 'First time?'

He's not smiling, or joking, or making fun of me, but instantly as he says it the weight of shame lifts the tiniest amount.

'Are you sure?' I ask. 'This only started yesterday and I've not had sex since . . .' I don't need to finish the thought. He knows I mean that Ruby is the last woman I was with.

'Symptoms can show after a week, or after a few months,' he says, diplomatically. 'Seems reasonable to me they could come now after, what, five or six weeks?'

I think to myself *six weeks and two days, but who's counting?*

'Have you had this before too?' I ask.

'Chlamydia? Oh yeah. Twice, mate. Most people have. It's nothing to worry about.'

'The burning, though . . .'

'That's why you've gotta order a test at the first sign.' He grimaces. 'There's a walk-in place by Bank station you can go to. That's your stop, yes? Go before work tomorrow – I'll send you a link.'

'Thanks,' I say.

'You know you're going to have to let Ruby know about this, don't you?' he says absentmindedly as he types in what he's looking for. It's the first time her name has come up. I deliberately haven't asked about her, and Jackson hasn't offered any updates on what she's up to. Maybe he's been waiting for me to say something first, to see if I want to.

'She must have given it me,' I offer. 'Before her, there was only Millie.'

We'd used condoms when we'd had sex the first two times, but by the time we did it a third neither of us had any more, and we were so in the moment that . . . okay, fine. We let it happen. We had unprotected sex because she

92

said she was on the pill. I never thought about anything like this.

'You just have to call her, admit it's awkward, and say it straight-up. If she had it already she'd have called you. Here, I'll send you her number. Or do you already have it?'

'No,' I grumble, taking my phone back. 'I don't.' We'd decided not to stay in touch, although I have looked at her Facebook profile a couple of times and searched for her Instagram. I'm a mere mortal, after all. It's probably a good job, too – if I'd had her phone number, I'd have undoubtedly sent a text by now. It was weird enough not being able to send her a message in the days after we'd got together. The polite thing would have been to check in, but I couldn't.

'Mate,' he says to me, in the way he does before yet more wisdom is about to be dropped. I brace myself for whatever 'Jackson-ism' he's about to extoll, hating already that I know he's going to speak an inconvenient truth. 'It's not like you've not been lovesick for her since you met. At least you've got an excuse to talk to her now. Think of this as an opportunity.'

'Weird paradigm shift,' I say. 'Using *it-burns-when-I-pee* as a way to flirt.'

'Never look a gift horse in the mouth.' He grins. 'Take your chances when you get 'em.' I pull a face, but his insight doesn't stop there. 'She told me you've been watching her Stories, by the way. You're lucky: she thinks it's cute.'

Ah. Well played there, Nic. Really smooth.

'Cute with the Clam,' I mutter. 'Sounds like a kids' TV show.'

'I hope it's not,' says Jackson. 'Potential Tinder bio though, innit?'

'Oh my God,' I reply. 'I hate this.'

93

He grins at me again. 'Really?' he asks. 'Because I'm kind of loving it.'

'Jackson?' I say. 'I'm really going to need you to piss off now.'

'No pun intended.' He laughs, backing away. 'But call her, all right? Don't be a twat about it.'

15

Ruby

JP lives on the outskirts of Manchester, in a small terrace that feels like an extended set for *Coronation Street*. Harry and I have no idea what he wants our help with, but we've got a small handheld camera with us and a couple of mics, just in case. I won't lie – that was Harry's idea. He said we should be prepared. He says he can smell a story brewing, and I can't explain it, but I think I can too. Maybe I'm developing a director's nose, as one of the storytelling lecturers described it. I'm learning to sniff out the magic of a potential something.

'Number 15,' I say, pointing, as we inch through the parked cars on each side of the road, trying to see the house numbers through the gaps.

'So around about here should be number 21.' Harry nods, slowing to a stop so we can see. A new curtain twitches and the shape of a person is just about visible, before the front door is flung open and a guy a few years younger than Harry and I waves a hand, letting us know we're in the right place.

'The grandson,' Harry says.

'I'd imagine so,' I reply.

We find parking around the corner and bring our stuff with us, welcomed enthusiastically by William, JP's grandson, who has a stiff demeanour and a firm handshake but a smile that reaches his eyes.

'Thanks so much for coming.' William grins. 'I know what a master's can be like – no rest for the wicked! I just graduated from LSE with mine. I don't think I slept for a year.'

'That's so impressive,' I say. 'Congratulations.'

'No idea what I'm going to do with it all now, though. I've been staying with Gramps for a while as I've been trying to get sorted. But, as you'll see, it's a lot of fun around here ...'

We step inside the shabby-chic terrace, decorated in various degrees of floral, mid-century furniture and velvet. It's the kind of décor that would have been fashionable in the Fifties, then horribly dated, and now has come back around to being stylish again, minus the carriage clocks and tiny pot bears everywhere. In an armchair in the corner, dressed in a checked shirt, chinos and a knitted waistcoat sits a man in oversized glasses, wisps of grey hair visible above his ears.

'JP, is it?' says Harry and the old man issues a wave.

'Come in, son,' he says in a broad Mancunian accent, and his voice is stronger and louder than you'd expect from such a tiny frame. 'What's the script?'

'He means how's it going,' William clarifies. 'In case you're not from round here.'

'Whaley Bridge,' I say. 'So not far.'

'Wigan,' says Harry. 'Spitting distance.'

'And yes—' I nod to JP '—things are going well, thank you. We're excited to be here.'

We fuss about with William making us cups of tea and JP supervising from his chair in the corner ('Crack on, I'm powfagged!' he says, with William retorting, 'Any chance of you learning to speak the Queen's English one of these days?') and when we finally all settle there's a pregnant pause of expectation, as if the big reveal can now finally come, where we all look at JP, waiting for him to speak and shed light on the calling of this meeting.

'So you make films, I hear,' he says, and we tell him that we do – or, at least, are learning to.

'Documentaries, William says,' he adds, and again, we confirm this to be true.

'What's the research like for that?' he presses, and I can't help but feel like we're being interviewed for a job we haven't even applied for. He wants to know an awful lot about the ins and outs of what we do considering this time yesterday he didn't even know we existed, and vice versa.

'It varies,' I say. 'Harry and I haven't made anything together yet – this is our first project together, for our course. But I've done some short-form stuff before – you know, half an hour or less. I told the story of four male swimmers who volunteered at Hampstead Lido for twenty years together, and I did another piece on a friend of a friend's bid for Eurovision. I like doing docs because people fascinate me. Harry and I were just saying, weren't we, that life can be wilder than the made-up stuff.'

Harry pulls a face from which we intuit that, yes, we were indeed just saying that.

'Well, I need helping finding somebody,' JP says then, apropos of nothing: 'And I've got a feeling you pair are the ones for the job.'

'Okay,' says Harry, slowly. 'Who do you need to find?'

'A woman,' JP replies. 'The love of my life, as it goes.' He pauses dramatically again for his tea, slowly drawing his mug to his lips for an audible slurp. I glance down at my phone. Abe. *You should let me come up for a visit.* I turn my phone over, so I'm not distracted again.

In the space between JP's words Harry says, thinking on his feet, 'JP, do you mind if we voice-record this? I don't know what you're going to say, but if we can help you it would be nice to have this conversation to refer back to. If you don't mind?'

JP looks to William, and William says, 'That seems okay to me,' and so JP nods. Harry places the voice recorder between us, JP has another gulp of tea, and the room is so quiet you could hear a pin drop. I'm impressed with Harry for being so direct and getting the voice recorder down.

'I need to find the love of my life,' JP says, and I feel Harry look at me with a sense of victory, but I can't take my eyes off of JP. The love of his life?

'I'll go back to the beginning,' JP continues, his voice weary with age and nostalgia. Harry's brow is furrowed, and William looks sanguine, as if he's heard what's about to be said multiple times. 'If that's all right?'

'Go for it,' I say. 'You certainly know how to capture people's attention.'

And with that, JP launches into his story: 'I was barely eighteen when I got called up to fight.' Immediately I understand that he means the Second World War. I've never met anybody who fought in the war before. My own grandad was a mechanic at Rolls-Royce, fixing engines for the planes. He never saw battle. I need JP to talk faster. He's got me, hook, line and sinker already.

'It was early spring when we shipped out, to France. My

convoy – about twelve of us – ended up living in the barn of a generous, kind family – dead lovely they were – for about three months. Down near Limoges. It was in the middle of nowhere. Peaceful and quiet. Our presence was supposed to keep people safe, protect them. And the daughter of the family, Amelie, well . . . We fell in love. I didn't speak a lick of French, she didn't speak any English, but it was absolutely love. Besotted, I was. She'd sneak me extra bread in the mornings, and we'd take long walks down by the river behind the village. She had the face of a movie star. And then I had to leave. We were called out to the front line, and the only thing I was able to take with me was her photograph.'

'Which I have here,' William interjects, handing over a small black and white image, barely bigger than a passport photograph.

'Whoa,' marvels Harry. 'She's beautiful.'

I look over his shoulder. Amelie has high cheekbones and a thick, wide smile with the kind of teeth most people would have to pay money for. Her eyes are soft and encouraging, and there's a sweetness to her, like she's embarrassed to hold the gaze of the person taking her photo and will look down into her lap any second now. She's wearing a dark-coloured blouse that covers everything, and yet it is entirely obvious that she is all boobs and hips. To be honest, I could fall in love with her too, on that still image alone. Bless JP. His heart mustn't have stood a chance.

'And that's not even the half of it,' says JP. 'In real life, she was a knockout. And so thoughtful, and sweet. I thought I'd be able to go back to her. I thought after the war, when it was all over, I'd be able to find her again . . .'

'But you couldn't?' I say.

'No,' he replies, shaking his head sadly. 'And I met Shelley two weeks after we got home,' he concludes, as if the war and his French love were always leading up to that. 'I was twenty-three, she'd worked on the factory line when we were all off fighting, and to be honest . . .'

He pauses, closing his eyes faintly. I wait.

'I'm allowed to be honest, aren't I?' he clarifies again, but mostly to himself.

I feel compelled to make it clear: 'JP, you only have to tell us as much as you want to. It's okay. I know you want our help, but don't get upset or anything.' I find myself desperately wanting his story, but not at the expense of making him distressed.

'She'd lost somebody,' he says, plainly. 'Shelley. Her Jonny never came home. I'm not saying we were second best to each other, but we had both loved before. And your first love never leaves you, does it?'

The Abe Thing flashes into my mind, a movie highlight reel of our best and worst moments. But as a first love . . . urgh. It can't have been love! It wouldn't have hurt so badly if it was. The right love makes you feel *more* like yourself – it doesn't strip you of who you are. I'm lucky Abe has me out of his grasp, now. I'm so proud of myself for that – for knowing my worth and sticking to my values. Where I actively want to exorcise him from my past, *Eternal Sunshine of the Spotless Mind*-style, JP is still thinking of somebody from eighty years ago. That proves the point of what love really is, doesn't it?

'You talked about that with each other?' I probe, as sensitively as I can. 'You and Shelley talked about Amelie and Jonny?'

He shakes his head and looks at me like he feels sorry for my immaturity, for the folly of my youth.

'We didn't have to,' he explains. 'But that didn't make it

any less true. It might seem strange to you. Maybe it is. When William found Amelie's photo in my wallet, he couldn't understand how I'd been married for seventy years to his grandmother but still could think of somebody else. It hurt him, I think.' He looks to William as he says this. 'He loved Shelley so much, and I think he was protective over her, even after she'd gone. But the things we leave unsaid – unfinished – they haunt us, don't they? That photo I carried in my wallet of her – it was a photo of a ghost, a sort of memento of who I used to be before . . .'

'Before the war?' I ask, when he waits so long to complete his thought that I think he might have even forgotten he'd started one.

'Something like that,' he agrees.

'I *was* upset,' William agrees, as it becomes clear his grand-father isn't going to explain any further. 'Nana Shelley was like a mum to me, really – my own mother drinks a lot, has her own stuff going on, and Dad doesn't really have what you'd call a high emotional intelligence. I've spent as much time here as I have in my parents' house, haven't I, Gramps?'

'You're a good lad,' says JP.

'Gramps told me all this, and then we got your email, like, literally two days later. Gramps says he needs to track down Amelie, and then two film-makers reach out? That's kismet, is that. It's fate.'

I look at Harry. Harry raises his eyebrows at me. Something the guy who bought my sofa said – Nic, the man I slept with before I moved – creeps into my head.

'Timing is everything,' I say, and everyone nods. 'So you want help finding Amelie?' I clarify, making sure I've not got the wrong end of the stick.

'Do you think you can?' William asks. 'I'm not mad

anymore. Gramps should be allowed to get a happy ending. I know he loved Nana, but it would be really cool for him to get to see Amelie before . . .'

He doesn't finish the sentence. I know what he means.

'Before I'm dead,' JP supplies. When we all look at him, horrified, he adds, 'I'm no spring chicken, am I?'

I've got tears in my eyes, threatening to spill over. Shouldn't we all be graced with the chance to tell the ones we love how we truly feel? Love is the simplest, most pure thing there is. If you feel it, expressing it should be a human right. Shouldn't it?

'Oh, JP,' I say, and my voice wobbles.

'Can I speak freely?' Harry asks, addressing the room. In turn, we all nod.

'JP, you want us to help you find Amelie, correct?'

'Correct.'

'And you're okay if we document this?'

'If it helps, yes.'

'How do we pay for it all? Aren't you supposed to be fundraising for the cancer charity? We were so sorry to learn about your son.'

'My Uncle Pete,' William says. 'Yeah. Our target is a thousand pounds, just to raise awareness that men should get checked for it, really. But that's not for you to worry about.'

'No,' JP agrees. 'It's not.'

I'm wincing at the crassness of talking money, but Harry is right. We've got our time paid for through the course, but if we need to travel anywhere – I mean, God, we could end up in France at this rate! Imagine! – we're students. We can't afford that.

'Nana left me some money,' William says. 'I think she'd want me to use it for this. I can cover any expenses. Assuming

102

we don't need to fly first class to the other side of the world or anything.'

I nod. Harry nods. We look at each other.

'Harry?' I say.

'I want to help JP find his French girl,' he says.

'So do I,' I say.

'I want you to help us, too,' says William. 'And let's get straight about this, nothing is off limits. You can film, record, whatever you need for your course. There's no secrets. We understand that you've got a job to do too. Gramps and me talked it all through yesterday, once you said you were coming. Just, from my point of view – don't tire him out? Be sensitive? That's my only stipulation.'

We look over to where JP has lightly closed his eyes, as if to emphasise the point.

'And it's okay if we set up an Instagram account for this too?' I ask. 'I think we should start there. People might be able to help us. The internet is the most powerful tool we have for all of this.'

'Absolutely,' says William.

I help clear away our dirty mugs and Harry fiddles with his phone whilst JP naps. In the kitchen William says to me: 'I know you probably won't actually be able to find her, but we have to try, you know? For Gramps. Do you see the way he talks about her? I just want him to feel some sort of hope. I think it will help him live longer, and God knows I need him around for as long as possible. He's been more of a dad to me than my dad ever has, that's for sure.'

'You're kind to help him,' I say. 'It's really sweet. We'll do what we can.'

'Done it!' calls Harry from the living room. We wander back in to ask what, exactly, he's done.

'I've set up the account,' he says, proudly. 'And guess what I've called it?'

I shrug, waiting for the answer.

'Finding JP's Girl,' he says. 'I've put your fundraising link in the bio, too. Now first things first, JP – wake up! We need a photo with you!'

'I'm awake,' says JP, the croakiness to his voice making it obvious he's just been woken up. 'I was just resting my eyes.'

'Come here,' says Harry. 'Let's get a selfie altogether, then you on your own too.'

We take our photograph, upload it with a caption about what we're about to do, tag everyone we can think of in the comments and then? We drink our tea and wait.

16

Nic

I don't think about Ruby much. I mean – obviously I don't *obsess*. But *occasionally* that night crosses my mind. And I *sometimes* think, *I wish we could have spent more time together.* *Intermittently* my finger lingers over the follow button on her social media, but I never hit it. I'm not even bothered that earlier she featured a tall, hairy, bearded man in a post. He's not tagged so I don't know who he is. I haven't thought about it all day. Fair play if she was just fobbing me off with that year-off blokes stuff – I would have been happy to call a spade a spade though. Or maybe she changed her mind. Or maybe they're just friends. It's none of my business, is it? Our time together was, well, *mind-blowing*, but honestly I don't care *that* much.

However . . .

On the three – maybe four, or twenty – times she's crossed my mind, no big deal, I think how I could have gone back to Maple Avenue for pizza that night and discovered that she wasn't kind or fun. I could have gotten close enough to understand she didn't believe in deodorant or made other people the butt of her jokes or farted, loudly and unapologetically.

But she *is* kind and fun. The love between her and Jackson and Candice was palpable, and seeing somebody's capacity for caring about the people they love was an unexpected turn-on. She's fundamentally good, and coupled with those legs . . . Fine, okay, *of course* I think about her. I've got eyes and a beating heart, don't I? I'm only a human man with blood in my loins. I'd have to be dead for her not to have left an impression. We fit together like two human jigsaw pieces, for pity's sake.

She'd said it was amazing precisely *because* it was for one night only. Knowing we'd never see each other again made it safe to be who we were, because we weren't trying to show off or impress each other. There was nothing to lose. I agreed with her at the time, out loud at least – secretly though it felt like lightning striking.

When we'd crept into the kitchen to make hot chocolate at 6 a.m., after we'd had sex for a third, even better time – the time without the condom, like the little STI-riddled idiots we are – she wore my T-shirt. It's such a truism: a woman in a man's clothes, half naked, looking the best you've seen her. But as she concentrated, heaping powder into the pan, finding a wooden spoon to stir it with, keeping the heat low so the milk didn't burn, I just remember looking at her and thinking *I think it might be you.*

And the way she looked back at me, I swear she was thinking the same. Surely she doesn't think a spark like that happens all the time. It's rare. Once-in-a-lifetime rare, I'm sure of it.

Anyway, like I said . . . I hardly think of her at all.

* * *

By the end of the day, I've come to the conclusion that if Ruby *is* sleeping with that hairy bloke from her post earlier she should have all the facts. And so once I've left the office and I'm walking down Fleet Street towards Bank station, on my way to Dodgeball, I text her. I'm awash in a sea of suits and heels and serious-looking people trickling out of Barclays and CIB, everyone with their head down and on their phone like I am. I used to be embarrassed to work in finance – all that stuff about what wankers we are – but if I'm going to work in the City, I'm proud it's for Hoare's. All that history, and the way historically they've supported the arts . . . it's not a bad gig. I wouldn't say I've made friends, but my colleagues are nice enough. Very proper. Sober, is probably the best word.

I type and walk at the same time, deciding to be direct and simple, even though reaching out to her makes me inexplicably nervous. It's not even telling her to go to the GUM clinic, really – I can own that – it's the heart-thumping that comes with having an excuse to talk to her at all.

I decide I have to make it a question, in case she doesn't remember me, so I type: *Hi – this is Nic, from your last night in London?*

Not that she must hook up with randoms all the time, but you know. She had a lot on, didn't she? The move, saying goodbye – all of that.

Oh my God, if she replies saying, 'Who?' I will scream. Scream! Bury me at sea, let the current carry my body.

Also even if she was hooking up with randoms all the time, that's obviously fine. No slut-shaming here. Not that she's a slut. Oh God. *Focus, Nic.*

I hope it's okay that Jackson passed on your number, I add, thinking that explaining it was via Jackson means she knows *how* I got it. That it's Jackson-sanctioned.

Just need to give you a quick call, if you can let me know when's good?

I REFUSE to tell her in a text . . . Now, how the hell to sign off? I labour for ages over whether to put on a kiss or not. Is it too familiar? Will it lull her into a false sense of security? Give her the wrong impression about why I need to call?

Eventually, I settle on: *Thanks.*

I round the corner and damn near have a heart attack when my phone bleats with the sound of a text and her name flashes up.

Now okay? x

I gulp for air. That was fast.

'Oh for God's sake,' another bloke in a sharp trench coat says, side-stepping where I've come to an immediate halt, right in the middle of the pavement. I'm actually shaking. I can kid myself that I've only thought about her on the odd occasion, but actually she's wandered into my mind every single day since the day we met. And not even because the sex was good – which obviously it was. That she cried? I can't get it out of my head. I'm not bragging, it's more that I think I could have cried, too. All those Nineties R'n'B songs about making love and holding tight and two becoming one – I thought it was hyperbole until Ruby. And even then, what we had was more than physical. I haven't made that connection up. I know I haven't. My imagination isn't that good.

I call her number.

'Hey,' she says, gently. 'Nic.'

I exhale. Even the sound of her voice is enough to make me smile, in spite of myself. She talks so lightly, easy-breezy. I can tell she's smiling too. I can't believe I get to talk to her again. 'How are you?'

'Hey,' I reply. 'Yeah. Good thanks. You know. Just finishing a hard day's work.'

'Breaking a sweat making the rich even richer?' she quips.

I laugh. 'The lefty artist taking a swipe at the capitalist banker? Ruby, I'm disappointed you'd be so unoriginal.'

She laughs too. 'You're right,' she says. 'I should have at least teased you for watching my Instagram stories without actually following me.'

It's a good job she can't see me. I've turned puce.

'Just hit the follow button and have done with it.' She giggles. 'Or were you waiting for me to follow you? In fact, hold on . . .'

I can hear voices in the background of her call get louder as I wait for her to do whatever it is she's doing.

'There. You have one new follow request.'

'Well, if we're pulling no punches,' I volley back, 'if I remember rightly it was you who got on the cyber-stalking train well before I did.'

'This is true,' she says. 'I have no problem holding my hands up and saying so. I'm woman enough.'

I step off down one of the little alleyways that litter the streets across the road from the station, lifting a hand to my free ear to block out the noise of roadworks still happening, even though it's 6 p.m.

'That's very admirable of you,' I coo. 'Not many people can admit to doctoring their truth.'

'The very essence of why film-making appeals to me so much,' she says. 'Your truth isn't mine; mine isn't yours. Nobody's version of their reality truly aligns with anybody else's. Not even the history books get it right. History is just written by the victor.'

'You're too clever for me,' I say. 'Multiple truths mean nobody can be wrong? That's a head-screw.'

'I probably am too clever for you – you're right,' she replies. There's a kerfuffle in the background then, gruff male voices laughing, talking a bit louder than they have been. 'Sorry for the noise,' she notes. 'We're at an interview. Well, we didn't know it was an interview before we got here, but it's kind of turned into one.'

'Sounds exciting,' I say. 'Reporting the story live as it's happening.'

'Breaking news,' she says. 'That's me.'

I want her to tell me everything: what the course is like and who she has met and crucially when she's next in London. She said not to make empty promises, but my mind can't help but concoct ideas and plans. Manchester isn't that far away from Liverpool. If I went home for a weekend would it be odd to ask to see her? It's just, this is already as great as I remember it. Why haven't we stayed in touch again?

'We think we might have found an idea for our independent project,' she continues, before pulling her mouth away from the phone and saying to whoever she's with, 'Can I have a bit more milk this time please, William? Not to be fussy but your last two cups needed a bit of creative direction.'

I wonder if William is the hairy man. He laughs, whoever it is.

'Sorry to get you when you're busy,' I say.

'No, no,' she replies. 'I have five minutes, for you. Is it about the sofa?'

The sofa?

'Oh no,' I say. 'Nothing like that.'

'Okay . . .'

'I feel really silly,' I blurt out, looking around to see if anyone from work might be able to hear what I'm saying.

'No,' she insists. 'Don't feel silly. It's nice to hear from you.'

'Is it?' I say, and immediately I know I sound too eager. Too happy. Too enthusiastic.

'Of course it is,' she says. 'I had a really nice time with you.' She lowers her voice. 'Several really nice times actually. It was definitely a night to remember.'

We obviously don't know each other well, but we figured out enough about each other that night to establish that she knew how to make me blush, and revelled in making me do so. I'm blushing now, again, my neck flushing and burning. I'm grinning stupidly, though, too. All I can do is laugh. I know she's flirting, now. I like it.

I hear her say thank you, presumably for her cup of tea from *William*. 'Five minutes,' I hear her say. 'I've got an idea on where to look first. And can you ask Harry to email the class list with the link?'

'I should get to the point,' I volunteer when she's done.

'Not that I'm not enjoying talking with you,' she soothes. 'But if you don't mind, yeah. I don't want to keep everyone waiting too long. We're on to a good thing here.'

'Uh-huh,' I say. 'Well, basically . . .' I scramble to land on the right turn of phrase. 'You need to get checked out. I've got . . .'

'Be right there!' she says. 'Sorry, Nic.'

There's a pause.

'You were about to tell me what you've got?' she reminds me.

'Right. Yes.'

Somebody shouts to her, 'Come on, mate! Can't you talk to your boyfriend later?'

She replies by shouting, 'Harry, your dad is just asking when he can see me again,' and it forces more laughter. Harry. So there's a William, and a Harry, and one of them says: 'It's not that shag you mentioned, is it? The one with the massive—'

The line goes dead for a moment, like she's either hung up or hit the mute button – then she's back.

'Sorry,' she says. 'Ignore all that.'

'Been talking about me?' I probe.

'Change the subject!' she insists, and my heart beats in double time at the notion of having been mentioned.

'Fine. Harry *and* William?' I say. 'Are you spending time with the royal family?'

'Ha, yeah, I didn't clock that. William and Harry.'

There's a pause.

'I really do have to go in a sec,' she prompts. 'Sorry.'

'Right,' I swallow. 'Yes.'

'So . . . ?'

'Well,' I tell her. 'Have a good day. I hope the interview-that-wasn't-supposed-to-be-an-interview-but-is-now goes well.'

'You rang me to tell me to have a good day?' she asks.

'No,' I reply. 'No, I didn't ring you to say have a good day. Chlamydia. You need to get checked for chlamydia. I've got it. You might do too.'

'Oh,' she says. 'I have had a bit of an itchy foof, actually. I thought it was thrush.'

I don't know how to respond to that.

'I'm really sorry if it's my fault you've got it,' she says.

'No, it could be my fault,' I reply.

'Oh,' she says, a bit disappointedly. 'Yeah, of course. I just thought if you'd only just had a break-up that . . .'

I realise what she means. She thinks she's one of many. 'You're . . . right,' I say. 'I just didn't want to sound un-gentlemanly. I had only been with Millie before you. If you must know.'

112

'Well, you don't need to protect me. I suppose I always knew my ex was seeing more than just me. If he was cheating with one woman, why not a harem of us?'

'Sorry to say it then, but maybe you should let him know?' I suggest.

'Fuck,' she breathes. 'I hate that you're right.'

'I'm sorry we're talking about your ex now,' I say. 'I didn't mean to bring him up.'

'It's okay.' She sighs. 'Sorry. I sound annoyed but it's not your fault. He's just been texting, that's all. I can delete those – but now I have to text back it will be like he's won, or something.'

'He's no winner if he's lost you,' I say.

She bursts out laughing. 'You should get T-shirts with that on,' she quips. 'Sell them on corny dot com.'

'I was trying to make you feel better!'

'It worked.'

'I'm glad.'

There's nothing left to say.

'I like talking to you,' I blurt out.

'Yeah,' she says. 'Same.'

It feels like we're both smiling, but neither of us speaks. If this was face to face it would make sense. You can stare at a person you like and grin like a loon but the effect isn't the same down the phone.

'Well . . .' she concludes.

'Sorry about the chlamydia,' I say. 'Let me know how you test?'

'I'll text you,' she offers, and the promise of it is enough for me. 'Bye, Nic.'

I'm smiling so much I think my cheeks are going to fall off. 'Bye, Ruby.'

We ring off, and I can't move. That was something else, man. It was really awesome to talk to her. My phone lights up in my hand.

Follow me back, asshole.

17

Ruby

What a gift to bring into my Year of Me, celebrating the entering of celibacy with an STI. I go to the clinic and within a day get the text confirming I've got it. It's as if the universe has just underlined my *memo to self* to keep away from men and focus on myself, and my work – not to mention proving the point that Abe is a cretin. It must be from him. I'd put money on him knowing, and having got treatment for himself, and not having told anybody else. I'd wager a million on the fact. How did I ever get seduced by a moral-free man like that? I must have been iron-deficient, or in a nightmare, or consistently drunk. Especially comparing him to a guy like Nic, who gave me a call and was charming as he delivered the news.

He's as lovely as I remember – he was even a gentleman when Harry yelled that thing about talking about him. I've only mentioned him once, in passing. Maybe twice. I've been wondering how he's doing down there in London – how he's finding settling in, and playing dodgeball. I'll bet he's made loads of friends already through the team. Jackson is crap on the group text, but I can't complain because I'm not much better. I do know Jackson sees him at practice though. I wonder if Nic has asked about me before now, when he needed my number. Not that he's left a lasting impression or anything. I absolutely don't regularly think about how he threw my legs over his shoulder like they were sacks of flour and I was dough about to be kneaded, or the way he used his tongue to tease between my legs long enough to make me come within about thirty seconds when he went down on me. I categorically do not think of him pinning down my arms above my head, so I writhed underneath him, when I am alone, right before I go to sleep and self-soothe with a little . . . well, you know. Self-soothing.

Before I can stop myself, I take another peek at his social media. I like that I can see what he's getting up to online now. Year of Me meant that I haven't looked at Nic's stuff because there was just no point: I'm never going to see him again, by my own volition. But our chat gave me the excuse, and I will say he's very handsome in his suit for work. Despite myself, I can't help but notice he always has his sweaty arms slung around a pretty girl in dodgeball snaps where Jackson is always doing something stupid and outlandish in the background. If they get to know him in the biblical way that I got to know him, all I can say is Godspeed. They won't forget it. I haven't.

I close the app, feeling wistful. It's been a few days since we met JP and started the Finding JP's Girl account, and I've been riding a high. I've been booked and busy: always something to do, something to say, and Harry and I have been hanging out a lot too. So tonight, in my tiny temporary one-bed flat, with furniture that came with the place and no concrete memories having yet been made with these walls, my aloneness hits differently. It's the first time I've felt this way since I arrived in Manchester. Lonely over alone. I think I must be tired or maybe I just need my dinner. Low blood sugar can cause a multitude of ills.

First, though, I try FaceTiming Candice, but she doesn't pick up. I've missed a couple more of her calls, too, so send a text that says: *Catch up soon?* Jackson rings out as well. I could call Mum, but I always have to do so much explaining about the master's and my life and keeping hydrated. I don't have the minerals for it, much as I love her. So I return to mindlessly scrolling on Instagram, rewatching the stories I posted from the day, and feel unreasonably disappointed that Nic hasn't watched them. *Sod it,* I decide, thumbing through my call log to get his number from the other day and saving it to my phone. You never know, I might change my mind. I'll keep the number, just in case.

My stomach growls in protest at going unfed, so I order extra-large mushy peas with my chippy tea via Uber eats, and cry, *again*, when I listen to JP's interview back for the millionth time. I've only had one glass of warm, cheap wine from a box too big to fit on the shelf in the fridge, but I stop myself from having any more, and then find myself opening up a new text message to type in JP's name to the top part, ready to write to him. William happened to mention that JP's phone is connected to his voice-activated speaker, and reads out texts for him because he can't see a phone screen. I type:

JP, it's Ruby from the other day. I just watched back our interview and wanted to say thank you once more for sharing so generously with us. You've really touched my heart, and made

117

me think, and I wanted to say so. I'm really excited to see if we can find Amelie!

As I lick the grease off my fingers from my last chip, my phone pings back:

The pleasure was all mine, Ruby. It was nice to have the company and do something different for a change. Stop by again if you've got time – I'm sure you have better things to be doing than seeing an old fart like me though, from JP.

The Year of Me isn't necessarily about doing as much as possible, as much as it is following my nose and embracing what excites me. I *could* do a fancy class tonight, or find out which pub everyone off the course is at, or even just wander the streets of Manchester like I've done several times already, drinking in the vibe. But if I did, I'd be breaking my own rule of tolerating things just to fill a hole. I know it's important to feel bored sometimes, or even a bit sad. But I also know that, if the Year of Me is about truly leaning into what excites me, simply because it does, I actually should be hanging out with JP some more. Surely you get to that age and have all the answers? I wonder what advice he might have for me and *my* life.

Even if I did have plans, I write back, *I'd still accept the offer of your company. You're a very cool man, John-Peter! xx*

I wait, excited, to see what he says back. I think I just asked out a ninety-six-year-old.

I've always been easily flattered, he says.

It makes me laugh out loud.

Do you know what L-O-L means in text speak? I tap out.

Lots of love, comes the response.

It means laugh-out-loud. So if I type LOL it means you made me chuckle.

Is that right? I've never really got on with text speak.

Well, I'd be happy to try and teach you!

He replies: *Ruby, I get two text messages a week. I don't think your efforts would get the pay-off you're expecting.*

I send back: *LOL.*

I'm happy you find me amusing, he says.

Did you really mean it when you said I should come round again? I ask. *Even if it's not for the project?*

How's the weekend? he says, and I tell him the weekend is perfect.

I'll bring cake, I add.

Ruby, sweetheart, he retorts. *We can do better than cake, can't we? Make it a can of lager with a lemonade chaser.*

I'll bring both, I sign off, marvelling at how the act of reaching out has resulted in feeling better about my life, and my loneliness, almost instantly – which is a Year of Me lesson in itself.

Connection is everything.

Connection is what it is all about.

Three days later and JP has got the port out, and his fancy glasses to go with it. I shouldn't drink because of the antibiotics, but I'm sorry: if a ninety-six-year-old man offers you his port you take it, no question. I don't make the rules, I just follow them.

'Life's too short to save them for best.' He laughs, as he pours out two rather large servings. He's a proper old-school gentleman with a real cheeky sense of humour – my kryptonite. I told Harry I was coming, but he has a date, so now it's just me and JP on this mid-October Sunday afternoon.

'You know, you're so right.' I laugh, accepting the drink. 'I should stop by in my ballgown next time.'

He laughs too. 'I'd say I'd get my suit on for you, but it hasn't fit since 1982.'

We clink our glasses against one another and in the gentle lull as we sip I look around his front room.

'This is a beautiful house,' I say. 'Really.'

'It'd have to be, for the amount of time I'm in it.' He chuckles.

'If you're trying to pull on my heartstrings, JP, it's working.' I grin. 'Do you want me to bust you out of this popsicle joint?'

'Do I!' he hoots.

'Caribbean do you?' I offer. 'Or are you more a winter sun kind of a man? Maybe Switzerland? The mountains?'

'You could pull me down over the snow in a big carriage,' he quips.

'I'm sure we could load you up on the back of a snow-mobile,' I retort.

'A snowmobile?'

I pull out my phone and google an image to show him.

'I see,' he says, squinting at the screen. 'I think you've got a deal then. You'll just have to give me a king's chair to get on the plane, but I shouldn't imagine that will be a problem. There's not much to me anymore.'

He's not wrong. He's not frail, not like a gust of wind would blow him over, but there's no denying he's not the strapping army man he showed us photos of. He must have been six foot back in the day, and strong enough to heave anyone he wanted over his shoulder. Now he moves slowly – purposefully, but slowly – with a walker most of the time, and even when he was pouring the port, I had half a mind to offer to do it for him. But I didn't because, already, I knew it'd piss him off. He's no less strong-willed for being old, and quite rightly too.

'How are you finding Manchester, then?' he asks, once we've listed all the different places we could run away to together. 'It's no London Town, is it? Not that I ever really cared for London. All that hustle and bustle. Everyone needs a fag and half a shandy, take a minute to calm down.'

'Yeah, I wanted to enjoy the hustle and bustle,' I admit. 'But to be honest, it ended up not being for me. Manchester is more my speed. My parents are across in Whaley Bridge – I think I said? – but that's a bit *quiet* for me. Manchester is proving quite the place to be, actually. Good restaurants, nice bars. Not that I have much time for that with my course. It's go-go-go most of the time.'

'Shelley liked a good restaurant.' He nods, appreciating my point. 'Every year on our anniversary we'd have carbonara at a little Italian place she used to love. Garlic bread, pudding after, a nice little jug of red wine. It was our treat.'

'I'm partial to an Italian myself,' I say. 'And not to brag, but I can whip up quite the carbonara. I don't even use cream – just eggs and parmesan cheese, the proper Italian way. I could make it for you one day, if you like.'

He nods. 'My appetite isn't what it used to be,' he concedes. 'But if it means having your cracking company again, how could I say no?'

'Shall we have it this afternoon?' I offer. 'For tea? What time do you normally eat?'

I laugh when he says 5 p.m. 'So you keep toddler hours then?' I tease. 'Up at dawn, bed at 7 p.m.?'

'Yes, actually,' he says, proudly. 'Nothing good happens after dark anyway. Anything that does is asking for trouble. And sometimes that trouble can be the good kind, but mostly it's the bad kind.' He sighs. 'Regardless, trouble is trouble. I know that much to be true.'

'Oh, I can get on board with that theory,' I chortle. 'Absolutely.'

'Go on then,' he challenges. 'Thrill this little old man's life with a story or two.'

'Absolutely not,' I say. 'I don't want you to think any less of me.'

'Come off it,' he scoffs. 'Try me.'

'Well,' I begin, with a sigh. 'I don't want to be boring when I say *boy problems*. This is a post-feminist era: I'd like to be able to talk about more than some idiot who almost broke my heart.'

'Be as feminist as you want,' JP counters. 'You'll still have a heart to almost break. You know, I get why you want all equal rights and whatnot, but don't let it make you hard. William had a girlfriend – awful woman she was. Got cross when he held doors open for her, things like that. Like manners could ever be rude. Being rigid like that – that's what'll cause a feminist to break. You've got to learn to bend, instead. Like tree branches in the wind. Work with what you've got, not against it.'

'I wasn't expecting to get into feminist theory with you, JP,' I say.

'No,' he concedes. 'And to be fair I'm not much into it. I'd rather you tell me some more about this wally that hurt you. Or about one who didn't. If you don't mind.'

'I don't mind,' I say. 'I'm over it. Ancient history can't hurt us, can it?'

JP doesn't reply to that. As soon as I've said it, I know it's not technically true. Our history informs our present, which informs our future. We *are* our histories – whether we choose to repeat it or rectify it.

'Anyway. There definitely used to be a man in my past who

only ever called after the sun had gone down, yes,' I admit. 'But it probably wouldn't be ladylike to give you the details.'

'Hmmm, I see,' he broods. And then: 'For what it's worth, though. I'll be dead soon. So if you did want a confidant, I wouldn't be a bad pick.'

'JP!' I exclaim. 'I've already told you not to talk like that!'

'Oh, stop it,' he bats back. 'You sound like my grandson. Like it isn't inevitable.'

I sit with his truth.

'Well, shit,' I say, finally, and my swearing makes him hoot out a laugh. 'Sorry,' I say. 'I don't mean to swear.'

'No, no,' he agrees. '*Oh shit* is the ticket. And for what it's worth: any man messing you about isn't a man at all. I hope you know that.'

'I try to remember that, yes.'

'Good.' He drains his glass. 'And now?' he says. 'Anyone on the go now? A pretty girl like you, I'm sure you must be fighting them off with a stick.'

I pull a face at him. 'You flatter me,' I suggest, and he grins.

'I always knew how to flatter a lady,' he sparkles, and I believe him.

I drain my glass as well, considering how much to reveal to him.

'I've decided something,' I settle on.

'How exciting,' JP retorts.

I roll my eyes. 'I'm going to tell you every gory detail, and if it gets too much you can just say . . . toffee sauce, okay?'

'Toffee sauce?'

'Toffee sauce is lovely, but if you have too much you start to feel a bit sick,' I clarify.

He winks. 'Gotcha.'

And so I regale him with *my* history: The Abe Thing, how

123

we were on and off again for years, my Year of Me – celibate, no dating, no casual sex, no *nothing*. I tell him about Nic, about spending one night with him that was actually pretty amazing. And then, when JP presses me about what's really keeping me from staying in touch with Nic or developing a friendship, I tell him something that nobody else knows – not Jackson, not Candice. Nobody.

'I miscarried,' I say, plainly. Relief floods my system to finally be talking about it with somebody. 'With Abe. I didn't even know I was pregnant, and then I wasn't, suddenly, anymore . . . it just made me think . . .' I turn my empty glass over in my hands so I can look down instead of at JP.

'I see.' He nods, solemnly, when I've finished. 'I'm so sorry. My granddaughter miscarried too. I know how deeply it hurts.'

'It's okay,' I say, softly. 'I totally don't have my shit together enough for a baby. Abe certainly didn't. But when something like that happens, it changes you. It changed me, anyway. Made me realise that I need to go after what I want, even if I'm not sure what that thing is exactly. That's why I left London, joined this course. And it's why I have been clear with Nic that I'm not interested in anything more – I won't let anything jeopardise this chance I have to find out who I really am and what I really want. I'm so embarrassed by this but . . .' I trail off.

'Go on,' JP encourages.

'The night with Nic? We slept together three times, but only used protection twice.'

'Hmm?' says JP.

'I just think . . . well, isn't that messed up? I had a miscarriage and then in a one-night stand I take a stupid risk? I'm on the pill, but I know three different women who got pregnant despite being on it. So I've always used condoms too. Then Abe said he didn't like them, that they didn't feel as good as without – and so we didn't, and bam. I got two blue lines. After everything that happened, you'd think I'd never risk it again and I did. It's so pathetic. Like I say I'm too young for kids, that I probably don't even want them at all, and then I test the boundaries just one last time? Am I really so void of character that I'd let life make the choices for me instead of making my own? It scared me. I scared myself. So I gave myself a talking-to. I feel like my life could be panning out a whole different way in some alternative universe where I *didn't* . . .'

I can't actually say it out loud again. I take a breath. God, I didn't think it would all still make me this emotional. 'All this to say,' I conclude, 'this feels very much like where I am supposed to be. Getting my answers. Being in charge. Not being a risky little bugger, but being strategic and purposeful about my life. I can't just be carried by the current.'

'Oh, kid,' JP says. 'You're not the first person to get too caught up to use protection. You won't be the last.'

I issue a weak smile. He's right, but, well . . . That's just not *me*. Or rather, that's not the me I want to be. A baby would ruin everything. My stepmum, Dee, never wanted kids and I grew up being aware of the vague inconvenience we were, that she didn't really want us around every other weekend and on Wednesday nights. I could never do that to a child. I can't believe my dad stayed with her, when he saw how she treated us. Not mean, or horrible, just . . . distant. Detached. Like, but not love. Children deserve to be drowning in love. Sometimes I wondered if Dee would have ever even throw us a life raft.

'Interesting that documentaries are your thing,' JP notes. 'How so?'

'Investigating how other people live like somebody, some-where, might give you a clue on how to live your life.'

'Oh, JP,' I exclaim. 'I'm counting on it!'

He laughs.

'Do you think I'm an awful person?' I find myself saying. I can't not. I have to know if he thinks less of me now – Abe's long-suffering girlfriend, who I never met, who I wondered about, sometimes. Did she know about me? Her boyfriend got me pregnant. I'd hate me, if I wasn't me.

'Why on earth would I think you're awful?' JP says, and I can see he means it. 'I think you've had a rotten time of it, and I can understand why you'd feel how you do.'

'Thank you,' I reply, softly.

'But . . .' he adds, and my heart sinks – I was waiting for the kicker, for the other shoe to drop. 'I do think life is shorter than we think, and I'd hate to see you miss out on something special because of this . . . *pledge*, you've made. Despite your reasons.'

'Fair point,' I concede.

'The minute I met Shelley,' he says, and I'm curious as to where this is going. 'And the minute I met Amelie, something clicked. With both of them. It was like opening up a new notebook and starting properly. Does that make sense?'

'I think so . . .' I say. 'As if everything before meeting them just faded into the background? Wasn't important anymore?'

'Exactly. Because it all brought me to them.'

'Hmm,' I muse, not sure how I feel about that. 'Are you one more port away from telling me to keep the faith, that love happens to everyone eventually, that my guy could be out there right now, wondering the exact same things, and we're just destined to be in the same place at the same time if only I can learn to trust in the mysterious ways of the world and stay open instead of closing myself off . . . ?'

'You might well take the Michael out of me, girl,' he chortles. 'But I'm not the one keeping my heart in a cage for a year to prove some *point*. It's a muscle – and we have to exercise our muscles to make them stronger or else they seize up. The heart must be used, or we risk losing its capacity.'

I think of Nic, suddenly. Maybe the next person I have a cute moment with I'll give a chance. It can still be The Year of Me, with added flirting just for fun. Right?

'Bang bang, I'm dead,' I say, clutching my chest like I've just been shot. 'If you were a younger man, I'd challenge you to a fight over what you're coming out with. Christ alive.'

'Privilege of the old.' He nods. 'Being able to say it like it is.'

'That's why I'm so pleased you're letting us film finding Amelie. The way you see the world . . . you're going to make other people, the people who watch this, hopefully, understand their own world a bit more too, you know.'

'I don't know how much use I'll be. Or if we'll even find her. But it's for William, really. He's a bit aimless since graduating. It's already given him a bit of purpose, thinking he can make his old Gramps happy.'

I start to clear away our empty glasses and dirty plates. I can sense JP is getting tired, but is too stubborn to tell me so. It makes me smile that he thinks he's doing all this for his grandson, but his grandson thinks he's doing it for JP.

'I should think I'd like to see it all in action, you know,' he says, before I pick up the tray with everything on it. 'How the sausage is made, so to speak. I'm interested. The way you talk about it has piqued my interest.'

'You want to come to campus?'

'Am I allowed?' he asks.

I consider it. I don't see why not. He's a lovely man, and it's not like he's any trouble. If he's part of the independent project, he can go wherever we go. Janet, the course supervisor, wouldn't disagree with that, surely.

'I'll check with Harry,' I say. 'Just no more truth bombs about *my* love life, okay? Your clarity is very inconvenient for those of us who'd like to blame their crappy love lives on matters of the heart being complicated.'

He laughs. 'All I'm saying is, darling – almost doesn't count. It's the ones who *aren't* afraid to commit to us that do.'

'Almost doesn't count? I like it.'

'Plenty more where that came from.' He winks, sleepily.

'No . . . seriously, JP . . . I think you've just hit the nail on the head.'

He blinks and waits for me to go on.

'I think you've just given us our title! Your almost wasn't enough, so you're going to get your answers, even though . . .' I trail off. I don't want to insult him.

'Even though I'm half a shock away from my heart stopping?' he supplies.

'Well, I wouldn't have put it like that, but yeah,' I say. 'Most people your age wouldn't feel compelled to get their answers, would they? You're special.'

'*Almost Doesn't Count*, you say?'

'Yeah. It works on so many levels. You refuse to leave this mortal coil on an almost, everything you've said to me about Abe – he doesn't count because he was an almost. It's as if, when somebody really matters, when it's really meant to be, you make sure there's no almost about it. You make it count. Anything else is just . . .'

'Cowardice.'

'Yeah,' I agree. '*Almost Doesn't Count*. Even just as a working title, for now. Something to anchor us.'

'Well. I'll take a five per cent cut, then. And executive producer. Is that what they call them? Like in the old Hollywood days?'

'Deal.' I giggle. 'John-Peter Morgan, Executive Producer and star of award-winning documentary *Almost Doesn't Count*.'

'That certainly does have a special ring to it.' He grins, and I grin too.

18

Nic

Tentative flirting via social media, thy name is Nic and Ruby. In the three weeks since our phone call, we've slowly started to like each other's stuff on social. We write the odd comment here and there, a 'cool!' or a 'lol'. I post a picture Jackson took of me at dodgeball, and I'll own it: it is a total thirst trap. I caption it, *For saying it's called DODGEball I don't half get hit a lot. Right-in-the-nuts-ball is more like it* ☹ and she leaves me the aubergine emoji underneath, which could be a comment on the caption or my photo. Feeling emboldened, later I put a pair of eyes under a mirror selfie she posts after a haircut, and she replies with the cry-laugh emoji. I feel a small sense of inexplicable triumph. Suggestive emoji use isn't exactly love letters across the seven seas, but it sure does keep hope alive.

Eventually, and out of the blue, she uses my phone number directly, sending a message that says: *Hey, if two people have the clam is that the beginning of a chowder?*

Corny, but it makes me laugh. I'm walking through Soho when it comes, fresh off a mooch around Foyles. When I hit the bottom of Old Compton Street, I have to side-step tourists and their umbrellas where they're gathered outside the theatre on the corner, and I feel a momentary pang of annoyance that they're littering the pavement, weighed down with bags of extremely early Christmas shopping. And then it hits me: I'm not one of them. Getting annoyed at visitors must mean I'm not thinking of myself as 'other' here anymore. That's a good feeling – I live here! These are MY streets! I'm a Londoner! It's a trivial thing to feel proud of, but I do.

I reply to Ruby: *I put the STD in STUD . . . All I needed was U.* My infection cleared up ages ago, so it's an odd thing to pick up on but I'll roll with it. She sends back a row of cry-laugh emojis, and then a photo of a bunch of computers with various stills from what I assume is material she has to study. *Student life on a Saturday,* she says. I can't figure out if I'm supposed to tell her what I'm up to as well, if this is an invitation for a chat. Communicating via proper texting instead of social media is immediately more . . . something. Intimate? Proper? Especially apropos of nothing. Whatever her reasons, I'm secretly thrilled, whilst also aware I don't want to seem eager – or too available. People say one thing and do another all the time, but it's important not to be so reactive that I'm like a toy she can pick up and put down at whim. There's nothing wrong with me playing it cooler than I naturally would and going in for the long game, no matter how much I like her name on my screen – especially considering that, in an unexpected but needed development, I'm dating now. I'm torn between wanting Ruby to be making the first steps in changing her mind about us staying in touch, and the self-respect of not holding my breath because what do I expect to come from it?

Anyway: to text back or to not text back – my decision is made for me. I'm already at Café Boheme, and I can see Audrey From Bumble – my date – waiting for me by the window. I put my phone in my pocket, text unanswered. I've wanted Ruby to act on whatever it is we had for over two months. She can wait for an afternoon.

'And so I said to her,' Audrey From Bumble is explaining, our pancakes long eaten and our coffee long drunk. 'That's just not cool. Like, okay you can be *inspired* by what I wear, but it's weird going out and buying all the same stuff, you know? Like, I work really hard to build a wardrobe that I love, and I was only sending her pictures for, like, friendly supportive approval, you know? A "yas, girl" or "slay, queen". I don't want to show up to work dressed like twins or whatever, you know? Anyway, then *she* said . . .'

Audrey From Bumble talks a lot. She's pretty, but I haven't said anything other than 'oh really?' and 'crikey' in about forty-five minutes.

My brother made me download all the apps. He said I have to progress to *dating* women, not just talking to them, but to keep it casual. Low-key.

'It's not like there's one soulmate out there for each of us, is it?' he insisted. 'Anyone can be our soulmate if we try hard enough.'

I don't know if that's the attitude I want to take, but seeing people is a great way to discover more of London and fill my weekends. The week is stuffed with work and the gym and dodgeball, but the weekends can be depressingly empty and that makes them feel long. I just turned thirty-one! I *should* be out there! I'm here for the adventure, after all those years not being very adventurous at all! It's time to sow my wild oats!

Except, I'm pretty sure I don't want to be sowing my wild oats with Audrey From Bumble, and so I gently decline the offer of going up to Wardour Street to see her friend's pop-up.

Kit From Tinder is a slightly better experience. She said in her bio that grand romantic gestures are her love language, so I take a punt and suggest that instead of drinks or lunch we go to Up at the O2, to climb the building and take in the view. We meet by a falafel cart and the banter flows pretty easily right from the off, but by the time we get to the top she's actually hit it off with another guy there, also on a date, leaving me and Carman From His Accounts Team to awkwardly chat as we stand behind them, watching their fireworks explode undeniably. Fair play to them and all – take your chemistry where you can find it – but bloody hell, these tickets were thirty quid each.

Priya From Happn says we should go on a twilight vigil for forgotten Victorian-era sex workers in a South London cemetery, which I attend because she's gorgeous and it's attractive to have a woman organise the date, but she brings a bunch of friends and I get the feeling there needs to be some sort of group sign-off before any affection for me can be established. I wouldn't mind, but they're all dressed in leather and purple lipstick, and the whole thing has a *The Craft*-like feeling to it, so I say I have to get up early for a work meeting and leave.

And then there's the IRL meet. On the day I'm meeting Zola from our dodgeball squad for coffee, Ruby is on my feed as I kill time on the bus having a scroll. She's prompting everyone to follow her work account, Finding JP's Girl, where she's chronicling the making of her documentary. I go through to the account and check out the posts on the grid. It all serves to remind me how cool she is. In the bio, there's her handle and an @harrynotbarry. Curious, I click on the one I don't know, and the profile picture is the guy who features on her social quite a bit. His bio says: *I hate it here, but @RubyPowell_101 made me.* There's three emojis: a video camera, a peace sign, and the LGBTQ+ rainbow flag. Interesting.

I get off the bus and take a photo of my box-fresh Veja trainers on the streets of Islington to send her, saying:

I have new shoes,

And that's breaking news.

I wish there was more to say.

You came on my feed,

As the bus picked up speed,

So I wanted to wish you good day.

A little 'read at 12:04' comes up underneath my message, and three dots to signify she's typing.

Hey there Nic,

I'm impressed with your pic,

Those shoes are truly stunning.

It's Candice's birthday next week,

And not to stick in my beak,

But I wanted to know if you're coming?

There's a party? At Maple Avenue? And she's going to be there? I call Jackson.

'Jumping Jack,' I say, using the nickname he hates when he says hello. 'How do?'

'All right, mate,' he says. 'Just on my way to a lunch date,

134

as it goes. The girl from work finally agreed to go out with me. Only took me six months of grafting!'

'Timing is everything,' I say. 'I've said it before, and I'll say it again.'

'Yeah,' he says. 'Plus she thought I was a dick for the first five months because of some stupid joke I made in a welcome meeting. Been trying to undo the damage all this time. She's seeing the light though. Just can't mess it up today, can I?'

'You'll do great,' I assure him. 'You know you're a top bloke.'

'Yeah,' he says, a small flicker of self-doubt in his voice. 'But it's whether she thinks that, innit? Anyway, what you on?'

'Rumours of a party next week, mate. Did my invite get lost in the post?'

'Candice's? Yeah, it's next weekend. How did you know?'

'Ruby.'

'Oh,' he says. 'Well, I was waiting to ask Ruby if it was okay to invite you – not being funny, but she might not want some dude she shagged at her big Maple Avenue reunion. But if she's the one who's told you about it . . .'

'Yeah, she texted me about it just now.'

'Texting, is it? I thought you weren't staying in touch?'

I shrug, but obviously he can't hear that down the phone. 'Occasionally,' I tell him, making a mental note of how she obviously hasn't mentioned our communications to one of her best friends. 'So I'm invited? Obvs I don't wanna intrude.'

''Course you're invited, mate! In fact, can you come early to help set up? Ruby won't be down until late because she's a tight-arse student who would only buy the cheapest ticket, so you can blow up balloons, make some drinks, that sort of stuff?'

'Sure,' I say. 'Yeah. Can I invite my brother too? He's good value at a party.'

'Yeah, no bother. You off seeing Zola now? She said you were meeting up. Great you finally asked her out.'

'Other way round, actually,' I explain.

'I wouldn't expect anything less from her,' reflects Jackson. 'Naturally *she* asked *you* out.'

'What does that mean?'

'It doesn't mean anything. That's just very Zola. She's assertive. Knows what she wants.'

'Is that a bad thing . . . ?' I push.

'Not up to me, is it?' he says. 'I'm not the one about to go on a date with her. Not that she'll get a look-in now you know you'll be seeing Ruby in . . . what? Seven days and four hours? Do yourself a favour: get a haircut before then. You look better when it's shorter off your neck. And wear those Veja trainers!'

'Okay, Queer Eye,' I say.

'Take my advice or don't,' he says. 'But ask yourself: when has Uncle Jackson ever been wrong?'

He's got a point. 'Text me the name of your barber,' I ask, begrudgingly.

'My dude does afro hair,' Jackson says. 'I'll ask at work for some reccs.'

'Awesome. Cheers, pal.'

I hang up and head for the coffee shop Zola has raved about. The jig is up, though. I can distract myself with as many women as I want. But now I know it's seven days, three hours and fifty-five minutes until I'll get to see Ruby again, I'm not really bothered about anybody else. I write:

Dear Ruby Powell,
Your text made me howl,

All this communicating in rhyme is just fine.
I'll be there at the party,
Dressed up kind of arty,
Anticipating a jolly good time.
She texts back one word: *Cool x.*

19

Ruby

Harry agreed that *Almost Doesn't Count* is a great working title for our documentary, even if it doesn't end up being the final one, and over an impromptu brainstorming session in the car we get into the details of what we're trying to achieve, what we've got so far and where we hope the main story blocs take us.

'Let's remember our anchor,' he says with his mouth full, salad falling out of the end of the sandwich he's holding in one hand, sprinkling garnish all over his lap. The other is resting on the steering wheel as he drives from JP's house – where we've picked him up – back to campus so JP can come see where we study. He might even stay for a lecture, if he isn't too exhausted. He's been asking and asking, and eventually William gave in and said it'd be okay. 'We're still not sure what our mission statement with it all is, are we, and I think keeping *Almost Doesn't Count* in mind could really help us decide on it.'

'Take the second left,' I instruct him, holding my phone in front of me. His car doesn't have sat nav, so he drives and I Google-Map, letting him know where we have to go next. The man might have a car, but without somebody telling him where to go next, we'd end up in Scotland. 'And you're right.'

'Wait. Second left, or second right?' He gesticulates wildly with his sandwich and a slice of tomato flies over into my lap.

'Oh, for God's sake,' I say, handing him a napkin. He swallows the last bite of his sub and takes it. 'This left here. And I mean: you're right about the anchor. I agree that we need it.'

'Something tells me you don't say that easily,' JP quips from the back seat, where he's strapped in around all our equipment. We took it to get some shots of him at home, stuff like getting his knitted waistcoat on and having a cup of tea. 'Colour', Harry called it, in case we need images to go with some of our earlier voice recordings.

'Hey,' I say. 'You ever hear the saying dance with the one that brought you, JP? Well, I'm the one who brought you. Zip it.'

JP holds up his hands. 'I might be old, but there's no need to shout,' he says. 'Give the old codger some credit. I've got at least forty-five per cent hearing capacity, you know.'

He's been like this all morning – cheekier than usual. I think it's because he's excited to be out and about with us. William made us promise that he'd never be left unattended in case he falls, and that we'd have him home by teatime. We have a list of what medications he takes and when, and instructions to text pictorial evidence of his wellbeing every hour, on the hour.

'That's the thing about getting old.' JP had shrugged. 'You've got to adjust your palate to appreciate humble pie.

The adults become like children, and the children become the ones in charge.'

We sit in silence for a bit, taking in the urban scenery.

'What are you smiling at,' Harry says, as I swipe off of Google Maps and read a text. 'If it's from that Nic fella, I'm calling it now: one-night stand my arse – you're smitten.'

'Co-signed,' says JP, the traitor.

'It's from Candice, actually,' I say. 'Thank *you* very much.'

Wearing heels, bodycon and face glitter Saturday, so I'm going to have to ask you to do the same please! Can't be the only OTT bitch in the room! And you'd better bloody reply to this Miss MIA!

I send back a thumbs up.

'Hmm,' says Harry. 'Hearing his name has made you smile, anyway, hasn't it?'

'Shut up,' I say. 'Left at the end here, then you should know the way. It's the main road there.'

'It's nice!' Harry retorts. 'You have a crush! Here?'

'Here.'

We pick up speed now that we're on the right road and Harry has got both hands lunch-free.

'He's funny, that's all,' I say, feeling oddly defensive. 'Nic's texts are funny, so yeah, I text him back sometimes. Not like fucking *Abe*. I need to actually block him. Every time I ignore him on one platform, he finds another way to get in touch. He reckons he's finally broken up with his girlfriend and wants to be with me. He DM'd me, and I saw that he's following Finding JP's Girl. Like dude, get a *clue*. He did both right after I posted a picture of us two, Harry, when the caption was just a love heart.'

'So he thinks you've moved on? With the handsome devil that is *moi*?'

'And he's making sure I don't . . . I reckon so, yeah.'

'All this texting,' says JP. 'Texting me, texting him. You want to get yourself out there, face to face. It's not good, all you youngsters on your phones all the time. When I was your age they talked about robot technology making life easier, not becoming a full-time job.'

'Astute point,' I concede. 'My screen time is pretty disgusting. Should I start a list of things I'm not doing well? That you can both refer to? I talk about Nic too much, I'm glued to my phone . . . what else was there? Oh, well, I got your order wrong at the sandwich shop, Harry – should I put that one down in pencil, or pen?'

The men don't dignify my faux self-pitying rant with a reply. They know I'm trying to change the subject.

'That's so passive-aggressive of you both, not saying anything now I'm mad. You're both a pain in my bumhole, do you know that? JP, you'd better stick up for me or else I'm going to undo the child lock on your door and leave you in a ditch. A shaded ditch, maybe with a bottle of water and a blanket, but a ditch nonetheless.'

'What about one of those apps?' JP asks, once again side-stepping my misdirected frustration. 'If you're going to be on your phone so much anyway?' I've been a bit short-tempered for a few days, actually, and I don't even think it's hormonal. I'm frustrated, I suppose. We keep adding to the Finding JP's Girl Insta and, in between classes, Harry and I have sketched out some important beats to hit in our storytelling depending on a variety of different outcomes in our Amelie search, but it's still far from taking shape; I feel like I've started a puzzle and maybe got the edges done, but haven't even turned over half the pieces to see where they go yet.

I'm constantly thinking about how to lace everything

together: I think about the doc before I go to sleep, as soon as I wake up, when I'm walking to Harry's. It's some sort of creative immersion, maybe, like Janet and I talked about, but I'm also getting a bit obsessed. Using *Almost Doesn't Count* as the anchor is great, and it means we're getting closer to figuring out the exact question it is we're trying to answer. If almost doesn't count, where does that leave us? Can people ever really be happy if they miss what was meant for them? Or was it never really meant for them if it passed them by?

It's a big question, and sometimes, unexpectedly, it makes me think of Nic. He wanted to see me again and I said no because of The Year of Me, so doesn't that mean it wasn't meant for me? Or am I getting in my own way? Maybe that's why I keep mentioning his name, now – I don't want to ask JP and Harry for advice, but I want someone to tell me what to do. I feel like I have to make a decision about how I'm going to play it when I see him, and I'm wondering what it means that I'm pretty eager for it to be the weekend already.

'I don't have time for dating.' I sigh. 'And I'm in my yearlong . . . you know.' I hate using sexual words in front of JP, even if those words are about the absence of sex.

'Oh, yes,' says JP. 'The Year of Me.' He says Year of Me as if it is in air quotes, like it's silly. It hurts my feelings, actually. Aside from this past week, I've been loving my Year of Me. I'm making things! Meeting people! Feeling more creative and innovative than I have in my whole life! I don't *need* a man right now. It would be a distraction. What's happening right now is too important to be distracted from. I'm using my heart in other ways, making friends and community and pouring it into my art. I see Harry glance up to the rear-view mirror with a smirk, locking eyes, I assume, with an unrepentant JP.

'What does he look like? Nic?' Harry asks. 'Just out of interest?'

'He has a face,' I say. 'And two eyes, a nose, and mouth.' I conjure up an image of him in my mind. I try to think back to that night, but it's easier to remember him from his social media, in photographs when I wasn't even there. 'Nice lips, I suppose. But whatever.'

To be honest, I don't remember how his lips looked. But I do remember how they felt.

'Tall?' presses Harry.

'Tall enough.' I shrug. 'Bit lanky. Nice hands.'

Harry keeps his face impassive. 'Nice lips *and* nice hands.' He nods, expressing his appreciation. 'And a funny texter to boot.'

'I gave him an STI,' I remind him, turning to apologise to JP. 'If you'll pardon my harlot ways.'

'Darling,' JP chuckles. 'I was a soldier, remember? The things I've seen . . .' He does a comic wince. It's enough to make me smile, and as Harry looks in the rear-view, he feels me looking at him and turns so that we smile at each other. They've won. I have thawed.

'Speaking of Abe and STIs, did you ever text him about it?' Harry says.

'No,' I say. 'I know I need to.'

The scenery outside changes back from the leafy suburbs into higher buildings pushed close together, shops and computer repair places and car parks and more traffic.

'Do you ever regret turning him down?' Harry asks, as we start to approach campus.

'Abe?' I say. 'Absolutely not. Christ.'

'Nic, you idiot,' he says. 'Because, excuse me for saying so, but: if you wanna snog him this weekend, you totally should.'

'Oh my God,' I say. 'You are way off the mark.' I'm shaking my head so furiously I think I might ping my eyeballs out of my head. 'I mean, yeah. If I hadn't had one foot out of the door, he'd *maybe* have been a prime candidate for something more.' There. I've said it. I actually feel a bit short of breath. 'But let's not forget,' I insist, trying to remind myself of the facts, 'HE WAS A ONE-NIGHT STAND. And that is *not* how the story of one-night stands go. Is it? But yeah, fine, maybe if I hadn't been leaving I'd have asked for his number or told him to ask me out on a date or played dodgeball again on my friend Jackson's team, knowing he'd signed up to play too. HE IS A VERY CUTE MAN WHO IS VERY KIND AND SENSITIVE AND HAS THE LIPS AND THE HANDS AND THE FUNNY TEXTS AND, FOR CRYING OUT LOUD, ARE YOU TWO HAPPY NOW?'

Harry shrugs. 'The question is,' he says, as if his work here is done. 'Are you?'

'Oh, for pity's sake.' I laugh. 'No! Okay! I'm not especially happy about being ships passing in the night, but I am happy that I'm here, and happy if he's enjoying London. So . . . He probably just likes a flirt and I like a flirt too. And anyway . . . there's nothing to be done now, so pack it in, okay? I'm fragile!'

'Is it any wonder?' mutters JP as we arrive back at campus. 'Denying yourself what you really want this way?'

I don't respond for a minute, until finally I say: 'Well, I tell you what. I'll go to this party, and on the off-chance what was there when I met him is still there, I'll consider taking a leap of faith and amending the rules to the Year of Me. Maybe. I'll take it under advisement, all right? I suppose we can just wait and see what happens, can't we?'

Harry nods sagely. 'I suppose we can,' he says, and there's

something about the look on his face that strikes me as the look of a man declaring premature accomplishment. The strange thing is though, I don't mind.

After the lecture, I check my phone to see how the Finding JP's Girl account is going. Harry and I have both asked friends and family to follow and share it, and in three weeks we're up to 478 followers already. There's loads of comments under our first post, basically all saying variations of: *Hiya JP, can't wait to find out if you find your girl!* Harry has uploaded a bunch of other photos – us in lectures, various camera equipment, and crucially a snap of him holding Amelie's photograph, with the caption, *It's a long shot, but does anyone recognise this woman? Châteauponsac village in Limoges region, France, spring of 1940. She would have been seventeen, here.* So far, there's nothing. This morning I posted a bit about JP's story, to get people more emotionally involved. It has seventeen likes.

'You know,' I say, staring at the Instagram page. 'If we had hundreds of thousands of followers, maybe somebody would recognise Amelie. Even then it would be a long shot, but it would be more likely, wouldn't it?'

'Have you got a plan to get us a few hundred thousand followers?'

'No,' I say, slowly. 'But I am thinking maybe what we need is a smaller net in a smaller pond.'

Harry looks at me blankly. Then he seems to have a thought. 'Military records?' he says.

'Oh, yes. That's astute. I was going to say we need somebody in the village.'

'Do you know somebody in the village?'

'No,' I say. 'But we can find someone, can't we? Maybe

there's a landmark with staff, like a local library or tourism office or post office. If we could get the photo to them, and have them ask around, that would be more targeted. It's still a long shot, but at least we'd be within batting distance of the farm. It could still be in the family.'

Harry nods, and then asks JP, 'And you still don't remember the family's surname, or the name of the farm? Google – or parish records – would be a lot more helpful for us if you did . . .'

JP shakes his head solemnly.

'What if we showed you a map?'

I switch my maps function to 'Earth' so it looks more like real life, and plug in the name of the town they were near. JP looks at it blankly.

'It was such a long time ago,' he explains, waving a hand.

'Of course,' I say. 'I don't think I'd be able to even pinpoint the family home I grew up in on here. It's confusing to look at unless you already know what it is you're looking at. Don't worry. It wasn't my strongest idea.'

'Who do we know who is French?' Harry says. 'Or who can speak French?'

'Well, that's something we can ask our followers,' I say. 'Surely out of five hundred people somebody can speak French?'

'William,' JP supplies, then. 'William speaks French.'

'Well, then let's get you home to William,' Harry says. 'He needs to make a phone call for us.'

And so we scramble back into the car and call William on the way, asking him to meet us there.

20

Nic

'I'm only here to get my steps in – you know that, don't you?'

Ollie is pulling a face beside one of the Beefeaters at Kensington Palace, mortified to be associated with anything close to 'touristy' but humouring me in posing for a snap.

'Mum'll love it. Don't be such a whinge,' I say, getting dramatic with my phone. I turn it from portrait to landscape and take a step closer, hamming it up to say, 'That's it! There's your angle! Yes! Yes! Make love to the camera, baby!'

Ollie relents with an eye roll and starts pulling poses, turning around to look back over his shoulder, hands on hips, and then spinning around to blow a kiss in my direction. I capture it all.

'There you go,' I say, selecting everything I've just taken to AirDrop to him, and then picking the most ridiculous to text the family WhatsApp group. 'You've got handsome lad for Mum, sexy for your apps, and a special one you could frame and mount above your fireplace at home, too.'

Ollie squints at his phone as they Bluetooth over to him. 'God, I'm a sexy bastard,' he says, and he's not joking. 'What's it like to have a brother as fit as me? You drew the short straw when it came to the gene pool, didn't you?'

'I got the brains,' I say. 'And the sense of social propriety.'

'Manners are for the boring.' He grins.

I've corralled him into a twilight walk in the dark around some London hotspots. I've cooled off on the dating this week, now I know I'm seeing Ruby. It's a waste of everyone's time when it's hard work, frequently disappointing, and I compare everyone to her anyway. Her texts have become more regular. They were erratically timed before, but now it's every other day, just to see how I am.

'She's totally bread-crumbing,' Ollie says. 'And look at you, following her trail like a hungry little mouse.' He mimics mouse-like behaviour by putting his fingers up to his mouth and making 'nom nom nom' noises.

'She is *not* bread-crumbing me,' I say, scowling. 'We're just *chatting.*'

'Yeah,' Ollie says. 'As a warm-up before this weekend.'

I deepen my scowl and reread what she's just sent.

All right there, me lad,
I'll preface with: I ain't mad,
But what the hell was that comment on Insta?
You're a little bit pervy,
You've obviously some nerve(y),
Hitting 'like' whenever you see me.

Is that foreplay? Okay, yeah. I think there's a bit of wordy foreplay happening before the weekend. A man can hope. I text back:

Hello and good day,
I fear I've got something to say,

These texts, they're getting quite frequent.
I may hit that 'like'
Making your heart rate spike,
But you have to admit that you love it.

It barely even rhymes but she sends back a photo of herself pulling a silly face – eyes crossed, chin pulled in so it's doubled, tongue hanging out of her mouth.

U think me pretty? it says.

I send back a photo of myself standing soldier-still next to a Beefeater.

U think me strong and sexy? it says.

She sends back the eye emoji, which is a total cop-out but has me grinning like an idiot anyway.

'I can't believe you've actually written a list of things we have to see,' Ollie complains, as we pace the Mall down to the palace. I put my phone back in my coat pocket. 'Can't we just go to the pub?'

'No,' I say. '*Time Out* said it's a romantic thing to do on a December's evening, seeing everything lit up when it's dark out.'

'You're not gonna try and shag me, are you?' he says.

'No,' I reply. 'But in lieu of an actual date, I am going to buy you a hot chocolate in a bit, and then we'll head down towards the river.'

'Fine,' he says, zipping up his jacket a bit further up. 'It's Baltic though, innit?'

'I know you're enjoying this,' I say. 'And I also know in about a week you're gonna text and say you've done exactly the same with some girl.'

'Probs.' He chuckles. 'Can't lie. I need to be on the South Bank at eight, though. Don't forget.'

'Ollie – when are you ever not meeting a girl?'

'Never,' he says. 'You say it with admiration,' he adds, knowing that wasn't how I meant it at all. 'But I don't mind telling you it can be quite the cross to bear. So many women, so little time.'

'And you don't fancy picking just one?'

'What, like at a time?'

I roll my eyes at him.

'Well what about you?' he says. 'It's all very well ticking off a list of London sights, but it's not exactly embracing the height of humanness, is it?'

'And humanness in your book is shagging, is it?'

'It's the most basic of urges.'

'You're a caveman.'

'A caveman with a high libido.'

'Hmm.'

We get to the palace and see the flag flying.

'They're in, then,' I say, nodding towards it.

'Archaic institution,' Ollie says, shaking his head. '*Vive la révolution*, that's what I say.'

'I think it's nice,' I counter. 'The royal family is an English tradition. Plus, they make us a mint in tourism.'

'Cost us a mint, too,' Ollie says, holding up his phone to snap a photo of me before I even have to ask. I don't know what I'm going to do with all these photos, but they're nice to have.

'All I'm saying is—' Ollie starts.

'I know what you're saying!' I interrupt him because he's already given me shit about holding out for Ruby, and it's boring me now. I already know what he thinks. 'Date! I get it!'

'But you're not dating, because of this sofa girl you think you've fallen in love with.'

150

He doesn't say it as a question.

'I don't *think* I've fallen *in love* with her. I just think if there's a chance to see if it's got legs, then maybe we should do that. I don't know. It's cool if you want to get your dick wet with somebody different every night of the week, but it's just not *me*. It's weird you're so hung up on my sex life anyway. It's creepy. You do you, bro.' He's smirking as I rant, and it forces me to smirk slightly too. The prick. 'And her name is Ruby.'

'And we're going to see her at the weekend?' he asks. 'At this party?'

I retort: 'Why do you think I'm trying to stay busy?'

Ollie blinks, like he doesn't compute. 'I just . . .' he says. I wait for the blow to come. 'I get that romance can be nice, but you're acting like a bit of a lost cause. You had one night with her. So what? People have one-night stands all the time.'

'We just clicked,' I insist. 'I would have let it go, but then when she said she'd be coming, and then the texting and whatever . . .'

'You got hard again?'

'Ollie.'

'Nic.'

I sigh.

'Just all sounds like a lot of hard work and earnest navel-gazing if you ask me.'

'I didn't.'

We head down towards the river, winding through some of the quieter streets where Ollie looks wistfully at a pub that has post-work drinkers supping pints outside, despite the cold. I motion for him to come across the road with me, to a van pulled up near Westminster Abbey, selling hot drinks and roasted chestnuts.

151

'How's work, anyway?' he says, once I've ordered the promised hot chocolates. 'I've got to admit, I love telling everyone that you work for a Hoare.'

'Ha, ha,' I say. 'The first person ever to make *that* joke.'

'My brother the banker,' he says. 'Doing us all proud.'

'That sounds dangerously close to a compliment.'

'It's not,' he says, cheerily. 'Don't worry.'

'What are you getting Mum and Steve for their anniversary, by the way?' I ask. 'And have you got your train ticket yet?'

'Not thought about it,' he says. 'The present or the train ticket. I'll just get one on the day.'

We linger on Westminster Bridge, looking out towards Waterloo Bridge, and Tower Bridge beyond it. The wind is icy, but the hot chocolate is warm and it's pretty, all the twinkling lights and looming dark sky.

'Shall I see what's on her Amazon wish list? We can go halfsies?'

'Sound,' he says, not taking his eyes off the view. I follow his gaze.

'I'm glad you're down here, you know,' he announces, suddenly.

'Aww, my younger brother getting soft on me?' I say. 'Surely not?'

'Piss off,' he retorts. 'I was just saying.' He goes back to looking out towards the water.

'I'm glad I'm here too,' I say. 'It's nice. Hanging out.'

'Yeah,' Ollie says, and he doesn't even make a joke.

I don't know what the future has in store for me – who I'll be in five years, or ten, or where I'll live or who with. But I do know that here, now, weeks before Christmas in the cold, with my brother, in a great city, texting a hot woman who, yeah, can't decide what she wants and lives miles away – but is texting me, me! I don't know. It feels right. Like I'm doing okay. It's all good.

'You look like you're gonna break out into a chorus of The Beatles' "Blackbird",' Ollie notes.

'"Blackbird"?'

'You know – blackbird singing in the dead night. Something about broken wings and flying.'

'*You were only waiting for this moment to arise,*' I say. 'Ha. Yeah.'

'You're doing all right, kid. You know that, don't you? I take the piss and that but . . . you know, Millie was great, et cetera, but you did the right thing.'

'Thanks for saying so,' I say.

'I know it was hard. You're a good lad, sticking it out as long as you did. She's a great match, just not for you. Not a lot of blokes would do what you've done. Work offered me the chance to go to New York for a year, and I said no.'

'Really?' I ask. 'Why?'

'I'm twenty-nine, mate. I don't wanna be in my thirties and Billy No-Mates in a wicked place but where I don't know anyone.'

'But New York,' I say. 'That's—'

'Like I say,' Ollie concludes. 'Not everyone has got it in them.'

I nod. I had no idea Ollie had turned down America. I'm surprised. He's so confident, so bloke-of-the-world. And he said no.

'Thanks for telling me that,' I say. 'About New York, I mean.'

'Just don't tell Mum,' he says. 'It's bad enough the stick I get about living down here. If she thought they were dangling the other side of the world in front of me she'd lose her head.'

'Your secret's safe with me,' I tell him.

'Anyway,' he says. 'I know I don't say it enough but I'm proud of you, brother. You're smashing it. I even envy your sad little romantic heart a bit. Only a bit, mind.'

'Well,' I say. 'You never know, you might be about to meet the love of your life on this date. What's her name, anyway?'

'Priya,' he says. 'Met her on Happn.'

'Got a photo?' I ask, taking the moment to bond. He fiddles with his phone and hands it to me.

'That's her.'

I look at it. It's the same Priya I went to the Victorian cemetery with and bailed on when she brought all her mates.

'Oh, Ollie,' I say, laughing. 'On second thoughts, I don't think you are. Good luck is all I can say.'

'What?' he asks, snatching back his phone. 'What?'

'Nothing,' I say. 'You have fun.'

'No, tell me,' he says. 'I thought she seemed all right. She's got bants.'

'Look,' I say, 'it's five to. You should go.'

He narrows his eyes.

'See you on Saturday? I'll send you the addy.'

'Fine,' he says. 'Maybe I'll bring Priya.'

'Maybe you will,' I say, still refusing to tell him what I think is so funny.

When I get home, I settle in on the sofa I bought from Ruby to watch some TV before bed. The flat is an okay size, by London standards, painted all white and with hardwood floors. It's part of a converted Victorian house, and has some great original features like a fireplace – not used, though – and interesting cornicing. If and when I buy here, it'll probably be closer to central. I only chose Ealing because that's where Ollie is. The flat is in a quiet block, with a couple about my age above me occasionally making their bed squeak on a Saturday night but otherwise I seldom hear them. Across the hall is a flat-share – two guys who never seem to be home at all. And the fourth flat is empty, I think, because I've never seen or heard anyone. It's not a bad set-up. Clean, tidy, just posh enough but not quite bi-folding doors onto a landscaped patio. One day, I hope. One day soon.

I look at my phone after choosing something to ignore on Netflix, using it mostly for background noise. Ruby hasn't texted back. I scroll through my socials, seeing if she's uploaded. She hasn't. I run a hand over the moss-green velvet of the settee, remembering the day I bought it.

Saturday can't come soon enough. I wander over to the wardrobe and pull out a shirt, a T-shirt and some cord trousers. I lay everything out on the bed and send a photo to Jackson: *Does this pass the Queer Eye test?* I type. *For Saturday.*

He sends me the squirting water emoji, which I think means yes.

21

Ruby

They've found the family! a text bleets on my phone as I carry my morning coffee from Mick's cart across campus. It's from William. I call him immediately.

'Talk fast!' I say, excitedly. 'Somebody knows who Amelie is?'

I'm walking up to the film studies department for the day, mentally planning what I need to pack for the weekend and still trying to decide how to play things with Nic. I think I've decided. I think that JP is right, and the heart is a muscle and I have to use it, and so if Nic's there alone and hasn't brought a date and wants a flirt and maybe that flirting leads to a snog . . . who's to say I won't enjoy it? Who's to say it's wrong? It's not! I'm old enough to know the rarity of chemistry and young enough to say sod it. Again. Then I can get on the train home the next day and continue to slay everything with my course, with the doc and my creative development as good as ever. In fact, my art could even be better

156

for living a little more, like Janet said back at my welcome meeting with her.

A woman can have it all, can't she, as long as she promises not to lose who she is over a man this time? I need to practise doing that. A key part of the Year of Me needs to be understanding that I can trust myself, that just because I chose a terrible man once, it doesn't mean I'll do it again – and even if I do, I'll survive. Look at Nic himself – he's the very embodiment of how life is for living. And JP: seizing his chances at ninety-six! I'm going to be okay. The Year of Me is about fun in *all* things. The celibacy rule can, like JP suggested, be bent. I won't lose out on anything else. I am making a promise to myself to be okay containing multitudes.

As luck would have it, I see Harry approaching right as William is about to start talking. Campus is mostly deserted because it's only just gone eight and most people don't start trickling in until nine thirty or ten. It's spooky how alike Harry and I are. He's an early bird who likes to catch the worm too, making us a badass team that gets things done. I wave him over.

'It's William,' I say urgently, turning the phone settings to speaker. 'They've found Amelie!' Then, to William I instruct: 'Okay, Harry is here now, William. Go.'

'Well, it was such a good idea to call the library,' William says. I'm holding up the phone in the air so both Harry and I can lean towards it, ear-first, holding eager eye contact. 'The librarian stuck our request to the books-out desk and somebody saw it, asked about it, and suggested she ask at the post office, because the husband of the woman who runs it is from a farming family, and a lot of the farmers know each other.'

'Uh-huh,' I say. 'Okay.'

Harry pulls away, then, to get out his own phone, and starts recording. Clever man.

'Sorry, William,' I say. 'Can you just repeat all that again? For the tape?'

William takes a breath and repeats it all a second time, for the benefit of the camera.

'So did the family know anyone? I mean, they obviously did. But who?'

'JP had got his directions wrong – the farm was east of the main town, by about twenty miles.'

'Ah, JP said north.'

'Well, luckily the village twenty miles *north* of the city had one person in it who had a box of old photos, and in that box of photos was another photo of Amelie, from twenty miles *east*, at a local street party when the war ended, only this photo had her full name on it AND the name of the farm. Honestly, the chances of that all lining up . . . I can't believe it. God bless French farmers with long memories and nosy natures.'

Harry and I look at each other, delighted. I almost don't dare ask what I really want to know. But that's going to be the decider. If Amelie is dead, the story ends here.

'And she's alive,' William says, pre-empting my thoughts. 'Amelie is alive.'

'Oh, thank fuck,' says Harry, smiling. 'Oh, that's amazing. I'll bet JP is made up!'

'He's processing, I think. Amelie lives in Paris, now. Her second niece once removed, I think it is, is still local and was the one to connect the dots for us. I spoke to her this morning on the phone.'

'Holy shit,' I say. 'All that happened this morning? It's . . .' I look at my watch. 'Not even ten past eight!'

'It was like pulling at a thread,' William continues. 'And now the whole mystery has unravelled. The only thing is, we don't have a Paris address. Some falling-out in the family or something. But surely it can't be that hard to find Amelie Renard? We're closer than ever!'

'Look,' I say, chewing the inside of my cheek in a terrible habit of nervousness that I just can't seem to stop. I've done it since I was a little girl. 'We have class this morning, but are you both free at about one? We'll come to you?'

'See you then,' says William, ringing off. 'And hurry! This is the most exciting thing to ever have happened to me.'

'Us too!' Harry says. 'I can't believe we found her!'

'I can,' I say, gleefully. 'Because everyone deserves a happy ending. And nobody more than JP.'

I barely take anything in during our activism and storytelling seminar, even though I'm normally on the edge of my seat taking notes and asking questions. Harry and I got coffee in the atrium and discussed what could happen next briefly, but we also had essays to finish so there's still so much to say. I think about JP and Amelie the whole time. I wonder how he's feeling – JP. Bless him. I'm nervous to see Nic tomorrow and it's only been four months – not to mention the fact we've spoken on the phone, and texted every other day. I don't know if that makes it better or worse, but the magnitude of waiting more than seventy years to see somebody who meant so much to him is growing on me. I don't know if I could do it. Holding on to hope for a brave ten seconds in order to maintain eye contact or even lean in for a kiss can be agony – holding on to hope for more than seven decades? I'm surprised JP isn't in physical pain.

Could they Skype do you think? I type into the notes app

of my phone, before passing it to Harry sat beside me. He glances down, careful not to appear rude to our lecturer, takes the phone and types back: *Nonagenarians on Skype? I just don't think it will work. Where's the drama?*

Yeah, I type back. *But we can hardly get JP to Paris, can we? Or ourselves for that matter . . .*

Harry pulls a face. He's dissatisfied with my negativity.

'There has to be another way,' he declares, on our way out of the lecture hall and towards his car. 'This is good. This is really, really good. Reunited World War Two lovers in the Twenty-Twenties? That's like, Hollywood-movie-level storytelling. It's epic.'

He updated the Instagram during class, telling everyone the latest news. We've both got 'the tingle' – the spidey senses that let us know we're on to something big. I have to tell Harry to slow down three times on the drive over.

'Don't kill us both before we finish this bloody documentary,' I say. 'Or it will have all been for nought.'

When we get to JP's house though, he's drinking tea, as is his standard way, looking like he doesn't have a care in the world.

'Aren't you excited?' Harry says. 'We've found Amelie Renard!'

'Née Renard,' JP points out. 'We don't know if she took a new name when she married. The great-granddaughter, or niece, or whatever she is, doesn't know. Breathe deep, lad. We've a way to go yet.'

'That's true,' I say. 'But we've asked Instagram now – we're up to eight hundred followers! And we've got a lot we can be googling. We're getting closer and closer, JP. I've got a good feeling about this.'

'We've been doing the same,' William says. 'Googling. It's

hard. I tried looking for parish records from the area like you said, I even typed in "how to do a family history search", lol. So this is amazing. I'm almost too excited to concentrate. But now you're here we can have a cuppa and then take a breath and brainstorm a bit, can't we? Come up with something strategic, like the librarian idea that got us this far in the first place.'

I take a mini-bow as everyone looks at me, what with that being my idea and all, and then we settle in, Harry and William making tea and JP watching over me as I set up filming equipment.

'I'm putting this on a time lapse,' I explain to him. 'So it won't record anything we say, just our movements, and then it will speed them up really fast.'

'And what's the point in that, then?' JP asks. 'More "colour", as you say?'

'You've got it,' I say. 'Texture. We can put something over the top of it – an interview recording – or use it as a stamp to signify time passing, or lots happening very quickly.'

'Lot to think about, isn't there?' he says.

'I love it,' I say, and we swap smiles.

'Right,' declares Harry, once we're brewed up and in our usual spots: JP in his armchair, me and Harry on the sofa, and William perched on the footrest. 'I think we'll have to go old-school.'

'Old-school?' I ask.

'Get the phone book and dial every number in there until we find her.'

William's phone pings. 'Chalamet!' he cries. We look at him. 'Married name: Chalamet. The librarian just sent a text. God, she's good.'

'Technology,' JP tuts, shaking his head. 'The world is in the palm of your hand, isn't it?'

'More's our luck,' I say. 'So what's the next move?'

'Spend all weekend going through the phone book for every Amelie Chalamet there is and call each one until we find her. That's my bet,' William says.

'I'm in,' says Harry. 'Shall we just work from here? JP, is that okay?'

JP waves a hand. 'We'll have to move my tarts and vicars party to next weekend,' he says. 'But yes, more the merrier.'

'Ha, ha, JP. I can come as a tart if that helps,' Harry offers.

'I'll hold you to that,' JP jokes.

Everyone is so motivated and animated that I get carried away for a moment, letting it bubble away inside of me, too, until I remember I'm in London this weekend.

'You won't be here,' says Harry, reading my face. 'That's okay. I can get what we need footage-wise. Don't worry, Ruby.'

'Okay,' I say. Fleetingly, I wonder about cancelling my plans. I think, *What if I didn't go to the party?* and then scold myself, guilt stabbing me between my ribs, because of course I have to go to the party. It's Candice! We've not been the best at staying in touch but she's my best pal, and not going isn't an option. It's just . . . this is such a cool development. It all feels so close. I want to be in the room when they finally make the call where the person at the other end says, *Yes, I am Amelie Chalamet and yes, I remember my soldier.*

'Let's do a quick search and see what we're working with whilst we're all together, shall we?' I suggest. 'I can at least help you come up with a plan, depending on how many we find. I don't even know if there's such thing as a French yellow pages online we can use, or . . . ?'

'I'll text the librarian,' offers William. 'Maybe she has access through there.'

'Superb thinking,' Harry says.

We spend the next two hours using the librarian across in Bessines as a sort of go-between as she uses her library's system to access the *Pages Jaunes*, copy and pasting what we need into a Word document that she eventually sends across to William, who then has to struggle with JP's largely unused and very old printer to get a physical copy out. There's 193 on the list with public numbers, and seventeen private.

'Here's hoping it's one of the ones we've got, then,' says William.

It's 5 p.m. by the time we've got everything we need to start making the calls, but JP is already sleepy and more or less ready to think about his small tinned-salmon sandwich and then bed, so we reason that Amelie, whichever one on our list she is, must surely be the same.

'Go,' Harry assures me as William gets JP on the stairlift and upstairs to help him change. 'Enjoy the party. All we'll do without you is make the call and establish her situation. I'd hate to miss it too, but I promise I'll keep you updated on anything significant, and you're back Sunday, aren't you? So we'll see you Monday, first thing. I'll even shout you a coffee and muffin in the atrium, okay? I'll walk you through every conversation we have step by step.'

'Okay,' I say, and I know I'm pouting. It means everything to me, and now we're making headway.

'And make me a promise?' Harry adds, reaching out to hold on to my shoulders so that he can look me square in the eye.

'What?' I say.

'Collect some stories of your own this weekend, Ruby. I think we're both learning to take our chances when they present themselves, aren't we?'

I nod, but don't say anything. I know he's right.

* * *

The next day I catch up on my reading for the course on the way down to Euston, before hopping on the tube to Ealing Broadway where I do my make-up. Ultimately, by the time I'm making a right out of the station, I look like a student dancer still in her warm-up clothes backstage: a full face of make-up and sweatpants on, textbooks spilling out of her backpack. I've done this walk so many times before; it's only five minutes on foot. I take a breath as I head down the dead-end street where the house is, taking in the manicured gardens of Mrs Higton juxtaposed with the rusty car parts and caravan resting on top of some bricks in Mr Birkin's. The winter leaves of the trees lining the pavement clag up the road where they've fallen and gone damp and soggy. I can hear music blasting from the house before I can even see it – I'm sure nobody is due to arrive until seven, and it's only half five. Tentatively, I knock on the door, wondering if they'll even be able to hear me. There's a scuffle, and somebody swears really loudly, and then I hear footsteps in the hall.

'It's you,' I say, when it opens.

Nic.

Nic being incredibly, incredibly handsome. More handsome than I remember. And he's in the house, all mischievous eyes and . . . wait. Has he had his ear pierced? His hair is shorter at the back, like it's been freshly cut, and his smile is wide and warm. There's a poetic symmetry to the first time we met, when he was the one waiting to be told to come in.

'Hey!' he says, opening his arms to envelop me in a hug. I pull away, noting how he smells like cedar and musk, because I'm unabashedly hungry to get another look at him. He's in rolled-up cord trousers, a cream T-shirt and open flannel shirt, wearing a beanie and stubble. He looks trendy and cool and not at all ill at ease like he did the last time I saw him.

We each take in the sight of the other. It's kind of adorable – we're grinning and staring and not knowing what to say, and it's there. Without a doubt, whatever has been fizzing in my tummy leading up to seeing him hasn't been wrong. I feel like I want to kiss him. I know that's totally over the top, but I do. There's not so much a spark between us as there is a blaze. I don't even question if he feels it too. It's indisputable: tonight I am going to hook up with Nic Sheridan again. I think it was decided before I'd even admitted it to myself.

'Can I take your bag for you?' he offers. He's tugging at the hem of his T-shirt as if he's chilly, and it occurs to me that I'm still in the doorway and it *is* pretty cold. I snap myself back into reality.

'That would be great,' I reply, noticing the way his forearm flexes as he takes the handle. I suddenly think of him in a suit, his tie pulled loose and his sleeves rolled up, all focused and concentrating. I'll bet half his office want to sleep with him. 'Thank you. I'm not sure where I'm sleeping? I don't think anyone has moved in yet, have they? But I'm happy on the sofa.'

Jackson sashays to the front door, then, hoots: 'Look what the cat dragged in! Here she is!'

Nic steps aside graciously to let Jackson flail out his arms for a bear hug. He looks as beautiful as ever, newly bleached cropped hair and all. He's in a sleeveless zip-up hoodie that's only done up to his nipples, revealing firm pecs and muscly arms. I notice he's got glitter on his cheekbones and is clutching a make-up brush in one hand, as if he's just finished doing it.

'I miss you so much,' I say, my voice muffled by his shoulder and a mouthful of his top. 'Too much. I miss you like oxygen,' I tell him. He pulls away and gets a look at me.

'Me too, darling,' he replies. 'I can barely even say your name without tears overflowing.' I roll my eyes, because he's being dramatic so that he doesn't have to be truthful.

'Earnest as ever,' I say, and he tells me to come in.

'I've not got time to gild an invitation for entry. Can you find whatever needs doing and do it? Nic has got the list. We've only got an hour before everyone is here and her highness is handing out instructions like party bags.'

'Your aversion to anyone with authority hasn't lessened then,' I joke, as Nic emerges from what used to be my old room, my overnight bag still intact.

'I've been instructed that you're bunking up with Candice,' he says. 'So I'll just take this upstairs?'

It happens again. We hold eye contact, and it ignites a storm in my stomach. I'm taken back to the lingering looks and coy smiles the night we met, but this is something else. If absence makes the heart grow fonder, the distance there's been between us has made our attraction sprout wings. He pushes his tongue to the side of his cheek in a way that I can only describe as very 'Ryan Gosling when everyone realised they'd given the Oscar to the wrong movie'. Smug, but not irritatingly so. Like he's in on the joke. It gives me – and there's absolutely no other way to say this – fanny flutters.

I watch him walk up the stairs, and I know that he knows I'm watching. Damn.

I peek my head around the corner of the front room, and Candice looks up from a tangle of wires and sockets, an empty shot glass at her feet and a radiant smile on her face.

'CANDY!!!!' I cry, and fall to my knees beside her so we can hug just as hard as Jackson and I did. We hold our embrace for ages, rocking back and forth and sort of squealing and making various noises of appreciation for one another.

When we pull away, we fuss over each other – she's already dolled up for the part and looks incredible in glitter eyeliner and glossed lips. I tell her so, but I'm not met with a compliment in return.

'Thank you, darling. But . . . you . . .' She gestures limply to my face. 'Are you okay? You look . . .'

'Knackered?' I supply. I can't fault a friend for being truthful, even if I'd prefer her to remind me what a sexy goddess I am so I feel good about flirting with Nic later. 'I am, a bit, truth told. But good knackered. Working on stuff that makes my heart sing knackered. Honestly, it's amazing. It was the right thing for me to do, for sure.'

'I'm excited you could come,' she says.

'Of course! Did you think I wouldn't?' I'm kidding, but there's a tiny movement across her face that suggests that maybe she did think I might not, and I get a flush of guilt for ever considering staying behind to help with the Amelie search.

'I don't know how busy graduates can be,' she says. 'I didn't go to uni, did I?'

I soften at her. 'I'll never be too busy for you. You know that, don't you?'

Her gaze has already wandered, looking around the room at what needs to be done. There's no bed, no furniture, nothing.

'I can't believe you've kept this room free,' I say. 'Isn't it costing you a fortune?'

'Rather it cost us a few hundred quid a month extra until we find the right person than end up with some of the bunny boilers and psychopaths that have stopped by to see it,' Candice says. 'Honestly. But we think that French guy might be a goer for when Bao leaves, don't we, Jackson?'

'Yup,' exclaims Jackson, from the doorway. 'Everyone else has been très dull, and we knew we were having this big party and could do with the room so . . .'

'So welcome to the dance room!' Candice finishes. I take it all in: the blinds are pulled shut and there's streamers everywhere, as well as balloons bobbing about across the whole of the ceiling – there must be seventy-five, maybe even a hundred, in silver and gold and red. It looks really cool.

'And check this out,' Candice squeals in glee as she stands. 'If I've done it right, anyway.' She plugs something in and it illuminates to cast stars of the galaxy over all the walls. It's really lovely.

'This room is for Spotify Roulette, as loud as we can go. The neighbours have gone away for the weekend, luckily for us. I just want everyone to really let loose tonight, you know? We were even going to use the bath as a big ice bucket for the booze, but because it's the only bathroom we decided we'd be locked out of it for most of the night. You know what people get like with their small bladders when they've been knocking them back.' And she motions having a drink, to illustrate her point. I feel my pulse quicken and my neck flush. I've needed a night like this. I suddenly want to already be backcombed and hair-sprayed to within an inch of life, wearing just as much glitter as Candice is, dancing the night away, drink in hand. Manchester is amazing, and I'm so, so happy there – but I've only just this second realised that I've also needed a night away from self-improvement and creativity against the clock. A night to just be free and dance.

'Who's coming?' I ask.

'Everyone,' she says, like that's detail enough.

Jackson says he's going to finish the jobs list, he just wanted to let us know there's drinks waiting for us in the kitchen.

When he's gone, I point through to the other room. I can hear Jackson saying something about Jack Daniel's – he must be supervising cocktail-making duties.

'So. Nic's here . . .' she says.

'Yeah,' I whisper. 'I mean, I haven't told you this yet because it's no big deal, but we've actually been texting a bit.'

Candice gasps, her expression strange. 'Well, at least you're replying to *somebody's* texts,' she says, and she means it playfully, I think, but it comes out sounding a bit mean. 'I'm only teasing,' she insists, when she catches sight of my face.

'You're crap at answering your phone, too,' I defend. 'It's not all me.'

'I work stupid hours, don't I?' she says, and then waves a hand to insist. 'Anyway, we're together now. That's all that matters. More details about Nic, please . . . I thought you were celibate this year?'

'That rule is under advisement,' I say. 'But all other tenets of the Year of Me stand.'

'I see,' she says. 'I knew you'd have some big epiphany because of what you're working on. How could anyone try to find the lover of a ninety-something-year-old without having their heart melt?'

I shrug. 'Exactly,' I say. 'I'm glad you understand.' She winks at me. 'And by the way – do you think he's had a glow-up? Is it just me or is he fitter now than he was on Bank Holiday?'

'I thought the same!' she exclaims. 'The earring, the cords, the fade? For sure somebody has had a word and dragged him into his manhood. He looks good for it. He helped zip up my dress earlier and said I looked fit and it actually made me blush.'

'So what, you fancy him now too?' It sounds girly and secretive, but I'll be fuming if she says yes.

'God no,' she says. 'But he's not the same bloke who bought your sofa, is he? There's something different about him. He seems a bit more confident, a bit more relaxed. It's hot – but hot for you. I don't care. Have you met his brother yet? Ollie. I quite fancy him, actually.'

'That'll be a fun cliché,' I joke. 'If we end up dating a couple of brothers.'

'Who said anything about dating?' Candice smirks. 'I don't do that, remember?'

'Is the postman here tonight?'

'Lost my nerve, didn't I?'

'Jesus,' I say. 'How can a woman be so sexually confident but so romantically timid?'

'Are you looking in a mirror when you say that?' she teases. 'Or . . . ??'

'Ha, ha.'

She pulls down the hem of her dress and throws a satisfied glance around the room, like it's all exactly as she wants it to be.

'Anyway,' she concludes. 'Remember: you're not here for Nic. You're here for me. I'm the birthday girl. You should shower me with nothing but love and attention, okay?'

'Deal,' I say.

22

Nic

We start out by making eyes at each other across whatever room we find ourselves in. Everyone has arrived by eight, is happily tipsy and relaxed enough to start dancing by nine, and by ten there's two different couples snogging on the sofa, a limbo competition happening in the dance room and Ollie has snorted a vodka shot out of some woman's belly button and weirdly, she seems to be finding it hilarious instead of gross. Jackson is here somewhere – last I saw he was creating cocktails in the kitchen, with an audience lapping it up, which is par for the course. I know only a handful of faces: Jackson, Candice, my brother and Ruby, plus two girls from dodgeball who Candice knows too. But I've been chatting as I sup a couple of beers, and fulfilled my role as chief rubbish collector as well, doing sweeps of the place for any stray empties. That ends up being a good way to talk to people, actually, giving me a pretext to interrupt people and chat but also a reason to move on as well.

But no matter what I'm doing and where I am, the magnetic power of Ruby never leaves. If I'm in the dance room I know that she's leaning near the stairs talking to someone who has just come in. If I'm in the tiny lounge I know she's by the door through to the kitchen, swaying to the sounds of the music drifting through. And when I'm on the way back from the loo, she's on her way up, saying nothing, only pursing her lips provocatively as I let her squeeze by. I feel the warmth radiating off her skin as she passes, wisps of her hair tickling my face. Is she swaying her hips that way for my benefit? She's like Marilyn Monroe with her tiny waist and rounded hips and an arse you could park a bike in – and I mean that in all the best ways.

We orbit the same spaces, each aware of the presence of the other, flirting with our eyes and smirking and it all feels so predetermined, so already decided, that after four hours of this game, she locks eyes with me, nods, and then slips out the back door. I know I'm supposed to go after her. Finally.

'Having fun?' I say, finding her out on the picnic table at the far corner of the patio.

'I am now,' she replies, grinning. It's cold, and she's wrapped her arms around herself to keep warm. There are goose bumps on her ivory skin, tiny dot-to-dots. She sees me notice and says, 'I didn't think this through. It's freezing.'

I take off my flannel overshirt and give it to her. It's heavy-weight – Jackson calls it a 'shacket', like a shirt-jacket. He's got names for everything, that man. I heard him compliment a woman's 'shoboots' earlier, and it took me ages to work out he meant shoe-boots, like that's even a thing.

'I wasn't expecting you to put clothes *on* me.' She giggles, as I drape it around her shoulders, enjoying my knuckles brushing against her lightly. I get to lean in just close enough to do it, from behind, and she doesn't quite turn the whole way as she registers my proximity, amusement dancing across her features.

'It's going to be like that, is it?' I whisper playfully. 'I see.'

Ruby shrugs, noncommittal and like butter wouldn't melt, but I know that look. I've seen that look before. I saw it that night.

'Can I have some of your beer?' she asks, and she's lowered her voice too. We're talking softly, as if we're postcoital. It does something to the air between us. I hand her my bottle. 'Thank you,' she enthuses.

She takes a long swig and I hop up onto the bench beside her, putting my feet where our bottoms should be, on the chair part. Her face sparkles where the light catches it – she's wearing the same glitter on her face as Candice and Jackson. Her hair falls long, in loose waves, like a mermaid, and the short, square nails at the end of her dainty hands are painted red. *I love red nails,* I think when I clock them, before realising that I only love red nails because they're on her. It's an opinion I've never expressed before in my life until now.

'How's Manchester?' I ask. Getting an update on her new life seems as good a place to start as any.

'It's even better than I hoped it would be, actually,' she says, talking to the moon. 'I mean, I'm shit-scared most of the time because I have this constant little voice in the back of my head asking me what I expect to come from all this, what am I going to do once I'm out of the uni bubble . . . but for now, I feel like more myself than I ever have done. I think . . . I'm scared and also driven by the fear? It's complicated.'

Sometimes Ruby's got the banter of an ice queen, but then

173

she suddenly switches to being open-hearted and authentic with something like she's just said. It's a killer combination, keeping me expertly on my toes. She's dizzying in the emotional highs and sarcastic lows she can scale from one sentence to another. I like it. It's mercurial but thrilling.

'You sound dangerously close to doubting yourself,' I observe, noticing how she's pulling at the label on the bottle she hasn't given back. Isn't that what the sexually frustrated do? 'Don't let it hold you back.'

'Yeah,' she says, still looking up at the sky. The moon is almost full, and casts bright light over the tops of the trees. 'But I don't mind a little bit of self-doubt if it spurs me on, I suppose. The problem contains the solution, and all that. Gotta feel my feelings before I can fix 'em, haven't I?'

'That's very mature of you,' I say, and she chuckles and says thanks.

'I'm doing my best on this spiritual quest for personal growth, or whatever it might be called,' she says.

'The Year of Me, isn't it?' I say.

'Well remembered,' she replies, impressed, turning her head to me and holding eye contact momentarily.

'I'm like an elephant,' I say.

'What else haven't you forgotten?'

'Hmm, let's see,' I muse. 'The fact that when we met you weren't wearing a bra . . . and that you look very good wearing my clothes and making hot chocolate. Or wearing my clothes and sitting outside a party on a picnic bench,' I add, stealing a sideways glance at her.

'And here I was thinking we'd get into the government's new economic policy, or unpicking the sartorial reasonings behind male ear piercings,' she quips, and then she nibbles the corner of her own lip, like she knows she's being cheeky.

174

It's so hot I feel a stirring in my pelvis. She's just . . . fucking gorgeous, man. 'We're just going right into it, are we? No shame.'

'Right into what?' I ask, feigning innocence. 'You were the one who asked what I remember . . .'

'And now we're talking about our thoughts on the night we slept together.' She sighs.

'I'm offended if you ever stopped thinking about it.'

'I didn't.' Her face is unreadable and thus proves my point about oscillating between the ridiculous and sublime. Whatever mood she's in, though, I'm here for it. I'm struggling to keep up, but the challenge is intoxicating.

'Well I'm glad then,' I bat back. 'It's not a spoiler to remind us both that we were pretty good at what we did . . .'

'No spoilers but the chlamydia was a nice plot twist.' She laughs, gently.

'Clean as a whistle now, though,' I counter.

'And what am I supposed to do with a whistle again . . . ?' she shoots back, and her provocativeness renders me speechless. She chuckles, knowing she's scored a point.

'You're doing that blushing thing with me again aren't you?' I ask.

She nods. 'Is it working?'

'I'm a man of the world now,' I say, stretching out my words like I don't have a single care, let alone have ruffled feathers because of the beautiful woman beside me. 'Four months in London will make a chap streetwise and ready to play.'

She cocks her head at me. 'You do seem kind of different, you know.'

'Really? I was only kidding.'

'You seem . . .' She tries to find the word. 'I don't know. Happy?'

175

I shrug and think about how to respond. So much has happened since this summer. I've found my stride, making me as proud of myself as Ollie said he is of me. I suppose if there are two types of people in the world – those who talk about doing, and those who do – I've been feeling pretty excellent about being a doer.

'Sometimes I feel a tiny bit different,' I admit, self-consciously. 'Don't kill me for bringing this up – you know, *again* – but that night here, the night before you left? Something clicked for me. I just had so much fun, and I realised that if I kept saying yes to everything that comes my way, maybe that was the point of it all. It's been cool. Meeting people, exploring the city.'

She sucks in her cheeks as if to stop herself smiling. 'Is that all I was then? An adventure?'

I laugh at that. 'Ruby,' I say. 'You're an epic poem of the seas.'

She laughs too. 'I don't even know what that means, but nice save.'

'Thank you.' I take a small bow from where I'm sat.

'Jackson says you're very lucky with the ladies of late,' she says. 'That must be nice. Dating and whatnot.'

I narrow my eyes. 'This feels like a trap, Ruby Powell.'

'It's not!' she insists, but maybe it is. I can't tell if she's getting the lay of the land so it's safe for her to keep being so inflammatory or she wants to write me off as being just another cad unworthy of her time.

'Well, let me tread carefully here anyway,' I say. 'Yes, I have been . . . well, not dating. Meeting people. Sometimes I even enjoy it.'

'Good for you,' she replies. 'Getting out there. That's what you came here for, isn't it?'

I carry on, noting the mild envy or jealousy, the edge to

176

her words: 'I met this gorgeous woman not long after I'd moved here, you see. Smart, charming, funny, hot . . . good chat. Set the bar high. Gotta kiss a few frogs to find my princess after that, you see.'

She makes a vomiting noise. 'You're such a bad flirt.'

'That's not what you said before.' My voice is soft. I'm testing the waters. This back-and-forth could go either way, but that's what is making it feel so worth the risk. Why else did she ask me to come out here? Why else is her leg pressed up to mine that way? Her chest pushed forward, her back arched seductively, like a cat? I almost kissed her when she stood at the door, earlier. The way her sweatpants hung low on her hips, the wild untamedness of her hair framing that picture-perfect face that she's got no idea is so damned *cute* . . . I knew it would have been stupid, but I wanted to. You can't fight chemistry. In fact, it should be law that all chemistry should be acted upon, just to make sure there are no missed chances, no almosts.

'No,' she concedes. 'I suppose I didn't. I liked that that was my last night, you know. It helped. Everything you said, when we were . . . you know. After.'

'After we fucked?' I say.

'Nic!' She rolls her eyes in a fake scolding.

'What?' I reply, as if I'm the most innocent person in the world.

She shakes her head. 'You're impossible.' She laughs. 'You know exactly what I mean. That night was helpful and kind and lovely and also you have a very nice penis. I'm not telling you anything you don't already know, I'm sure.'

'I don't mind hearing I've got a nice penis as many times as you care to tell me that,' I chortle. 'By all means, keep the compliments coming.'

177

She looks at me properly, now. 'Seriously,' she says. 'This confidence! That night, you seemed . . . I don't know. A bit intimidated by me?'

'I'm sure that was all part of the turn-on.' I grin.

'Nothing wrong with a little thrill of the chase,' she says lightly. 'Is there?'

'Zero complaints here,' I reply, holding up my palms in surrender. 'And for what it's worth . . .'

'Yes?' she says.

'You still scare the hell out of me.'

It makes her burst out laughing. 'Excellent,' she replies.

I grin back at her.

'So here we are again,' I say, seizing my chance. 'This house. You and me. Clock ticking close to midnight . . .'

My hand moves an inch so that my pinkie finger brushes gently against hers.

'A little bit of history repeating itself, perchance . . .' she replies, lowering her voice so that I have to dip my head to hear her.

'Imagine that,' I whisper.

'Hmm.'

We look at each other, and I lean in for the kiss I've been craving all night. The kiss I've been craving for weeks. Months.

I hold my face millimetres from hers, that last linger before closing the gap, a delicious pause of teasing. It makes her do her half-smile, nervousness and amusement personified, and then our lips touch.

She tastes like my beer. It's chaste, at first. A gentle tickle through mutual smiles, and instinctively I reach out a hand to her neck to pull her in closer. Now it's happening, I want her as close as possible. It makes me hard when she reaches out back to me, those red nails raking through my hair and sending shivers down my spine. We stay like that, holding each other, letting our tongues meet slowly, deliberately, and then it's more passionate, like the restraint we've shown all night can now be shed.

I move from beside to sit in front of her, where our bums should have gone in the first place. I push her knees apart and she looks at me as if to say, *not here?* But it's not what she thinks it is – I reach around to scoop her up so that she shifts off the table and into my lap, her dress pushing up around her thighs and legs wrapping around me.

She shifts her weight so that the warmness of her crotch pushes against the straining part of my trousers, and she grinds into me like we're teenagers dry-humping before curfew. If she keeps doing that, I'm going to come in my pants – like, seriously – so I move my hands to the tops of her bare thighs to press down, my thumb close to the fabric of her knickers, only just hidden by her clothes. I pull away from her lips and she looks at me, her chest rising and falling with deep, heavy breaths. I wait, staring at her, noting how her inhalations and exhalations become more shallow. I move my thumb the tiniest bit. She freezes. I stop. We stare. I move it the tiniest bit more, so that it rests between her legs, over the fabric that's now wet. I move it once, twice, three times, and she tips her head back, showing me her neck, and moans.

That's it. That's done me. I work my way under her knickers until I can feel her properly, and she throws her head forwards so that her forehead touches mine, and I work fast. She stays statue-still, and from a distance, in the shadows, I don't think anyone can tell what we're doing. We look just like the others did earlier, like we're kissing in a quiet corner, away from everyone else.

'Look at you,' I whisper, pausing, just for a second.

'Look at *you*,' she whispers back.

'I want you in bed,' I tell her. 'You're going to have to come home with me.'

She shakes her head, but only just. 'I want to,' she says. 'But Candice – it's her birthday . . .'

'Hmm,' I say. 'When do you go back?'

'Tomorrow.' And then, when I start to move my hand away she clamps her legs together and says, 'Don't you dare.' I smile, looking her dead in the eye as I resume the movements of my fingers. She makes another appreciative noise.

'This,' she says, softly. 'This is what I remember.'

I grin.

'Ruby?'

The voice comes from the double doors of the kitchen, loud and clear as a bell.

'Candice,' Ruby whispers.

'Ruby!'

I half expect Ruby to ignore it, considering where my hand is and the noises she has been making. But she doesn't. She whispers to me, 'Sorry,' and then calls Candice's name in return.

'On the picnic table,' she continues, and I take my hands out from under her, and because I don't know what else to do I sit on them as if to deny having ever touched her in the first place.

Candice wears a furious expression, muttering loaded nothings about how cold it is.

'Oh,' she says, when she sees that I'm there. 'I see. Sorry to intrude.'

She's slurring her words, and looks pretty out of it. I glance from Candice to Ruby, and immediately know that I need

180

to leave. As if to underline the point, Candice stares at me with eyes so hard I have no doubt she's staking her claim and silently letting me know to sling my hook.

'I'm just going to search out another beer,' I declare, disappearing – albeit disappointedly – into the bright lights of the kitchen. I look back before I dip inside, but I can't see them anymore, hiding in the shadows.

23

Ruby

'You having a good night?' I ask Candice jovially. 'Everyone seems on really good form.'

'Well,' she says. 'I'm a bit annoyed, to be honest.'

Surely she's not pissed that I've been outside with Nic for half an hour? When I slipped out, she was dirty dancing with his brother in the music room, his face pressed into her neck and her eyes closed. It was a calculated move – she was busy with a bloke, so I took my opportunity to be, too. I'd been inside with her for all the rest of the night. We danced, we lit a match to some sambuca, we took several wees together, gossiping as one of us sat on the loo and saving water by not flushing before the other had her turn too, like all best girlfriends do.

'How come?' I ask. The last of Nic's drink is still beside me on the table, so I finish it off.

'You just missed the cake cutting. Did you know that?'

I didn't, actually. I look again to where Nic just disappeared and, yeah, now I think about it I suppose everyone else has cleared off from the back door, where all the smokers had been. My attention had been a little divided, what with me sat on Nic's lap that way.

'Oh, pal,' I say. 'I'm sorry.' I'm ready to be as effusive in my apology as I need to be, but as I take a breath, it appears she has more to say.

'You've not been very present all night, to be honest. I've barely spoken to you since you got here. For a best friend you're kinda letting the side down. Jackson thinks so too, so it's not just me.'

Her words come thick and fast, like she's been saving them to fire off all at once. I don't get it, though. I *have* been with her tonight.

'It's your party!' I reply, stung. 'You've been a social butterfly! I was letting you get on with it! But for the record I've not been more than six feet from you since I got here, Candice. Come on.'

'Hmm,' she says, in response.

'Hmm what?'

'Well, never six feet from me physically, but mentally you're basically shacked up with Mr Sofa aren't you? Is that the only reason you came down – for him? You don't even reply to my messages anymore, but apparently you message him back and forth like your life depends on it.'

I'm taken aback. I know emotions get high whenever drinking is involved, and obviously it's late so we're all tired and we've been drinking, but she's gone a bit far. I wonder if this is about something else, but I just don't know what.

'I'm not being funny,' I say, and I know I sound defensive even as the words are coming out of my mouth, but that doesn't stop me. 'But I did say this would happen. Not the Nic thing, but the not getting proper time together thing. That's why I offered to come down last night or stay tomorrow night too. It's you who told me not to, because you had to save your time off for the hen party tomorrow. The hen party of a person I've never even heard you mention before I left, by the way.'

'So this is my fault now?'

'That's not what I said, is it?'

'You're unbelievable,' she says. 'Just take responsibility for being a bit of a crap friend,' she says. 'It's my birthday!'

'I'm here, aren't I?' I say.

'Barely.' She pouts. 'Like I said, it's obvious what your priorities are tonight. So much for your Year of Me or whatever you're calling it. Aren't you embarrassed you can't even last a few months?'

'Ouch,' I say. 'Okay, you're shooting from the hip now. I'm going to assume this is about more than just this, and give you the benefit of the doubt, but one more hurtful thing like that and I'll change my mind.'

I can tell she still wants to be mad at me. I just can't unpick why. This isn't about Nic. This isn't the whole story. Is it just the booze? She's swaying as she talks, but I can't fault that what she's saying seems to have been on her mind for a while. Maybe the booze means she finally feels able to tell me.

'Fine,' she says, in a tone that suggests it's anything but fine. 'Can you just come and dance and, like, not be huddled off in a corner with a man? It's my birthday, and I want your attention.'

'Yes,' I say, feeling instantly guilty if I've broken the girl code of birthdays. 'Of course. That is exactly what I want to do,' I say, but after being yelled at, I'm not really in the party mood anymore. I paste on a smile and head inside anyway. She's right. It *is* her birthday.

We pass Jackson and Nic in the kitchen as she pulls me past them and through the living room to dance. I close my eyes and give in to the dirty rhythms of some old R 'n' B records, swaying back and forth and then when it switches to some ABBA spinning and moving in circles with my arms out wide around me. At one point I think I see Nic loiter by the doorway, but when I look back around he's gone. I don't know what to do – if I go and find him, Candice will get upset, and I don't even know where my phone is to text him. Last time, Candice practically pushed me into bed with him and now she's all but forbidden it.

We dance some more until I realise there's only a handful of people left. I wonder if he's gone. All these weeks of build-up to seeing him, all this existential angst around what it would mean if I had a good time with him, and I've been cock-blocked by a friend who wants my attention and my conscience that knows she's right. I am here for her. But it still crushes my soul a little that I haven't even been able to say goodnight. Who knows if a chance to see him will come up again?

24

Nic

'Well, well, well. Fancy seeing you here.'

I know her voice before I see her face. In fact, I think my body feels her presence before my ears hear her words. Hairs prickle on the back of my neck. I'm smiling before I even turn around.

'Ruby!' I exclaim, as I take her in. I can't believe she's here in Euston station too. It makes no sense. 'What's a nice girl like you doing in a dark, miserable train station like this?'

Her hair is piled on her head and she's got smudges of black make-up under her eyes. She looks tired, despite her megawatt smile. I probably look even worse though. I barely slept. I stared at the bedroom ceiling after I got home, trying to figure out how to make this work, what my next move could be. She's there, I'm here – long-distance is one thing, but we actually don't even know each other. You have to have a relationship to go long-distance with, right? But how do we build a relationship from afar? The pieces are all there, they just don't add up – and it's baffling me.

'I've got to get back to Manchester,' she says, indicating to the trains with her thumb as if to say, *That's me*. 'I think I said last night – I've got a morning train?'

'Oh yeah,' I reply. 'I mean. I know Jackson and Candice miss you so much. I thought you'd maybe be down here a few days. But you did say, you're right. Candice had to get off for a hen party, didn't she? I was distracted . . .'

She smirks, but she's blushing. 'Yes,' she says. 'Sorry about the interruption last night.'

'Not as sorry as I am,' I say back. 'I was going to text you later. Was everything okay with Candice in the end? She seemed . . .'

'Upset? She was,' Ruby concedes. I swear she might have tears in her eyes, but the strip lighting of the train station is so bad it makes things deceptive. It might be tears in *my* eyes from the lack of sleep. If I have time, I might even get some eyedrops and some sort of sleep-ease pill to help me drop off on the journey. I can't let anyone see me like this – anyone else, I mean. I need to get sorted before I get to Mum and Steve's for their anniversary party.

'Well,' I say, steering the conversation away from Jackson and Candice, just in case. 'Soon be Christmas. Maybe you can all meet up then?'

She nods solemnly. 'Yeah.'

'Will you be back then?' I ask, hopefully. If she is, I'm taking her out, no questions asked.

'No, actually.' She shrugs. She's not herself; something is off. 'I'll be at my mum and stepdad's, up in Whaley Bridge.'

Dammit.

There's a beat where neither of us seems to know what to say after that. She's clearly side-tracked, and it makes my stomach drop. I should probably wish her a good day and get to Boots, if she wants to be alone. I get the feeling she does. It's just, less than twelve hours ago her tongue was in my mouth and my hand was pulling at her knickers. There's a bit of a yin-and-yang going on here. A bit of oh-this-is-awkward-in-the-cold-light-of-day.

'Why are you here, anyway?' she says, coming back to herself. I'm relieved she's making the effort to keep me talking. We're both hungover, but I don't care. This is a bonus bump-into. I don't want to waste it.

'Family party,' I say. 'Mum and Dad – my stepdad, really, but he's always been Dad to us – are celebrating twenty-five years together. Ollie should be around here somewhere, but knowing him he's in a ditch somewhere. Hey – did he hook up with Candice?'

'If he did, he doesn't take up much room in bed. I slept top-to-toe with her last night.'

'Oh,' I say. 'That's good, then. Be weird if there was some sort of foursome happening. You and me, him and Candice.' She screws up her face in a way I cannot decode so I change the subject. 'Hey – I've got a rail replacement route because of works on the line. You're not on the 10.03 by any chance, are you?'

'Actually,' she says, glancing up at the departure board. 'Yeah. I am! Oh, that's so strange. What are the odds?'

'That should be the tagline of our whole relationship,' I quip, immediately regretting saying *our relationship*. I know we don't have one of those. I just mean, her and me. Me and her. We're not an *us*, but after last night we're undoubtedly a something, even if that something is just a couple of horny bastards who snog whenever they happen to be in the same place as each other.

'Calm down.' She giggles. 'Last night was . . . nice.'

'A gentleman never kisses and gloats,' I say, grinning. How do we get so *into it* every time? It makes me chuckle to think of how daunted I was by her that first day. All of that has gone, now. As soon as we chat again, all my doubts evaporate. She's so *awesome*.

Ruby pulls a face and I laugh.

'Are you boarding now?'

'I was just going to grab some snacks, first,' I say. I look at my watch. 'Except . . . Oh, I probably don't have time. Dammit. I'm starving.'

She opens the paper M&S bag she's carrying.

'Lucky for you,' she says, 'I have more than enough to share. Check this out.'

Her bag is loaded with sandwiches, sweets, drinks, and . . .

'Are those eyedrops?' I say, almost excruciatingly enthusiastic.

She raises her eyebrows. 'Yeah . . .'

'Ohmygosh I could kiss you,' I say. 'My eyes feel like sandpaper!'

She takes a step back from me and pulls a face again. 'Please don't kiss me,' she says. 'I'm not even sure I've brushed my teeth. I'm mortified you're seeing me like this, truth be told.'

I laugh again, and it's everything I've got in me not to sling my arm over her shoulder and call her *mine* as we head to find our carriage.

'You're beautiful to me,' I say, and she makes a gagging sound even though she's smiling.

* * *

She's got the snacks, the eyedrops, some headache pills *and* the Sunday papers – although, as we settle them out on the table between us, I can't help but hope we don't read in silence and get to talk instead. But then her phone rings and after texting Ollie to check he is, indeed, alive, I pick one up as she takes the call from her mum, so I don't simply sit and stare at her – as much as I want to. (That face! I just want to look at that face!)

'That movie is really good,' she says, hanging up and seeing that I'm reading the culture section. 'It's a hard recommend from me.'

'This critic says it misses the mark, and far more experienced screenwriters have addressed the same issues with more nuance and aplomb.'

'What!' she exclaims. 'Can I see?'

I hand over the paper and feel vindicated that whilst I couldn't openly stare before, it feels appropriate to now. Her face crumples and expands as she reads the review, and by the end she's shaking her head and says, 'What an idiot. He's only been so harsh because she's a woman, and because it's already been nominated for an Academy Award. Why do middle-aged blokes have to hold young women starting out to a higher standard than they do their own peers? It drives me absolutely potty!'

'Fear and worry,' I say. 'Nobody likes to think they might be irrelevant. Especially not the demographic of society that has been told the world revolves around them their whole lives.'

Ruby blinks slowly and looks at me like I'm a dog that just started explaining the theory of relativity.

'Well, that's astute,' she says.

'I'd be less offended if you said that without sounding so surprised,' I shoot back.

'Fair comment, calmly administered.' She nods, holding her hands up in surrender. 'My apologies.'

'Ha!' I say. '"My apologies"? That's *so* not an apology.'

She narrows her eyes, and finally the train starts to pull out of the station. 'I think you'll find it is,' she says. 'It literally has the word *apology* in it.'

'People only say *my apologies* when they don't really mean it. Normal people who are actually sorry say *I'm sorry.*'

She rolls her eyes. 'I'm *sorry* then!' she intones, but she's taking it in good humour. 'Jeez.'

The light is more orange than it is yellow, shy in the sky and hiding through trees shedding the last of their amber and nectar-coloured leaves. It peeks through the gaps in between the buildings that start out high-rise and packed together, and slowly become more spaced out and eventually turn from flats to terraced houses and then sprawling plots of land.

'I hate Euston station,' I say, watching the world go by. 'But I really love this stretch of railroad coming out of it. I love how you can see right into people's gardens, and sometimes even right into their houses.'

She follows my eyes to where I'm looking and nods.

'Yeah,' she agrees. 'I see what you mean. All those different lives playing out that otherwise we'd have no idea about.'

'It sends my head into a spin,' I say. 'How can every single person on this earth have the starring role in their own life? How is it possible that every single person has – I don't know – a breakfast routine and a birthday and plans for the weekend and unfulfilled aspirations?'

'Hmm,' she says, considering it. 'Do you have those things?'

I look at her. 'Well, yeah . . . That's my point.'

'What are they?'

'Erm,' I say, trying to remember what it is I've just listed. 'Breakfast is a spinach and celery smoothie—' She scrunches up her nose when I say that. 'My birthday is in October, so I just turned thirty-one and celebrated at dodgeball, and my plans for the weekend are undecided because it's still *this* weekend. Oh, and . . . unfulfilled aspirations? I don't think so. Not anymore.'

'Because of the move?' she asks. She's pulled out some lip balm from her bag and uses her pinkie finger to run some over her mouth, making her lips look plump and moist from across the table.

'Did I not rub that all in?' she asks, self-consciously putting a hand to her face again and looking at her reflection in the glass of the window when she spots me looking.

'No, you did,' I say. 'Sorry. I didn't mean to . . . you know . . . look. At your mouth.'

She smiles with half her face in the way that I'm learning drives me up the wall with how seductive it is.

'You were saying?' she prompts, and I think about moving to her side of the table in our little configuration of four. I weigh it up: if I sat beside her I wouldn't be able to look at her, but I *would* be able to touch her . . . In the end, I can't find my nerve and stay where I am.

'I'm not telling you anything you don't already know,' I say, focusing on her question. 'Leaving Liverpool was the best thing that ever happened to me, mostly because it didn't happen *to* me; I made it happen. If I hadn't taken that leap then, yeah, I'd have unfulfilled aspirations.'

'And what do you want your future to look like?'

'We're tackling the small stuff on these mutual hangovers and sleepless nights, are we?'

'I'm curious!' she says. 'I like learning about you.'

192

Fuck. I wish I could record her saying that. *I like learning about you.*

'I want my future to look like everyone wants their future to look like! Happy marriage, kids, nice house. Although, you know, that's the long, long game. In ten years. Fifteen. For now, I've got everything I need, you know? I'm enjoying *living*. It's harder than they make it sound but it's worth it, to me. I'm happy.'

'It shows,' she says. 'It's very attractive.'

And there we are again, flirting like our lives depend on it.

'And what do you dream for yourself?' I ask her.

She mulls it over. 'Not too much planning,' she settles on. 'All of this – on the course, I mean – is opening up thoughts and ideas and doors I didn't even know were there. So I think I have to stay open, which I've not been very good at doing before.'

'The world is your oyster.'

'A flippant term for a very real fact,' she bats back.

'I admire your vision,' I tell her. 'I think we have the same ambition.'

'Yeah,' she says, chewing on her lip once more. 'I think I'd have to agree with that. We do.'

'A nice thing to know,' I say, teasingly.

She mockingly rolls her eyes. 'What am I supposed to say to that?' She giggles.

'You don't have to say anything,' I tell her. 'Making you laugh is enough for me.'

'You're terrible,' she says.

'Luckily you're no better,' I tell her, and she lobs a Percy Pig at me.

25

Ruby

I get to learn a lot about him in these two hours. There's nowhere to be, and as the scenery changes it's rife for idle chit-chat.

'Do you still do the live action role-play?' I say, trying to steer us onto less flirtatious ground. I remember his LARPing from the photo we'd seen of him before we met. 'You used to do it loads in Liverpool, didn't you?'

He considers the question. 'You know . . .' he said. 'This is the longest I've gone without LARPing since I was a teenager. I love it, but I suppose I've just been doing other things.'

'Playing tourist?'

'Is that a guess, or a cyber-stalk again?'

'No comment.'

'I've looked at your page sometimes too. And I follow the Find JP's Girl account.'

My heart soared when he first followed the account. I'm touched that he'd take an interest.

'I'd imagine film-making taps into the same feeling I get from LARPing, now that I think about it.'

'How so?'

'You know, getting to try on another character for size, using a story to learn about yourself . . .'

'I'd never even heard of it before. It does seem pretty cool. There's something about finding an interest or a passion and really going for it, isn't there? The difference between, I don't know, going to a football match once in a while and plastering your bedroom in team colours, researching the formations, following the transfers or whatever.'

'Listen to you, it's like tuning in to *Match of the Day*!'

'Shut up,' I say. 'We can't all be Alan Shearer.'

'To be fair,' he replies, 'I played a bit of footie before I moved, but it wasn't exactly a passion. It was just what everyone else did and it kept me busy. I'd prefer to lift weights or listen to a podcast on a treadmill to keep fit.'

'Which you obviously do.' I grin.

'I try to keep in shape, yes,' he says, flexing an arm like Johnny Bravo.

It killed me, having to walk away from him last night. He keeps looking at me now, and he thinks he's being stealthy and that I haven't noticed, but I have. I mean, I look *awful*. I feel like I've not slept in a decade and I'm really mad at myself for not taking off my make-up last night, and for not washing my face this morning. Candice was gone when I woke up, and so I hit snooze more times than I should have, leaping out of bed at the last moment. I didn't expect to run into anyone, but of course the laws of the universe dictate that whenever you look like you've been dug up from a grave you *have* to bump into everyone you know. I don't normally have trouble getting up, but I felt heavy and sluggish today. I guess I'm a bit sad, really. Candice and I have fallen out before – we've had silly disagreements and big screaming fights, but they didn't feel like this. The energy to this one is different. It's more . . . sinister.

When I was waiting for the tube, she messaged me: a great big wall of text that was so long it came through as an attachment. It said all this stuff about how she was upset with me for disappearing on her outside with Nic. She said how it was great that I was pursuing my master's, but that I'd left them all behind and I wasn't allowed to be cross that she was making new friends or that she'd saved her time off for them instead of me. There wasn't any warmth to it all, and I felt sick the whole way to the train station, reading it and rereading it. It's left me feeling really delicate, and when I saw Nic across the departure hall at Euston I almost didn't say hello. I thought the second I had to speak I might cry, and I knew he'd be able to tell because he's good like that. He's a good man. His kindness is humbling.

After the booze, and the flirting, and the kissing outside, and now this big fight with Candice, I'm worried even human touch would disintegrate me, somehow. Like I could blow away. Of course, Nic gets it out of me in the end, less than half an hour into the journey, and maybe I knew all along he would. But the thing is, he makes it feel safe to tell him. How is it possible that he's had this big glow-up, and kisses me like he means it, *and* listens as well as he talks?

'It sounds like she really misses you,' Nic comments from across the table we've snagged. Neither of us have first-class tickets, but there's no conductor on the train that we can see, and it's so empty that it doesn't feel like we're doing anybody any harm by finding a cosy spot where we can spread out and chat.

'I miss her too,' I say, green fields lit by winter sun whooshing past, my hands occupied by pulling apart some strawberry laces. I'm not even embarrassed by how much crap I got at the shop: strawberry laces and egg sandwiches and ham sandwiches and Percy Pigs and mini Colins and water and cloudy lemonade and little sausage rolls and apples. 'But the thing is, she's mad I left. She feels abandoned, and ... well, I did abandon her, didn't I? For three years we've been inseparable and then the way she sees it is that I split because of a man.'

'A man?'

'Abe.' I hate saying his name.

'Ah,' Nic says. 'I see. But wasn't he just the catalyst? You've wanted to get your master's for ages, haven't you?'

'Yeah. I mean ... I suppose I could have applied for London City, or even Brighton.'

He holds out a hand for a strawberry lace. 'Why Manchester then?'

'It's the best course, but even if it wasn't I was drawn to being closer to family,' I say. 'It's where I'm from, you know? Just knowing my family are up the road, even if I don't see them – it's a comfort.' The penny drops, then. I see Candice's point. 'I think she thinks I sort of ... used her. She was my family when I was in London, and now I've gone back near to my actual family, which sucks for her because she doesn't have one of those. They're all estranged.'

'Big weight for you to carry,' he notes.

'Yeah,' I agree, soothing myself with a mini Colin and a lemonade chaser.

'Want to go halves on the egg sarnie?' he asks. We eat in

companionable silence and consuming something proper that isn't just sugar helps me to feel more grounded. More centred. We share the ham sandwich, too, and by the time I've had a bottle of water and an apple, we're half an hour from Manchester and the world is no longer ending. I can fix this thing with Candice. Friends are allowed to get upset with one another and allowed to be mad. I really did give her a lot of attention last night, and I understand why giving Nic some attention would bother her, but we'll have to agree to disagree on that. Surely in a few days we'll be able to talk rationally.

'It's okay if you feel happy *and* sad,' Nic says. 'I don't mean to play amateur shrink, but . . . feeling conflicted, it's normal. I seem over the moon about my new life in London, but like I told you it was awful deciding to do that. And I don't go back enough for visits – but I didn't leave so that I could spend all my weekends on a train back up, visiting.' He looks around the carriage. 'All evidence to the contrary excluded.' He smiles.

'Have you taken the week off work?' I ask. 'When are you going back down?' It's crossed my mind that if he's just down the M62, maybe there'd be the chance to spend some time together. I know both that there's a connection between us, but also that our circumstances make it hard to explore. But if Lady Luck was on our side and he was around for a few days, I *did* decide to make my 'rules' malleable ones.

'Tomorrow morning,' he says. 'Here today and back tomorrow. I don't feel like I've been in the job long enough to ask for time off, you know?'

My heart sinks. 'I'm with ya,' I say.

'I'm "working from home" tomorrow morning, if they ask.' He says 'working from home' with air quotes. He opens his mouth as if to elaborate, closes it again, and takes a second to decide what to say next.

The scenery gets more urban, and before long we're pulling into Manchester station and our time together is up.

'What have you got to do now?' I ask.

'Wait,' he replies plainly. 'My connection to Liverpool isn't for a while. And to be honest, I'm in no rush. My family will go on into the wee hours, even if they start celebrating at lunch. I'm not saying they're all functioning alcoholics, but if you saw them you'd definitely be wondering where, exactly, all ten pints are going.'

I don't know if I'm imposing if I ask him to hang out. He knew all the right things to say about Candice, and I've got nothing waiting for me at home. The only reason I got the 10 a.m. was because it was the cheapest ticket. It occurs to me that it wouldn't be very appealing, admitting to having an empty diary. People like people who are in demand and desired and wanted, don't they? Of course, I don't need this man to think I am any of those things, because I'm not doing that this year, anyway, and . . . and . . . and whatever. If he was a girl, I wouldn't be overthinking everything this way. Look at me and Candice: we met in the smoking area at an event and ended up living together. It shouldn't be any different with Nic, just because he's a guy. I can still be enthusiastic about wanting to spend time with him, can't I? I'm getting in my own way, otherwise.

'I don't suppose you want to grab a coffee before you have to go?' he says then, reading my mind as we gather our things and stuff the rubbish in the bin. He adds, with an impish grin, 'I'm buying?'

I try not to sound too desperate as I reply, 'Oh yes, that would be lovely.'

He moves back from his chair to let a woman with two young children get past, to the doors.

'Here,' he says to her. 'Let me grab the buggy.'

She looks at him gratefully as she's able, then, to pick up the kid who is crying and hold the hand of the one who isn't, finding room now to have kind words for them.

'I'll get your bag,' I say to his back, and I can't help but glance at his arse as I do.

I allow myself exactly five seconds to take it in, and then pull my eyes away and follow him off the train.

The sun is low but eager, the streets by the station surprisingly busy with people coming and going laden down with shopping and fast-food bags.

'I honestly think a Big Mac would be my death-row meal you know,' Nic declares, as the salty scent of nutrition-free meat fills our collective nostrils. 'In fact . . .' he begins, and I think I know where he's going with this.

'Filet-o-Fish with large fries and vanilla milkshake,' I agree. '*My* death-row meal.'

'McDonald's it is, then.' He nods.

We join the queue in the McDonald's on the corner, and when he offers to pay, I gladly accept. He's the one with the job, after all. I'm a mere student. We find a bench in the tentative sunny warmth and chew and slurp and people-watch. After all my train snacks it's a wonder I've got the room for it.

'Ice cream van driver by day, dog breeder of champions by night,' Nic says, nodding his head in the direction of a chap walking by with an ice cream sundae on his T-shirt, a raft of fluffy Finnish Lapphunds trotting like tiny geishas just ahead of him.

'Too easy, that one.' I giggle, looking around to see how I can trump him. I spot an ageing woman with smeared lipstick and a beehive lighting one cigarette off of another, and whisper, 'The developer of the UK's first non-flammable hair setting agent,' and he laughs, gleefully.

'Perfection,' he says, looking right at me as I shovel the last handful of fries into my mouth like an anaconda swallowing a bison.

'The jaw dislocation is especially sexy,' he notes, chowing down on his own chips. 'Ten out of ten for that one.'

I deliberately answer him with my mouth full. 'I don't exist to be sexy for men,' I say, food spraying everywhere.

'And yet,' he remarks, and there's a moment as I swallow my food and self-consciously wipe the salt from my lips with the back of my hand that we could kiss. My tummy drops as we look at each other and he swallows and then I lose my nerve and it's too bright, too *daytime* to launch at him – especially when I'm hungover and haven't even brushed my teeth.

But I want to.

'Look,' he states, and at first I think he's giving me an instruction to look across the square, but then he keeps talking and I realise it was a stamp on my attention. 'This ...'

'This,' I repeat, understanding we're going to have A Talk.

'Well, it's nice, isn't it?'

'A Smaccy's on a hangover is a God-tier cure, yes,' I say, being deliberately obtuse.

He shakes his head. 'If you had to list your top-three hobbies, why do I feel like torturing Nic Sheridan would be right there at the top?' he says.

'Because Nic Sheridan sometimes refers to himself in the third person,' I say. 'Nic Sheridan deserves it.'

I'm doing it again – getting silly and sarcastic so I don't have to be genuine and sincere. I can't help it. I couldn't stop it, even if I wanted to. But this feels like dangerous ground.

'I'm going to take you out,' he says. 'You know that, don't you?'

'I'm not dating, remember.'

'The Year of Me,' he laments.

'Yup,' I say. 'No men for a year. Just me, myself, and I, in a relationship with film-making.'

'That seems like an awful shame.'

I could almost waver. Last night, today . . . what if I did go out on a date with him? I have JP and Harry's faces floating through my brain. I know they think I'm being silly with my Year of Me, but I feel so happy, so fulfilled. A date with Nic would be a huge risk to all that.

There's a vibration in my pocket.

'Saved by the phone,' he says, as I pull it out of my pocket. It's Harry, and I scan his words.

'Holy shit!' I cry. 'They think they've found JP's girl! They've done it!'

'Oh wow, that's amazing! At least somebody gets the girl,' Nic quips, issuing a fake pout.

'Look. I owe you all the information, right?'

'You don't really owe me anything,' Nic says, shrugging. 'But I'll still take it.'

'I thought this was just sex,' I say. 'But a date would be . . . not that.'

'No,' he agrees. 'It wouldn't.'

'Exactly . . .' I say.

He looks at me, big brown eyes like a puppy's, all wide and wet and captivatingly cute.

'Ruby, I don't just want to sleep with you. I want to take

you out, on a date, properly, because I know we're great in bed together, but I think it's obvious we'd be great outside of bed together too.'

I take a breath. 'Ten out of ten for honesty,' I say. 'I wasn't expecting that.'

'Well, then you're an idiot.'

'I love it when you talk nasty to me.'

'Plenty more where that came from.'

He waits for my answer. I don't know what I want to say. I'd thought about flirting with him, and snogging him, and maybe even sleeping with him again. But not about *dating* him. But then I think about Candice refusing to make herself vulnerable to the postman and how ridiculous it seems to me, and everything JP has said to me about staying open in matters of the heart.

'Can I think about it?' I ask. 'You know my story, you know my deal. If I say yes, I want to mean it. I'm not going to mess you around.'

'Take as long as you need,' he decides, waving a hand. 'Because then I've got even longer to plan something worthy of you.'

His words rattle around in my head for a full twenty-four hours until finally I have to talk to someone about it.

'Houston,' I say to JP and Harry, 'we have a problem: I fancy the pants off of Nic. We kissed – well, a bit more than kissed to be fair – and now he wants to take me out and I'm scared.'

We're setting up in the studio for a formal interview with JP so that we can get his take on everything that's happened so far. We need to ask him about how it feels to have located Amelie now, and what his hopes are for moving forward.

Does he want to Skype her, visit her, or is he happy just knowing she's out there? He might not want to do anything, or choose to keep it simple with a letter. For true authenticity we haven't asked him any of this off-camera, so that we get unrehearsed footage.

Harry and I move lights and figure out angles as JP 'supervises'. I send William a quick message letting him know his Gramps is okay.

All Harry had idly asked as we moved tables and chairs and lighting was how my weekend had been, but because I didn't know who else to tell – Candice isn't speaking to me, Jackson is Nic's friend now too – I was almost bursting to reveal the gossip about myself. Not talking about Nic is agony. I've thought about nothing but him for days now, and I can't lie to myself any longer: I have a crush. A big old crush, and I need to talk about it.

JP hoots, 'At last! She sees the light!'

I roll my eyes. 'Don't gloat,' I warn him, wagging a finger. 'It doesn't suit you.'

'My wife used to say the same thing,' JP replies.

'Shelley was a wise woman to keep you in check.' I smile. He clucks appreciatively at my reply. Finding excuses to mention the person you were married to for seventy years is as much of a thrill as mentioning a new crush. He gets me. I get him. I issue him a wink.

Harry and I set up the boom mic and decide a wide shot from one end of the meeting room to the other works best, with the glass wall behind our subject and the rest of the co-working space in the background.

William texts back a request to make sure JP is hydrated, has had a snack, and taken his heart medication.

'Oi, JP, where are your pills?' I ask. He motions to his bag, and I retrieve them. Harry gives our set-up one last look-over through the viewfinder of the camera and decides he is satisfied.

'Okay,' says Harry. 'You sorted, JP? Ready?'

'As I'll ever be,' JP confirms, and I help him get up from the corner and into the armchair we need him in.

We decide the lighting and the angle and the sound are all good, and I settle in to talk to JP. He is on camera, and I am just off, so that he is looking to the right of the lens. We don't know yet if we'll keep in my questions or edit them out so that it simply seems like JP is recalling everything of his own accord. I have to be careful to leave gaps between JP answering a question and then asking my next one, to make editing easier later on.

'JP,' I start, once I know we're rolling. 'You asked us to help you find Amelie, a woman you knew seventy-eight years ago and haven't seen in person since then. We've done that. Can you tell us a bit about how that makes you feel?'

JP nods, a sign that he understands what I'm asking.

'I knew we'd find her,' JP says, and he looks right at me as he says it, unflinching. 'When you emailed us, it was like a sign from the heavens. Two young film-makers have questions about me and my life? You couldn't make it up, could you? And then when you came to the house, I could tell you'd do it. I'm an old man, and William – my grandson . . .' His gaze moves an inch directly to the camera then, like he's making sure the invisible audience is up to speed on who is who. It's quite endearing. Charming. 'He's my best mate in a lot of ways, but he didn't know where to start. He's book-smart, not street-smart. But he knew to invite you over, so I give him credit where credit is due.'

I smile.

'It was clever of you to have him call the local librarian, and the weekend we spent calling every Amelie Chalamet in the phone book was the most exciting of my life – and I've had five kids and fought in a war.' He lets himself have a little chuckle, there. 'Her housekeeper answered. William was on speaker so we could all hear, but obviously I couldn't understand a word. You'd think I'd have spent all this time learning French, but me and Amelie, we never needed words before. Why start now?'

'And what did the housekeeper say?'

'The housekeeper said Amelie isn't well. Lung cancer.'

We let that hang in the air.

'She never even smoked, so riddle me that,' he adds.

'I'm so sorry,' I offer. 'Do you know the prognosis?'

'She doesn't have long left, they say.'

'Does she know you called?'

'I believe so.'

'And what did she say?'

'She said we'd better get there quick.'

I freeze. 'And . . .' I venture, and I honestly don't know how he is going to answer. 'What do you think to that?'

'I think we'd better get on the Eurostar.' He grins, and his eyes sparkle with hopeful tears. 'I want to go and see her,' he adds. 'Finally.'

Nobody speaks after that. Eventually Harry says, softly, 'And cut,' marking the end of the interview. I look at him. His mouth is set in a firm line, but his eyes are crinkled, happy.

'Did you know this?' I ask him. 'Did you know JP wants to go to Paris?'

'I did,' he admits.

'So we're going?'

I look at JP, who nods. 'William is finding my passport and booking the tickets as we speak. Harry said to just go ahead and get sorted.'

And so get sorted we do.

On the way home, my head spinning with the news of an impending – and university sanctioned, Harry assures me – trip to Paris, I'm thinking about Nic, and a date, and how lovely love is, when my phone rings. It's a withheld number, which I usually make a point of not answering, but it could be anything to do with Paris or JP or the trip, and so I press accept.

'Hello?'

'Ruby,' his voice says, and I'd know it anywhere. 'It's me.'

It's typical of him not to announce himself. My throat constricts and when I speak it comes out harsh and hard.

'I don't want to talk to you, Abe. Which I think you know, otherwise you wouldn't have withheld your number.'

'Don't hang up,' he pleads. 'Please don't hang up. Just listen, please?'

In spite of myself I stop walking and hesitate. I don't speak – but I don't end the call, either.

'We made a baby together, Ruby. And then you left, and cut me off, and it's not fair. I love you. The baby didn't make it, but us . . . we should be together. We're both messy and fucked up and crazy and I know you love me too, in your own way. It's you and me, Rubes. You know it is. Talk to me. Come on.'

'Are you kidding?' I find myself saying, somewhere just past Mick's coffee cart on campus. It's almost dark already, even though it's only mid-afternoon. 'Are you actually kidding?'

'No . . .' he replies, uncertainly.

'Abe, you were fucking awful to me. You picked me up and put me down and gave me scraps of your attention and affection. Not to mention chlamydia, by the way.'

'If you'd answered any of my texts, I was going to tell you about that,' he says.

'Classy,' I snap. 'Making it my fault I didn't know. Really classy.'

'Don't be mad, darling,' he says. 'Please. I've left Carly. It's over. I told her I want to be with you.'

'I don't want to be with you, Abe. Sometimes I can't believe we were ever even together. Do you know that?'

'We made a baby!' he cries down the line. 'How can you walk away from somebody you made a baby with?'

'A baby we lost,' I shout, and a girl fiddling on her phone looks up as she passes, forcing my voice into a low hiss. 'And where were you when I found the blood in my pants in the toilets at work? Where were you when I texted and said I needed you? Where were you when I had to visit the doctor, and then go home to just *let it happen*, with nobody in the world to hold my hand? Where were you then, Abe?'

'I'm here now,' he says. 'I'm sorry.'

'No,' I spit. This is everything I ever thought I might want to say to him, before I decided he wasn't worth the oxygen. Well, since he's tricked me into talking to him he can have my speech. I don't care. 'You don't get to be sorry. You don't get to be absolved from guilt. I *do not* forgive you. Listen to me very, very carefully,' I seethe. 'Because we are never going to speak again after this. Okay? Do not text. Do not email. Do not slide into my DMs, and certainly do not call me. Forget you know me. I've already forgotten that I know you.'

And with that I hang up.

It's only then that I realise that I'm crying. Tears are

streaming down my face silently and a bloke passing by reaches out a hand to my arm and says, 'Hey, are you okay love?'

'Yeah,' I say, wiping my face. 'Yeah, I really am. Thanks though,' I tell him. He frowns but says okay and carries on walking. I pull my scarf closer around my neck, shake my head clear, and keep on with the walk home, my eyes fixed on the pavement.

Being abandoned by Abe as I miscarried was the loneliest and the lowest I have ever felt. But thank God, I think, that I did not have his baby. That I have not been tied to him indefinitely, that our lives have not been inextricably linked forever. I knew for a week before it happened that I was pregnant, and I hadn't even told him. I didn't know what to do, what to think, what to feel. And then I went for a wee and the blood was already there and it was all over before I'd decided what to do and *I felt relieved*. I knew, as I lay in bed for a whole weekend when Jackson was away and Candice was working two twelve-hour shifts, that not only was I thankful not to have Abe's baby, I was thankful not to have a baby at all. I don't want kids. I don't want to feel bad about not having kids. I want my freedom and intend to use it now I've come so close to losing it.

And then it hits me.

With Abe, I didn't know how to stand on my own two feet. But with Nic, it's different.

You can trust him, I think to myself as I arrive at my front door. *You can trust Nic. He's not Abe.*

I consider it. I promised I wasn't going to mess him around. But . . . I'm okay, now. I'm the strongest and happiest I've ever been. I need to seriously consider the possibility that Nic in my life might actually be a positive, instead of worrying how it could become negative. He could be an asset. Letting somebody in could actually be *good*.

I will not be held hostage to who I used to be.

I am moving on.

I think I needed one last have-it-out with Abe to understand how different what's in front of me is. I don't *need* a man, but when a great one wants to take you out, it's stupid to turn him down because the last one was awful. I want to change my narrative; it doesn't have to be about how hard love is – or can be. Everything else about The Year of Me still stands, just with added romance.

I've thought about it, I text Nic when I get inside. *Let's go out.*

He texts back a gif of a little kid jumping up and down in excitement.

Or should I say, he texts, *excellent. Not to be too enthusiastic but how's this Friday?*

This Friday is perfect, I reply, *because I leave for Paris on Saturday. We've had a JP breakthrough!* and I'm not crying anymore. It's safe to be happy.

I let that sink in.

It's safe to be happy.

26

Nic

'Just don't fuck it up, that's all I'm saying,' Ollie insists with his typical diplomacy, the news of tomorrow's date with Ruby out there for all to comment on. He's barely out of breath as we hurtle from one end of the dodgeball pitch to the other, warming up. Since the party, where he met everyone, he's come three times to play. He seems to love it. I never anticipated it would be his thing – but then there *are* a lot of girls here. I perhaps overlooked that part.

'Have you ever considered a career in motivational speaking?' Jackson asks, as we touch the end line and switch directions again. I can't be sure, but I think he's mildly competing with Ollie, trying to stay a tiny bit in front, just to let him know who the boss is.

'All I mean is,' Ollie contends, ducking to touch the line right before Jackson does, leaping ahead. Over his shoulder his continues: 'You've played the long game, and so when

211

you finally get what you've wanted it can make you nervous. And nervous people drop the ball.'

We stop doing laps and start stretching out our hamstrings, quads and arms. I don't mean to look at Jackson as Ollie makes his point, but I do. He scowls. He's just done exactly what Ollie has said: the girl he was trying to seduce at work has told him, in no uncertain terms, that she's not into him. He's normally so upbeat, but he's been totally dejected these past two weeks. He claims it's a case of sore ego over sore heart, but either way he's been licking his wounds.

'I'm not going to drop the ball,' I grunt, touching my toes. 'You've both been very helpful in giving me pointers when I've needed them, and I'm grateful, but the student is ready to become the master. You're single,' I say, gesturing at Ollie as I stand up again. 'And sorry, Jackson, but you are too.' He clutches at his heart at the reminder. 'And I'm the one who met a woman *months* ago now, made an impression, gave her space, and now she's asked to go out properly. It's been a slow burn, and that's all right, you know? And . . .' I add, 'we've already slept together, so we know that works. We've already hung out at the party, and on the train, so we know it's more than physical. Lads, I'm telling you: I've got this covered. Focus on yourselves.'

Ollie pings his sweatband at me and Jackson mutters darkly, 'Pride comes before a fall,' but he's half-smiling, so I know he's a tiny bit impressed. I don't mean to be braggy or big-headed, I just don't see the need to pretend it could all go wrong. The obstacles have slowly been removed. What's wrong with assuming the best could happen, over fearing for the worst?

'Okay,' announces Zola, our co-captain with Jackson, who doesn't meet my eye now, after our coffee date that didn't

212

pan out. She said no hard feelings, but we haven't gone back to how we were, swapping flirty comments and teasing one another. She largely avoids me, now. 'Tonight is just us, no rival team, so we'll split up and play best of three games, team captains being Jackson for the reds and Ollie for the yellows.' She holds out the bibs for them to take, and each of them stand either side of her, facing the rest of us. 'I'll flip a coin for who picks first,' Zola continues. 'So, Jackson, heads or tails?'

'Heads,' Jackson shouts.

'Good,' quips Ollie. 'Because I'm good at chasing tail.'

Nobody laughs, but he doesn't need anyone to.

The coin comes down on tails and Ollie chooses Zola, leaving Jackson to choose me.

'You'd think blood would be thicker than water,' I say to Ollie as I walk to join the opposing team. He grins. 'You're a goner.'

We play hard and fast, our team winning first, Ollie's second. It's neck and neck for the third match too, and in the end we just miss out on the win – but it's close enough that Jackson doesn't even seem to mind. Ollie does a handstand into some sort of handspring over his side of the pitch, shouting and whooping and generally making an idiot of himself, sucking up all the attention in the room.

'Your brother is a dick,' Jackson says, but his features are soft and he's shaking his head lightly, like a mother who can't control her unruly son but loves him anyway. 'An absolute dick.'

'Yeah,' I agree. 'But he'll also probably get the first round in, so there's that.'

'Oi! Sheridan!' Jackson bellows across to him. 'You coming to the pub or what?'

Ollie peels off his bib, taking his T-shirt with it, and jogs over to us topless. He's ripped, and knows it. Jackson narrows his eyes in a way that shows he knows it now, too. ''Course I am,' he says, jogging on the spot. As he moves off towards the lockers he adds, gallantly, 'I'll even get first blood in. That's what you call it, isn't it, Jackson?'

'It is,' Jackson says, and we both watch Ollie dash off ahead.

'Dick,' Jackson reiterates once again. 'Dick, but also a charming bastard.'

'Frustrating, isn't it?' I reply, satisfied that he can see what I've been dealing with my whole life.

I don't stay long at the pub, choosing instead to leave Jackson and Ollie arguing over the series finale of 24, and everyone else drinking and laughing – even Zola, who managed her first smile at me across the bar when we were both ordering at the same time. I decide I want to walk through the city, meandering through Shoreditch down to Clerkenwell, finally ending up at Tottenham Court Road, the city changing from hipsterville to furniture design studios to the West End, theatres lit up with flashing lights and clothes shops still blasting pop music, even at 9 p.m. I don't even listen to music as I walk; I want to admire where I live.

My mind turns to tomorrow and the date with Ruby: I already know what we're going to do, and I'm excited. I wonder how things would be if I hadn't met her. Our night together gave me the balls to date other women down here, and every date made me more confident, more sure of what I want. Through Ruby I met Jackson, and the dodgeball team, and that's half my social life. Ollie hearing me talk about those dates, and the team, has given us new common ground. I've gone from sporadically seeing him a few times a year to

214

now, especially since he started playing too, to twice a week or more. Buying Ruby's sofa on my second day has had a knock-on effect on so many things, and now it feels neatly like we're coming full circle.

If I hadn't met her, would I be another lonely loser down here, a millennial man who only cares about his job and anything that orbits around it? Work barely scratches the surface of my life here. It's rich, and full, and more than I hoped it would be. I lived in or near Liverpool for my whole life, but it's only been lately that I've truly felt it: the feeling of being home.

I can hear the gurgles of chatter coming from the flat above when I get home. I think they must be having a dinner party, because there's the occasional scrape of chairs and the smell of cigarette smoke at the back window. I flick on the telly and take a long hot shower, washing the day away, and when I get out I open my wardrobe to pack for the weekend. I told Ruby I was up seeing family, but that's not strictly true – I just knew I couldn't wait. She's worth the special trip.

I have my bag with all the equipment we'll need, but I also lay out clean pants and socks, my baggy corduroys with the cuffed ankles, some coloured socks and a long-sleeved T-shirt to go under a heavy flannel shirt. I get a thin body warmer that I can wear under my coat if it's especially chilly, and my hat, scarf and gloves as well. I might not need them, but maybe Ruby will.

When I'm done, I sit on my second-hand sofa and scroll through some work emails, umming and ahhing over whether to text her. I decide that yes, as a grown man with very specific intentions I am allowed. *I've got our equipment ready,* I text her. *If you're in the market for a date-shaped hint.*

She sends back a single question mark. She's cool as a cucumber.

Just make sure you're wearing layers, I tell her then. *I don't want you to get cold.*

Right away she replies: *So we're going for a walk?*

Putting one foot in front of the other will help, yes, I reply.

You're being obnoxious, she says.

Terrible habit of mine, I reply.

I get the eye-roll emoji back.

Okay fine. I'm just looking for an excuse to keep you texting me, I type. *Call it a crush.*

I'll call it infatuation, I think, she retorts. *Sounds more grown up.*

Mild infatuation, I send her. *For my ego.*

That's settled then, she says. *Mild infatuation.*

And then: *You know I'm never going to live up to the Ruby you've got in your head, don't you?*

How horribly self-depreciating, I say.

I'm not as wonderful as you imagine, she replies.

Only because my imagination isn't that good.

Touché, she replies. *And yes, I'll be sure to dress warm.*

I can't wait, I type. *For the record.*

For the record, she messages back, *neither can I xxxx*

216

27

Ruby

Nic spends twenty-four hours sending hints about what he's got in store, but is refusing to fully divulge what we're doing. It's driving me mad. I'd like to be prepared, and look nice, and generally just treat this as the occasion that it is. I'm not anxious or anything, more just . . . it's important to me. It took me a second to get here, and now I am I want to revel in it. I'm proud of myself for taking a chance, taking a leap of romantic faith. JP has rubbed off on me. This deserves to have attention paid.

Also: I'm not going to shout this fact from the rooftops, but I've never actually been on a proper date. I found myself in the same place at the same time with lads at school, and at uni it was mostly about getting drunk and snogging somebody at the student union so frequently that eventually it was a given that you were 'together', for however long that lasted until it all started again. And then when I moved to London, there were some one-night stands, a few things with guys from work or whatever, and then Abe. Abe always just came over to my house, or occasionally he'd tell me he'd booked a mid-level hotel for a Sunday night, if we were seeing each other again after another break. I've seen it in films: getting dressed up, being picked up at the front door by a smiling paramour bearing flowers, something special all planned out and ending the evening with a kiss. I've just never experienced it. I text him:

Nic, dear boy, I hope you know
That for this date I don't need a big show,
Drinks and dinner for me is just fine,
Some flirty chatting and decent wine.
I suppose my biggest issue, if I'm going to be clear,
Is *exactly* what to wear, if you'd be so dear,
To at least tell me that so I can prepare,
And if you don't: YOU'LL HAVE TO BEWARE!

I follow it up with the knife emoji, as if I'm threatening his life. I just want to know if I should be in heels or flats, jumper or strappy top. I don't know what 'layers' means.

'You nervous?' asks Harry, nodding at my phone where he can see Nic's name at the top. We're waiting for a 'perspectives' class to start, and are both sat with the reading in front of us, various Post-it Notes sticking out, thick binders that carry reference notes that might prove relevant wedged beside us in our chairs. Our laptops are balanced on the tiny individual tables in front of us.

'Nervous?' I ponder. 'No, actually. Not really. Obviously I want it to be nice and go well, but I'm not *nervous*. It's not like an internet date, or a blind date, or that awkward follow-up meeting where you have to greet somebody hello who you were balls-deep in last time you saw them. It's Nic. After the weekend, especially on the train, I just feel . . .'

'Yeah, it's written all over your face.' Harry laughs.

I grimace. 'What is?' I exclaim, defensively.

He fixes me with a look that is the equivalent of smacking me upside the head and saying, *I'm not an idiot, pal.*

'You're in lurrrrrrve,' he teases me, rolling the 'r' to be especially dramatic.

'Hardly,' I say, keeping my voice flat. If I react too much, he'll only use it as fuel for the fire. 'That's taking it a bit far.'

'Don't be shy about it,' he insists. 'I think it's nice. Inspiring, even. Seeing another person embracing their warm and fuzzies makes it easier for me to embrace my warm and fuzzies.'

'Inspiring? Are you in love too?'

Harry's expression brightens. 'In love *too*? I knew it!'

I narrow my eyes. 'You know what I meant,' I say, drolly. 'I *meant* . . .' and I have to steady my voice, because I didn't mean for that to slip out and it's taken me aback and I hate that Harry picked up on it. I'm not *in love*. Jesus. 'Are you seeing somebody?'

Harry pulls a face now, making his lips all thin and flat and looking shiftily from side to side.

'Possibly,' he says.

'How can you be *possibly* seeing someone? Actually, don't answer that.' Without warning, Abe flashes into my mind. I've told him to fuck off, but it's like detoxing from heroin, or sugar. I've got the Abe-sweats as he finally leaves my system and leaves me alone. I can't believe I finally got to tell him what I think of him. 'And why is this only the first I'm hearing about it?'

'You know what it's like when something is new. It's delicate.'

'Do I at least get the vital statistics?' I probe. 'It's only fair . . . How long has this even been going on?'

'A month or so,' he says, shyly, because a month is a really long time to keep a secret and he knows it. 'Beau. Twenty-eight. He's an English PhD writing his thesis on whether poetry expresses emotions or elicits them. End of top-line information.'

'He goes here?' I press.

'Like I say, end of information.'

I hold up my hands in surrender. 'Boundary established and respected,' I say. 'But, just before we close this secret liaison off can I just say: I'm very happy for you. And I look forward to either more information whenever you're comfortable *or* maybe meeting him … one day. Soon. Around campus. Since he goes here.'

'Your man has replied,' Harry says, changing the subject with a smirk and nodding at my phone. He's right. It's lit up.

Okay I get your point,
What to wear is always an issue.
My advice would be to stay comfy,
Flat shoes, activewear, some tissues.
I don't want you to feel scared,
Or intimidated by the plan,
All will be revealed,
I've told you as much as I can.

'Clear as mud,' I mutter, tucking away my phone as the lecturer enters.

When he arrives at the flat to pick me up, he's holding a sword.

'We're going LARPing, aren't we?' I say, the penny dropping. I flashback to the photos of him and his sword back when Jackson, Candice and I looked at his profile. He's taking me to play dress-up. I don't know if I'm touched he'd share that with me or bloody terrified. Good for him if he likes spending his time that way, but am I really going to be expected to take part? Maybe I can just watch. LARPing seems very intense.

'Ding, ding, ding! Give the woman a prize!' He grins. 'Yup. We are. And don't look like that – honestly. This is going to be a gateway drug for you: swear down, you'll love it. And I'll look after you.'

We embrace with a hug and he kisses my cheek briefly, pulling away to look at me again.

'Really, Ruby, you're going to enjoy this.'

In the forty-five-minute drive to our secret location – 'Actually just some woods about halfway between here and Liverpool,' Nic informs me, 'Just off the M62.' – we idly chit-chat about the news headlines and the scenery. He asks about Candice, and I tell him I still haven't heard from her, despite several pleading messages on my part. It doesn't feel forced or formal. Just nice. Like we're a couple of people hanging out, enjoying each other.

And then, as we start to drive through canopies of trees, I realise all over again that I have zero reference point for what to expect from all this LARPing business and can't pretend otherwise. I'm used to directing the action for screen, not acting everything out. How is it all supposed to work? Is it like being an actor? Being the actual character? When do you know if somebody is being themselves or playing a role?

'I feel nervous,' I blurt out, as we round a corner. A few people are already milling about in their costumes. Nic reverse-parks into a spot at the far end of the gravelled dirt box that sits off the edge of the woodland where he says we're going to play. When he's put on the handbrake and turned off the engine he says: 'It's not *serious, serious.*' He takes off his seatbelt so he can turn to face me better. 'It's like, seriously fun. You have to stay in character and let your inhibitions go for it to work and feel enjoyable, that's the only rule. It's like sex: the more you get carried away with the feeling of it all, the better it is.'

'That's all well and good,' I say, pointing out of the window, 'but that man is wearing an actual bearskin.'

Nic follows my gaze and notes the man dressed in a kilt and boots, no top (in this weather!) and what look like genuine furs.

'I should have warned you,' he says, taking in the magnificent sight. 'That you have to go big or go home.'

'Why am I suddenly concerned about whatever outfit you have for me back there in the boot?'

'Because you're slowly understanding that this is a thing you cannot control, and it's killing you already,' he shoots back. 'How about trusting that something new can be something excellent, Ms I'm-going-to-taste-everything-life-can-offer-in-my-Year-of-Me?'

'Ouch.' I laugh. 'Is this the police? I'd like to report a character assassination.'

'Lol.'

'Urgh. You just said lol unironically. I hope bear man gets you.'

'Come on.'

We get out and he pops the boot, pulling out a flask of warm tea he's brought with him. We half-lean, half-sit in the trunk, a blanket over our knees, watching everyone transform from regular Richie in IT and Carla mother-of-four-and-tired-with-it into characters in the game. People greet each other with waves and hugs, and I catch snippets of conversa-

222

tion between folks dressed as witches and harlots, warriors and clergymen, about everything from cryptocurrency to dog-training tips, and off-hand comments about an impending orgy for somebody's in-laws celebrating seventy-five years together. There's all kinds of people, from all walks of life, all united by this strange, foreign hobby.

'Ready for your costume?' he says, once we've dunked our biscuits and finished our tea and eavesdropped on everyone and everything.

'Just about,' I say. 'Can I emphasise again that I'm trusting you?'

'Can I emphasise again that that is an honour I do not underestimate?'

He gives me the bag of stuff he's brought for me and I disappear into the public loo where everyone else got changed. It's empty, so I don't even go into a stall, I just stay by the sinks, assessing my costume. Nic has given me a peasant blouse with a corset that laces up under the boobs and a long flowing skirt. I'm wearing trainers, which rather spoils the look, but the skirt is long and flowing enough to hide them, mostly. I have a pashmina, as well, that I put around my shoulders for warmth.

'That's for your head, actually,' he says to me as I walk back to him. He takes it from me. Gently, he loops it across my crown, fastening it behind my neck so that it to flows down my back as a loose headscarf. He smiles as he does it.

'You look good,' he comments. 'Mediaeval and pretty.'

'I hate that you're kind of right,' I say, smoothing everything down. 'I feel weirdly feminine? I quite like it. Even the corset.'

He winks at me. 'It is kinda showing off your best assets,' he says, with a pointed nod to my boobs. 'This is your character sheet,' he adds, giving me an information pack one of the non-playing characters has handed out. 'The NCPs are the ones who don't play the game, but who assist us in playing. If you need anything, ask them, okay?'

'You keep talking about the game,' I say. 'But what *is* the game? That's the bit I don't understand.'

'That's the thing,' he replies. 'We make it up as we go along. Your character uses magic, and there are certain things you can and cannot do – it's all on that paper – but you've just got to roll with the punches, baby.'

My eyes widen: there's no plotline to finish? No story to complete? No big narrative story we flow through with a beginning, middle and end?

'If you think that's scary,' he says, pulling out his shield from the back seat. 'Wait until I tell you I have to go and get my weapon checked with the safety marshal. I'm engaging in live combat.'

'You're not!' I gasp. 'You actually fight? Will you fight bear man?'

'If I do,' he says, grinning, 'may the sweet and fair maiden know that it is testament to her spell that I am able to both fight and take victory over those who must be conquered.' He's hamming it up, putting on a silly voice for me. 'And for that, the maiden shall be but rewarded,' he adds, and it makes me laugh.

'I honestly thought we'd go for a pizza and then to the pub,' I say. 'I was *not* expecting this.'

'I know,' he replies, cheekily.

'May I act as your guide, dear ones?' a Benedictine monk offers at the edge of the wood. I look to Nic.

'Praise be,' Nic says to him. 'Let us follow.'

Apparently the game has begun.

We weave through the tall trees, careful not to trip on any of the tree roots as the full scale of the day comes into focus. Other characters pass us, but there's also what I decide to mentally call 'set pieces', too: a few small bonfires in little clearings with old bowls and utensils and some wooden structures serving as small huts. We walk for about ten minutes, maybe fifteen – long enough for it to become meditative and trance-like, like walking further and further into a storybook, so that when we reach a clearing it feels like happening upon magic.

'Whoa,' I say, not entirely in the character of a local healing woman from the ages, but it's my instinctive response, and if authenticity is what is called for it doesn't get much more authentic than that.

It's like a mediaeval village. All around us, men in armour, from chain mail tops to full-on helmets and shoulder pads, tend to their weapons – fake ones, Nic assures me, designed to look as real as possible. Nic has said that as a warrior himself, it's important to enter battle but the rules of this particular set-up mean non-contact. If I'm captured, I've been told I must go quietly and know that my boundaries will always be respected. It's not re-enactment, Nic said, just fantasy.

This is the craziest thing I've ever done in my life. As we move through into the woods, it's apparent that there's loads of us here – some in costume and some not, who are apparently the guides. Nic told me to just go with the flow, and so when he says goodbye, that he must meet with the men to discuss their wares, I watch him go and let myself get swept up in all that is on offer.

* * *

'A seat, my dear,' a woman in a costume not dissimilar to mine says. 'They are sure to win today. Much depends on it, but nevertheless let us cast a good luck spell to aid them. To protect them.'

I surprise myself in that . . . I do. I help with a potion that we sprinkle on the fire that's been made, and I give directions to some elves, and bear witness to an argument between two shopkeepers over who has right to the land in front of their stores. I lose myself in it all, in totality, embodying the story of this strange new world where we have to cooperate, help each other, and where each of us contributes to the new reality we're building. It's full immersion into a make-believe world that the hundred or so people here have created as a team, like live-action theatre but with no script.

'That's exactly right,' Nic whispers to me as we siphon off from the in-character area. Apparently there's nothing worse in LARPing than being out of character in the middle of the action because it spoils it for everyone else. Which is fair, really. We pour more hot tea from the flask, catching our breath, and make sure to keep our voices low.

'You see that guy there?' Nic is gesturing to a walking suit of body armour. 'He's a primary school teacher who enrolled in a welding class to learn how to make his own gear. Paul, I think his real name is.'

'Christ,' I marvel. 'He made that?' Honestly, if I saw it in a museum I'd have been impressed.

'I'm sort of breaking the rules by telling you who people are outside of their characters,' Nic says. 'We're not supposed to fully identify each other really.'

'I'm in awe,' I say. 'All of this creativity, and not for money or fame or whatever. Everyone has come together to weave this world within a world with proper artistry.'

'That's why I like it,' says Nic. 'There's a sort of devotion to it.'

'Devotion,' I echo. 'Yeah. It's beautiful. How does everyone come up with their characters?' I say. 'From books?'

Nic tuts. 'Absolutely not,' he says. 'We're forbidden from being a character that already exists – although after the first *Lord of the Rings* movie came out that all went out of the window for a while. It was a scandal within the community, actually.'

I smile.

'You can be inspired by books or TV or whatever, but it's more about trying out sides of yourself you can't or don't in real life and making up something new entirely.'

I nod in understanding.

'And they're all this mediaeval vibe? Soldiers and warriors and whatnot?'

'Oh no,' he says. 'There are zombie LARPs, army-of-steel sort of stuff . . . I mean, you want to get out to somewhere like Croatia or Germany. If you think this is impressive, out there is another world. It's like a cross between a film set and your weirdest I've-eaten-too-much-brie-before-bed dreams. Expensive, though.'

We finish our tea and Nic slips the cups and flask back into the picnic bag with his initials on.

'Hey,' I say. 'So if your character is supposed to symbolise stuff you don't or can't express in real life, what's your deal?'

He grins. 'Bearing in mind I've had this character since I was at school,' he says. 'It's a sort of desire to be a go-getter, to go after what I want.'

'That tracks,' I say. And then: 'So wait. What's mine?'

He pulls a face. 'Well . . .' he starts, and I can tell he thinks he's about to get into trouble. 'Your character is about

227

surrender: she can't control anything; she can only respond thoughtfully to what happens.'

'Which is unlike the real me, who is a grade-A control freak,' I say slowly.

He pulls on his helmet and through the mouthpiece shoots back: 'You said it, dear. Not me.'

And then the game resumes. I'm more into it than I have been all day.

28

Nic

'That was AMAZING,' Ruby says, as we clamber back into the car at nearly 6 p.m. We've been playing for six hours, and every time I've caught a glimpse of her, she's genuinely looked invested – in fact, it was me who said to her it was time to go. We've enjoyed the same day today, but haven't had enough one-on-one time, which I'm now keen to rectify.

'I cannot tell you attractive it is that you got into it,' I say, and she looks up with wide eyes from where she's fixing her seatbelt. I lean in and kiss her.

'Mm,' she says. 'I was wondering when you were going to do that.'

'Were you now?' I say, and she grins.

'So, what shall we do now?'

'Well . . .' I reply. 'We're actually pretty close to another place I love, if you want the full Nic Sheridan experience.'

'Of course I do,' she says. 'Show me everything you love, please.'

I click in my own belt buckle.

'Yes, ma'am,' I reply.

I take her to the boardgame café.

'Because if you're going to know what really thrills me,' I tell her as we arrive, 'you may as well know that after a hard day's LARPing, I like nothing better than a couple of Vik's malt milkshakes and a round of Cluedo.'

'I can't believe there's a whole café dedicated to playing boardgames,' she says. 'That's genius.'

'Isn't it?' I enthuse. 'I've been coming here for as long as I can remember. Maybe since I was thirteen? I'll bet there are some games here as old as we are, maybe older.'

'Aww,' she says. 'Little teenage Nic!'

'I was a car crash, really,' I admit, as we wander through the low and dim lighting of the main part of the café to the back, where you can stay as long as you want as long as you keep ordering food and drink. We pick a corner with two small sofas facing each other, a low wooden table between them. I give a gesture that says, *after you.* She takes off her coat and hands it to me, saying, 'If you put that over there for me, you can sit here?'

I follow her lead.

We order grilled cheese toasties and a couple of malt milkshakes and look through the games under our table to see what we fancy. There's Scrabble, Cluedo, Monopoly, Backgammon and the *Friends* version of Trivial Pursuit.

'Go on then,' she says. 'What were you like when you were thirteen and coming here at the weekends?'

I think about it. 'Braces,' I say, and she replies, 'Of course. Same.'

'I had mates at school and stuff, some I stay in contact with even now. I wasn't a loner, but I didn't really stand out.

I went with the flow, kept my head down, never really caused a scene but never got the spotlight either. I very quietly got great grades and then slipped off to university.'

'Is that a good thing, or a bad thing?' she asks.

I consider it. 'Probably good, overall,' I say. 'I think your school years can traumatise you, can't they? Either because you never reach those dizzying heights of popularity again, or you get bullied and spend your life never really being able to forget it.'

'School was an escape for me,' she says. 'When Mum and Dad split up, they were both pretty miserable for a while, so me and my sister found all these different reasons to be out of the house: school, breakfast club, hockey, chess, drama – you name it. We ended up being the most extra-curricular girls in the school's history, we did that much.'

I cock my head to look at her. She's laughing, but: 'That's so sad!' I say, giving her shoulder a nudge. 'Ruby. Not feeling like you ever wanted to go home. I wouldn't wish that on any kid.'

'Me neither,' she says. 'It got a bit better once Mum remarried, but then Dad married Dee. They're still together, though Lord knows why because they don't seem to even like each other that much. And Dee hates us. We joke about it, but it's been the same since I can remember. I'm fairly certain she tried to have her own kids with Dad and couldn't, so her resentment for us got even worse. In the end we stopped going around, you know – when we were old enough to put our foot down.'

'You see him now?' I ask, picking up my malt milkshake and using the soggy paper straw to stir the dregs. It was better back when I was a teenager and we could have plastic ones that didn't disintegrate, even though I prefer a planet not dying from unrecyclable overconsumption.

'Occasionally,' she says. 'I try to go over when I know Dee is out. He doesn't really do a lot. Watches TV, mostly.'

'And your mum and stepdad?'

'I see them more,' she says. 'Yeah. Though I have been a bit naughty and not really been home as much as I should have since I moved up here. The course has been so all-absorbing. I know it's selfish, but I haven't wanted to tear myself away.'

'I'm sure they understand. Especially knowing you're so happy.'

'I am,' she says. 'And now we've found Amelie, I mean – can you bear it? We go to Paris to meet her tomorrow! That's worth missing Sunday lunch for – even if Mum's Yorkshire puddings are as big as my head.'

She reaches out to me as she says that, touching my forearm, and I want her to leave it there. We've not even picked up a game to play, just got comfy and started chatting and now we're not stopping. If it weren't for the waiter occasionally checking to see if we need anything else, we could be in our own world.

'The Instagram is amazing enough,' I tell her. 'To see this all play out on film is going to be even better.'

'Thanks, yeah. We've got faculty support and everything. Even our classmates are supportive. I guess I thought there'd be competition, but with this, because of the social media stuff, people seem more invested in JP than what that means for mine and Harry's success.'

She says 'success' in air quotes.

'We're on the train to London tomorrow, then onto the Eurostar into the Gare du Nord. We're going to film the whole thing, and then hopefully that's our story. Anyway . . . Sorry, I'm hogging the oxygen.'

'Please don't apologise,' I insist. 'It's honestly fascinating. I used to *love* my work and feel dead proud of being so fancy in my suit and doing my banking and whatever. Making rich people richer, as you once said to me.'

She does an *uh-oh* face.

'No, you're right,' I press. 'That's what I do. And I thought moving to Hoare's would make me feel even more like that, but to be honest moving was for the place, not the job. It's amazing and everything, but it's all the other stuff in London. I'd serve sandwiches or try and write adverts or be a street mime if it meant living in London.'

'See, I just didn't feel that way,' she says. 'I tried to, but . . .' She shakes her head.

'It's Marmite, isn't it? You like it or loathe it.'

'Candice and Jackson love it, but most of the foreign students we had in the house seemed to simply tolerate it. I know it's not just me.'

'I totally get that, like, she's a tough nut to crack – London. And I think people are either made for it or not.'

'Yes!' she says, and this time when she touches my arm, she stays there, her fingers lightly dancing on the underside of my forearm. 'That's bang on. I don't know if I'll stay in Manchester, but I'm pretty certain I won't go back to London. I don't have the fight in me for it. Or the money.'

I let myself look at her.

'What?' she says, automatically reaching to her face like she thinks I'm going to tell her she has milk on her chin.

'It's a shame I arrived as you were leaving,' I say.

She shows me her dimples. 'You're there . . . I'm up here . . .' she says. 'At least you actually come up and visit your family.'

I look sheepish. 'Well . . .' I admit. 'I didn't technically have

233

a reason for visiting them this weekend. I just didn't want to wait to see you.'

'Am I freaked out by that, or do I find it sweet?'

'Oh,' I say, leaning in just the tiniest amount, and she leans in a bit too. 'You definitely find it sweet.'

'Is that so . . . ?' she murmurs, and then we kiss again, deeper, this time, more passionate than earlier. I love how she feels. Her lips are soft, plump pillows, and she's nearly always smiling for a moment as our lips meet, before she suddenly gets serious like she has to make the decision to let herself go. I live for the sigh she gives when that moment comes: a deep, guttural sound of surrender.

'I like kissing you,' she whispers.

'I like kissing you too,' I tell her.

We make out a bit, stopping occasionally to push our foreheads together happily, or exchange long and lazy smiles.

'Can I get you both anything else?' the waiter asks, I don't know how much longer later. I look up to meet their eye and realise there's nobody else left in the café. 'We're closing in twenty minutes,' they say.

'We're good,' I confirm, and then turn to Ruby. 'Well . . .' I say.

'Well,' she replies. Then she smirks. 'I don't want to be too forward,' she coos. 'But would you like to come home with me?'

We hold hands on the way to the car. As we reach it, I open her door for her, and she rewards me with another kiss. I drive with my left hand reached out across the back of her chair, and then, when I need access to the gear shift a little bit more readily, on her knee, where occasionally she lifts my knuckles to her mouth. We don't speak much. The radio plays and the dark sky hovers and the lights of passing buildings glimmer.

'This way?' I ask, when signs for the university start to show up. I had my sat nav on earlier, but male pride forbids such assistance right now.

'And then the second right,' she says. 'I'm the tower block right there if you remember. You should be able to park right outside the door.'

We go inside and hang up our coats, take off our shoes. The apartment is a small one-bed. From the entry hall there's a bathroom on the right, a bedroom on the left, and right ahead is the kitchen-diner. The walls are white, but it *feels* very Ruby: she's got framed film posters leaning up on shelves and on top of drawers, with smaller pictures of friends and family scattered throughout too. When I lived with Millie everything was shades of beige, all very neutral. Here there is a woven rug on the lounge floor and colourful crockery stacked on the open shelves over the sink. It surprises me that pride of place is given to a poster for *The Miseducation of Lauryn Hill* album.

'I loved that album too,' I say, pointing. 'Back when CDs were a thing.'

She looks up. 'Yeah,' she says. 'I think it's the first piece of music I listened to as a body of work. I was only ten or something when it came out, but I must have been an early teenager when I snaffled a copy in a charity shop. I just liked the cover. But it was a revelation. Before that album I'd buy CDs and only be interested in the songs that had been released, and then with that one she told this whole story, all her heartache and wants and longings. I got obsessed with her relationship with Wyclef Jean – about how he led her on, how they'd have these high passions and blazing rows that basically ended up breaking up the Fugees. She still went to his wedding, though, when he married somebody else. I just thought: there's a woman leaving everything on the court. Giving life everything she has.'

'Wow,' I say. 'I just liked it because Ollie did, and he's cooler than me.'

She smiles. 'Tea?' she says. 'I've got beer, if you want a beer. Warm milk?'

'Will you make me a hot chocolate?' I ask. 'Like you did . . .'

'That night?' she says, smiling. 'I will. Yes.'

I watch her like I watched her last time. She's barefoot and in leggings, pulling off her jumper when she gets too hot so she's only in Lycra and a white T-shirt. I can't help myself. I walk behind her and wrap my arms around her, leaning in to kiss her neck.

'I've had fun today,' I say, after she kisses me, shooing me away so she doesn't burn the bottom of the pan. She pours the liquid into two mugs and we stand, both leaning against the countertop, blowing the steam from where it escapes the cups.

'I've had fun too.' She smiles.

'I can't believe you thought I was only after sex,' I tease. 'What a filthy mind.'

'We had a one-night stand, Nic. Of course it was only sex.'

'Until it wasn't.'

'Until it wasn't.'

'And so,' I say. 'This is nice. You. Me. Us.'

She smiles. 'So, what's the plan?' she ventures. 'Not to sound like a girl or anything. Or, actually, yes, I mean to sound exactly like a girl. I'm old enough to ask that question and shoot right to the point, aren't I?'

'You are.' I nod. 'And so am I. I don't want to screw this up, so let's just agree to that now. We don't make assumptions, and we ask what we need to ask.'

'That's very healthy and mature,' she says, taking a slurp of her drink. 'So . . . I won't assume you're spending the night, I'll ask: Nic, are you spending the night?'

I put down my drink. She puts down hers. I lift her up so that she is in my arms and reply: 'If I could just show you to your bedroom, ma'am, I can confirm the answer to that.'

It's gentler, this time. Not as feral. When we first slept together there was an unspoken knowledge that we'd only get one night, and so anything went. This time, it doesn't feel like a finality, it feels like something is just beginning, and so I take my time. We lie in her bed opposite each other, both naked, both touching and stroking and caressing. I tell her she's beautiful. She tells me I'm hot. She jokes about my sword, about having watched me all day, but it's all done in whispers, making everything we say intimate and confessional. If we raised our voices, we wouldn't be saying the things we are saying but because it's just us, hushed under a duvet, it's safe to say them.

I pull her into me so that she's on her back, my arm scooped under her and her head on my chest, where we can kiss with ease. With my other hand I push open her legs and let my fingers wander. She squirms, saying it tickles, but I push them open again, and tell her firmly: 'No moving.'

She lies still and giggles as I tease her with my fingertips, finding a rhythm that makes her breathe heavier, and then almost pant. We kiss until she melts into me enough that it stops even really being that – she's breathing into my mouth as I touch her, a little bit faster and then a little bit slower, until her legs buckle and kick and she shudders and moans into my mouth, 'Yes. Yes.'

I put on a condom and then roll over onto her and fit

237

myself between her slick legs, and we hold eye contact as it happens until she pushes her head up and back with a deep groan as I enter her. She wraps her legs around my back and pulls me into her, again and again, again and again, and it doesn't take long before I groan in release myself. I stay there, on top of her, catching my breath and shrinking inside of her, and then she laughs. And it makes me laugh.

'Why are we laughing?' I ask. 'I know I'm laughing too, but why?'

'I'm laughing because I'm happy,' she says.

'I like that,' I tell her. 'I like making you happy.'

She grins.

'Can I see you after Paris?' I ask her. 'If you're coming back into St Pancras, I could meet you off the train? Get lunch, or dinner, or a drink? Anything.'

'I'd like that,' she whispers. 'Yes. See you after Paris.'

29

Ruby

'Hey,' says Harry, as I climb into his car. Harry is driving us to the station, and we're on the 2 p.m. train to London Euston with William and JP, who'll meet us there. The Eurostar leaves from St Pancras, so to break up the travel we're in the hotel opposite there tonight, and France-bound tomorrow. Within twenty-four hours, we'll be at Amelie's house and JP will finally, after all these years and all this excitement, be laying eyes on his girl.

I am beside myself – and mildly exhausted. Nic and I didn't get much sleep last night. It was such a thoughtful and fun date, and we chatted so easily, had sex all night . . . I'm officially smitten. Absolutely, two hundred per cent, no-way-back-now smitten. I believe in love again! Me and Nic! JP and Amelie! Harry and his secret lover, Beau – whenever he's ready to talk about it! The breeze feels softer. The sun seems sexier. Smells are more potent. Life is good and happiness can be real. Would I have allowed myself to let Nic in if it weren't for JP shining a light into my dark fears? Honestly, I don't think so. Which is why it is so incredible to me that we can bring his magic to as many people as possible. I buckle my seatbelt and accept the coffee Harry has brought for me. Did coffee always taste this good? Ahhhh.

We drive in companionable silence, the radio on, and for the tenth time I reread the text message Nic sent after he'd left this morning.

Fuck me, Ruby,
Last night was exquisite,
Your tits, your arse and your mouth.
But more than that
It's everything about you,
Your kindness, your humour, your laugh.
I hope Paris is great,
JP's story gets a conclusion.
But for you and me, baby,
We're just beginning,
(About that
Let's have no confusion) xxx

'Jesus,' Harry teases as we hit some traffic. 'I can practically smell the shagging beating off of you. Yesterday was that good, huh?'

'I don't mean to sound smug,' I tell him, not really meaning it, 'but the whole day was that good. Falling in lust, pal – there's no feeling like it.'

'You're going to be insufferable for this whole trip, aren't you?'

'Most likely,' I sing-song. 'If I'm going to be honest. Yes.'

I plan to linger in this part as dreamily as possible. Real life can be hard, and so when the magic happens I feel like it's my duty to pay attention and savour it. Savour this all I will.

240

We meet JP and William and climb aboard the train. We've decided that Harry will film anything we deem pertinent, so I'm likely to end up on camera as conversations naturally weave in and out of talking about the purpose of the trip. I check my reflection in the selfie camera of my phone, just in case. I'm flushed and my eyes are bright, even if I do look tired. I put on some tinted lip gloss, rubbing some into my cheeks for good measure to perk myself up. It'll have to do.

As a group we've got nervous energy, all of us tapping our fingers or crossing and recrossing our legs, unable to settle. Well, except for JP – who has nodded off beside me. I keep picking up my phone, even though I know Nic won't have messaged because I haven't replied to him yet. I didn't know what to say. It was all said last night. And this morning. In the end I settle on: *I really fancy you.* That's it. No kiss, but straight facts. I can see immediately that he's seen it, with a *read: 2:01pm* coming up underneath it. He sends back a smiling emoji.

I idly check my email as well, and my heart leaps when I see one from our supervisor.

'Has Janet emailed you too?' I ask Harry, not looking up from my screen.

'Hmm?' he says. He's scrolling his own phone, not really hearing me.

I scan the contents of the message quickly, answering my own question when I see Harry cc-ed in and addressed at the top.

'Mystery solved,' I say. 'It's to both of us.' Harry finally looks up. I read it out loud. '*Hi Ruby, Hi Harry. I'm emailing because you're being spoken of very favourably amongst the staff. Just wanted to lend my voice to say the application with which you're pursuing your studies is admirable, and we are*

241

all very proud to have you in the department. Good luck in Paris! Janet.'

'Oh,' says Harry, waving down the buffet trolley person for a drink and some crisps. 'Well, that's unexpectedly nice.'

'Yeah,' I say. 'I wonder what's been said though?'

He considers it. 'I mean, we are doing a great job of showing up. You can tell most of the lecturers enjoy us being in the seminars. We do the reading, have interesting things to say . . .'

'God, do you think everyone hates us?'

'Who cares? I'm there for an education, not a popularity contest.'

'Fair enough.'

'On that note, actually, I'll start recording. I know we're not saying much, but just in case. Maybe we can just go over what's about to happen, how we're all feeling? JP, that okay?'

'It's been a long time since I've left the postcode,' JP replies, as he rouses from resting his eyes. 'Paris. Blow me down.'

'Via London,' I remind him.

'Two capitals in one trip,' he marvels, and he's on good form now he's awake. 'Good job we are getting this on camera. I wouldn't have believed it all otherwise.'

Harry settles back down, camera in hand.

'Don't worry about this.' He gestures. 'I'm just going to get you all chatting naturally. We might not even use the sound with the footage, just the images of travelling with other audio overlayed.'

'Texture,' JP notes, winking at me. I've taught him well.

William goes wide-eyed, and JP laughs.

'I never pegged you for being camera-shy,' he says to his grandson.

'I've never been in a position to find out,' Harry says, and I swear he's even sweating a bit. When I'm on camera I tell myself that it's me editing, too, so we don't have to use anything I don't like. I guess when it's all out of your hands it's harder to relax.

'Let's just chat, when it feels natural, like Harry says,' I suggest. 'Don't worry about the camera. Erm . . . what did everyone get up to this morning?'

Neither JP nor William speaks.

'Okay,' I say. 'Well . . .' I want to break the tension. 'I've been so emboldened by your story JP that yesterday I went out on a date with Nic, who as you know I have turned down before, despite having slept with him, because I was keeping my heart in a big old cage and thought that was the best way to protect myself.'

William nods, thankful I'm filling the silence.

'But doing all this with you has opened my eyes to how seemingly protecting my heart can actually cause more pain. Anyway . . . Long story short, I took a chance, Nic is incredible, and I've been up all night shagging, the end.'

I declare it a success when William laughs and JP shakes his head with a smile. The ice has thawed. Before long we're chatting and swapping stories and we forget the camera is there at all. We're a motley crew: JP, small and slight in his wheelchair; William, dressed like he's about to take the Labrador to the vet's in the Volvo; big and beardy Harry, tall as a tree and a heart like marshmallow; and then me, wearing Nic's jumper that I am ninety per cent sure he didn't leave behind as an accident, and that I immediately commandeered as my own.

The time passes quickly after that.

'The next station is London Euston. Please make sure you

243

have all your belongings as you disembark,' the announcer says over a crackly line to the carriages.

'Game on,' says Harry, standing to put on his backpack and film us getting all our stuff together too. It's like being watched by the paparazzi.

'I was thinking about getting last-minute tickets for a show tonight,' Harry tells me as we wait for the wheelchair ramp once the doors are opened. 'You up for it? Or are you seeing friends or something?'

'I texted my friend Candice, but she's not free,' I tell him, and it's half the truth. The full truth is that she never replied at all: I'm still in best friend purgatory. Jackson says not to worry, that she just needs time, but I don't like it. I'm in London without seeing her – it's just not right.

'Her loss is my gain.' Harry smiles and I smile back. I suddenly feel very sad, though.

'Do you fancy a movie night instead?' I ask. 'Conserve our energy? We can hook our laptops up to the TV and bring back a Pret a Manger picnic? Even do it in our PJs?'

'Movie students having a movie night.' Harry chuckles. 'How original.'

'If it ain't broke.' I shrug, and he puts his arm around me with familial love.

'She'll come around,' he says. 'Candice. I know it's shitty now, but your friend Jackson is right. She'll come to you when she's ready.'

'Hmmm,' is all I say in reply.

When we arrive, Paris takes my breath away.

'Holy crap,' I gasp in awe after our unremarkable but efficient Eurostar across the Channel. We've stepped out of a big, carpeted metal box and into a postcard come to life.

Gare du Nord is like a huge London market hall on steroids. Neoclassical, William says it's called. There's a central hall with all the local platforms on that we see as we come down in the lift from where the Eurostar terminates. Thin green iron pillars line two sides of a slate glass roof that reveals thick grey clouds, heavy with the threat of rain. There are small little carts dotted around selling crepes and croissants and coffee, a Francophile's wet dream. Everyone seems to have somewhere to go and somewhere to be, which is the same the world over, obviously, but there's something so magical about the fact that all the people I can see going places are *French*. They walk differently – insouciant and slouchy. The dial marked 'elegance' is turned up to eleven out of ten, here.

'Is this your first time?' Harry says.

'Yeah,' I tell him. 'And now I feel stupid. Who knew this was two hours away this whole time?'

'Wonderful, isn't it?' joins in JP from his wheelchair. Harry and William exchange a look, amused by our childlike wonderment. I never thought my master's would lead me here.

Outside, we search for the driver with William's name on a small whiteboard: because of JP he decided to book a cab in advance. A man with white gloves and a driver's hat greets us in grunts, and we're mostly quiet as the cab heads west to Chaillot, the neighbourhood Amelie lives in. We now know, after being able to talk to the housekeeper and a few emails Amelie's granddaughter has sent us, that Amelie ended up living in Paris because her children brought her here to be closer to them when her husband was sick and it looked likely she would become a widow. It becomes obvious as we turn off from the Arc de Triomphe and into somewhere more residential that it's a moneyed area.

'Not like the farm out here,' JP notes, his eyes as wide as everyone else's.

The streets are wide and quiet, lined with cars that all seem to have dents in them, like a badge of honour. Most of the buildings are two or three storeys tall, all grand bay windows and pillared entrances and small, neat gold plaques beside doorbells signalling that once-illustrious abodes have now been carved up into only slightly less illustrious apartments. It gets quieter and quieter the deeper into the streets we get, odd dog walkers and meandering couples punctuating the place like actors on a film set.

'Do we know what Amelie's children do?' I say, noting the clear view of the Eiffel Tower through the buildings. And I don't mean in the distance – we can't be very far from it at all. It's huge. Small shops, cafés, bakeries – it all seems surreal. How is this a place where people live? How is this real? Different shades of white and stone are punctuated with wrought-iron balconies and railings. People are actually wearing berets and trench coats! If we'd made up the script to our documentary as a movie we couldn't have chosen somewhere more picturesque and romantic for the lovers to finally be reunited. I understand what all the fuss is about.

'*Nous sommes arrivés*,' the driver says from up front, pulling up to the small hotel, around the corner from Amelie's house.

'Let's drop off our stuff in our rooms,' William says, once we're out on the pavement. 'Have a rest for an hour or so, then meet up in the lobby at just before three? Google Maps says we're six minutes away on foot, and it's flat.'

'Perfect,' Harry and I say in unison, looking at each other and saying *jinx*.

'What do you reckon to the chances of a decent brew?' asks JP. 'I'm gasping.'

'I've never known anyone knock back tea like you do,' Harry jokes. 'You should get buried in a teapot.'

'That's not a bad shout.' JP smiles. 'My heaven is either a nice hot cup of tea or half a shandy, but I imagine there'd be more room in a teapot.'

On account of us being in our thirties and not our nineties, Harry and I don't much feel call for a rest, and so on dropping off our bags in our shared twin room we decide to go to a café on the corner for an authentic Parisian pastry and coffee. We huddle up on two chairs side by side, facing out to the road, and without us even saying anything the waiter gives us a tourist menu written in English.

'I've heard the French can be *un petit peu* passive-aggressive.' Harry grins after I issue a small *merci* in what I hope isn't too mortifying an accent.

'I can't believe we've made it this far,' he continues, after we order. 'Three months ago, we didn't even know each other, and now we're balls-deep in this project, in another country, with emails from the department wishing us luck. I'm pretty proud of us, you know.'

'I'm proud of us too,' I say. 'It's vindicating to me. I made a commitment to myself, and that commitment is paying off.'

'Sure is,' says Harry. 'Oh, hey, let's update the Insta page,' he adds, pulling out his phone to take a selfie of us. He narrates the caption as he types: '*This is it. We're in Paris, an hour and a half away from reuniting JP with his girl. Paris is beautiful, albeit rainy, and we can't wait to show you what teenage war-ravaged sweethearts look like after more than seventy years of wondering after each other. Who says true love is dead? For JP and Amelie, it has survived decades and distance.*'

247

'Beautiful,' I say. 'And we're up to fifteen hundred followers now? That's so cool.'

'I've hash-tagged it *soulmates* and *to be continued*,' Harry says, posting the image. 'And yes, fifteen hundred. Some cool people are in that list too – some film people.'

We scroll through the followers list and note some arts councils and creative talent hubs in amongst our friends and friends' friends. I see Nic's name in there as well.

'That's him,' I say, pointing. 'Nic.'

'Ooh, let's have a look then,' Harry says, clicking on his avatar like Candice and Jackson did back at the end of summer. 'Handsome. Geek-chic.' Harry nods appreciatively. 'Looks like he's loving London life. Jeez, I want to be living it up like he is!'

'Yeah,' I say. 'He basically did the same as us: wanted a change and took the leap to make his life better. He should be proud of himself too.'

'So you're going to long-distance it?' Harry asks.

'I guess,' I tell him. 'We haven't talked details, and it is still early days. As long as it doesn't interfere with the master's, I'll go with the flow. That's what JP wants for us both, isn't it? To enjoy ourselves, to know that when it's right it's worth making the room for?'

'Beau and I agreed the same,' Harry says. 'And yes,' he adds, noting my intrigued expression, 'I am volunteering more information about my love life. I think I might be danger-ously close to happy.'

'Ha,' I hoot, causing the stern waiter to shoot me a look of unbridled who-the-hell-are-these-classless-tourists disgust. 'That could be the name of a novel.'

'Well, my memoirs will be called *I Did A Thing, And I Regret It Already*.'

I giggle. 'Mine will be *Sorry, I Couldn't Hear You Over My Internal Monologue*.'

'Overthinkers?' Harry mock-marvels. 'Us? Never!'

'Overthinking about how to get the happy ending they deserve,' I say. 'By which I mean JP's, not our own.'

'Yes, let's not jinx *that*,' Harry says, making the sign of the cross over his body. 'Dear Lord, do not smite my happiness – by which I mean JP's – amen.'

'But, Lord, please do give us some great footage for our doc, thank you.'

'Yes,' says Harry, looking skyward. 'We're huge fans of your work, my Lord. We know you'll look after us.'

'I'm so pleased you came to talk to me that day in the atrium,' I say, peeling open a sugar sachet and pouring it into my empty cup. 'I think a lot about JP affecting my outlook, but it all came from your encouragement. I'm thankful for that.'

'Awwww, Ruby!' Harry exclaims. 'Are you trying to make me cry?'

'Maybe.' I wink. 'How close are you?'

'I'm a bit on the edge, truth told,' he says. 'Seeing you so happy as well, knowing that we're breathing the same air as Amelie right now . . .'

'I know. I get impatient when my food takes too long to arrive in a restaurant. Imagine having the patience to see an old love again after all this time.'

'I don't even know if I could let myself get old,' Harry says. 'JP is the life and soul, but the salmon sandwiches and endless naps? Put a bullet in me when I'm seventy – that's what I say.'

'My stepdad is almost seventy and there's life in him yet,' I insist. 'I think it must be nice, finally slowing down, taking stock of it all.'

'Hmmmm.' Harry checks the post he's just published. 'Lots of excited people,' he notes, changing the subject. And then: 'Holy shit, Ruby. Guess who is following us?'

I shake my head.

'The pope?' I offer.

'Veronica Bloody Latimer,' he says.

'BAFTA-award-winning BBC producer?' I say, pulling his phone from him. 'No. No way!'

I look at the screen, and there she is. *This is so cool!* she has written.

'Christ,' I say. 'That makes me feel . . . pressure. Does that make you feel pressure?'

'Let's just say,' Harry laments, pulling his gloves back on and starting to stand up, 'that it makes me want to go and check I've got back-up batteries and all our gear is ready to go,' he says.

'Yeah,' I agree. 'We really cannot screw this up now.'

Back in the lobby, JP is wearing a bright red knitted waistcoat under his winter coat, and a tartan scarf that William has tied in a knot to keep the breeze out. He's tapping his fingers on his knees slowly with one hand, holding on to the photo of Amelie in the other. I can feel his energy: upbeat and happy, eager and anxious.

Harry already has the camera rolling and so I ask JP how he's feeling.

'Ready,' he says, with a nod, a tentative smile playing on his lips.

'And before it all happens, let me ask you this too: what do you want people to know about love?' I prompt. 'Reflecting on this journey you've been on, what lesson have you learned that you'd like to save somebody else from learning the hard way?'

JP considers his response. 'I think it's very simple,' he says after a lull. 'Not knowing what could happen next means that anything could. Grab on to love with both hands when it appears. Don't take it for granted. That I have a second chance to lay my eyes on Amelie puts me in the minority. Let ye be not so stupid.' He grins. And with that we're off.

We reach the address that William has saved into Google Maps, and look for Amelie's surname on the shiny engraved plaque. It activates a phone, and a youngish voice answers with: '*Oui?*'

William announces us in what sounds like fluent French, and there's a pause as the person at the other end sounds annoyed, and then she switches to perfect English to say: 'Hold on, please. I will come down to you.'

We wait, the cold gathering around us as the weather prepares to rain. JP's eyes are searching through the small glass strips between the weighty wooden door and the walls, and then a woman who looks almost identical to the person in his photograph appears. Her cheeks are flushed and her eyes red-rimmed, as if she's been crying. I'm surprised I haven't cried yet myself; it's an emotional day for all of us. No doubt I will.

She opens the door and stands, looking at JP. She doesn't even have to speak for my heart to sink. She waits just a beat too long, and it shifts the weight of the air between us. In half a second, my eyebrows drop and my forehead creases, because something isn't right. I have an ominous feeling. The young woman looks at JP sadly, and then at the rest of us. She's shaking her head.

'I'm Sophie,' she says, her accent making it sound impossibly glamorous. 'Amelie's granddaughter.'

We all make subdued noises of *oh!* and *nice to meet you!*

but she doesn't smile. In fact, the longer I look at her the more it becomes clear. She looks devastated.

'I'm so sorry,' she says, in the quiet of our expectation. And it's weird, but I know what she's going to say before she says it. We're too late.

'My grandmother died this morning,' she confirms. 'You just missed her.'

30

Nic

'Sorry,' Jackson says to me, his pint centimetres from his lips. 'What do you mean?'

'Millie is pregnant,' I repeat. 'With child. Having a baby.'

He puts down his glass.

'Millie, your ex Millie?' he clarifies.

'Millie my ex.'

'And . . . sorry, I don't think I'm understanding here,' he says. 'And it's yours?'

'Yes,' I say. It's enough to make me pick up my own drink and down two-thirds of it. Jackson watches me chug it, glug after glug after glug. It barely touches the sides. I wave a hand at the barperson to signal two more. Both are going to have to be for me.

'Mother of God,' Jackson says, when I'm done. 'You're going to be . . .' He doesn't say the word.

'A dad,' I supply. 'Yup.'

It's his turn to down a drink. We sit.

'I thought it was weird she text, and even weirder that she knew I was up,' I say. I'm shaking, and my voice is high-pitched and strained. I keep rubbing under my eye, like a new tic from the shock. 'Turns out Mum had told her, after seeing her and her bump in Asda. Millie didn't confirm anything, but you know mums – they connect dots faster than anyone else sees them. So . . .'

'So it's soon? If there's a bump . . .'

'She's five months,' I say. And then: 'Oh God, what am I going to do, Jackson? I'm not ready for any of this. Especially not with her.'

'But you said she doesn't expect anything from you,' he confirms.

I nod. 'That's what she said. I mean, it's not like I can just abandon her or whatever. She's seeing somebody already, but I mean surely he's not going to stick around? It's all a bit of a blur to be honest. I went over to hers, to her new place, and she made coffee and I complimented her wall-paper and then she said that when we had sex before I left, she'd got her cycle wrong. We always used a sort of natural method of contraception – she takes her temperature every morning and puts it in an app and it lets her know when she's ovulating. It worked the whole time we were together. We never even had a scare. And then before I moved I went to pick up a box of my things she'd accidentally taken to her new place, and in the most frenzied, spontaneous act of affection we've known as a couple I went to kiss her cheek goodbye, somehow hit her mouth, and then we did it, right there in her hallway. It lasted less than ten minutes. We didn't even talk about it afterwards – we just said see you around and good luck. I'd even pushed the fact that it happened out of my head, because it didn't mean anything other than a full stop to everything.'

'And now the full stop is a dot, dot, dot . . .'

'Ha, ha.'

'Sorry,' Jackson says. 'I shouldn't be making jokes at a time like this.'

'The whole thing is a joke,' I say. The barperson puts our drinks on the end of the bar and Jackson goes to fetch them. When he sits back down I say, forlornly, 'You know, walking over here, I saw my reflection in a shop window and I just thought to myself, like, who am I? The new shoes and the way I've styled my hair – has it all been a performance, a big game of dress-up? Everything I'd told Ruby, and you, when we've chatted and whatever, it's been true: how it felt to take a chance on myself, to trust I could thrive here. I've been so proud of myself. And now I've got all these thoughts in my head and none of them are nice.'

'Like what?' asks Jackson.

'Like: men like me don't get to make it in places like this. I got too big for my boots. Who am I to think I could escape anything? Who am I to imagine I deserved adventure, a new start, everything my heart desires?'

'Mate,' Jackson starts. 'No. Don't think like that.'

'This has ruined everything,' I say. 'This has ruined my whole life. I'm screwed. I can't be a dad. Can I?'

Jackson doesn't speak for a moment, and we continue our drinking. Eventually he says: 'You did the right thing to text me.'

'You've been a good friend to me,' I say. And then I burst into tears. 'God, I'm sorry,' I say, wiping them away as fast as I can. 'It's just – everything was going so great. I didn't even tell you – I mean, it felt grubby to talk about it or whatever, but Ruby and me, we hooked up. After our date. I got about three hours to think that it could all be the beginning of something and then bam.'

'Don't be worrying about Ruby,' Jackson insists. 'She can wait. She's a separate issue. Let's unpick the pregnancy, first. Also: let me get us some water.'

'I know self-pity is boring,' I tell him. 'I just . . . this isn't what I signed up for, you know? I've been loving it down here. It's hard to make friends and tough on the tube and to be honest I preferred my old office, but there's a vibe here that isn't like anywhere else in the world, and I *feel* different. I feel so much closer to how I've always wanted to. That sounds so stupid, but I've had two pints and a shock, so I'm just going to go on ahead and pour out all my feelings, okay?'

'Exactly the point,' says Jackson. 'We can go for pint number three if you need it. I can see it's helping.'

I raise my almost-empty glass in a salute of cheers.

'It feels unfair,' I say. 'This is a decision out of my hands. I'm not saying she shouldn't have the baby – I don't mean that. The baby is coming, fine. But, like, Jesus. I didn't think it would all happen this way, you know? I feel so helpless, and I'd only just started to *not* feel that way. It's one step forward, two steps back.'

'It took a lot for you to move here, mate, I know that. The bloke who bought Ruby's sofa is worlds away from the bloke sat in front of me now – you've fucking *bloomed*, mate. Like a flower.'

I look up at him, tears in my eyes. That's exactly how it feels.

'Have I?' I say, and it's not lost on either of us that my voice is quivering.

'Yeah,' he says.

'I don't want responsibilities,' I say, sadly. 'I wanted to just *be* for a while. Have one of those movie montages of crazy nights where people snort vodka out of the belly buttons of lithe models in their underwear and swing around poles on bridges, the twinkling lights of the city behind them. I wanted to be piled into the back of a cab with a bunch of mates and laugh hysterically as we have to pull over so one of us can be sick. I wanted to run up a bar tab that's higher than my monthly rent, and do a runner on it – just once. I wanted to make friends with the table next to me at a pub and end up at a warehouse party in a part of London where the tube stops running until the next morning, and I wanted to have to fake being sick for work when really I'm on the Isle of Man with no idea of how I got there.'

'You wanted your twenties back then, basically.'

'Yeah. The twenties I never had. I was so sensible. It's a horrible feeling, knowing I wasted them. I've never even got a last-minute plane ticket to a new place or been slapped by a woman in the street because I never called when I said I would. I just wanted to laugh and feel free. Unburdened. Really properly laugh and not feel so weighed down by who I am and all the responsibility I feel that other people – Ollie, you, the guys at dodgeball – just don't seem to suffer from. Why am I like this?'

'You're bloody wonderful, mate. You're a proper sort. Don't shit-talk yourself.'

'It's been four months of finding my way, like I might actually be able to loosen up a bit after all, and now I feel like I've been building hollow dreams. To think I could change who I fundamentally am just because I live somewhere else seems laughable to me.'

'You're already changed,' he says. 'No matter what happens next.'

'Yeah,' I lament.

'Nothing is over. You have choices.'

'It doesn't feel like it.'

'That's the shock talking,' he says. 'I'll help you, all right? We'll make a list – when we're sober – and think about all the ways this could pan out, and we will NOT panic, okay? No good actions were made from fear.'

'Okay,' I say glumly.

'But for now – more beer.' He nods his head towards the third glass I've drained. 'And some chips, too. If you're going to drink like this, you need to line your stomach.'

'Can you just make it all go away?' I say, sadly.

'Afraid not, pal,' he replies. 'But I can sit opposite you and let you know you're not alone, and that's not nothing.'

'You're right,' I say. 'It's not. Thank you.'

31

Ruby

JP is silent. Sophie has invited us upstairs to her grand-mother's apartment, which feels incredibly intrusive and yet we all understand that it's as important for the woman who has just passed away as it is for the man Sophie has only just met. It's the kind thing to do. He looks distraught. I can't believe that even five minutes ago we were laughing and joking and bloody *filming*. We've been treating this as one big story and it's not make-believe. This is people's *lives*. I'm ashamed. We take the lift up to Amelie's floor without speaking and Sophie's mother and her husband are there, too, dressed sleek and sophisticated as if they've come straight from work.

'Hello,' the woman says, 'I'm Brigitte, Amelie's daughter. This is my husband, Claude.'

We shake hands, express condolences, accept offers of coffees and teas and then sit. The apartment is light and airy, with herringbone hardwood floors and ceilings that meet the walls with ornate cornicing. Modest art is on the walls. It's a far cry from JP's Manchester terrace in terms of style. It's European and chic. JP's house feels more like a home, but there's a serenity to Amelie's apartment. It makes me wonder what she's like. Was like. Oh, God.

'We've heard so much about you,' Brigitte says, gently, once we've all got drinks and seem settled. 'The Englishman who had her heart. I've known about you since I was a little girl.'

JP smiles, and it seems genuine. I think it must be a comfort to hear about her from one of the people closest to her in the world. 'All good, I hope.' His voice sounds translucent and thin. Tired. I suddenly have a thought – I think: *I hope this doesn't kill him.* I try to shake it off.

'It was a sort of legend in our family,' Brigitte continues. 'It's impossible, I think, to imagine a life for your parents before you are born – we children are so selfish, aren't we? – but with *Maman*, she was different, you know? She loved life, was so calm and at peace with herself. She had a smile, like she had a secret, and I always thought whenever she drifted off into one of her daydreams that it was to spend time with you, especially since she found out you had been looking for her. It brought her so much happiness.'

'Did she ever talk of finding him too?' William asks.

'No,' Brigitte says diplomatically. 'She was a practical woman. To find a soldier called JP in all of England – she told me once she wasn't even sure you were alive. I think her memories were safer. But goodness, when we found out you were alive and had been looking for her – I've never seen her so happy! She's not been well for a long time, but it's true – is it not, Claude – that when she knew you were coming, she seemed better. She stayed awake longer, started to hum her little songs like I remember as a child.'

Out of respect, we're not filming, but our voice recorder

blinks in interest as she tells us all this. It's awful, thinking about the project when JP is so heartbroken, but it was Harry who whispered to me as we got out of the lift that whilst we are JP's friends, we're also here for work and the work is to document this journey for everyone who has followed us so far. I didn't reply, but I know my silence makes me complicit in the decision to keep getting our 'content'. That makes me feel ashamed, too.

'There's value in telling this part of it too,' Harry had whispered. I don't know what to think.

'Would you like to see her, JP?' Sophie asks then. 'She's in the bedroom. Perhaps you'd like to say hello again after all this time, before you say goodbye?'

Crikey. I did *not* know that she was still here. I don't know what I thought. I knew she'd died in her sleep, but I thought the body had been moved already. Isn't that what happens? I don't have any experience with death. All my grandparents are still alive. I don't want to have to see a dead body. The hairs on my arms stand to attention, letting me know that I really do feel unsettled.

'She will stay here until tonight, when the rest of the family can visit to say goodbye,' Claude explains. I wonder if anybody will sleep in the apartment with her.

'Yes,' says JP, after considering the question. 'I'd like to see her.'

We give him his privacy, William helping him to the bedroom door but letting him take the last few steps alone, loitering only to make sure he gets into the chair Brigitte has put beside the bed.

'This is a beautiful home,' I offer, to fill the silence nobody else seems to mind. I do, though. It's too devastating, being here mere hours too late. If we'd have come yesterday instead

261

of breaking up the journey, or come straight from the station on an earlier train, would she have even died at all? Would it have been enough to keep her alive, refilling her heart? Or is that too much to hope for? I don't know if I'm being silly, or romantic. I hate myself for wishing Nic was here, but I do. I want to hug somebody, or be hugged.

'She loves it,' Sophie offers. 'Loved,' she then corrects. We exchanged wounded looks. 'Sorry,' she says, welling up.

'Were you very close?' William asks her, and she looks up gratefully, pleased he's asked, I think.

'Very much so,' Sophie tells him, and they exchanged a knowing look.

'Gramps is my world,' William says, and Sophie nods.

'She always moved at my speed. How do you say? We were *in step*.'

'There's a poem about that.' William nods. 'About how children need their grandparents because grandparents move slowly, don't rush around as much as parents. Little people and old people have a commonality.'

'Yes!' Sophie agrees, gesticulating in glee at being understood. She seems to catch herself then, remembering that this is a solemn day. 'Sorry,' she says. 'I've just always thought this. To hear you say it brings me a lot of joy.'

William smiles at her again, and she nods.

When JP reappears we all turn to him, awaiting his guidance, and he announces, 'I think we should give the family their privacy.'

We leave.

I feel sad for JP, and sorry for Amelie's family, but the next morning it's a small comfort to know that Nic is going to meet me off the train. I texted him last night, telling him we'd just missed Amelie, and he left me a garbled voice note saying he was incredibly drunk with Jackson, but very sad to hear that news. It made me smile. He didn't sound wasted, just a bit slur-y, and he signed off by saying, *Anyway, see you tomorrow. I love you. Well. Not love you, but – you know what I mean. Shit. Okay. Bye.* I did know what he meant.

We get into St Pancras and the others go across to Euston to go straight up to Manchester, but I make a right. He's waiting right by the exit, holding a sign that says 'RUBY' with a heart and arrow through it drawn on.

'Hey, you,' he says, as I approach.

'Hey, you,' I reply, nuzzling into his neck. I stay there, suspended in time, enjoying the solidness of him, the fact that he said he'd show up and did. And then it feels safe to have a little cry, in a way that felt wrong and inappropriate in Paris, in front of JP.

'Was it shit?' he said. 'It's so sad.'

'It's awful,' I say. 'He missed her by a day. More than seventy years of waiting and we were a day late. It's just not fair. It's not fair at all.'

He strokes my hair.

'Ruby,' he says, then, and his tone has changed. 'Do you think we could go and sit down somewhere? I know you're upset, but there's something I need to tell you. And it can't wait.'

I pull away. 'Are you breaking up with me?' I say. 'Not that we're official yet, I know, but – just say . . .'

'Let's sit down,' he insists.

'Just say it,' I counter. 'Say it.'

'It's Millie,' he tells me, right there in the train station with a hundred people moving in a million different directions around us. 'My ex. She's pregnant. By me. But . . . can we

263

talk about it? Because I really hope that doesn't change anything.'

'Change anything?' I say. 'Nic.' I can't believe what I'm hearing. Thoughts of tears and cramps and blood and loneliness engulf me. *I don't want kids.* 'That changes everything.'

32

Nic

Ruby blinks rapidly. It reminds me of when the little wheel comes up on my computer when I've asked it to do too much and it needs time to think. I wonder if that's how I looked when Millie dropped the bombshell. If it is, I need to be as gentle and slow with Ruby as Millie was with me.

'Let's sit there,' I say, pointing to an empty bench by the station's communal piano. I take her by the wrist. She's still blinking. I try to read her mind, find clues for how this is landing. I need to hold on to hope that this can all work out.

'I didn't want to go a second longer without just coming out with it,' I explain. 'I didn't know. It happened in the summer. We'd broken up, but . . .' I don't want to give too many details. She doesn't need to know the date and time and what position. 'It happened before I left,' I settle on, deliberately vague. The details probably don't matter that much to be fair. The fact is: a baby is imminent and it's got my DNA.

Ruby narrows her eyes, crinkles her brow. She's beautiful. I want to hug her and take her home. I don't want to be saying any of this. Or, at least, I want to skip the part where it's a shock and get to the bit where it's awkward, but we figure it out. She's worked so hard to be happy. I know that. I hope this can add to the happiness, somehow.

'I know it's not ideal,' I say. 'But I don't want this to change anything. Millie is seeing somebody already and doesn't want anything from me. I haven't sorted out any details or anything, but even if I lived next door I'd still just be co-parenting. I'd be able to have a life, you know?'

'You're moving next door to her?' Ruby asks, coming to.

I shake my head. 'No, I didn't mean . . .' I trail off. 'There is no plan yet. I just meant that even if I did, I'd hope we could still do . . . this. Us.'

'Hmm,' Ruby muses. Her face is impassive. I can't read it. If Ruby thinks I show every emotion that channels through me, she's the total opposite. I haven't got a clue what she's feeling. I've never seen her look this vacant, though. It's not ideal that I'm telling her all this right on the back of what happened in Paris.

'I know you'll probably need time to process all this,' I say. 'I found out two days ago and still feel like . . . whoa, what?'

I'm trying to get some sort of reaction. A smile would be nice. A comfort.

'I mean,' she says, closing her eyes briefly. 'I'm, you know, I'm having a big reaction to what you're saying here. Erm . . .'

I don't speak. I wait for her to put how she's feeling into words.

'I don't want kids, Nic,' she says plainly.

'No . . . ?' I say. 'Well, that's okay. You don't have to like, be a stepmum or anything. I wouldn't ask that of you.'

266

'But you *should*,' she replies. 'That's exactly what a dad should ask of his partner. You should want me to be involved, and to love your kids like you love your kids.'

'Okay,' I agree. 'It's just, we're not even together-together yet, so I don't want to sign you up to something when I don't even know what the deal is. But yeah, I suppose you're right. This baby, she'll need a good team. If you think . . .'

'She?'

'Yeah. Millie says it's a girl.'

'When's she due?'

'May.'

'Wow.'

'Yeah. Soon.'

Ruby pulls a face, and then looks sad. Every time I think she sounds like she's erring on the it-isn't-a-big-deal side of things, suddenly I'm not so sure. She doesn't have to be involved at all. I can separate church and state. But if she wants to be involved that's cool too. It's a lot, but why not? People have unusual and strange set-ups all the time. Who is to say I can't figure out being a parent at the same time as starting a relationship? This is the Twenty-Twenties. Anything goes.

'My stepmother never really liked me and my sister,' Ruby announces. 'And we knew it. I always hated Dad for marrying somebody who didn't want us around. It's like when it came down to it, when he had to choose a side, he picked her, not us. And that was a really shitty feeling.'

I don't speak.

'You're a good guy, Nic,' she says. 'And you won't ever make the shitty choice – I know you won't.'

'Ruby . . .' I begin, but I don't know what I'm hoping to say next.

'Do you know what catapulted me into this Year of Me thing?' she says, rhetorically, holding up a hand to signal I need to let her finish. 'It was finishing with Abe, yes, but the reason I finally had the strength to end it with him was because I had a miscarriage.'

'Oh, Ruby,' I say. 'I'm so, so sorry.'

She's staring at a spot on the floor, just beyond our knees. She doesn't look up at me.

'I hated myself for months afterwards. But not because I lost it – I hated myself for months because I was secretly pleased that I hadn't had to make a choice. I knew that I was half-living up to my potential and calling it my twenties, calling it fun, calling it just-what-you-do when you live in London, in a big city, with your friends and get drunk and do stupid things and all of that. But then miscarrying right before I turned thirty and realising that it was a fucking close call? That was awful,' she says. 'It was a shock to the system, like *wake up! Go and do something with your wild and precious days!* I realised what I want to do is make art, and live on my own terms. I've never even had to talk to a partner about building a future because I've never had a partner I was building something with. But if I was to put a stake in the ground now, it would be: I don't want children, I don't even know if I believe in marriage. But I do believe in myself, and the stories I want to tell, and that deciding to take myself and those dreams seriously is the most important thing to have ever happened to me. What happened yesterday, in Paris – meeting JP and chronicling his story. That's made me even more sure. It makes me feel more alive than anything in the world.'

'Can't this be different?' I venture. 'This isn't *your* baby. I'm not asking you to stay home and warm my slippers by the fire and cook my dinner. I'm not like that.'

'You're not listening,' she counters.

'I am!' I say. 'You don't want kids! That's okay! I don't even know if I want kids!'

'But you *are* having one,' she says, kindly. She's not angry. 'And you'll be magnificent. You'll be thoughtful and patient and you'll build a life that works for you both, and I can't be in that. I'll be with a video camera and a boom mic in a forest somewhere, or on the beaches of Seville, or on a rig off the Atlantic. And even if I'm not, even if I never leave Manchester again, I know that when I see you . . .'

'It's not going to be for soft play and bath time.'

'No,' she says. 'Two paths diverged in a wood,' she whispers, 'And we took a different one each.'

'You say yesterday with JP has made you feel more connected to storytelling than ever before, but what about real life? Didn't yesterday prove that when you find your person you don't let anything get in the way?'

'JP had a beautiful life,' Ruby says. 'Seeing Amelie again would have been the cherry on top.'

'I'm just a cherry?'

'No,' she says. 'You're wonderful. But you can be wonderful and it still not be right. I won't make you choose between me and your daughter. My own father did that and made the wrong choice.'

I think about what she's saying. For a brief second, I wonder what it would be like to not be involved with my kid at all. To leave Millie and her boyfriend to it. But then just as quickly, I know I'll never do that. A future I didn't plan for is coming for me, but it's a future I won't run from.

'I don't want to stop you from having everything you want,' I say.

'I don't want to hold you back either,' she replies, and we stare at each other sadly.

'I really am sorry about what happened to you. The miscarriage.'

'Thank you,' she says. 'I've made peace with it now. I'm okay.'

She reaches out for my hand and kisses my knuckles, in the way that she does. As it happens, I already miss it.

'So this is it?' I say. 'It's so unfair. I didn't ask for any of this. I've had ten minutes of knowing what it's like to fall into something fucking brilliant, like the stuff they write the songs about, and now, because of something that happened before we even met, we have to break up? I really do have to choose?'

'Yeah,' she answers, sadly. 'I think so. I'm fucking gutted, for what it's worth. Like, I'm going to get on a train in a bit, and as soon as I get home cry really hard, for a really long time.'

'Oh, well . . .' I say, smiling unhappily. 'As long as you don't get over me for six months to a year. Maybe two. That will help, to know you pine for me.'

She chuckles, bittersweet. 'I'll think of you every time I have a film premiere,' she says. 'I'll pray for your google search history whenever I've had good press.'

'You're the cyber-stalker,' I remind her. 'And God. I'm going to have to unfollow you now, you know. I cannot see your face every day. I just can't.'

'No,' she agrees. 'That's understandable. Same.'

We sit.

'Dammit,' I say.

She shakes her head. 'We really did do our best at trying to thwart the old bad timing,' she laments. 'But apparently, fate knows what she's doing.'

'Chuffing fate,' I spit.

'Millie has really been growing a baby inside her this whole time we've known each other?'

'Yeah,' I say.

'And you really didn't know?'

'I didn't have a scooby.'

'That's crazy,' she says.

'Film-worthy,' I say, and she wrinkles her nose.

I walk with her through the evening twilight, down to Euston so she can get the train up to Manchester. As a police car speeds past us and a group of yummy mummies in heels shriek something about the penthouse suite at the St Pancras Hotel, she asks: 'Will you stay down here?'

I take a breath. 'I don't know,' I say. 'I love it here. It feels like I'm only just finding my feet.'

'You'll figure it out,' she says. 'Clever bean.'

'Just not as clever as you,' I concede, referencing an earlier joke about how her intellectual prowess trumps mine.

'I don't know,' she says, coming to a stop to look at me, reaching out a hand to my cheek. I grab it and pull it to my lips, depositing a kiss onto her palm. 'You do okay.'

'Good luck with everything,' I tell her.

'You too,' she says.

And then she's gone.

33

Ruby

'I wish you'd have told me about the miscarriage when it happened,' Jackson says to me over FaceTime. 'Everything makes so much more sense now. We could never figure out why everything seemed so drastic. No, that's not fair actually. Not drastic. Just . . . Candice and me couldn't understand why the Abe heartbreak seemed worse than any other heartbreak. But now . . . I'm just so sorry you went through all that, Rubes. I wish we could have helped you more.' He pulls a face to emphasise his point, and I can tell he feels for me.

'It's okay,' I say, taking a deep breath. 'I don't think I had the words for it as it happened. It's a hard do-not-recommend from me on a secret pregnancy, and a secret everything-that-came-after. I just wanted to start over, and do things properly for myself. And it's worked, for what it's worth. I've felt like a new person. I'm happy. That's why I can't do this with Nic. I'd have taken the risk if it was just him, but now . . .

'The path he's about to go down isn't one I want to walk.

272

I think it's better that we're both clear about that now instead of once a little human is involved.'

'That's true,' says Jackson. 'But . . . you're sure?'

I sigh sadly. 'No,' I say. 'But only because it hurts. Let's be honest though, our timing hasn't been right this whole time. It's okay. Or, it will be.'

I notice the time in the top corner of my screen.

'Is it preview o'clock?' Jackson asks, when he realises I'm suddenly distracted. 'Do you have to go now?'

'The time is now,' I say, putting on a silly voice. 'Gah! Oh my gosh, I'm so nervous. Thank God I've had editing to distract me.'

'Lol,' says Jackson. 'That sounds like heartbreak justifying itself.'

'Your point?'

He waves a hand. 'None,' he says. 'I have nothing further to add.'

I roll my eyes at him. 'Wish us luck?' I request.

'You don't need it.' He winks. 'And also: surely I must be able to see a cut soon? Please?'

'Not until it's perfect,' I insist. 'Bear with.'

'Will do.' He smiles. 'I love you, Ruby. I'm proud of you.'

'Thank you,' I say. 'I'm proud of me too. I think.'

I fill Harry in on the break-up, minus the miscarriage story. I've kept quiet these past few days because it's all been about finishing the first draft of the project, but I tell him now that Nic is having a baby and I don't want kids in my life that way, and so we've decided to hit pause.

'I'm sorry to hear that,' he says as we wait outside the screening room. 'I know the leap of faith was a big thing for you.'

'Yeah,' I say. 'But *c'est la vie*, et cetera.'

'There's more than one way to have a romantic life,' he offers.

'Says the man happily coupled up,' I retort.

He shrugs, faking being coy. 'I know. There's nothing worse than seeing somebody happy when you're . . .' He trails off.

'It's okay,' I tell him. 'You can say it.'

Harry asked Beau to be his boyfriend when we got back from Paris, probably right at the moment I realised Nic couldn't be mine.

'The good news is you can finally meet him,' Harry offers. 'I'm not hiding him away like a dirty little secret anymore. Not after what happened to JP.'

'Could be a hashtag to get trending,' I quip. 'Hashtag JP-made-me-do-it.'

'That's actually a pretty good idea,' Harry concedes. 'Let's add it for the list for after. I think we should seriously cut one-minute bits of the interviews up for the Instagram account too. Little shareable pearls of wisdom.'

'That's smart,' I say, nodding. 'Agree.' And then I feel the recurring gurgle in my stomach that's been making an appearance all morning. I've not been able to tell whether it's my bruised heart or the impending big reveal. Probably it's both.

'Are you nervous?' I ask, nodding towards the room where we'll have our first audience outside of anyone involved with the thing. 'My stomach is very much telling me that I am.'

We know what we've got needs work, to an extent. We've done our best, but we can't really move forward until fresh eyes have seen it, and that's the whole point of sharing it with our peers. We're too involved, now. JP has wanted a little bit of space from it all, which is understandable, so he hasn't seen it, nor have he and William contributed any further thoughts to it. We've kept a respectable distance since we came home, letting William know via text that JP is in our hearts, and that we'd like to see him soon. William said he's okay, just quiet. And we haven't said on social media that Amelie has died, because it gives away a key point of the doc. That's why it will be good to get the minute-long snippets up there – we can share parts of the story without giving more away about its conclusion. At least until we've tightened the whole thing up, anyway.

Our fellow grad students mill around as we wait to be called in. We're third on the list of six. I know everyone will be feeling the same, although I doubt everyone had Janet, the course leader, emailing them to say they show great promise and are an asset to the department, to be fair. It feels like the bar for Harry and me is a tiny bit higher than it is for everyone else.

'Look,' Harry says calmly. 'This is all designed to make us better, right? Everyone feels the same, because everyone wants to knock it out of the park first go-around, but you know as well as I do that that isn't part of the process. The process is being uncertain and unsure and patching stuff together and being embarrassed of it until a fresh pair of eyes connects dots we haven't. And not for nothing – don't forget that for as talented as you and I are, so is everyone else in that room. We'll probably end up saying thank you. You know. Once we get over our feelings being hurt.'

'You're so much more gracious than I am.' I sigh and check my phone.

Some gossip to cheer you up: I think Candice is sleeping with our new French roommate, Jackson has texted. *Maybe that's why she hasn't messaged. More details to follow . . .*

He doesn't understand why she's still blanking me, either. Apparently, she's been out a lot, sleeping in late, and there's been a lot of popped bottles and twerking in clubs on her stories, which is fine, except for the fact that she's never really been a clubber before. Maybe the pub, or at a push a noisy bar with a tiny dance floor – but the clubbing is new. And we had one rule in Maple Avenue: don't shit where you eat. If Candice is sleeping with another housemate, Jackson won't be happy. I hope for everyone's sake he's mistaken. He's saying it lightly, but it will cause trouble.

'Okay, gang,' Janet says, sticking her head out of the door of the screening room. 'Do you all want to come through? Let's get started.'

We shuffle through to the tiny cinema-like room and I tug on Harry's sleeve to steer him towards two seats second row from the front, at the edge.

'I don't want to be able to see everyone's reactions,' I explain.

He rolls his eyes at me. His skin really is way thicker than mine.

Janet welcomes everyone and gives us instructions for the forms in front of us. She reminds us all that we're on the same side, and even though it probably feels like it, we're not actually in competition with one another. The point of the early screenings, she says, is to give constructive feedback to each piece, wherever it is at in this moment in time, but we also have to remember that the act of *giving* feedback will make us think more critically about our own projects too.

'Don't skimp out on helping your colleagues and cohort,' Janet warns, 'because then you're only skimping out on helping yourself. Being as detailed as possible with your notes for everyone is actually a deeply selfish act, because it will force you to understand your own projects from the audience's point of view too.'

It's a fair point, and as we watch various cuts and edits from everyone, it quickly reveals itself as being absolutely true, because I know what I am critiquing in others' work is exactly what I am worried about in my own.

I'm not sure the stakes seem high enough – I want to care, but I am struggling to.

Where is the heart? The warmth? Life is hard enough, I'd like to feel a bit more comfort, I think.

It feels to me like you're dancing around the point you want to make. Is there a central question you're avoiding? I only say that because we've had the same discussions around ours.

It's no surprise, then, when we get our anonymous forms back and the truth is there in black biro and white. Harry is calmer about it than I am.

'Feedback isn't personal,' he reminds me. 'We are not our art. The art is the art. If they think we can make it better, we probably can. That's a compliment, really – isn't it?'

'How have you found a compliment in *do better*?' I marvel. I'm upset that we let everyone see a rough cut with so many holes in it, mostly because I knew those holes were there and couldn't find the solution myself.

'They think we can do better is the point,' he says. 'There's some really workable solutions here.'

Basically the theme of our notes is that we need to heighten the stakes to really make viewers care about JP's journey, because if we do that people will understand how it reflects their own. There's a few suggestions about getting some more background on Amelie, interviewing JP's wider family, or maybe asking other interviewees about their love lives, and I can see the point, but none of those feel like the answer.

Almost Doesn't Count. Hmmmm. I ask myself what else there is to say about that, feeling a slump in my heart at getting my almost with Nic. I sigh. Making a film about love isn't exactly having to do twelve-hour shifts down the mines, but it's still hard, and confronting, and takes a lot from me. It's been a nice way to distract myself this week, after Nic, but it forces me to do some emotional excavation as well, and that's a lot, especially on the back of having my heart crumpled.

'Let's take a walk,' Harry suggests, noticing my mood. 'Get some fresh air. I've got an idea.'

I follow him.

We pace through the concrete blocks of the university, picking up a couple of hot chocolates at Mick's coffee cart and heading out to the canal because, Harry insists, there is no problem that cannot be solved by looking at a body of water.

'World hunger,' I offer. 'The issue of how to force billionaires to solve the climate emergency instead of exploring space. Mosquitos,' I say. '"There's no problem that cannot be solved by looking at a body of water" might sound poetic, but it doesn't stand up under even the most basic interrogation.'

Harry remains sanguine. 'Just bloody enjoy it,' he says, refusing to lower himself to my cynicism. 'Your problem is that you're so clever and articulate you can talk your way into contempt like it's a badge of honour. You use your powers for evil instead of good. Just walk, and breathe, and marvel, please.'

'Yes, Mr Buddha.' I sigh, but I give him the tiniest hint of a smile. He's a good partner in all this.

When Harry thinks I've calmed down and can actually

hear his words instead of spin them into something I can make fun of, he finally says: 'Can we stand here? And as my behind-the-scenes footage, can I put my iPhone here and capture this?'

We're by a big stone wall and the day is moody and it's quiet, where we are. Atmospheric.

'I don't get it.' I wave. 'But if you must.'

'I must.'

I stand, getting chilly, as Harry gets his phone and decides on an angle, checks the sound is okay and then hits record, standing off camera himself.

'I'm going to ask you some questions, and I need you to be honest, okay? Not funny, not self-effacing, not silly – just honest.'

I pull a face at the camera to get it out of my system, and Harry patiently waits for my features to become neutral again and for us to continue. I register the arrangement of his own into 'I'm Being Deliberately Kind and Tolerant', as if I am a four-year-old who won't brush their teeth for the mere fact that they just don't like being told to brush their teeth. I'm fighting back against him because I know he's about to be right; even though I don't know what he's going to say, I just know he's been building up to this for ages. Clearly, my way isn't working and so, in the true rules of partnership, whatever he suggests now I am going to have to at least try, so we can say we have.

'I promise to take this seriously, and answer your questions accordingly,' I say, after a few deep breaths. My palms are sticky with nerves. Why do I feel light-headed and faint? It's just Harry. It's just a movie. It's just a project that could possibly decide the rest of my entire career.

He looks at me.

'What if almost *does* count?' he says, eventually.

'Uh-huh,' I reply, eyes narrowed. 'Go on.' How can almost count? That's the very definition of almost . . . that it doesn't quite *get there*.

'You started afresh here after a bad break-up. Right?'

I get defensive. 'I started afresh to start afresh,' I begin, my tone harsh.

'You didn't run away from something, you ran towards an opportunity, yes, yes, yes, I know,' Harry retorts. 'But essentially, Abe was the catalyst. Correct?'

Begrudgingly, I agree. I'm not putting more details onto camera than I need to, so I leave it at that.

'I think *you* are the story, Ruby,' he offers, then.

'Me?' I balk.

'Yeah.'

I wait for him to explain, but when nothing is forthcoming add: 'That's why you've been filming behind the scenes so much, isn't it? Have you been thinking this for a while?'

'To be honest, yes.' He nods. 'I just didn't realise how right I was.'

I wait for further explanation. A cosy, hand-holding couple traverse the corner nearest to us. She's gazing up adoringly into his eyes, and they're laughing but not really saying anything in a way that means either the joke is private and they don't want us to hear, or they're so in love that even the mere presence of the other is cause for ebullient, fizzing laughter. My eyes flick up to catch theirs as they mutter 'Excuse me' and 'thank you so much' and 'lovely day for it, isn't it?'.

'So, what do you say?' Harry prompts. 'Do you get my point?'

'Erm . . .' I falter, suddenly painfully aware of the camera.

I'm sure he's just caught me literally gawping, double and triple chins galore. Me as the story? But how?

'I think you're making me out to be a lot grander than I really am,' I begin. 'I don't think I'm the interesting one, here . . .'

'It's interesting to me – the pursuit of love after an almost. There's bravery to it. JP is great, but JP's effect on *you* is even better. You could interview me as well, since JP's effect has been that I've opened myself up to love too. But that's a neater resolution. You and Nic have decided not to be together, even after it took you all that courage to give it a whirl. I still don't understand what happened – I know there's something you're not telling me, and that's fine. But the idea of JP so closely missing out, me getting a relationship, and you trying but . . .'

'Failing,' I supply.

'Not in a horrible way. I'd much rather you be happy. I'm sorry you aren't yet.'

I scoff, cheeks pinkening. 'You feel sorry for me?' I ask.

'The opposite,' Harry insists, his voice gentle. 'That you admitted how you feel for Nic is remarkable after the heartache you had . . .'

'Yeah, and look at how that turned out,' I say.

'Do you feel braver in love though? Even though it didn't work out? Did JP make you realise it was worth the risk, even though . . . ?' Harry trails off, but it's such a good prompt. I'm tempted to give him a pithy one-liner, but when I open my mouth, I find I can't. Jesus. It's so bloody terrifying. It's so out of *my* control. I think of everything I thought I'd pushed myself towards – letting it be okay to bend the rules of the Year of Me, taking a chance with somebody new. And still knowing, now Millie is pregnant and Nic is about to be

281

a dad, that joining him on that journey is absolutely not right for me . . . it's not ended up how I thought, but oddly, magnificently, despite the heartache, standing in my own truth has made me feel more myself than ever before. Do I feel brave in love?

'I do,' I say, nodding, letting the pride wash over me. 'I took a chance, but it didn't break me.' I remember what JP said to me, that time I went over his house for port. 'The heart is a muscle, and we have to use it.' I start smiling, and embarrassingly tears well up in my eyes too. 'It's pretty badass that I did, even if it didn't work out.'

'Bingo,' says Harry. 'So almost *does* count, after all.'

'Holy shit,' I say. 'Almost is the whole friggin' point.'

Harry nods. 'Exactly.'

34

Nic

I have dreams about her. The sofa is always there. Sometimes Millie is sat on it, holding a baby and smiling, but I never hold it. I just observe. I watch Millie cradle it, sing to it, stroke its tiny cheek with tenderness and love. Ruby stands behind her, watching her too, or sometimes reaches out a hand to me and pleads with big, wide eyes: *Come with me, Nic. Come with me.* In our dreamworld the baby cries and I don't know what to do, how to help. Millie looks at me and says she doesn't need me, she's got it under control. *Why don't you go and take a bath?* she says, but she doesn't look at me when she says it. She can't keep her eyes off the baby. My mother appears then, and Millie hands our blanket-wrapped child to her. Then she walks with her dressing gown unfastened towards Ruby. They kiss, and then Millie opens her mouth so wide that Ruby's head disappears inside of her throat.

* * *

Millie's bump is growing by the day.

'Tea?' she says, as I stand awkwardly in her new house, just around the corner from where we both lived together. It's a small semi-detached, opposite the park, with a nice flat garden at the back and an open-plan kitchen/living room. It's quiet. Safe. Family-friendly.

'Water?' she continues. 'I have sparkling. I know you prefer it.'

Millie must have got that in especially, because I've never known her to drink anything other than tap water, and occasionally champagne on special occasions. Millie doesn't like to lose control, and drinking nearly always leads to losing one's inhibitions. Millie likes to keep a clear head, and an organised mind, and doesn't understand the concept of blowing off steam or misstepping or even making the odd mistake. She's a planner. A type-A. Logical and sensible, and as practical as they come.

Well, actually. Obviously she makes the *odd* mistake, present condition duly noted. Not that the baby is *mistake*, but insofar as it was unplanned.

'Water would be great, thank you,' I reply. 'However it comes.'

She grabs a glass and slices a piece of lemon.

'You don't have to hover so . . . strangely,' she says, as she pulls out a glass bottle from the fridge. 'You're welcome here. Don't stand on ceremony. It's just me. I won't bite.'

I perch on a stool at the breakfast bar and she slides my drink across to me.

'Do you want some toast, or a sandwich?' she asks. 'I've got some cheese if you want cheese on toast.'

My stomach growls at the prospect.

'I can tell you need it,' she pushes, smiling. She's doing

everything she can to help me relax. I can tell by how accommodating she's being that she knows I'm still catching up to everything.

'I'll make it,' I say, standing up. 'You sit.'

'No, no,' she insists, waving a hand to signal that I should sit back down. 'I've got it.'

I sup my water and watch her potter about, and she watches me in return as I eat, leaning against the countertop and nursing her peppermint tea. Eventually we make eye contact, and it forces my hand and I speak properly for the first time since I got here.

'So this is really happening,' I say, pointing at her belly.

She rubs a hand over where I'm gesticulating and smiles.

'I'm happy about it, Nic. It's not the best circumstance, but you know how my mum struggled to conceive and had a stupidly early menopause – I've always worried it would be the same for me. That's why I wanted to settle down and get to it.'

'I know,' I say. 'And I'm sorry for falling off the radar a bit since you told me. It's been something I needed to get my head around.'

'I know that,' she tells me. 'Like I said the other week – it's okay. I understand that this isn't what *you* wanted. Not like this. And that can be true at the same time as the simple fact that . . . well, it's happening. It's all in motion, now.'

'Can't fight city hall,' I say.

'And I don't want to,' she replies, simply. 'You didn't seem able to really take in the details before, so sorry if I'm repeating myself . . . but for what it's worth obviously I'd miscalculated my cycle. Best I can work out is that for some reason I'd ovulated late? I don't know. But, like I say . . . Mum entered the menopause in her early thirties so . . .'

285

She doesn't have to fill in the blanks. I don't need her to explain why she's having the baby. There's a baby, and it is coming, and that's the end of that.

'But I am sorry I didn't tell you sooner. I was stuck between a rock and a hard place – you'd already left, already moved to London. And I knew whenever I told you it would be a bit of a bomb going off in your life, and so I waited, and then suddenly all this time had gone by and . . .'

'It's okay,' I say, and it is. I could get mad if I wanted to, but it would be like trying to bite the wind: pointless. 'I think I might be strangely grateful I got to have my fun,' I add. 'In blissful ignorance.'

'We can paint it as an altruistic move on my part if that makes what else I have to say easier,' she replies and, as I eat the last part of my food and push the plate away, I frown in question.

'Is this the bit where you tell me it's twins?' I joke.

'It's the bit where I tell you I've been seeing someone,' she responds. 'I mentioned it when you were here last time, but you just seemed so overwhelmed by the pregnancy that I thought that was enough for you to be digesting . . .'

'I remember,' I say. 'Does he know?'

'He knows and wants to be involved.'

I blink.

'You're seeing somebody who wants to keep seeing you after the baby is born?'

'I know it's odd,' she says, with a lopsided smile. 'It's Sandeep, from work? You met him at a few parties? We've just always got on, and he was so kind to me after you left, and then I knew pretty early that I must be pregnant because I take my temperature every morning, don't I, so I knew something was different because of that.'

'Sandeep from work knew about this before I did?' I ask. 'And he wants to stay with you after the baby comes?'

A wave of envy washes over me. Ruby wouldn't stay because of the baby, but Millie gets a new boyfriend out of it all? It's not a fair thought, but it's the one that I have.

'Like I said – it's all very odd. But yes, essentially. He's been amazing, and it's not like I've only just met him. We've known each other so long that when it got romantic it didn't feel rushed or too soon or anything. It just felt normal, really.'

'Right,' I say. I don't know how else to respond.

'I was thinking that he could come over one day, when you're here, so you could get to know him. He's going to be a part of the baby's life. We both want it.'

'As a dad?' I ask, and it's a question that sneaks out before I can stop myself.

She shrugs, but not dismissively. Kindly. I know her well enough that I get that she's trying to soften the blow. There's no reason she shouldn't get everything she wants. I just wish I could too.

'He's asked me to marry him and I've said yes. You're off the hook, you know – if you want to be,' she declares. 'There's absolutely no obligation. I'm fine. This is less than ideal for you. I'm not trying to trap you. I'm not expecting anything from you.'

I want to tell her that she can expect everything from me, but I don't. I wipe my hands on a piece of kitchen towel and nod, absorbing what she's saying. Finally, I settle on the only absolute truth I can say with conviction.

'I'd like to meet Sandeep too,' I say. Then I add: 'Let's take it from there.'

* * *

'But you've only been in London ten minutes,' my mother says to me as she clears away my plate. She's fed me a full English and a cup of tea in a giant *Sports Direct* mug. I don't think she's made me a fry-up since I was a teenager, but today, because I've said I've got news, she's pulled out all the stops.

I pick up my cuppa and take a big gulp now it's at the right temperature. It buys me some time, too. I've not exactly been looking forward to this.

'Well,' I start. 'As it happens. I've got a bit of an unexpected responsibility.'

My mum looks at my stepdad pointedly and when I clock it says plainly, 'Is this about Millie and the baby?'

I furrow my brow. 'You know about the baby?'

'Saw her in Asda,' Mum says. 'You can't tell from the front, but when she walked away her walk was different.'

'And she told you . . . ?' I falter. 'You understand that I'm the father?'

'Mother's intuition.'

'Right,' I say. I assumed I'd get fireworks. An argument. A big old telling-off. Everybody seems remarkably calm. I say so, out loud.

My mother shrugs, my dirty plate still in hand. 'Nobody can be mad about a baby, can they?' she says, plainly.

I don't mean for it to come out, but it does: 'I was pretty mad when I found out.' When Steve and Mum look at me like I'm the devil I clarify: 'It was the shock. It's not exactly the perfect family set-up, is it?'

'Let me get rid of this,' Mum says, nodding at the scraps of my food. I wait for Steve to say something in her absence but I get nothing. He raised me – he isn't *Stepdad*, he's just *Dad*, really – but he'll often await Mum's nod that he's okay to express an opinion to us. Like me and Ollie are her boys first, but we get to be his by a close second. I wonder if all mothers are like that with their children. I've got nothing else to compare it to. I don't know my biological dad, nor his second family.

'So you reckon you'll move back, do you?' Mum says, as she pops down a plate of digestives arranged in a circle on a doily-topped plate.

'I mean,' I say, 'Millie is having my baby. I sort of have to, don't I?'

Mum narrows her eyes. 'And this other fella – this Sandeep. You don't think he might get in the way of you playing happy families?'

'Are you saying I *shouldn't* get involved with raising my own child?' I ask in a measured tone. 'You're going to be grandparents. I thought you'd be thrilled!'

Mum exchanges a look with Steve, issuing silent permission for him to speak. 'Nobody would blame you if you didn't,' he says. 'In theory, of course you should move back and be in your child's life. But from what your mum heard from Sally-Anne—'

'Who sees Jeanette every Sunday evening for darts,' Mum interrupts, referring to Millie's mum.

'It's really serious with Sandeep. You're not biologically my kids, you and Ollie, but I'd take a bullet for you, wouldn't I? If she's marrying this man, it's going to . . .'

He looks to Mum.

'Edge you out a bit, that's all,' Mum finishes, sighing and coming to sit beside me on the sofa. 'We know it was never right between you and Millie – we know you were unhappy, especially towards the end.'

'And so all we mean,' Steve says, leaning forward to put a

hammy palm on my knee, 'is that the baby is being taken care of. Millie is being taken care of. We're managing our own expectations, too, about being grandparents. If you and Millie were together the pair of you would be popping over all the time, but if there's Jeanette and Clive, and then Sandeep's parents too, we'll be pushed down the list.'

'So I should just let them get on with it? Let another man raise my kid?'

The penny is dropping now, and I'm able to access the anger that I'm pretty sure is two hundred per cent justified. The thing with parents is that they know us, and love us, and value us and they raised us and so should know us best. It's easy to default to what our parents think because when you're a kid, what they say is the law, and the world. So it doesn't come naturally for me to tell them that they're out of their minds.

'Mum, you can't be serious. I mean – Steve has been everything to us, but you can't say that's the preferable choice, surely?'

'Have you ever felt less than totally loved by him?' Mum says, and I acknowledge that I haven't. Dad did a runner and Steve stepped up, and once, drunk at my cousin Flora's wedding, she did once tell me that she shudders to think how different everything could have been, that Dad leaving was the best thing that ever happened. The memory comes back to me in technicolour.

'You think this baby would be better with Sandeep than me? You think I'm as bad as Dad?' I press.

'No, no, love, of course not.' She puts her arm around me. 'All I mean is that you've got options, and we support those options. Moving back here when you're so full of life, now – nobody would expect that. You can come up every other weekend for the day and spend time with the baby, see what happens. If Millie does need you more, then think about moving. But we're just worried it's going to go the other way for you – that she's actually not going to need you very much at all.'

I can't believe what I'm hearing. Millie is telling me I don't have to get involved, my parents are telling me I don't have to get involved . . . this feels like the twilight zone. I've made a baby with a woman who I did love, once, but I feel like the protagonist in a Greek tragedy, the chorus telling me in surround sound that that doesn't matter and I can pretend it's not happening, if I like. It's all so bizarre.

After another awkward hour of hashing out my responsibility in everything, I finally go to bed. When I can't sleep, I pull out my phone and do some googling, plugging *how do dads bond with their baby* into the search bar.

The measure of it is basically cuddles. Dads need to cuddle their kid loads. Which of course means actually being in the presence of my child – there's no hugging over FaceTime, is there. In a forum for single dads somebody has posted about getting 'skin-to-skin' contact, too.

Yo, it sounds crazy but you've gotta tell the midwife it's what you want!! That little fresh-out-the-oven bb has got to feel your heartbeat and learn what you smell like. They do that with Mummy all the time when they breastfeed but Daddy gotta get his too! Real talk!

Honestly, what made me feel closest to my son was done even before he was born. I was so so scared that I wouldn't know what to do with him, or he wouldn't like me or that we wouldn't bond since I didn't grow him in my body for basically most of a year. They say women become mums as soon as they know they're pregnant, but men become dads only when the thing is born. I didn't want to miss out on a second. I read that babies can hear from like, 4 months or something really early like that, so I'd talk to her bump all the time, reading books to it in bed and singing wake-up songs in the morning. Sang every lyric of Frank Ocean's first album to him almost every day, and I swear down (he's almost a year old) if we put that on in his room he calms down immediately. Coincidence? I don't think so!!!

Touch is so important – even as they get older and you don't want to be carrying them all the time – touching their face, tickling their hand or toes, all of that . . . It sounds so lame but I do it all the time and I can feel the bond getting stronger.

I'm known as the baby whisperer in our house. Our daughter wants Mommy for almost everything – except when she's upset by something, and then only Daddy can fix it. My girlfriend hates it!! So I'm not allowed to say out loud how needed it makes me feel because it upsets her, but it's true, I do. She's 3 soon and still calls for me in the night or when she has a boo-boo, and her favourite thing to do is hold either side of my ugly old bearded face and push her forehead to mine. It melts me every time. I think about her on her wedding day. I know it's so archaic and marriage will probably be a dead concept by the time she's old enough but I just think about holding her even when she's grown, twirling her around the dance floor in

a white dress and putting my forehead to hers, to tell her
that I'll never not be her daddy.

Shit. A big fat splash of something pulls me out of the forum and back into the single camp bed pulled out in Steve's 'office'. I'm crying. The splash is a tear, and then another one, and another one. I use my fingers to blot them away, and it's so clear to me then, in that moment, what I want and how it's going to go from here. Everyone else is wrong. I get to be in this kid's life. I'm going to move back to Liverpool. I'll leave London and face up to my responsibilities. There's absolutely no doubt.

I call Millie.

'Hello,' she says, obviously confused as to why I'd be calling out of the blue when texting exists, but too polite to ask as much. 'Are you okay?'

'Millie,' I say, urgently. 'I want fifty-fifty, all the way, okay? I want this baby to call me Daddy, and Sandeep is going to have to figure out another name to go by okay? I'm Daddy. Me.'

'Okay,' she says, simply. 'I hear you.'

'I'm Daddy,' I repeat again, and I think I'm waiting for her to fight me on it. I hear her excuse herself over the noise of the telly, telling Sandeep she'll be right back, and a door close behind her.

'Listen,' she says, and I almost don't let her talk because I don't want her to try and convince me of anything other than what I've decided. But her tone – she's speaking softly. I swallow, forcing myself to let her say her piece. After all, I just did.

'I'm glad,' she tells me. 'I could never have asked this of you, and I wouldn't have done. I love you. Not like I did.

Differently, now. But it's love, and it will never go away, and it's there because you're a good man, Nic. And I'd be an idiot not to want you around to show this little girl what that looks like.'

'But . . .' I say, 'why didn't you just tell me that?'

'I didn't want to ever wonder,' she says, kindly. 'You deserved to move and have the life you wanted for yourself. If there was a way for us to be in London, I'd consider that, but there just isn't. I want to be near Mum, my friends. My support network. But if you're going to move back here of your own accord, I won't ever let myself feel guilty about it. You're a big boy. A man. This is all on you. I offered you a get-out clause.'

'I don't think I was ever going to take it.'

'I know,' Millie says. 'Like I said: one of the good ones.'

I don't want to be edged out. I'm having a baby, and I'm going to be a father. And what's more, I'm going to be a brilliant one – close by. It's going to hurt, but I'm moving back home.

35

Ruby

'Oh, love,' JP says over, predictably, a cup of tea in his front room. 'I don't know what to tell you. What a choice to have to make.'

'Thanks, JP,' I say. 'I'm better than I was with it all.' I catch William's eye as he sets his phone down from where he's been typing something with a smile on his face.

'Sorry,' he says. 'I was listening. I promise.'

'Don't worry,' I insist. 'And I'm okay. The point, mister,' I gesture towards JP when I say this, 'is that you made me brave enough to put myself out there, and as you've extolled all along, that is the point, isn't it? So . . . I'm fine. I just wanted to come by and make sure that *you're* fine. We've been so worried. Paris wasn't at all what we expected. We're sorry if we caused you pain.'

JP has bombarded me with questions since I arrived, having got wind of my break-up via William, with the news that came via Harry. At first I felt selfish only talking about myself, but I think he's been grateful to have the distraction. I do need to know he's all right, though – or as all right as can be.

'No, no. You're not to take any responsibility at all. I asked you to take me there. I keep trying to remind myself of the exact same thing you are.' JP smiles. 'Trying is the point. Harder to remember when everything feels a bit shit, though, innit?'

I smile sadly. 'I can't imagine how you've been feeling,' I tell him. 'It's not fair, what happened.'

'No,' says JP. 'But we tried. We tried.'

'We did,' I agree. 'I just wish . . .'

JP shrugs. 'So do I,' he says. 'But wishing doesn't get you owt, does it?'

He meets my eye and pulls a face.

'Did Gramps tell you about the fundraiser?' William then asks, suddenly, changing the subject. I shake my head. 'Five grand for the cancer charity, for my uncle. Our target was only one, and we've got five! Because of the Instagram account!'

'Really?!' I say. I grab my phone to pull up the account. Harry and I did what we talked about, cutting a series of short clips, out of context but each one sounding fun and wise, and people are sharing them and tagging us. It's all quite exciting. Our follower count is up to six thousand, now, so every day we add another clip, and try to push it higher. Harry and I have had brainstorm after brainstorm to figure out how to action all the notes we got from the initial screening, and in the meantime we decided that sharing more on the Finding JP's Girl account means we keep building an audience for the project when it's done. Plus, it keeps us accountable.

I click on the link we've still left in the bio for the fund-raiser and see the total.

'Five and a half,' I exclaim. 'Oh my God!'

'A tidy sum,' notes JP. 'He'd be happy.'

'That's really cool,' I say. 'That's all because of you, JP. You're a gift to this world. I promise you, you are.'

He shakes his head, but smiles too, as close to accepting the compliment as we're likely to get.

'Onwards,' he says. And then, to William: 'With another cup of tea, I reckon.'

William departs to the kitchen with a tut and half-hearted grumbles of being like the in-house waiter service and JP takes the opportunity of his absence to whisper, 'Can you keep a secret?'

I tell him I can.

'I reckon he's courting Amelie's granddaughter. I hear him on the phone, whispering in French. I'm sure he said *Sophie*.'

My jaw drops. 'Really?' I ask. 'He's still talking to her?'

'I'm certain of it,' he says with a wink. 'Every day since we came back.'

'That's two weeks,' I remark. 'He's spoken to her every day for two weeks?'

William pops his head around the door. 'Are you staying for lunch?' he asks, brightly. 'It's tuna paste sandwiches, everyone's collective favourite!'

Harry and I are assisting with class at four, as requested by Janet, but I've got time.

'Sure,' I tell him. 'That would be lovely. Thanks.'

JP does an enthusiastic thumbs up once he's gone again, signalling his enthusiasm about what he's just revealed, and I stifle a laugh. It's nice to see him as his old self. It's comforting to know that for both of us, life will go on.

* * *

The module Harry and I were asked to assist with is an undergraduate module called *Intro to Documentary Film-making*. There's a small payment involved, but more than that it proves that the head of department really does believe in our potential and our value. It's an honour to be asked. We don't have to do too much – sit in on the class, be available for three office hours a week to help out anyone who has questions or needs guidance on what's been asked, and at Easter we'll have to mark some essays that make up fifty per cent of their grade. There's a set syllabus to go off, with notes from previous graduate students who've done it before us, and so it's really less about what information we deliver and more about how we do it – namely, with enthusiasm and kindness, was Janet's instruction.

'That was pretty cool, wasn't it?' Harry says afterwards, as we watch the hundred or so students file out of the seminar hall and the lecturer thanks us and says she'll see us next week.

'Yeah,' I say. 'It's bonus learning, too – I didn't know that stuff about late-nineteenth-century film and cinema inspiring a new diversity of writing.'

'My favourite geek.' Harry smiles.

'Always and forever.' I smile back. 'So . . .' I say, glancing at the lecture hall clock. 'It's half five. Should we do the student union and have this chat over a drink, or risk a coffee and sit in the atrium?'

'Atrium,' Harry says. 'I want your head clear.'

It takes thirty seconds after we sit down with our decaf lattes to understand why.

'That's me,' I say. 'That's footage of me,' I say, looking at his laptop where he's pulled up two months' worth of rough footage. 'There's so much footage of me,' I add, using my right hand to move the mouse to check what I'm saying is right, 'that you've given me my own folder.'

'Correct,' Harry says. 'And I'm telling you: this is the solution.'

'I mean . . .' I start. 'I could act like I need some big persuasion, but honestly, whatever makes the doc sing. I'll do whatever it takes.'

'Okay great,' Harry says. 'You feeling up to being on camera now? For a formal sit-down?'

'Now?'

'You look great, before you start.'

'I mean, okay. Let's do this before I change my mind then.'

'Superb news. I've booked a filming room, just in case.'

We film for about an hour, on and off, with Harry turning the tables to ask me questions, with me just off centre of the shot, looking at him left of the middle like we had JP do too.

'And so that's the long and short of it,' I say, wrapping up a summary of my own love life. 'I got out of a really crappy non-relationship with a man I never should have been with in the first place and decided to take myself seriously. I had a one-night stand who I kept bumping into, and it was JP who taught me that no matter how much I think I need to protect my heart, what I actually need to do is play faster and looser with it. Almost like building up heart loving strength. If we act like our love, and our attention, is some rare, must-be-hard-won thing that's finite, we end up more miserable than if we just take a chance and give it away freely. I did that. But then his situation has changed with the baby. It's okay. I'm okay. Well, I mean . . . I will be. I kind of get a kick out of JP being proud of me for it too. *Almost Doesn't Count*? I don't know. I think it all counts. I'm learning all the time.'

'Okay, cut,' Harry says, when I've finished.

'Have you ever seen *When Harry Met Sally*?' I ask. As I've been talking, I've formulated my own idea about what could really make the documentary perfect. Harry issues me with a look. 'Okay, yes, of course you have. My apologies,' I say. 'Your film education is spotless.' Harry nods, but doesn't interrupt me. He's all action, now – he's excited about how we're wrapping up JP's story in a comment about my own love life, but I want to go one better.

'You know how they intersperse the story with snippets of other people's love stories? Maybe we need something like that.' Harry narrows his eyes. 'Or other people's reservations about love?' I add. 'That gives what we're trying to do context. Get a bunch of talking heads. People could even send little videos of themselves through Instagram – don't forget we have that ready-built audience of people invested in what we're doing – or they could send in their stories written and we can put them on screen or voice-over. That might be easier in terms of how much time we have left. But if we set the narrative arc up as: so many of us guard our hearts thinking it will stop us from getting hurt. Enter, me, whose wider story we can tell if you really think it's interesting enough, which . . . well . . . Let's see how that shakes out in an edit. We're getting down to the wire now. Juxtapose my reticence to let Nic into my life – or anybody for that matter because now I'm saying all this, I have to ask myself why I chose to fall in love with a man with a girlfriend? Did I pick Abe precisely because I wouldn't have to open myself up to him? Oh my God.' My words are crashing into each other now. 'This is like therapy! Shit! Okay. Where was I?'

'Juxtaposition.'

'Okay, right, yes, so a bunch of people saying they guard

their heart, me exploring guarding my heart and how my thoughts on that change as I meet JP. We show JP's journey: telling us about Amelie, the search for her, and the heart-breaking dénouement of what happened in Paris. Then the footage of me and JP chatting about life, love, the meaning of it, something uplifting about JP choosing to live his life as open as ever, despite being robbed of the one thing he's wanted for almost his whole life . . .'

'And bam, by homing in on the smaller stories of you both, we speak to a wider, more universal audience, exactly as we hoped, like this is crazy how it's all come together, imploring them, through our powerful, authentic, uplifting documentary . . .' Harry says.

'To be brave in love themselves. Humans are supposed to get battered and bloody and bruised in their pursuit of happiness,' I say. 'End scene.'

'I think that's it,' Harry says. 'We've got everything we need. We don't need to film anything else.'

36

Nic

'Right,' says Jackson. 'Follow my instructions to a tee, all right? There's an art to this.'

'Yes, boss,' I say, deseeding the pile of peppers he's given me as he sweats onion in a pan to make his self-proclaimed 'famous chilli'.

We chop and cook in companionable silence, music playing, focusing on our tasks. Then Jackson says, 'So, now all the dust is settling . . . how are you? Like . . . really?'

It's been three weeks since the big bombshell.

'I'm . . . I dunno. Still working everything out. I need to have a conversation with my boss and see what my options are. The job is actually the least interesting thing about my life down here so it's the thing I would be least sad to say goodbye to – but, okay, so what? I ask my old boss for my job back?'

'Does the prospect of that excite you?' he asks, opening up the bag of mince we picked up from the butcher to add to the onions. I put the diced peppers into a bowl and start to slice the courgettes as thinly as I can without losing a finger.

'Going back? Absolutely not,' I reply. 'I just keep thinking, surely there's a way to do this that feels like a step forward instead of a massive leap back.'

He uses the spoon to point at me. 'Now you're talking,' Jackson says. 'I was about to say the same thing. You've loved being here because you've gotten to try new things, try on new parts of your personality, even try looking a bit different.'

'Yeah,' I say, slowly, because at first it feels like an accusation. 'I'm not trying to be somebody I'm not though.'

'I know that, idiot,' Jackson says, firing up another pan to cook off the vegetables I've prepped for him. 'But the things that did that for you – can you name them?'

My cheeks sting hot.

'You know it started with Ruby,' I say. 'And to be fair, you, that night I got the sofa, inviting me over. I made my first friend, and it felt pretty easy. Everyone back home is coupled up, and not being part of a couple means I quickly felt like an outsider in my own friendship group. It feels more common to be single later down here.'

'And the guys at your old job?'

'Yeah, some of them were cool, but it's not like I'm twenty-five. I'm management, now, so it's frowned upon not to have a sense of boundaries.'

'I get that,' says Jackson. 'It's the polar opposite to my job where we're out with the talent all the time and have to be almost like BFFs with them. It can be quite fake, really.'

'Do you enjoy it though?'

'It makes good money,' says Jackson. 'And I get to shape culture, in a way. I know that sounds wanky, but this new

303

generation of influencers: they're not just hawking handbags and spot creams, they're activists and they stand for something. One of our clients has been on the bestseller list for nearly half the year with her book on gender theory, and another just went viral for a Ted Talk on helping new mothers back into the workforce.'

'Okay, yeah – that's pretty badass.'

He takes the veggies off the heat and boils the kettle, getting out a jug and some stock cubes once he's finished.

'Do you have to move back to Liverpool?' he says. 'Do you even have to leave London? It's a quick train ride, all things considered.'

'I know for sure I don't want to be a part-time dad,' I say. 'I'd like to be a drive away, not a scheduled train trip away.'

'So maybe the chat you need to have is with a recruitment specialist, not your old boss . . .'

I nod, enjoying what he's saying.

'That, I can do,' I say. 'Yes. That makes total sense.'

'I'm not just a pretty face, see.' He smiles.

'Oh,' I say back. 'I thought people said you're not *even* a pretty face.'

'Ha, ha.'

The chilli needs time to simmer and so Jackson puts the TV on and I google recruitment agents on my phone, because it's really not a bad shout. It's important to remember I don't *have* to slip back into how everything was. I can get a new job, see about a dodgeball team up there. I could live in a nice apartment by the water, even, spend weekends and maybe some weeknights with the baby. I need to talk to Millie officially, but I assume we'll be able to do a proper fifty-fifty arrangement. I've met Sandeep over FaceTime and I'm not worried about him taking over.

The more I talk about it, and the more time that passes, the more I can believe it might all be okay. I don't feel as hopeless, now.

Once we've had our chilli and I've issued several overt compliments to Jackson confirming that yes, it really is sublime and world-class and should be featured in a recipe book, somewhere, maybe Jamie Oliver's, or at a push Gordon Ramsay's, we head out. Millie says she doesn't want me holding her hand at her NCT class. She says it would be like a budget version of an ITV drama where she has her right hand held by her lover, and the left by the baby daddy she's no longer with, and none of the nurses knowing who to refer to as 'daddy'.

'There must be something you can go to on your own,' she said, her face as neutral and pragmatic as ever over Skype as I checked in to see how she's feeling. 'Or with a friend?' she added.

And that's how I end up in a cold, draughty hut in Bethnal Green with Jackson, who is laid between my legs pretending he's in active labour.

'Oh for God's sake,' I hiss at him as I mop his brow with a pretend damp flannel. 'Can you stop making this worse than it already is?' I'm so embarrassed that I'm hissing.

What we're actually at, in lieu of my going with Millie to her class, is a very specialist sort of NCT for couples using a surrogate – it's mostly same sex couples, but there's a few hetero couples too, all of whom have assembled to feel part of a more traditional journey despite the fact that nobody in the room is pregnant themselves. There's weak tea that tastes like it hasn't so much been made from a boiling kettle so much as tepid bath water, and biscuits that, when I reached out to pick one up, Jackson batted out my hand.

'Absolutely not,' he muttered to me. 'I could help you with the clam, but who knows what you'll catch from a limp rich tea on an unwashed community centre plate.'

I dropped the biscuit in question, watching it later get picked up by a squat man with a teardrop tattoo on his left cheek, here with his partner Rochelle, a trapeze artist who genuinely once ran away and joined the circus. If Millie wanted to avoid Sunday night drama by disinviting me to her events, I've managed to rustle up my own Netflix comedy special.

'In this moment,' says Derek, the balding yet strangely virile-seeming chap running the event, 'hormones run wild, like horses dancing in a forest's stream, dazzling in delight and causing all sorts of sensations. Your job is to be the calm farmhand, here with food offered on an outstretched hand, fully prepared to be bitten.'

I do not get the metaphor *at all*, and as he clocks me and my confused face he adds: 'Which is to say, if the person giving birth wants to scream blue murder at you, it's your job to take it on the chin and await further instruction. You are a cool, calm leader, here to remain steadfast in the face of the arrival of new life. When the aliens come you do not scream, you do not yell, for they come in peace. Same with babies.'

'Okay,' Jackson whispers over his shoulder to me. 'He's even losing me, now. Did you shag E.T.?'

'Breathe,' intones Derek, taking up his place behind Velma, his wife and partner in running the class, who is currently on all fours and executing variations of a cat-cow yoga pose, occasionally issuing low, guttural moans. Apparently it's rare for women to give birth on their backs like they do on TV, and it's our job as birth partners to support any position that feels comfortable, even if that means taking the weight-bearing load of a squat, or seeing the whole shop window from behind as they roll on an exercise ball. I don't even know if I'm going to be in the room when all the action happens – Millie hasn't decided yet.

Velma starts to howl, then, moving to lie on her back with her legs in the air, gently rocking from side to side on her spine.

'Ow-owo-owwwwww!' Jackson mimics, and I hold the 'cold compress flannel' (it's actually just a bit of paper towel as we play make-believe) over his mouth and say, 'Don't even think about it, pal.'

He pulls it down.

'The way I see it,' he tells me, 'is that you can either surrender to this madness and get fully involved, or keep acting like there's a stick in your arse and end up giving yourself a stress nosebleed.'

I know he's right. He's very good at reminding me that life is ludicrous, so one may as well get involved.

'Ow-ow-owwwwww!' I howl, and Derek looks across the room in surprise and I think I'm going to get told off for taking the piss, but his face bursts into a smile.

'Excellent,' he says. 'Yes! Try that – what our glorious friend Nic is doing. Howl to the moon, embody the energy of your warrior, embrace the chaos!' he instructs, and before I know it everyone is squealing in the highest notes of their register, and it feels pretty damned cathartic.

'That was good,' says Jackson after, as we wander through town and to the pub. It's a cliché, two blokes worried about the future getting a pint after a particularly traumatising

307

unveiling of the self and its vulnerabilities, but one we're happy to roll with. 'It was helpful, I reckon, in that way that nothing that happens at the actual birth can be as bonkers as what you've just weathered.'

'I knew you were hamming it up to make me uncomfortable!' I say, and he breaks into a mischievous smile and shrugs.

'Gotta find the bright side, haven't you?' he says. 'And I will say, mate, you were a trouper in there. You're being a trouper about all of it.'

The thing about life after formal education is that nobody gives you an appraisal on how you do life – after school there's no marks out of ten or grades on a scale of A to Ungraded that let you know you're doing it right. And I've been so pent up and stressed, what I've needed is somebody to say: *Hey, this is a shock, and not ideal, but you're doing it well anyway.*

'Thanks,' I say, swilling my drink in my glass. 'That means a lot, to be honest.'

'Good,' he says. 'You should be able to recognise that I mean it because it's true. That's very emotionally healthy.'

He says that in a doctor-to-his-patient-on-the-fainting-couch sort of a way, so we're both clear he's being both genuine, and tongue-in-cheek about how he's done it.

'Don't,' I say, shaking my head. 'I got one of those Timehop alerts the other day? It's a photo of a bunch of us at a wedding a year ago, and I'm so thin. I just look miserable, even though I'm smiling. And I *was*: I had anxiety, mood swings, loss of appetite – all because I knew I wasn't happy. Anyway, my point is . . . well, I don't know what my point is.'

'This isn't a full-circle moment, you know,' Jackson says softly. 'You don't have to go back to being that guy again just because you're physically back there. There's the freedom of commitment, too, innit? I admire you.'

'That doesn't make sense,' I say. 'How is there freedom in commitment? They're literally opposites.'

'Au contraire,' says Jackson. 'That's the lie we're told. But actually, holding ourselves back from commitment is the true constriction. When we fully invest ourselves in something, we are free to bloom, unrestricted, and so there's a beautiful sovereignty to it when we decide to go all in.'

I look at him.

'Bloody hell,' I say. 'Did you just make that up? That's brilliant. It's so true!'

'The girls got me a subscription to a psychology magazine a few birthdays ago. I've learnt a few things.'

'I'll say,' I agree. 'The freedom of commitment.'

'The freedom of commitment,' Jackson says again, and we let the magnitude of his theory sink in.

It's dark by the time we finish our drinks and head for the tube. We're messing about, swapping quips and jokes and Jackson keeps calling me Daddy, which was cute at first, then annoying, and now he keeps saying it with a strange sexual sound in the vowels. He doesn't stop, and I finally have to issue a good-natured punch to his shoulder as I tell him to pack it in.

'Sorry, Daddy!' he says, stepping out of the way of another one of my shoulder punches and into the road, so that he's almost mowed down by a double-decker bus.

'Jackson!' I cry, reaching out for the corner of his coat and pulling as hard as I can.

'Dude.' He laughs, stumbling into me. 'Chill your beans. I'm fine.'

Another inch more and he'd have been flattened to the tarmac. His cheeks have flushed like he knows it.

'See?' he presses, flinging out his arms and doing a little hop to one side.

Everything after that happens in slow motion. I see it frame by frame but can't do anything about it.

Jackson spins on his heel. Another bus misses him by less than an inch – again. But then he looks down to his arm in disbelief at the second close call of it all, then hears me say his name and looks up with a face of shock and euphoria.

And then instead of walking towards me on the pavement he falls to the ground, a cyclist flying over his head, kicking the side of his face as they crumple in a heap beside the kerb, the bike splaying out beside his leg and Jackson's eyes closing, knocked unconscious before he's even hit the ground.

37

Ruby

How do you feel about going out-out? ☺

It's Harry. At 8.34 p.m. I am in my pyjamas, toothpaste deposited onto three spots I appear to have been growing throughout the day and half a tub of Ben and Jerry's still to plough through on my lap. I'm watching *Dawson's Creek* – the episode where Joey enters the Miss Capeside pageant and Dawson realises she's beautiful for the first time. I text back: *Is this meant for me?*

I only have one friend here, doofus. Yes, it's for you.

I am puzzled. Going out-out is not something we have done before, nor talked about potentially ever doing, nor have referenced ever.

Beau's friends are going out for somebody's birthday, and I just thought maybe you'd want to come with? We BOTH need to let our hair down. WDYT???

I start to write a message saying I'll just see him tomorrow – I don't want to go out. Why would I want to schlep out into the cold when Joey is about to give her speech about it just being hairspray and lipstick? Why would I want a hangover tomorrow, when I've been loving early to bed and early to rise, getting all my work done with a clear head and fresh eyes, rinsing every moment with as much clarity as possible? And then I remember the Year of Me, and saying yes and taking chances and sometimes doing things just to see what happens, realising that all my reasons for not going out make me sound like I'm a forty-five-year-old exhausted by her three kids, dog, and absent husband. Isn't the point that I'm supposed to be out having fun? And so I delete my sarcastic response and instead try with earnestness: *I am surprising myself here, but: yes? I'll come?*

The question marks make you seem super invested, Harry types back. *Meet us at the edge of campus, where Mick's coffee cart is. 9.30. We're going to Mayfield Depot first, and then we've got VIP for Chinawhite, apparently.*

I take a last spoonful of ice cream and hit pause on my laptop, then pad through to my wardrobe. I've got a few 'dressy' things I could wear, but nothing majorly fancy. I was pretty ruthless when I left Maple Avenue, streamlining as much as I could because I knew I wouldn't have room nor occasion to wear full bodycon and heels. I left most of it for Candice – although a lot of it was cheap tat. I'm pretty sure cheap tat is exactly what tonight calls for though. My hair is clean enough, but I have a hot shower and shave my legs, moisturising all over and whilst waiting for the steam to clear to do my make-up. If I put some dry shampoo on my roots and a bit of argan oil through the ends I can pass off the volume as artfully dishevelled, and it's easier to pick an outfit with lipstick on. I choose a backless top with a deceptive high neck and full balloon sleeves from the front, high-waisted careful. I can love him, and not be with him. I know that seems controversial but it's possible.'

'Like Kevin Costner and Whitney Houston at the end of *The Bodyguard*,' Jackson offers.

'Exactly that,' I say.

'Didn't he drive to Manchester to come get you when Jackson had the accident?' Candice says.

'Haven't you been sharing a bed?' Jackson says.

'Don't you panic when he's not nearby, and jerk your head up all fast and crazy until you locate him again?' asks Candice.

I hold up my hands, laughing. 'Okay,' I say. 'I mean this with all the love in the world but both of you need to piss right off, okay? Just piss off.'

'Which bit do you think hit a nerve?' Jackson stage-whispers to Candice, whilst maintaining eye contact with me.

'I don't think it was anything we said,' Candice stage-whispers back. 'I think she just misses her *boyfriend*,' she adds, using the word with all the force she knows it will elicit from me. I give them the middle finger.

When Candice and I have to leave for Jackson to get taken to the loo, she holds my arm and says: 'Can we have that chat now?'

I look at her. 'Yeah,' I say. 'Shall we get coffee? There's a Costa downstairs.'

We get our drinks – Candice pays – and we shuffle about getting comfortable with chairs and coats and finding some-where for our bags.

'Okay look . . .' Candice begins, when it's apparent we're all sorted and there's nothing else to do but address each other. 'I just wanted to say—'

'You know you don't have to, don't you?'

'Don't interrupt, okay?'

I make a zipping motion across my lips and mime throwing away the key.

'You didn't deserve me ghosting you. That wasn't cool. I know it wasn't. I just . . . I don't know. I missed you, and I felt like you didn't miss me, and I felt stupid for that. And then at the party with Nic I got jealous, which I'm not proud to admit but I did. I couldn't understand why you'd have time for him, but not time for me. So I punished you. But maybe really I was punishing myself?'

'Oh, Candice,' I say. 'Of course I miss you. I hate that this is what it took for us to get to see each other properly. There's so much I've wanted to tell you about.'

'Me too,' she says. 'And I know things change. We're growing up. We've got dreams. Well, at least you have. I don't know what I'm going to do with my life, but I can't envy you for your ambition. Ambition isn't bad. You moving to do this master's wasn't bad. I was just being a big baby. I was having a tantrum and I didn't use my words to tell you. And that was shitty, and I'm sorry.'

'It's okay,' I tell her. 'I know it's been hard. But are you okay? Like actually okay? Jackson said . . .'

'That I've been drinking a lot and shagging Jacques? Yeah. I have. I broke rule number one.'

'Was it worth it?' I ask, trying not to sound judgemental.

'No,' she admits. 'Hence why it's time to move out and move on. Jackson hasn't been home much, but when he has, he's been kind. I think he's been waiting it out. Waiting for me to get it all out of my system.'

'A true friend,' I say. 'Knowing you'll come back to him.'

'Am I forgiven?' she asks, sadly.

jeans and my leather-heeled boots. With some nice jewellery I surprise myself with how like my old self I look. I haven't been fancy in months – it's been all big jumpers and messy buns. Harry is right. I have needed this.

'Oi oi!' he says as I approach the group waiting at the allocated place. 'Here she is. You look really pretty.' Harry gives me a kiss on each cheek flamboyantly, and I can tell he's already had a few drinks.

'Ay up,' I say. 'Why do I feel like I need to play catch-up?'

'Because you do,' the man beside him says. He's petite, glasses and cultivated blonde stubble contrasting with his obvious chiselled physique. He has delicate hands, like a pianist, that he outstretches as he grins, friendly, and says, 'I'm Beau. Harry's boyfriend.'

At the word boyfriend I shoot a look at Harry. He raises his eyebrows in pride, and then pulls Beau in for a kiss.

'I would say I've heard so much about you,' I tell him, 'but Harry has kept his cards very close to his chest.'

'Yes,' Beau says. 'He's a squirrelly sort, isn't he?'

Harry juts out his front teeth and pulls his hands to his mouth, a terrible impression from a man at least four drinks to the wind.

'Let's have some fun tonight, Ruby-Booby. Come here. I love you. You know that, don't you? I love you so much. We're going to take over the world, you know. Do you know that? I know that.'

I give him a kiss on his cheek, aware that his effusive profession has drawn the attention of the others. There's a tall, dark-haired man holding a rolled-up cigarette, two women holding hands, and a spitting image of Beau that confuses me so much the look on my face must be obvious as I whip back to check I'm not imagining things.

313

'Seb,' he says. 'Beau's twin brother.'

The others are identified as Manroop, and Leticia and Woody.

'Let's crack on,' says Manroop to us all. 'It's Baltic.'

We all chat as we wait to get into the bar, passing around a flask of vodka between us that burns as I swallow. We're a bit further removed from the student area where the undergrads go out, and it's a strange feeling to be surrounded by people who obviously work for a living, some in suits having obviously not been home after the office, people from more creative jobs in shirts and chinos with trainers. That will be me again, soon. I'm six months in with six more to go, which means every day that passes is one less day in the safe cocoon of a university and one day closer to hopefully making this documentary stuff work for me. Somehow.

'You're not drunk enough,' Harry says, wagging a finger at me. 'Stop thinking about work.'

'I wasn't thinking about wo—'

He thrusts the flask at me, not buying what I'm saying, and I take another fiery gulp.

'Harry says you're a fellow film-maker?' Manroop offers, as I pass the flask off to Beau and his brother.

'Yeah,' I nod. 'Trying to be.'

'He got us all to follow the Instagram account,' he continues. 'I have no idea what it was about, but he stood over us and made sure we did it.'

'I hope you like what you see,' I tell him. 'Waste of a follow if you don't.'

'I don't really use social a lot. I prefer the real world.'

I screw up my face at him. A man with a topknot who protests about social media and thinks he's special for knowing it's rotting our brains? That's so boring to me. I can tell he wants to get chatting, but he is *so* not my type at all. Too self-aware, trying too hard. Not like Harry, being his loveable self, or somebody like Nic, awkward but genuine, asking questions to find out things, not asking questions as a way to talk about himself.

'What?' Manroop says.

I shake my head. 'Nothing,' I say. 'It's just, everyone knows social media is a black hole and a time suck.'

'So why is everyone on it then?'

'Including you?' I bat back. 'You just said you followed us.'

'But I try not to,' he counters. 'My mate, he's got a screen time report of like, four hours a day. That's over a hundred hours a month. Imagine what he could do with over a hundred hours a month!'

'Maybe that's the point,' I say. 'He doesn't want to be maximising his time, achieving every second. Maybe smart phones are the new TV. It's just we don't get screen time reports for watching TV, do we?'

'No.' He laughs. 'Just that little box that comes up and says *are you still watching?* when you got past five episodes of something.'

'Ahh,' I say, and we're at the front of the queue, now, our group next to be let inside. 'So you aren't so perfect. You do have some bad habits . . .'

'I never said anyone had bad habits,' Manroop defends. 'Only that it's a lot, isn't it, four hours a day?'

'But four hours of TV is okay? That's different?'

'If you're learning something, yes.'

I laugh. 'How do you know your friend isn't following accounts about something he's passionate about? That he hasn't found his community online through a special hashtag that's unleashed a whole new world to him?' Manroop goes

315

to speak but I don't let him interrupt. 'You know social media is a key element for grassroots political movements, don't you? Facebook and Twitter played a key and meaningful role in bringing down the Mubarak regime in Egypt.'

'Russia targets the LGBTQ+ through the rainbows they use in social media profiles.'

'Black Lives Matter.'

'That's true.' He nods. 'Videos of injustice make people act in a way reported still images in newspapers don't.'

'If it ever gets to the newspapers,' I say. 'Anyway, I don't even have skin in this game. I don't care if you hate social media or not. I just think it's a weird hill to die on – making out like people who enjoy it are stupid.'

'That's not quite what I said, is it?'

He's smiling as he speaks. I'm getting all riled up by this pompous idiot saying things just to maximise his oxygen use, and he's laughing.

'You're debating me for sport, aren't you?' I say, my tone neutral.

'Just killing time until we're at the bar.' He shrugs, and with that the bouncer gestures for us to go inside, where the low lights and loud music kill any chance of meaningful conversation at all – which is just as well. I was almost in danger of enjoying the arsehole, which would have been a step backwards in terms of my taste in men, that's for sure.

Seb gets the first round in, drinks for everyone with a matching shot.

'I haven't done shots in months,' I tell Harry as Seb sets down a tray at our table.

'Not exactly JP's scene, is it?' He grins, as he raises a glass to signal to us all that it's time to get tipsy – or tipsier, to be fair – and I take it down like a champ. It's a nice place, all dark wood and glass front and bar staff whose employment is undoubtedly based mostly on how attractive they are. We sit around a big round table, talking across it, trying to keep everyone involved but ultimately ending up slipping into a two- or three-person offshoot conversation because the music keeps getting louder and we keep getting drunker and at some point Manroop is sat beside me asking how my night is going.

'Fine,' I say. 'Good!' I have to shout to be heard so he leans in close enough for the citrus tang of his cologne to permeate the air around me.

'I like your top!' he yells, and at first I think he says something about liking to mop, so he repeats himself and I look down at what I'm wearing and yell a thanks.

'The backless thing!' he continues. 'It's hot!'

I nod thank you, and realise his arm is snaked around over the back of the booth, a finger lightly tracing the side of my spine.

'I hope that's okay to say!' he continues to yell over the music. 'I just wasn't expecting Harry's friend to be you.'

I don't really know what to say. I do not fancy this man. Maybe the old me, the one who hadn't realised her worth and had never met Nic – been changed by Nic – the one who had never saw to it that she changed herself – maybe she'd flirt back with this man. But I don't want to. I don't want to pretend to appease him, or to prove to myself that somebody finds me attractive. The back-and-forth in the queue, the seedy comments that wouldn't sound seedy from somebody I actually like but from Manroop feel generic, designed to elicit a specific reaction from me that he's still waiting for as he dips his head to try and make eye contact.

I don't want any of it. I didn't come out for a man, to try and have a casual hook-up. I came out for me. To dance. To let loose.

'When are we going to the club?' I shout across the table, to anyone who might hear me.

Beau stands up and addresses us all: 'Now, little ones. Let's go!'

We pile out of the booth and work our way through bodies and tables to the outside, and I hook my arm into Harry's and walk ahead of the crowd, telling him: 'Do *not* leave me alone with Manroop, okay?'

Harry looks back over his shoulder.

'He's staring at us,' he says.

'He's vile,' I tell him. 'No, no, no.'

'Not even as a distraction from Nic?'

'Harry,' I tell him plainly. 'I don't need a distraction. I need to dance.'

Now we're talking. The club has three levels, each one playing a different sort of music with a different sort of vibe. We head to the top floor, where it's Nineties and early Noughties R 'n' B so we can bump and grind and drop it like it's hot. Just off from the dance floor we have a table, another booth wrapped around a big circular glass thing, and I have no idea who in the group knows somebody sending us champagne, but Harry assures me the tab is taken care of and all we need to do is have a nice time.

Manroop hasn't taken the hint, approaching Harry and I on the dance floor a few times, but I'm so into the music that I spin away from him without causing too much of a scene. The bass is loud and the room dark, occasionally lit up with laser and flashes of coloured light. It's busy, but not

38

Nic

She ignores my first calls. I mean, I assume she's ignoring them. We haven't been in touch since that day at the train station, almost a month ago now. I told Jackson not to fill me in on her life unless I explicitly asked, and that if I did explicitly ask, to remind me I don't really want to know.

Fuck, man. Jackson.

It was awful: the sound of the bike hitting his flesh; the bend of his leg as he lay on the ground, the lights of the ambulance; the cries of the person who hit him. I spent the whole ambulance ride thinking to myself: *This isn't happening, this isn't happening,* even though, on another level of thought, I knew it was, and that I needed to be calm and tell Jackson everything was going to be okay. I can't remember if I did or I didn't. I don't remember anything else.

At some point Jackson went one way and I was sent another to be checked over. It was after midnight when a nurse came to find me to say he was in a critical but stable condition, and that he was being closely monitored. He has a broken leg, sprained wrist, cracked ribs and lots of swelling. He seems to be responding to stimulation, but they won't know about any cognitive damage until he wakes up. That for now his coma is induced to make sure his body can heal. The nurse has to repeat all this three times for me to understand. They say his parents are coming. They accessed his emergency contact through his phone. I didn't know that was possible. I don't know what his parents look like, or what I'll say when they get here. I'm told to wait in the family area, since I'm the one who came in with him. It's got strip lighting and hard plastic chairs with arms. I couldn't lie out if I wanted to. I don't. I sit, a scratchy hospital blanket over my arms and legs, replaying everything over and over and over. I never saw the cyclist coming. If I'd have just looked to the left, I would have done. I could have stopped it. But I didn't look to the left, and now Jackson is hooked up to monitors and I'm not even able to see him.

It's not until 2 or 3 a.m. that I think to text Ruby. I hold my phone, the shakes I had earlier subsiding but still there. I should eat something. I'm in shock. Sugar? Do people eat something sweet after a shock?

Urgent, I type. *Call me back. It's Jackson.*

I unfollowed her everywhere I could and don't ask about her, but I never deleted her number. I thought about it. But I didn't.

Accident, I type. I can't make words stack up to make sentences.

Call me. Doesn't matter what time.

I flick the button at the side of my phone to make the ringer loud. I hold it. I wait. At 4 a.m. she rings.

'What's happened?' she says. 'I'm drunk. I'm sorry. Are you okay?'

'Jackson's been in an accident,' I say, my words sluggish, coming from somewhere not me.

'What?' she says. 'What do you mean?'

'He got hit by a cyclist who was going like, a million miles per hour or something crazy. She's unconscious too. I'm at the hospital now but I'm not family, so I don't know much else. I can't see him. I'm just waiting.'

'Are his parents there?' she asks.

'They're on their way.'

'Okay,' she says. She pauses. She's in shock too. It's a lot to take in. 'Hit by a cyclist?' she says eventually. 'He's just bruised, surely. He's not unconscious or anything?'

'Ruby,' I tell her, as calmly as I can but needing her to understand. 'It's bad. He was unconscious in the ambulance.'

'Fuck,' she says.

'Yeah.'

'Are you okay? You were there?'

'Yeah,' I says. 'I was there when it happened. It was . . . I mean . . . Ruby.'

And then I burst into tears. Big, guttural sobs that make the person snoozing opposite me in the waiting room jerk awake, look at me, and then close his eyes again. His arm. The whimpers. I can't escape it. It's all there behind my eyelids when I close my eyes, but it's there at the front of my brain too, whether I like it or not.

'Nic, I'm so sorry,' she soothes. It's animalistic, the noise I'm making, as if I'm traumatised. My tummy heaves in knots.

'Hey, it's okay. He's going to be okay.'

I sob down the line to her, and she lets me. The other people in the waiting room are staring, but I don't care. I can't stop.

'I'll come now, okay?' she says. 'I have to be with my friend. I have to come down to London. I'm coming.'

I sniffle down the line. 'On the train?' I ask. And then, because I can't do anything else, it becomes wholly clear to me what I *can* do. 'Let me come get you.' I breathe deeply enough to steady myself, to calm himself down. Yes. I'll get in a hire car and I'll drive and that is a thing I can control. 'I'm no good here,' I say, my head clearer now. 'I can't do anything. Let me drive up. It won't take long at this time.'

I look at the clock on the wall. It's 4.30 a.m. It'll take four hours without traffic. I'll be there by morning.

'That's ridiculous,' she says. 'I'll get the train.' She pauses, doing the maths of it. I can practically hear her decide that there probably isn't a train now. She'll have to wait until at least 6 or 7 a.m. anyway, and then get across London from the train station – not to mention the cost of it.

'I'm coming now,' I insist. 'Please? I can't sit here. I want to see you. I need you.'

'I need you too,' she says, quietly. 'Okay.'

My hands are shaking. I feel sick.

'All right, all right,' she decides. 'Just drive steady, okay? And take breaks. I don't want anything happening to you, too.'

I'm operating on pure adrenaline. I don't stop the whole way up the motorway, I just put my foot down and turn the radio up loud and let the words of songs I don't know wash over me. I try not to think about what I saw. Jackson's leg at that angle. The blood. The screams of the woman on the bike, which were awful. Until they stopped because she passed out and everyone thought she was dead. Then her silence was worse.

When Ruby opens the door of her flat to me, I hold her tighter than I've ever held anyone.

'It's okay,' she tells me, her voice muffled by my armpit. I cry, and I hold her some more, and we end up on the floor of her hallway in a tangled embrace until I finally stop, and she says, 'Let's have some tea, shall we? Come on.'

I'm shattered and end up falling asleep on her sofa, waking up to fresh coffee and a clean T-shirt folded on the edge of the sofa, on top of the throw she told me she got in Thailand.

'Morning,' I say, barely able to open my eyes. They feel practically welded shut in puffiness from the crying.

'How did you sleep?' she asks, and she's barefoot in black skinny jeans and a V-neck T-shirt, not a scrap of make-up on her. *I want to wake up to you every morning,* I think to myself, and she smiles at me softly as if she can hear my thoughts.

'Fine,' I croak. 'Deeply. Is there any news?'

'Candice called me,' she explains. 'She has him on the Find My Friends app and saw he was at the hospital – a nurse answered his phone. So she's at the hospital now – said she was his sister. He's in an induced coma. They need to give his body time to heal, and they think it's better that way.'

'It was so bad, Ruby. Honestly. It was just awful. I know it sounds like he's going to be okay but God, in that ambulance I just kept thinking, if he spent his last day on earth at an antenatal class with me, I will personally have to cross over into the afterlife and swap places or something because . . .'

She sits on one of the dining room chairs the wrong way, her arms across the top holding on to her coffee cup. Her eyes are wide and soft, her hair falling in waves down her back.

'You don't have to make a joke you know,' she says.

'I'm not,' I tell her. 'I thought he was going to die.'

She nods. 'I'm sorry you had to go through that.'

'Me too,' I say, and the image of him on the pavement blasts behind my eyelids once more, seared onto my brain.

'We're still not allowed to visit,' she says. 'I called. So maybe we don't go down today? We await the bat signal?'

'Okay,' I say. I'm still basically asleep.

'Do you want to move to my bed?' she asks. 'It's comfier.'

I look at her. I feel like we should be at the hospital, waiting. But I'm tired. So, so tired.

'All right,' I say, wearily. 'Maybe just for another hour.'

I stand up and head towards her bedroom, and as I pass her I reach out to her shoulder. I do it without thinking, reflexively. She responds quickly, putting her hand on top of mine kindly and I lace my fingers around hers. I pull, just a little bit, and she stands up. She follows me, climbing into bed with me without a word so I can wrap my body around hers from behind, clutching her closely, listening to her breathe.

39

Ruby

Nic and I hold hands through the winding corridors of the hospital as we find Jackson's room. We've been touching in one way or another since this morning, when we cuddled in bed. It helps. Everything feels dream-like, or only half-true. His hand was reached out to behind my neck as we drove, or my fingers held his belt loops when we stopped for coffee. It's like if we don't hold on to the other, we might float away, and so we take turns in acting as gravity for the other, so we don't disappear like Jackson almost did. It's the same when we see Candice in the waiting area on his corridor – I fling myself at her like I might never let go. Everything feels thin as paper and transient as air. Life is too fickle, too easily gone. I want to wrap everyone I love in cotton wool and keep them close forever, so everybody is fine and nobody can hurt.

'I know,' Candice says, into my hair. 'But he's fine. He's going to be fine. The coma will let him heal. But he will.

Everything looks hopeful, the doctors say. Tentatively, anyway. They won't know for sure until he's awake, but the signs aren't bad.'

I'm crying, she's crying, Nic is crying – we're sad and relieved and still anxious to see him and hear his laugh, hear him tell a stupid joke or issue an inappropriate comment.

'I'll go and find a nurse,' Nic says to us, wiping at his eyes. 'I'll see what the visiting situation is.' He leaves Candice and I to it, walking right past the nurses' station and back the way we came. My heart leaps at his emotional intelligence, that even in a time like this he knows how to do the right, thoughtful thing.

'Have you seen him?' I say to Candice.

'Yeah,' she says. 'He doesn't look . . . you know. He's sleeping, but it doesn't even really look like him. He's tired. His body is recovering from the shock, I think. Broken leg, sprained wrist, some cracked ribs. Everything else is swelling. Trauma from the impact.'

'Nic said it was horrible. He was beside himself.'

Candice pulls me in for a hug again, and we stay that way for a while. I hate that it's taken this for me to see her, but I sink into her arms willingly. Maybe now we can talk. Maybe now we can put our stupid fight behind us. Nothing is worth not speaking over. I can tell she feels sorry, too.

'I've been an arse,' she says, eventually, pulling away and looking for a tissue in her pocket. She blows her nose. 'I'm sorry. I know I've been awful to you.'

'It's okay,' I say. 'It doesn't matter.' I wave a hand to make my point, but she shakes her head.

'We'll talk, okay? Not now. But we will.'

'I'd like that,' I say.

* * *

328

I take an immediate leave of absence from the course – Harry is going to assist our class and take over my workload, because he is amazing and kind and wonderful. I stay in Jackson's room at Maple Avenue, and together the three of us – me, Candice and Nic – hold our breath and say our prayers. We go to the hospital every day, take meals for his parents who are beside themselves with worry, and we sneak in, occasionally, depending which nurse is working, to say hello and tell him we love him, knowing that he must be able to hear us in some way, even though he can't respond. The swelling is going down, but it's still too early to wake him.

Meanwhile, Nic and I hold hands. We hug. We snuggle. We do not kiss, and we do not sleep together, but for seven days we operate in each other's orbit constantly. We are not back together, but in this time he stays over, curled around me in Jackson's bed. We do not talk about it, it just happens, two question marks wrapped around the other, no answers necessary. Not right now. Whoever wakes first gets up to make the coffee. Life feels precious, and we all treat each other like we're bruised and heartsore, measuring our words and trying to be thoughtful, and even Jacques and Meg – the other two housemates who moved in, Jacques taking my old room and Meg, from Argentina, taking the box room – keep vigil, quietly entering and leaving the house, leaving us space for our worry. If Candice really is sleeping with the French guy, I don't get wind of it.

Six days after the accident they reduce Jackson's medication to wake him up. Candice, Nic and I sit impatiently, looking up every time somebody new enters the waiting room in case it's one of his parents come to tell us some news. Finally, his dad comes through.

'He's okay,' he says. 'He has full cognitive function, and he just asked for some water. The doctors say no visitors today, but we told him you're all here and he smiled and put his hand over his heart.'

That night in bed, I roll over from my position as little spoon so that I'm facing Nic. His face is barely visible, but I can feel his strong profile, the shape of his nose and mouth and chin.

'Thank you for being here,' I say quietly, when I know he is awake.

'Thank you for letting me,' he tells me, and we fall asleep facing each other for the first time.

It's almost like old times when Candice and I hang out at Jackson's bedside. Normally Nic comes with us, but tonight he has to work later than usual and so it's just the three of us. Jackson will come home tomorrow, all being well, and he seems more jubilant than he has all week at the prospect.

'I'll have both casts for six weeks, but I've got a widescreen TV in my bedroom at Mum and Dad's. It's right by the bathroom, and work have told me to take as long as I need, which is quite right too – the pay certainly isn't a perk there, so sick leave better bloody be.'

'I wish I could stay longer,' I say. 'I can come down some weekends, but—'

Jackson holds up his cast. 'You've got a documentary to be finishing,' he says. 'There are plenty of waifs and strays back home who will keep me company, and Candice can visit, can't you?' She nods. 'My good hand is cramping already from all the texts and voice notes I've had this week. I've got a whole dodgeball team who miss me already, don't forget.'

'And I'll be here,' chimes Candice.

'You don't even need to ask,' I say. 'I mean, am I forgiven? Can we just go back to normal?'

'I want that,' she says. 'Whatever normal is.'

A man with a face like Nic's approaches us then, striding across the café to where we're sat.

'Hey, sorry, hi. You're Jackson's housemates, aren't you? I'm Ollie? Nic's brother? I was at a birthday party for one of you last year. I play dodgeball with Jackson.'

'Yeah, I remember,' says Candice. 'Life and soul,' she adds.

'I didn't know about his accident. He only texted today. Do you know where I have to go? I didn't know.'

'Nobody at dodgeball knew,' Candice says. 'We didn't know what to say, so we just had Nic message the WhatsApp group to say he'd had a small accident.'

'Why didn't Nic tell me?' Ollie says. He seems frantic, dazed. I had no idea he and Jackson were friends either.

'He's been holding everything together for us,' I offer. 'I'm sure he didn't mean to omit any information.'

'He should have told me,' Ollie says. 'I should have known.'

'Okay,' Candice says. 'Well, the nurse is in there now but it's third floor, take a right out of the lift. The nurses' station is right there.'

'Thanks,' he says.

He leaves without saying goodbye.

'That was weird,' I say. 'I didn't know Jackson was even friends with Nic's brother.'

'He's always weaving tangled webs,' Candice says. 'We'll get the gossip later.'

'Yeah,' I say, watching him walk away, wondering what that was all about.

40

Nic

Lights twinkle on the inky snake of water looping around the development, the night-time sky punctuated by the lights of people arriving home after work. I stand and look out over the manicured lawns surrounding the smaller of the three apartment blocks, and the walk the length of the place back to the sliding doors of the kitchen.

'You could put a swing set there, a little slide, maybe,' Ollie notes, coming up behind me. 'It's fake grass, so at least you won't have to mow it. You're not exactly the "get the mower out" sort, are you?'

I screw up my face. 'Is anybody a get-the-mower-out sort?' I say. 'Shut up.'

'Steve is,' he replies, and I see what he means. Get-the-mower-out sorts are the dads who can't make a lasagne but disappear for all of a Saturday afternoon to sort out some old tree branches nobody cares about at the back of the garage.

'Are you?' I ask.

'Nah, mate, get fucked. I'm proper thinking I might be even more of a babe magnet with my little niece in tow, though.'

'God help us all,' I say, turning to take in the kitchen again. Polished marble-esque floor, big breakfast bar and nice wooden cabinets. I've seen a handful of places in a couple of different spots in Liverpool city centre, out on the quay, and here, a bit more suburban. This is the only place that has had a homely feel.

'Loads of places have been all right, haven't they?' I say to Ollie. 'But this actually feels homey? Do you know what I mean?'

'I like it,' he declares. 'You're close to town, close to Millie's, able to jump on a train to come see Uncle Ollie whenever you want.'

I pull a face. 'Or I'll come to you,' he says, holding up his hands. 'New babies don't travel well, I know. I've read *What to Expect When You're Expecting*.'

'Have you?'

'Jackson lent me his copy.'

'Jackson?'

'Yeah,' Ollie says, shrugging. 'I went to see him at his parents' place in Sevenoaks. He *is* recovering from a coma, you know.'

'I know that,' I say. 'I just didn't know you visited people recovering from comas.'

'Can you knock it off?' he says then. 'I know you think I'm stupid and irresponsible and only ever in it all for a good time, but in case you haven't noticed I'm *trying* to be a good friend to somebody who needs it, and I'm bloody here, aren't I, trying to be a good brother. Pack it in.'

'You're right,' I say, quietly. 'I'm sorry.'

'You're forgiven,' he says, and we both stand. Then: 'I think you should take it. It's a nice place.'

We walk through the open-plan kitchen and living room through to the hallway.

'Two bedrooms,' he continues. 'You can cook whilst she plays. It's big enough for a massive sofa bed for when I come and stay . . . Decent price, decent location.'

'Yeah,' I say. 'All of those things.'

There's a knock on the front door and the estate agent lets himself in.

'Sorry about that,' he says. 'It was the office. So, what are we thinking? I've got one other couple interested, so you'll have to move quickly if this is the one.'

I look at Ollie. He nods encouragingly. 'It's the one,' I say. 'I'd like to officially put in my offer. I'll take it.'

After making such an enormous decision, I feel compelled to tell the one person I can't stop thinking about. Ruby.

A photo of my new place,
I've only gone and bought it
I'm taking steps to build a life
Just not in the way I thought of
I don't know if it's allowed
For me to text hello
It's just when something big like this happens
It's you that's in my mind.

I see three dots on my screen to indicate she's typing back, but then they disappear, like she's changed her mind.

'How exactly did you leave it?' Ollie says, as we walk up the drive to Mum's.

'With no formal conclusion,' I say, ringing the doorbell. 'She doesn't want to be with a man having a baby, and that is obviously very final – but none of this feels like the end. I can't explain it. It's like some sort of invisible pull between us.'

'Does it come from your trousers by any chance?' Ollie quips, right as Steve opens the door.

'How do,' he says, reaching out a hand for us each to shake in turn. 'Your mum's just in the kitchen. Come in, lads. You're letting the cold in.'

Ollie and I dump our duffel bags and kick off our shoes – rule number one growing up: no shoes in the house. We traipse through the front room with our stinking feet and kiss her hello.

'My two home,' she says. 'And it's not even Christmas. Should I be worried?'

'Worry about that one,' I say, pointing at Ollie. 'He's being unnervingly considerate.'

Ollie steals a lump of cheese from the block Mum has left out by the grater. She bats his hand away. 'I've been upping my game, Mum, since your eldest is having an illegitimate child and can't stay in one place for more than five minutes. You need to be proud of one of us, don't you?'

'I'm proud of you both,' Mum says, loyally, but I know she's still unsure about everything. I think she's too afraid to be excited – I know she's going to be an amazing grandmother but it's like she can't believe it's really going to happen. My phone pings.

'Is that your girlfriend? Or your baby mama?' Ollie teases, and Mum shoots me a look.

'Has he got a girlfriend now?' I hear her asking him, as I focus on what it says. It's my recruitment agent, asking me to call her.

'I don't have a girlfriend, Mum,' I say. 'He's just being an arse. I do have to make a call about a potential job, though. I'll do it upstairs.'

I move past Steve watching the six o'clock news and sit at the top of the stairs.

'Nic, hi,' my recruitment agent Sinead says as she picks up my call. 'Thanks for getting back to me so fast.'

'No worries,' I say. 'Any news?'

'Well,' she says. 'I just wanted to sound you out about a potential role that is a bit left of the middle.'

'Says every recruiter ever,' I joke.

'I promise you'll want to hear about this,' she says. 'I only get my cash if you stay in the role, remember? So I'm not fobbing you off here.'

'I trust you, Sinead,' I say. 'I've heard nothing but great things.'

'That's because I'm nothing but great,' she retorts, and I can hear the smile in her voice as she talks.

'I'm listening,' I tell her, and I'm smiling too. Am I flirting with my recruiter? I pull the phone from my ear to see if Ruby has replied. She hasn't.

'There's a year-old company who need a chief financial officer. With everything you've said about being willing to sacrifice money for time, but also wanting to do something socially conscious if you can, I think culturally this is a great fit. I know the founders socially, actually, through my husband, and they're great – but they need a proper money man. They've got talent and vision and are attracting great press, but somebody needs to steer the ship, financially speaking. It's a generous enough package, a four-day week, and they do a lot of remote working too. It's not all in the office – so for childcare stuff, by the time your daughter starts school, all of that, it's a good fit for you. They want to meet you. Are you up for it?'

'I mean, yeah, of course,' I say. 'You've basically checked off my job requirement wish list.'

'I really am as good as they say,' Sinead replies. 'I'm sending you the details now. It's thirty days' notice in current role, correct?'

'Correct,' I say.

'Okay awesome. Check out their profile and I'll call them now to arrange. Any limitations on your schedule tomorrow?'

'I can stay flexible,' I say. 'That's fine.'

'Dream client,' she says, and I can hear that smile again.

I get a text at 10 p.m. telling me to be in the lobby of one of the central hotels at 8.30 a.m., for an informal meeting with the founders who, Sinead reiterates again, have read my CV and heard all about me and 'love' me. I wear my suit, which I almost didn't bring, and drive myself into town. John and Craig, the founders, are already there when I arrive. They're about my age, both wearing wedding bands, sat in a corner table with a couple of ring binders and a laptop each. They stand up as they see me approach.

'Nic?' and I nod, reaching out a hand. 'Great to meet you. I'm John, this is Craig. Sit, sit. Do you want coffee? Thanks so much for coming on short notice.'

They're nice enough, and are obviously passionate about what they're doing.

'The world probably doesn't need another mental health app,' Craig acknowledges, 'but we've almost got funding for the next five years, and you can take this away with you – this is the whole plan, the full insight into what we're trying to do. We just need somebody the investors can see knows how to keep us fiscally tight. We're both dads, both uninterested in the hustle or the grind, but both care deeply about adding something to the world.'

John shrugs. 'Sappy as that sounds.'

'Sappy as that sounds,' Craig echoes.

I take a walk around town after I've said goodbye, fairly certain they're going to give me an offer. I'm not hugely bothered about what I do – I've done corporate, I've done impressive business cards, all of that. I suppose I feel like there's been a bit of an internal shift since finding out about the baby. Ruby called it. She said I'd feel this way. How strange to know she knows me well enough to get that before I do, but we still can't be together. My phone rings. It's Sinead.

'You impressed them,' she tells me. 'They want to make a formal offer. The question is, then, what did you think of them?'

I accept. By the time I'm back in London and ready to hand in my notice at Hoare's, I've got contracts for my new mortgage and my new job lined up, both in Liverpool. I don't waver on this next step at all. Am I ready to be a father? Fuck knows. Am I ready to try anyway? Abso-bloody-lutely. I thought I'd be in London for so much longer and experience so much more, but if I have to leave, this is the very best reason.

so busy that people bump into each other, so Harry and I sing lyrics into each other's faces, sway our hips, and as a few more glasses of whatever's on offer at the table course through our veins increasingly close our eyes to sway and sing and be at one with ourselves. A good night out can be like a meditation. I've forgotten that. When it's past midnight it's like free time. Sure, like JP once said, nothing good happens after midnight but to be fair, ensconced in the throng of sweaty bodies moving and shaking, it doesn't feel like anything bad can happen either. The worries of today are forgotten but tomorrow hasn't yet begun, making it easy to breathe deeper and laugh louder. Nothing matters in the middle of a great night out.

I open my arms and spin on the spot, getting dizzier and dizzier and only stopping when my hand accidentally brushes the hair of another dancer.

'Sorry!' I say, happily, and just as happily she yells back, 'It's okay!'

If I could bottle this feeling, I could make a fortune. Thoughts come to me and then are just as easily washed away. Nic ebbs in and flows back again. Abe. The miscarriage. JP. What I'll do after. The new Instagram followers, some development people at production companies amongst them. I should see my family more. I should go and see Candice, force her to fix what's up. Jackson. Lovely, lovely Jackson. It's all what makes me, and it all matters, but none of it matters either. I'm just a person, doing her best, who likes to dance.

By the time 3 a.m. crawls around, we're in the kebab shop on the corner, Manroop with his arm around a woman he met on the way out the club, Woody and Leticia sharing cheesy chips, Harry and Beau stealing kisses as they sit on the windowsill and bark orders at Seb and me at the counter.

We have fizzy canned drinks and questionable meat and greasy chips, and it's perfect. I'm laughing at nothing, happy just to be here, against all the odds, making strangers into friends and my own body, my own soul and mind and heart my home. I live here, I think to myself. Not in a place, but within myself. And that's exactly what I've been chasing, this feeling. Peace. Not in spite of everything that's happened, but because of. It's all made me who I am. Alone, but not lonely. Not anymore.

'She says, threateningly,' Jackson teases, and Candice narrows her eyes at him.

'Anyway, I'm glad all it took was my near-death experience to get you two back talking again,' Jackson notes. 'And . . .' he adds, nodding towards Candice, 'I'm glad you're finally out of the deep dark hole you decided to hide yourself in.'

'Yeah, well.' Candice shrugs. 'I needed to feel sorry for myself for a moment. And now I'm ready to deal with things head on.'

'I know all about that,' I say. 'Burying my head in the sand is my superpower.'

Jackson and Candice look at me, waiting for me to elaborate.

'Oh,' I say, 'I didn't mean . . . you both think I'm talking about Nic, don't you? I just meant in general.' They both continue to stare. 'I'm not sleeping with him,' I press. 'I know you're looking at me like that because you think we're hooking up, but we're not?'

'I hear you've both been sleeping in my bed,' says Jackson. 'So I'd prefer it if that was indeed the case. Do feel free to buy me new sheets if not, though. In fact, you can buy me new sheets either way. I'll accept them as a housewarming gift?'

'Housewarming gift?' I ask.

Candice nods. 'We're giving up the house,' she says. 'Meg is going to take on the lease and find two more housemates. We've talked, and decided it's time to grow up and move on.'

'But that will make it the end of an era?' I exclaim. 'You can't leave!'

'It's already been the end of an era,' Jackson points out. 'We're the ones playing catch-up?'

'But that means . . .' I say, and Jackson nods.

'Honey, you were never coming back. It's okay.'

I ask them where they're going.

'We're going to find a two-bed somewhere, a flat maybe, closer to central. Somewhere where we can have a proper dining table.'

'That *is* grown up,' I marvel.

'It's time,' says Candice. 'We're ready for the change, aren't we?'

'We are,' says Jackson. 'And now we've covered that off the "to discuss" list, can we go back to you and Nic? What are you going to do, darling? I can barely bear the tension between you! Just get back together already!'

'I don't know . . .' I start. 'It's not what I want. I'm really sure of it . . .'

'I wouldn't date a man with a kid,' says Candice. 'At least, I don't think I would. Can you honestly say that you would, Jackson? It's a lot to take on?'

Jackson shrugs, then seems to remember that the shrugging causes him pain and winces as he readjusts himself into a more comfortable position.

'Depends on the person,' Jackson insists.

'It'll end in tears,' Candice says.

'And so what, it's not worth the risk?' Jackson counters.

'Jesus, I thought they said your head was okay? Nurse! Doctor! Jackson has a head injury!'

'Ha, ha,' says Jackson. 'How long is that going to be a running joke please? Because I'm bored of it already.'

'Look,' I tell them. 'I'm getting the train back tomorrow and then I just don't know. I thought it would be too painful to see him as a friend, but he's been amazing with all this. It hurts we can't be together, but I just think I need to be

41

Ruby

'I think this is it,' Harry says, squinting at the computer screen through his glasses, which he switched to about ten hours ago – nine hours after we first sat in the editing suite together and got to work. We smell, we're tired, and we're also wired. We hand in the doc in the morning. I lean back in my chair and go to put my arms behind my head before I think better of it. Harry notices me change my mind. We've been working and working – it's been three months since Paris, Christmas and New Year passing in a blur – our new deadline for submission mere hours away.

'Do I stink?' I ask.

'I didn't want to say anything.' He nods to my armpits. 'But yeah.'

'You stink too,' I retort. 'But truly, this might be the smell of . . .' I struggle to find the word.

'A story pretty bloody well told?'

'As somebody who features in this quite a lot,' I say. 'I feel

weird saying this. But yes? Maybe? I don't even know what my own name is and might be on the verge of tears through sheer sleep deprivation but . . .'

Harry reaches out a clammy hand and grabs my own. 'It's good,' he says. 'I think we can be proud of this.'

JP agrees. We submit it to the department and then drive to his house after a couple of hours' sleep at each of our homes, not to mention showers. William stays to watch it too.

'Wow,' William says once it's done. 'Guys, this is actually really, really good.'

'Actually?' I say.

'I knew you'd get all those kinks sorted through in the end,' says JP. 'And before I kick the bucket, too! How's that for good work!'

'Gramps, I do wish you'd stop saying things like that. It's not . . . normal.'

'Ah.' I smile. 'He's a dead man walking. Let him have his gallows humour.'

William looks shocked, and then amused. 'Jesus,' he says, shaking his head. 'I can't believe I ever agreed to let him spend time with you fools.'

'They're my fools.' JP smiles.

'It's a proper journey you take us on,' William presses. 'It's really clever. We think it's going to reveal one truth about love to us, and then it reveals something else that was there right in front of us all along, we just didn't see it.'

Harry revels in the insight. 'Say more about that,' he goads, and William obliges.

'*Almost Doesn't Count*, you know – you're actually saying almost absolutely counts, because it can often bring you closer to the love you're supposed to be with. Although, I

344

suppose . . . well, it's a shame Nic isn't in it, really. He's so obviously in love with you that it doesn't make sense, now I think about it, for him not to say so on camera. Unless . . .' William takes in my expression, which I assume is one of agog fly-catching. 'Oh,' he says. 'Sorry. Did you not know? I thought everyone knew.'

'How *don't* you know?' Harry says to me, and I shoot him a look that prompts him to clarify: 'You *do* know that he's in love with you?'

'This is an awful lot of speculation,' I say. 'Come on now. Let's not talk ill of somebody not here to defend himself.'

'Oh, darling, he's in Liverpool, not the ground,' says JP, drolly. 'Did you really not know?'

'No,' I say. 'And even if he was . . .' I feel like I've been backed into a corner not of my choosing, and we've gone from a wonderful celebration of a job well done to shining a light into the nooks and crannies of my personal life, which has been painful enough to get on camera. I don't now need three bloody men making impertinent assumptions about my heart.

'Honey, it's okay,' Harry says, gently.

'I thought you loved him too,' says William, and I lock eyes with him and then burst into tears.

'I do,' I admit, finally, in between sobs. 'But there's nothing I can do about it.'

'You can tell him,' Harry says, and after everything – Jackson, how he was there for us all – I know I have to. I might not be able to be with him, but the one least thing I have to do before I let him go for good is tell him exactly what he means to me.

'I want to meet him,' JP says. 'Can't you have a get-together? After all these stories we've heard about him, surely we can put a face to the name. For an old man, love, you can do that, can't you?'

I think about it.

'That's very weird,' I say. 'He's not a dog in a dog and pony show.'

'Make him the pony in a dog and pony show then.' Harry grins. 'I'm with JP. I want to meet him. How did you leave things when you left?'

I shrug. 'We just said see ya,' I say. 'No promises. No reference to anything really. Just see ya, good luck, et cetera.'

William pipes up: 'You could hold a screening party? Put out a few nibbles or make some pasta, and we can all watch it together?'

'I can't believe you're all making me do this,' I say. 'Jesus.'

'We're not making you do anything.' Harry laughs. 'You're itching to make the call! Look at you!'

It *has* felt very unfinished with Nic. We said our big goodbyes after Paris but now, after Jackson and everything else, it's like we've picked a scab off a wound that hasn't healed.

I pick up my phone. I still haven't replied to his last message – I just didn't know what to say. I decide to just go for it.

Of course it's fine you'd text
These past few weeks have been wild
I've just been talking about you actually
Don't worry, I kept it mild.
JP himself is wondering
If you'd like to see the doc.
I don't know if you're north or south,
But we were thinking five o'clock . . .

He texts back immediately: *Tonight?*

Tonight, I say, texting him back. *YOLO, et cetera.*

I sigh dramatically, but I'm secretly a bit glad somebody

else has pushed me into reaching out to Nic. Everything feels so unfinished, even though before Jackson's accident we drew a line under it. I suppose the line was more of a paragraph break though, after all that hand-holding and spooning, and so now I need to go back and get my closure.

'See you all at mine in a bit then,' I announce to the room.

'Looking forward to it,' JP says, and when he catches my eye, he looks pleased as punch.

I tell Candice all about it when I get home to prep.

'I can't believe it's in and done,' Candice tells me over FaceTime. 'I wish I could celebrate hand in with you too.'

We've been trying to talk at least once a week since we made up, and with Jackson still in recovery he's been way more active on the group text, so it feels like the band is back together – or at the very least, have weathered their stormiest clouds yet.

'The doc sounds great, getting closure with Nic sounds great. All you need now is a plan for once the course finishes. What is it, a few more months? Wait. Sorry. Should I know better than to ask?'

'No, no,' I say. 'You can ask. I think I'm going to stick around here, actually. Just for a term, anyway, before I know next projects and whatnot. Janet, my supervisor, has asked if I might be interested in continuing to do some associate lecturer stuff for the undergrads, and I like it up here. I feel like I've got space to make things. Harry is going to stay too so . . . yeah. That's the option. I need to submit coursework for the other modules, but it all feels doable – to think about what's next whilst finishing stuff here. We're submitted *Almost Doesn't Count* to a few festivals and things, so I know I talked about travelling, perhaps, but in actuality I think some roots up here would be nice.'

'I just like to prepare myself for what's to come,' Candice says. 'If there was even one iota of a chance you'd be coming back down this way . . .'

I know she's going to tell me that they wouldn't leave Maple Avenue if I was, that I could have my old room and this past seven months would have served as a lovely musical interlude before returning to everything I knew and loved.

'Nah,' I say. 'But make sure you keep a blow-up mattress nearby for me, won't you? I intend to visit *a lot*.'

'Well, I do have somebody down here I'd like you to meet,' she says, and I swear to God she's almost coy. Candice acting coy is like the Queen doing a striptease – an impossible feat of imagination. It's so rare, so unheard of, that . . .

'Candice. Is this about a man?'

'I asked out Sterling.'

'The postman?' I cry. 'You did it?! Oh my God, tell me everything.'

She goes into forensic detail about him dropping off a package for Jackson one morning, and how they laughed and chatted but he had to get on with his rounds, and something in her made her ask if he wanted company. So she did his round with him, talking non-stop for hours, and by the end of it they'd agreed to drinks at the local.

'I'm pretty nuts about him,' Candice says, and I grin approvingly.

'Well, well, well . . .' I say. 'Who's the old romantic now?'

'Still you,' she says, but she's beaming, obviously very much in the early flushes of falling. 'But I'm trying.'

'I see that,' I say. 'I applaud it.'

'And you?' she asks. 'You think this dinner really will be closure?'

I nod, slowly.

She sighs. 'That man.'

'I know,' I say. 'But it was so great to hang out as friends throughout the whole Jackson thing, and the baby comes any day now, I think, so I honestly don't think we'll see each other after that. Tonight feels like a nice goodbye. Again. Our second goodbye.'

'Sounds like a second break-up,' says Candice. 'But you do you.'

'I do feel for him – it *is* a less than ideal situation. I think he wants to draw a line under everything so he can enter this next . . .'

I say 'chapter' and Candice rolls her eyes and makes a gagging sound.

'Well, what else should I call it?'

'I don't know, but it sounds like you're about to dissect his "journey" over an instrumental version of a Westlife single any moment now, and that's taking it *too* far.' She smiles.

'You're impossible,' I say.

'I am,' she replies. 'What's your point?'

'My point is that I'm okay. If the documentary taught me anything, it's that being brave with my heart makes me a superhero, not a needy wet cabbage or somehow less feminist or empowered. Talking to all these people, seeing myself on camera – God forbid – I just feel . . . stronger, I suppose.'

'But . . . the love,' she says. 'What are you going to do with the love?'

'Feel it,' I say. 'Love him as a friend, maybe, or love him from afar. I don't know. That's the beauty of it. I don't need to know.'

* * *

'I come bearing gifts,' Nic says that night, waving a couple of carrier bags from the corner shop at me after I open the door. He'd sent a follow-up text asking what he should bring, and we ended up deciding that since I'm hosting, he'd happily cook for everyone.

'Come in, monsieur,' I say, unsure why I've pulled out a 'monsieur'. 'I've got the champagne on ice.'

It isn't champagne, it's cava, and it isn't on ice but rather in the lettuce drawer of the fridge, because that felt coldest. I've washed my hair and took almost an hour to do my make-up in a way that looks like I'm not wearing any at all. It feels strangely like a first date – I've got those same nerves, gurgles in my tummy, and I can tell he's made the effort as well. He's in a shirt and jumper with jeans, and exactly like the first time we met he insists on taking off his trainers after he hangs up his coat. But there's an element of goodbye to the evening too: I feel like we're two protagonists in a season finale of a Emmy-award-winning show.

'This is nice,' he compliments, taking in the vibe of the room. I've lit some tealights and got music on, put some crisps in a bowl. I agonised for ages about snacks – it seems so grand to decant Morrisons Mature Cheddar family pack as if I'm entertaining the neighbours over a friendly game of bridge, but he'd already buzzed in downstairs before I could change my mind.

'I figured you're worth it,' I say, shrugging.

'I am,' he replies, and the edge to his voice is perilously close to flirtatious.

We pour the drinks and nibble at the sliced cheese and he makes a prawn jambalaya.

'You're looking good,' he says, covering the rice to let it

cook and turning to take a breath in between cooking steps. 'If I'm allowed to say that.'

'You're allowed,' I say, from my perch on the dining room table where I've got my feet up on a chair. 'You look good too,' I add. 'Sort of, at peace.'

'Yeah.' He nods, taking a big gulp from his glass. 'I'm happy.'

'Good,' I say. 'I'm happy you're happy.'

He looks at me, goes to say something, and then changes his mind.

'What?' I press.

'I was just thinking that this is nice. I like being in your kitchen. I like you watching me cook.'

'Well, I can wholeheartedly say I like being cooked *for*, so this is some good teamwork.'

'I cook, everyone else eats. Got it.'

'I can set the table, though,' I say, hopping down to hunt down some cutlery.

I have to lean across him to open a drawer for the forks and as I do so he says, 'You smell like you.' He says it softly. Quietly. It makes the hairs on the back of my neck prickle with something close to desire. I can feel his eyes on me, waiting for my reaction.

'Don't,' I say, stepping away from him.

'Sorry,' he says. 'I didn't mean to . . .' He shakes his head. 'That's a lie, actually. I did mean to. I don't know how to be around you as your friend, Ruby. I'm trying, but shit, look at you. Your hair and your eyes and your smile and your stupid jokes and inability to use a piece of furniture properly. I can go, if you want. I don't mean to mess you around.'

'So don't mess me around,' I say, clear as day.

He looks up.

I move my shoulders up and down as if to say, *It's really that simple, dude.*

'What does that mean?' he says.

'I don't know.' I sigh.

'Come here,' he says, reaching out a hand and pulling me towards him.

We're interrupted by my phone: it's Harry, waiting to be let in via the buzzer, with Beau, JP and William in tow too. I free myself from my Nick-induced trance and hit the buzzer, opening the front door onto the third-floor corridor where I can hear the lift grumbling.

'Where is he!' Harry says, as way of greeting.

We eat, we chat, we drink a little bit of the wine Beau has brought after toasting to completing the project with the champagne. I don't remember much. Nic keeps looking at me when I'm talking, and when he's talking I keep stealing glances at him, and so it all feels like a giant prelude to the inevitable. JP announces that we're idiots not to be together, and it makes us both laugh, and as everyone else says their goodbyes Nic doesn't make a move to leave, and I don't expect him to.

'That was cool,' he says, when we close the front door and hear the lift take them back down.

'It was,' I say. 'I'm glad you've been able to meet everyone.'

'Me too,' he agrees softly, and then we do what we didn't do for those ten days we shared Jackson's bed, and it is tender and gentle and emotional and perfect.

42

Nic

Millie is in labour. Everything I know about dads and hospital waiting rooms is what I've seen on TV. If I expected the same whisky-and-cigars anxious cheersing, a sense of reluctant camaraderie amongst men, I'm disappointed. Everything is clean and efficient. On arrival I'm directed to Millie's suite where she's make-up-free and in a hospital gown, flicking through a magazine.

'Hey,' I say, lingering in the doorway. I don't know how much space she'll need or want and I wait to be invited and instructed.

'Nic,' she says, brightly. 'Hello.' I feel a presence behind me.

'Sandeep,' I say, nodding.

'Nic,' he says.

'Gang's all here,' Millie declares, before patting her belly and adding: 'Well, almost the whole gang. Things are moving slowly, I'm afraid.'

Sandeep fusses around her, moving her pillow and cooing loving, encouraging words about how lucky the baby is to have her, how proud he is of her, how he'll be just outside the theatre waiting for her. I feel like an intruder on their private and personal moments, and have to remind myself that this is my moment, too. I'm a part of the process as well. I've got just as much right to be here as he has.

'And you,' says Sandeep, as if he's telepathically tuned in to the bad thoughts I'm having. 'You're wonderful too, Nic. I know this isn't easy. I really appreciate you giving us the space to let our love grow at the same time as this baby. It's not how I imagined becoming a parent, but I want you to know how committed I am – how committed we both are – to making this as loving a family as possible.'

'Three parents,' Millie says, patting her bump. 'How much love is that?'

'More than she'll ever use up,' I say, smiling, and I really do think that the three of us – the four of us – are going to be okay.

Sandeep and I walk into the birthing suite at the same time, and I feel so emotional and light-headed I swear it's all I can do not to hold his hand. I want to hold *somebody's* hand, right up until the moment Millie puts Lila Grace Sheridan-Greene in my arms, and then I realise I don't need anybody else in the world. I'm a daddy.

'She likes you,' Millie says softly, and she looks exhausted, but happy.

'You're a hero,' Sandeep tells her. 'The nurse said you didn't even tear!'

Millie is uncharacteristically sardonic. 'Doesn't mean it didn't hurt like a motherfucker,' she retorts, and as if to emphasise the point shifts her weight to make herself more comfortable.

The baby is . . . I don't even have the words for it. Hypnotic. I can't stop staring at her, and she's not even doing anything. She's sleeping, and pink, and scabby and weird-looking and perfect. I'm aware of the size of her, and of the size of me. She's as light as air, and I know, right away, that I would lay down my life to protect her. Whatever she needs in this life, I will provide. She'll want for nothing.

'Can I . . . ?' asks Sandeep, gesturing to her, and you know what? I want her to be loved by as many people as possible. I don't feel possessive or like nobody should have her but me. I mean, I want the snuggles, and I'm working up my nerve to take my top off for some skin-on-skin contact like the blogs said, but Millie is right – she's so loved, and that's all you want for your kid, isn't it? Love. Love cures everything. Love is preventative. Love is.

The baby wakes up in Sandeep's arms, and I feel a flush of vindication that she seemed so at peace in mine – and instantly feel regret that I'd even silently point-score. I suppose I am only human. I pull out my phone to snap a photo and send it to my parents, Ollie, and then Ruby.

I thought people who gave birth had to stay in hospital for days. Maybe even a week. But Millie is discharged that afternoon and just like that, our baby is out there in the world.

'Careful, careful . . .' I say as we navigate the hospital together. Sandeep has gone ahead to get his car, and we're to meet him at the front. Millie is being pushed in a wheel-chair by a nurse, and I can tell that despite the brave face she's tired, now, and wants her own bed and house and shower. She still seems uncomfortable.

'I'm being careful, Dad,' the nurse says back to me. 'You just focus on that wee bundle of joy you've got there.'

I can't believe I am carrying a baby out of here. Yesterday she was *inside Millie's body* and now she's here, outside of it, marvelling at the world and breathing on her own and making these adorable little croaky noises that break my heart and fill it up, all at the same time. Millie doesn't even have to stay. She's just *going home,* with a baby.

Shit. She is breathing, isn't she? I slow down and reach out a finger to check. Okay, yes. Still alive. I'm doing pretty well so far.

We get around the corner and the nurse helps Millie up as Sandeep gets out the driver's side and fusses with bags in boots and reassuring me that the hospital have already checked it and certified it safe.

'I'll . . . see you tomorrow?' I say to Millie. She looks exhausted. The thought of being apart from my baby tears me in two, but I know I'm supposed to be respecting boundaries.

'Listen,' she says. 'For tonight – for her first night. Why don't you come and stay? You can't miss her first night.'

'Are you sure?' I ask, and Sandeep winds his window down too.

'We insist,' he says.

I stay at Millie and Sandeep's for four nights, and driving home to the new apartment feels so strange. We've agreed that for three months the baby will stay at Millie's and I'll see her there, and after that we'll assess if she's ready for sleepovers with me or when the right time for that might be. But being home now, with everything still in boxes and my new job having not yet started, I feel the weight of it all for the first time. I send Ruby a photo of the baby. I don't even realise I'm doing it until I'm scrolling for her name. She calls me immediately.

'She's beautiful,' she says. 'Congratulations, Nic.'

'Thank you,' I say. 'She's very tiny, and very cute.'

'You sound happy.'

'I am,' I say. 'Are you?'

She pauses. 'Some producers at the BBC have seen *Almost Doesn't Count*. I'm actually just about to go into a meeting with them, with Harry.'

'Shit!' I say. 'That's amazing. Ruby!'

'Yeah,' she says. 'Wish us luck.'

'You don't need luck,' I tell her.

We pause.

'I just wanted to say,' Ruby offers then, 'that even though we've decided not to be together, I love you. That's it. You don't have to say it back. But I wanted to say it. I love you. You've changed me. And I will carry that with me forever.'

'You changed me as well,' I say. 'And I love you, too. I don't understand how this doesn't get to work out, but I know it's right. Maybe in our next life the timing will be right.'

She laughs, snotty and cute. 'Maybe,' she says. And then: 'Be well, Nic.'

PART THREE

FOUR YEARS LATER

43

Ruby

'That was a beautiful memorial, wasn't it?'

I knew he was coming. He'd read the announcement online, the algorithm on his news app issuing an unexpected blast from the past. Jackson told me last week, at Candice's wedding as we waited for her to finish getting her bridal photos done. They aren't in touch often, partly because of Nic's move, partly because of me, and partly because Jackson and Nic's brother Ollie had an ill-fated month-long secret shag-fest of a relationship two years ago that left Ollie heart-broken when Jackson didn't want any more than that. Ollie's first heartbreak. Nic chose blood over water, despite Ollie ultimately being happier than ever after embracing his full sexuality at Jackson's encouragement – or so I heard. Still, it ended up being a bit of a mess. Everything got reported to me second-hand, through Candice, in breaks on set or writing binges with Harry.

He looks almost the same – Nic. There's a softening

around the eyes, a thin new dent between his eyebrows, almost as if a thumb has run the breadth of his face and smudged his wide-set features. His eyes sit pool-like and dark, those full, pink lips parting just enough to reveal his enviably perfect teeth, that thick neck sloping deep into his starched white shirt, the black tie loosened by a centimetre or two, his top button undone in the smallest nod to casual, despite the expensive-looking suit. His broadness hasn't changed, but it's settled into something less lithe, less gangly. What I'm saying is, I suppose, is that he looks exactly as old as he is, and I'm suddenly aware of it because I wonder how different I look to him. I'm just shy of thirty-five, but the late nights, early mornings, endless meetings and working weekends – all of that means I know, factually speaking, I'm not as fresh-faced as I was. That's not me being paranoid. It's true.

'I hope it's okay that I came,' he adds.

I pull up my sunglasses and perch them on my head.

'Of course it is,' I say. 'That film was as much a story about you and me as it was JP. He'd be touched that you made the effort.'

'It seems he touched a lot of people,' Nic comments, motioning to the dispersing crowds outside of the church. It's a beautiful day: there's a cloudless June sky, and it's warm enough that men have shed their suit jackets and a few people are sitting on the grass, waiting for the pub across the road to open at midday.

'Are you coming to the pub now?' I ask. 'There's food, and coffee.'

William and Sophie walk past us, her bulging pregnant stomach coming into view before anything else. William touches my arm and smiles, Sophie saying *bonjour*, but they

362

don't slow. They told me earlier that they're having a boy, and he'll be called Jean-Pierre: a French nod to his great-gramps. Life goes on, even in death. JP would be thrilled at the namesake, of that everyone is sure. He loved that William and Sophie had the chance for the love story he didn't, and whilst he might not meet his great-grandson, he did get to watch William walk down the aisle at least.

'Erm,' Nic says, smiling at William and his wife. 'I don't know. Yes? I don't want to intrude. I just saw the piece in the *Guardian*, and then downloaded the doc to watch again, like everyone else I suppose, and I had all these *feelings*. He was so kind to me at that dinner. I don't know if you remember. Probably not. But we had a dinner, at your flat in Manchester, and he was there and . . . I don't know.'

'I get it,' I tell him. 'That's how JP made me feel too. Thank you for coming. It's really nice to see you.'

Nic looks chuffed to hear me say that, and I feel chuffed to be saying it. I've thought of him, over the years. Especially in the beginning. I always assumed he'd found someone, probably got married, probably had another kid. I look down at his left hand reflexively: no ring.

'Nic? Hey!' Harry waves as he approaches, Beau by his side, and everything unspoken between us vanishes as Nic reaches out a hand and greets them both exclaiming, 'Harry, mate, how are you? Beau, isn't it? Hey, Beau.'

'Lovely service, wasn't it?' Harry says, and he looks between Nic and me pointedly, knowing full well that in the foot between us there's a whole history waiting to be properly acknowledged – or totally ignored. I don't know which way the conversation will fall, yet.

'Where's baby Mirabelle today?' I ask Beau, as Harry and Nic talk about the architecture of the church and how much money has been poured into the region's waterside redevelopments. I hear Nic say he's been following the projects we've done, too, giving him a big congratulations.

'With my mum,' Beau says. 'Overnight, too. So if we want to drown our sorrows, we're able to.' He makes a little 'drink' sign with his hand, and Harry catches it, interrupting himself to say, 'Beau! It's not a fucking party, Jesus!'

I smile. 'I think JP would have actively encouraged partying, to be fair. He wouldn't want us maudlin.'

'"Good innings, me,"' Harry says, mimicking what JP had taken to saying after the documentary came out, referring to his age, the fact that he had a bigger spring in his step than ever, that he kept on keeping on. They played some of his footage in the service, clips of him telling his story, and the minister referred to JP's last-minute claim to fame in his eulogy. He loved the attention he got after it was properly released. He was on the news a couple of times, and we were all interviewed by *The Times* for a Saturday supplement piece too. He ended up raising a hundred and fifty thousand pounds for the cancer charity that took his eldest son. They said that in the eulogy too: a hundred-and-one-year-old man raising thousands for charity and getting national press to boot.

William had quoted another thing JP liked to say over these past few years, as well: *It ain't over til it's over, sunshine.* I look at Nic again. Snapshots of everything flash through my mind, a hundred different touches and smiles and moments that meant something in the blink of an eye. Looking at him, I know that to be true. That what we had was real. The magnitude of it. It's funny how a stranger can come out of nowhere and affect so much of your life in only a few months.

We all hear the pub door open at the same time, turning in unison as the giant creaking wooden door shifts and a tiled hallway floor is revealed, a gilded mirror on the wall reflecting the light of a coloured glass ceiling lamp that hangs down in pride of place.

'So – the pub?' I repeat.

'Yeah, I'll come,' says Nic, and we walk in loaded silence behind Harry and Beau, filing into the building along with everyone else.

We find a small table in the corner, Harry and Beau on the banquette, Nic and I on small stools, impossible to sit on with any kind of elegance. I feel self-conscious in my dress. It's mid-calf and sleeveless, very Audrey Hepburn in *Breakfast at Tiffany's*. I got it through one of those dress loan websites in a panic. It's so much more demure than anything I'd usually buy.

Ostensibly we're all talking together, catching up, swapping stories about JP, but Nic keeps looking at me, and I keep looking at Nic, and I know, now, that we really are going to capital-T Talk, later. Maybe not before we've had the buffet, and probably not until somebody has spilled a pint, or one relative has yelled at another, but at some point, we'll have our moment. He reaches out and lightly touches my knee when he asks if I want another drink. He may as well have doused me in petrol and lit a match: I flush with heat as everything comes flooding back.

JP's niece is playing the piano, performing any and all requests that we give her as we squish into the back room and sing loudly and out of tune, drunkenly celebrating the time that we all had with the cheeky, loveable, full-of-life JP. I slip out to the loo, and when I return rest against the doorframe, gazing into the back room right as a rousing chorus of 'Wonderwall' reaches its crescendo. I feel him before I see him.

'Another drink?' he says, waving an empty bottle at me.

'Sure,' I say, and we walk through to the back part of the bar, where there's fewer people. The barman nods, signalling we're next.

'How's your little girl?' I say, resting my forearms on the bar. He mirrors me.

'Not so little,' he says. 'She starts school in September. Wipes her own arse now and everything.'

I laugh. 'You surplus to requirements then?'

'Something like that. She's brilliant, though,' he says. 'Good value. Two nights ago, I was getting cross that she wouldn't go to sleep. Most nights I lie with her until she's fast on, and it's nice, you know, feeling like you're sending her off into sweet dreams or whatever. But she'd had sweets, and was high as a kite, and I said, "Lila, come on. Close your eyes and go to sleep." And she sat upright, looked at me, and said, "Daddy. I just don't think that's going to happen."' He shakes his head at the memory.

'Oh, she's got you wrapped around her little finger,' I say.

'She did from day one,' he replies, looking at me. My whole body responds to that look.

'What can I get you?' the barman asks, and Nic gestures, letting me go first.

'Pint of water,' I say, 'And double gin and slim. Lime as well as lemon, if you can.'

'Beer for me,' Nic says, tapping the rim of his empty and fishing in his suit jacket for his wallet. When we're served, we stay standing, right where we are, taking long pulls of our drinks. Then he says: 'You did everything you said you were going to do.'

366

'Me?' I ask.

'You,' he says. 'Making your mark on the world.'

'Oh,' I say. 'Yeah. It's good. I've been lucky.'

'Funny how lucky hardworking people can get,' he says, and I smile.

'That's very generous of you. Cheers.'

We clink glasses, a nod to two old friends.

'What are you working on now?' he asks.

'A few things,' I tell him. 'Two projects in development: one in pre-production to start filming in the autumn, another pretty much ready to go. Directed one, wrote and directed the other.'

'Jesus,' he says. 'Ever hear of doing one thing at a time?'

I shrug. 'Doesn't work like that,' I say. 'Plus, you know . . . Of course I'm terrified it will all go away. And I once walked away from the best man I've ever known in the name of my own creativity, so . . . I try to make it count.'

I turn around so I'm not forward-facing anymore, flipping to rest my back against the bar instead. I can't believe I just said that. I didn't even know I thought that. I take a beat. Is it true, what I just told him? I realise, with a startling clarity, that it is.

'And does it?' he asks, softly, as if I haven't just lit the fuse on a bomb about to go off.

'Does it count? I mean, I'm enjoying myself, yeah. It's a lot. Harry thinks I'm mad and need to slow down a bit, but he's got Beau and Mirabelle. I've got . . .'

I don't know what I've got.

'Everything you ever wanted?' Nic supplies. I can't look at him. I don't know what's happening. What I've tried to hold together for such a long time is unravelling, dropped toilet paper spooling out away from the cardboard roll.

'What about you?' I change the subject. 'I'm boring. Tell me about your life.'

'Me?' he repeats. 'Same old, really. Lila starts school, like I said. Millie and Sandeep had another kid, so she's got a brother, whom she loves until she doesn't. I think she likes that she's got me, who she doesn't have to share. And then she misses him and wants to see him again.'

'Cute,' I say.

'I dated a bit, even got pretty serious with one woman, but . . . well, it didn't work out.'

'I'm sorry,' I say, and I mean it. I want him to be happy.

'I'm not,' he says. 'Not really.'

'How's your brother?' I ask. 'Candice passed along the details about him and Jackson. I hardly see Jackson, but when we do it's like no time has passed at all.'

'Yeah,' he said. 'He's good. Happy. Happier than I've ever known him, truth told.'

'That's nice.'

'Yeah.' He nods. 'And Candice? Jackson said she was getting married?'

'Got married,' I say. 'Last weekend. On her honeymoon now. I don't know if you remember, but our postman? She finally made her move.'

'I remember,' Nic says.

'I'm surprised you're not telling me that you remember everything. Wasn't that your line?'

'It was never a line,' he says, deadpan. 'And for what it's worth, I do.'

I finally look at him. He's smiling with half of his mouth, just like always.

'God,' I tell him. 'It's so weird seeing you. Good weird, but . . .'

'But misty watercolour memories?' he says, quoting lyrics from the Barbra Streisand song.

'Of the way we were,' I say, supplying the song's title. 'Exactly.'

'Work good?' I ask.

'Work's fine. Living in Liverpool is fine. Lila is fine.'

'So what you're saying is?'

'It's weird seeing you too.' He smirks. 'Good weird, but . . .'

I pull a face. What am I supposed to say? He looks as good as he does in my memories. He smells like he always smelled. Existing in his orbit feels *great*. And what? We agreed we wouldn't hold each other back.

But it's the damnedest thing: I can't remember what we thought we were holding each other back from.

44

Nic

'You couldn't bear the thought of having a child anywhere near you,' I remind her, after accepting her offer of a walk to get some air. It's one of those still summer nights that really belong to an August evening on the continent, a rare gift from the weather gods where the air is warm but not suffocating, the sun setting pink behind the full trees. The churchyard where JP was buried is across from us, and so we turn right to head around the back of it, seeing if we can make a big loop back to the pub.

'Oh my God.' She laughs. '*That* is not fair, sir. I was trying to spare you and her from . . .'

'I know,' I say. 'There were things you needed to do.'

'Yeah,' she says. 'Exactly.'

'And for what it's worth, I absolutely could not have dated as a new dad. You were totally right there. I think I forgot my name for about three years? I was just . . . Da-da, and then Daddy. I don't know what I thought it was all going to look like but holy shit, honestly . . . I don't know how people have a baby in their house every night of the week. Millie and I have pretty much been fifty-fifty since Lila was a few months old and even then, I was exhausted, I felt like crap . . . Millie was the same. It was, like, the moment you catch up with yourself it's your turn again, and then you're back where you started. Not that I'm complaining,' I add, hurriedly. 'I'm illustrating your point. She was my world. Still is, but it's a different rhythm now. She's so independent.'

'You'll always be Daddy, though,' she counters.

'I will,' I say. 'But I'm getting myself back a bit, you know? How you knew what would happen and I didn't is a source of embarrassment. I was *very* blasé.'

'You're welcome,' she says, slowing to admire the last of the blossom on a particularly stunning tree. 'That feels very vindicating.'

'Vindicating?'

'That even if I was a bit grand declaring that I needed to go off and change the world with my art, it was right for you to be alone and figure out parenthood.'

'I don't think you were grand for declaring that,' I say. 'Especially not because . . .'

'It all worked out?' she supplies.

'Just like we said, yeah.'

'Hmm.' She lingers by a village bench, resting on it lightly and then pushing off in a burst of energy.

'I just keep thinking,' she says, 'that it's so nice to see you. Easy, you know? And if you'd have asked me this morning why I walked away I would have had very clear answers. The miscarriage is a distant memory now, but it wasn't back then. Back then it defined me. I was so sure I couldn't be around

371

kids. But now, talking like this, walking with you through this fucking picturesque fucking village, everything with JP ringing in my ears: don't miss your chance, love with your full chest, the thing he started to say about it's not over until it's over . . .'

She catches herself then, suddenly embarrassed by her outburst. She shakes her head, emotional. 'I'm not my stepmother, am I? I'm me. I just came off a project with the most amazing kids and I thought: *Oh. They love me.* It was fun. I enjoyed them. Why did I ever think otherwise? Oh my God,' she adds. 'I sound crazy, don't I? It's this deadline. I don't think I've had a day off in, like, four years. I tell stories for a living and now I'm trying to write the story of us and – are you seeing anybody? You could have a girlfriend for all I know.'

'I don't have a girlfriend,' I tell her, amused.

'I don't have a boyfriend,' she replies. After a beat she adds: 'Hey – do you still have the sofa?'

'I do, actually,' I tell her. 'It's in Lila's room at the house. We do our bedtime stories on it.'

'I'd have thought you'd have got rid of it.'

'Why?' I say. 'It's . . .'

'Go on,' she prompts. 'What?'

'I was going to say it's a memory. Everything that happened sort of spurred me on, didn't it, and London came and went so fast it was something I could bring with me. Something tangible.'

She nods. 'That's nice,' she says. 'That you read stories on it.'

'Every night she's with me,' I say. 'She likes the velvet of it. She likes to stroke it to self-soothe when we sit together.'

We start walking again.

'I don't regret any of it,' I say, our pace slowed, now. Our hands brush just enough to not be accidental, but I don't know whose fault it is. I feel the same about her as I ever have done. And everything she's saying makes me wonder if I'm not alone in that.

'Am I imagining what's happening here?' I say, finally.

She steals a look at me. She stops walking. She shakes her head. 'No,' she says.

'Ruby,' I start. I take a step towards her.

She opens her mouth to speak but changes her mind.

'Say it,' I implore. 'Say it because I'm about ten seconds away from kissing you and I need to know how much of a bad idea that might be.'

'Nic. I honestly don't think the reasons I gave you back then hold up. I don't care that you have a child – I think . . . not that it was an excuse. I meant it at the time. I was so traumatised by whatever came before that I wasn't ready to believe this would work. But I think about you. And I was excited to see you. And I knew when I asked you if you wanted to go for a walk that I was hoping you'd kiss me. In four years nobody has even come close to you. I'm not sure that they ever will . . .'

'I've wanted to kiss you since I saw you walk into the church,' I tell her.

'I've missed you,' she says. 'I don't want to miss you anymore.'

I step towards her, reaching for her wrist so I can tug her towards me. She comes willingly. I hold her face close to mine and she parts her lips as she looks at mine, like she's wanted this. Like she's hungry for it. I'm hungry for it too. I hold her head between my hands, my thumb caressing her cheek. She leans into my touch, closing her eyes and sighing deeply.

Our mouths meet, crashing into each other. It's not gentle. It's a furious, passionate, intoxicating kiss, where she's pulling me into her and I'm pulling her into me.

'Jesus,' I say, coming up for air.

'I'm filming in Manchester in September,' she says. 'I'm going to be around.'

'Oh really?' I say.

'And not to be presumptuous, but . . .'

'But we're finally in the same place, at the same time, with the same attitude about how we were idiots for ever walking away?'

'Pretty much,' she says.

'Let's do it,' I say. 'Wide-open optimism first, okay? No excuses.'

'None.'

'No freak-outs.'

'Zero.'

'Just you, and me.'

'And your daughter every other weekend?'

'Exactly,' I say. 'I never for a second thought you'd be to a child what your stepmother was to you. For what it's worth. You're just not like that.'

'We're about to find out, aren't we?'

'I trust you,' I say.

'I trust you too.'

'I'm going to kiss you again now,' I say.

'Let's make up for lost time.' She grins.

And so there, underneath the maple tree behind the churchyard where JP has just been buried, we kiss again like it was always going to be this way. Like it was always leading up to this, here, now, finally. I breathe her in and let the knowledge wash over me that this time, now, after everything, the timing might just be – possibly, maybe – right.

Publishing Credits

It's my name on the front of this book, but there's a whole world of people who make that possible. That includes:

Ella Kahn, and everyone at Diamond Kahn and Woods Literary Agency

Team Avon:
Molly Walker-Sharp – Commissioning Editor
Katie Loughnane – Senior Commissioning Editor
Becci Mansell – Press Officer
Cara Chimirri – Senior Commissioning Editor
Elisha Lundin – Editorial Assistant
Ella Young – Marcomms Assistant
Ellie Pilcher – Marketing Manager
Hannah Avery – Key Account Manager, International Sales
Hannah O'Brien – Senior Marketing Director
Helen Huthwaite – Publishing Director
Lucy Frederick – Editor
Oli Malcolm – Executive Publisher
Radhika Sonagra – Editor

Sammy Luton – Key Account Manager
Thorne Ryan – Publishing Director

Freelancers:
Anna Barrett from The Writer's Space – Freelance Editor
Anne Rieley – Proofreader
Giovanna Giuliano – Illustrator
Helena Newton – Copy editor

HarperCollins:
Alice Gomer – Head of International Sales
El Slater – Marketing Manager
Anna Derkacz – Group Sales Director
Ben Hurd – Trade Marketing Director
Ben Wright – International Sales Director
Caroline Young – Designer
Catriona Beamish – Production Controller
Charlotte Brown – Audio Editor
Claire Ward – Creative Director
Dean Russell – Design Studio Manager
Georgina Ugen – Digital Sales Manager
Holly Macdonald – Deputy Art Director
Melissa Okusanya – Publishing Operations Director
Robyn Watts – Production Controller
Tom Dunstan – UK Sales Director

Rights and international:
Emily Gerbner, Jean Marie Kelly and the Harper360 Team
Lana Beckwith – Film & TV Team
Michael White and the HarperCollins Australia Team
Peter Borcsok and the HarperCollins Canada Team
Zoe Shine, Emily Yolland, Olivia Ter-Berg and the HCUK
    Rights Team

And to Leah TerVoorde who won a pre-order competition
to name a character in the book, and chose Ollie. Thanks, Leah!

Nose in armpit.

Elbow in back.

Not every romance starts with flowers . . .

Don't miss the international sensation *Our Stop* – a not-quite-romance of near-misses, true love, and the power of the written word.

Available in paperback, ebook and audiobook now.

Penny has to choose between three.
But are any of them The One?

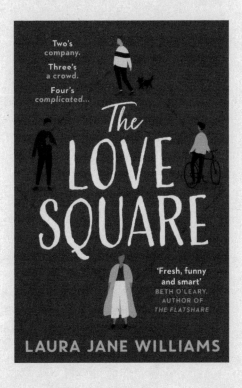

Laura Jane Williams will have you laughing, crying and cheering Penny on in this funny and feel-good exploration of hope, romance and the trust it takes to finally fall in love.

Available in paperback, ebook and audiobook now.

The wedding? Cancelled.
The bride? Heartbroken.
The honeymoon? Try and stop her . . .

Escape with this gorgeous read, full of effortless banter,
sizzling sexual tension and, above all, an overwhelming
sense of hopefulness – in life as well as love.

Available in paperback, ebook and audiobook now.

When you lose your luggage, the last
thing you expect to find is love . . .

A warm-hearted novella packed with lust, longing and
luggage, this is the perfect bitesize treat from the author of
the smash-hit bestseller *Our Stop*.

Available in ebook and audiobook now.